'Didn't you see the papers? Fellow's supposed to be loose on the East Side with a blockbuster in his satchel. An A-bomb, no less. Me, I think it's a lot of hokum to take the people's minds off the mistakes the Government's makin' — '

'It could be,' said Tony sagely. But crazy laughter had begun to bubble within him. It was quite true that a killer was at large in Manhattan. But his weapons were far less spectacular than atomic energy.

EAST SIDE GENERAL

Frank G. Slaughter

ARROW BOOKS

Arrow Books Limited

An imprint of Random House

20 Vauxhall Bridge Road, London SW1V 2SA

First published by Jarrold Publishers (London) 1953
Arrow editioin 1955
Reprinted 1961 and 1967
This edition 1974
Reprinted 1977 and 1988

Printed and bound in Great Britain by
Mackays of Chatham PLC, Chatham, Kent

ISBN 0 75 299908 7

CONTENTS

Thy Eternal Providence has appointed me to watch over the life and health of Thy creatures. May the love for my art actuate me at all times; may neither avarice, nor miserliness, nor the thirst for glory, nor for a great reputation engage my mind; for the enemies of Truth and Philanthropy could easily deceive me and make me forgetful of my lofty aim of doing good to Thy children.

May I never see in the patient anything but a fellow creature in pain.

Grant me strength, time, and opportunity always to correct what I have acquired, always to extend its domain; for knowledge is immense and the spirit of man can extend infinitely to enrich itself daily with new requirements. Today he can discover his errors of yesterday and tomorrow he may obtain a new light on what he thinks himself sure of today.

O God, Thou hast appointed me to watch over the life and death of Thy creatures; here I am ready for my vocation.

FROM THE OATH AND PRAYER OF MAIMONIDES,
JEWISH PHYSICIAN OF THE TWELFTH CENTURY

I—EVENING

I

THE ambulance cut through the First Avenue traffic like a
homing banshee—shaving taxi mudguards with only inches
to spare, streaking past the looming menace of trailer-trucks.
Sirens were muted in New York these days, on orders from
above. This particular ambulance needed no advance warning
to open a path before it. The legend—*East Side General
Hospital*—painted on its cream-coloured flanks proved that
its errand was urgent. The orderlies, riding the back step
with ease, stared down at motorist and traffic cop with the
same aloof contempt. White demigods, with the power to
snatch life from the brink, they seemed to take omnipotence
in their stride.

Within the swaying tonneau, Dr. Anton Korff looked just
as bored as he sat on the jump seat. Even his garb seemed
appropriate to the setting—an asbestos suit was routine on
calls of this sort. So were the lead-lined gloves that still
encased his arms to the elbow—and still bore witness of the
task he had performed on his two emergency victims.

Tony wasted no further glance at those charred lumps
of flesh. He had stripped them of their last rag as they lay on
the platform of the warehouse. While the police cordon
restrained the crowd, he had transferred them to this ambulance with a minimum of lost motion. One cadaver, ticketed
for pathology. One breather, ready for the table—if he
survived his check in the emergency room. So much for the
realities that met the eye. A busy intern—assistant resident
doctor—could hardly dignify such jetsam with personality.
Nor could he pause to speculate on the cause of their plight.
The thing, at the moment, was to win the race to the operating
room. Or so Tony reasoned, while the ambulance roared out
of the traffic, to take the short cut between tenement steps
and the back wall of the Rilling brewery.

It was true that death had struck in a weird guise today—
claiming one victim instantly, and all but snuffing life from
the other. In all his years of war (and the evil that came
before and after) Tony could hardly remember a more
grotesque sight. Fortunately he had been inured to shock
from his youth. The carapace that shielded the real Tony
Korff from the world had been adequate for a long time.

Yes, it was enough to keep the facts in order, until he
could relay them. Thereafter he would be free to resume the
more exciting business of planning for tomorrow. As always,
his dreams leaped time and space, ignoring the crushing
iniquities that plagued him. It was a pleasure as real as the
sharp aroma of hops that swept from the door of Rilling's
brewery—pure as a chord of music, evocative of the past he
could never quite forget.

For that moment, he was in Munich again. Back in the
cave of the Hofbrau, one with the legion that packed the huge
beer hall, shouting the Horst Wessel from bursting lungs.
One with the faith that gleamed in every eye. One with the
fury that raised each heart from despond, fusing it into the
same giant beat. Of course he had been only a boy in that
distant day: he had learned long since to classify that madness
under the microscope of science, to thank his stars that he
had escaped it in time.

He was an American today, with the papers to prove it.
Even his war record had been earned on the winning side.
Yet America had given him no hope to transcend that
madness. No dedication to match that early, fanatic faith.

The emergency case moaned faintly, and he bent forward
to soothe the near-dying man with an ease born of long
practice. He made the gesture mechanically, just as he stared
out at the looming bulk of his hospital. They were skirting
the red brick walls of the old outpatient ward—a sunless
domain that now housed the morgue, the ambulance bay,
and the laboratory where the pathologists laboured. Tony
grinned as he thought of Dale Easton, the department head—
and the chore he was about to deliver on Dr. Easton's doorstep. Then he raised his eyes to the soaring battlements of
the main building.

Seen at this angle, East Side General was a colossus blotting the eastern sky. The great rectangles of Livingston and Warburg and Madison (each ward was sacred to the memory of its founder) shouldered each other for space in the glow of sunset. The spire of Schuyler Tower (the private wing), lifted a good ten storeys above the buildings at the river's edge, was the inevitable climax to this vast temple of healing. Tony Korff scowled at the windows of the operating theatre, high up in that immaculate cliff—and wondered if the resident was working there, at this late hour. He hoped that Dr. Gray would be free to take over what he had just found at that warehouse.

The ambulance whined under its marquee, its doors wide to permit the transfer of the two wheeled stretchers to the cork-floored corridor beyond. As he shed his asbestos shell Tony Korff found time to wonder why he should choose Andy Gray as the focal point for his hatred. Knowing the answer in advance (and insisting that hate refreshed the soul), he shoved the first stretcher into the hands that waited to receive it. He began his orders as he wheeled out the still breathing victim—in a quick, clipped diction that had all but lost its foreign overtones.

"The D.O.A. goes to pathology. Please to keep clear of this ambulance till Dr. Easton comes. I'm taking the breather to emergency myself. Put in a loudspeaker call for Dr. Gray——"

From the corner of his eye he saw the squad car glide up to the platform, saw the blue-coated sergeant clump out and follow his lead. The system is meshing, he told himself—and favoured the horror under his hands with a contemptuous glance as he whipped the stretcher into an elevator.

Rocketing to the emergency operating room, he felt his pulse steady to a familiar rhythm. The hospital claims its own, he thought. To those who serve within its walls it gives direction and meaning. Even to outcasts like Tony Korff.

For one brief moment he felt a strange, all but human stirring in his heart. He could almost pity Dr. Andy Gray for the ordeal he would soon be facing.

II

"Dr. Gray. Dr. Andrew Gray."

The operator's voice on the loudspeaker was soft and coaxing, as if begging for an instant answer. *"Dr. Gray, please. Dr. Andrew Gray."*

Already the call had probed into the farthest reaches of East Side General, over the network of wires that knit the whole great hospital to its central switchboard. It had stabbed at the interns' quarters—where the nightly poker game was just beginning; at the wards—where a hundred nurses moved with muted precision, finishing the evening cares; at the lounge of the operating suite; at pathology where Dr. Dale Easton had just answered his own summons.

It found its target in the canteen just off the main rotunda —just as Andy Gray was settling on a stool to order the sandwich that would suffice for his evening meal.

"Dr. Gray here——"

"Dr. Korff calling——"

He waited for Tony to come on the line—and jiggled the receiver while he waited. It was a habit that had become automatic in these crowding days of overwork.

"What's become of Korff, Operator?"

"He's on another line now, Doctor. Dr. Easton, I believe."

"Didn't he say what he wanted?"

"He's calling from the emergency O.R. Shall I ring another phone?"

"Thank you, no. I'll go up myself."

But he did not leave the booth at once. A familiar lassitude (as dangerous, in its fashion, as the hypertension that had begun to snap his nerve ends) made him hesitate a moment more. So Korff was in trouble. Then let Tony come to him direct, as protocol demanded. After all, he was the resident. Korff was still an intern, albeit a skilful one, with a background that all but matched his own.

He came out of the phone booth, permitting his eyes to linger for an instant on his image in the fountain mirror. He bowed vaguely to the gaunt, Lincolnesque figure who stared

back at him from the glass with uncomprehending eyes.
Perhaps it's the life I've been leading, he thought. Four
major operations since noon—and another on the table now,
if I know Korff. Since when have I had time to breathe deep
and call the next quarter of an hour my own?

The hell of it was, he still loved operating—more than
food or drink or love itself. Once the lights and the problem
had claimed him, externals scarcely mattered. His eyes sought
the mirrored image once again before he turned away from
the soda fountain—and the snack supper he'd have no time
to order now. The surgeon's life, he repeated, is a short and
not too merry one.

Johns Hopkins and the clinics, he thought, put those
worry wrinkles in your forehead. Blame the Marines for a
skin brown as an old saddle, and almost as weather-worn.
Blame the Brass Hats for the eyes that study friend and foe
alike—grey as your own name, and cold as outer space.

The Army had used and broken him—in ways that only
the Army knew. He didn't blame the Army in the slightest.
After all, he had seen the world at its expense. He had learned
his lessons the hard way—before the Army discarded him.
'Invalided' would have been the word in the old days. But
he wasn't really an invalid. Merely a trained surgeon—a too
trained observer of human folly who had found his berth
at last. East Side General was an excellent place in which to
overwork—with no time out to dwell on one's dreams.

"*Dr. Gray. Dr. Andrew Gray*——"

He snatched the phone in the booth. This time Tony
answered instantly.

"Can you come up to emergency, Andy?"

"What's up?"

"A dilly I just brought in myself."

Why did he distrust Tony when the intern ventured into
slang? Certainly this wasn't like Tony. His junior had always
prided himself on handling his own cases with dispatch.
Even when it was clear later on that he should have asked
for help.

Andy kept his voice mild. "Since when have you gone
back to riding the ambulance?"

"This is my speciality. A burn case." Even on the phone Tony seemed to lick his lips. "Two cases, in fact. One dead on arrival. We may save the other, if we move fast——"

"Can't you move fast without me? I'm off duty."

"I still feel this will interest you, Andy."

Again Dr. Andrew Gray curbed his impatience. This would not be the first time Korff had teased him into a job that Korff himself was well able to finish. He frowned at the phone as he pictured the handsome blond intern, with his changeless smile. Tony's smiles always began and ended in his eyes. Only the Baltic, thought Andy, could produce that blue marble stare.

"Did you bring Dale into this?"

"Dr. Easton agrees. This is your job, not mine." There was no mistaking the provocation in Tony's voice. "I've called Dr. Ash, too, of course. We'll be ready for you in ten minutes——"

"Can't you be more definite?" If Tony had called the hospital head on his own, that meant Tony was sure of his ground. Dr. Martin Ash was not a man to disturb lightly.

"Sorry," said Tony. "My diagnosis is reserved, until Dale reports. As for the burns themselves—well, they are something you must see to believe."

"Who's scrubbing?"

"Talbot and Ryan, praise God."

Andy found that he had echoed Tony's sigh. The nurses just mentioned were graduates; indispensable in cases such as this.

"You'll assist, of course?" There was no rancour in Andy's voice now. No matter how they shouted on the phone, he and Tony Korff were still a team.

"Of course, Andy," said the intern, just as quietly. "Dale will stand by—at his own request."

"I'll be right up."

"My report's on the scrub-room board," said Tony. "The O.R. will be ready when you're gowned."

Andy found he had banged up the receiver after all. He did not regret the impulse. Nor did he regret the urge that sent him across the rotunda at the double—and into the

elevator. The pressure between his shoulder blades had
vanished. Work was waiting in emergency. The work he was
born to do.

III

*... Sgt C. Donnelly, of Traffic B, whose squad car discovered
the bodies, reported to emergency. Ambulance 17, with self in
charge, took off at 6.43, arriving at destination 4 minutes later. ...
Thanks to Donnelly's alertness, area was roped off, and a CD
unit on its way. ... The two victims, both burned so violently as
to preclude identification, were tumbled on the platform of the
shuttered warehouse of the Premier Box Company, long dis-
used. ... No sign of fire, no other visible marks of violence ...
Working with gloves, I removed all clothing, and checked with
counter to be positive the bodies themselves were not dangerous. ...
Ambulance returned to emergency at 7.01 with both victims—one
D.O.A., the other near moribund. Dr. Easton summoned to
confirm findings: Ambulance 17 delivered to decontamination unit
for further check. ... Proceeded to emergency O.R. at 7.03,
alerted Dr. Gray, and set up for débridement.*

T. K.

Dr. Dale Easton, scrubbing side by side with Andy Gray
at the long sink just off the operating theatre, scowled at the
report pinned on the scrub-room board. A long, thin man
in his thirties, with the face of a melancholy martyr (and a
twinkle behind his horn rims that belied the martyr's role),
Dale was more saturnine than usual tonight—and more wary.
He had acknowledged Andy's arrival with an off-centre grin.
He had waited patiently while Andy read through the intern's
report. Like most scientists, Dr. Easton was not a man to
waste words. ... When Andy spoke at last, Dale merely
raised his shoulders a trifle, as though disclaiming an opinion
in advance.

"If this is a radioactive job, why couldn't Tony say so on
the phone?"

Dr. Easton grinned. "He got you to take over his case, didn't he? That's what counts."

Andy did not answer as he bent over the zinc-lined basin. Watching his friend's corded muscles ripple under the short-sleeved surgeon's gown, Dale folded his own arms into a sterile towel and waited. I must look like a praying mantis at this moment, he thought ruefully. A caricature of the laboratory gnome, a trifle larger than life. Too grotesque to inspire laughter. He could still marvel at his acceptance of events—no less than he marvelled at Andy's own acceptance of the healer's role.

His mind pursued the thought fluently, in a soundless monologue that was part of the lonely career he had chosen. Probably we were both dedicated from our creation, he thought. Andy will go on healing until the last trump sounds. I, for my part, will surely be crouched over a microscope when man achieves his ultimate destruction.

His eye strayed to the operating room, where Dr. Tony Korff (sterile for five minutes now, and strutting like some acolyte at a mystic shrine) supervised the final details of their emergency. By the same token, the intern was slated to do spadework for his betters. To see that the knives were sharp and the last scrub nurse on her toes. Between such high moments as these he was free to eat his heart out with envy.

Tony Korff's tragedy, thought Dale, was the tragedy of the small man everywhere, who yearns hopelessly for greater things. The little man who was also stubborn—and too blind to realize that he must be for ever satisfied with second best. Because his training (and his wartime honours) matched Andy Gray's, Tony could still dream of besting the resident surgeon at the table—to say nothing of winning the battle for promotion that went on here without ceasing. He would never admit that his was the genius for background planning rather than the bold initiative of the surgeon.

Meanwhile, fighting his way to his degree, Tony would blame a thousand enemies for his failure—refusing to admit that the failure lay within. This evening's coup, of course, was typical. An outside observer, looking at this race with death, would never guess that Andy, not Tony, was in charge. Yet Tony's organization had been more than efficient. Thanks to his handling of the ambulance call, a trail of radioactivity had been cut off, well outside the hospital walls. Within the last half hour he had sluiced down their patient, prepared him for surgery, and set up the operating room itself with an offhand ease that Dale observed with envy. Martin Ash (or any other hospital head) would have cause to be proud of his senior intern tonight.

And yet, thought Dale, Tony had been wise to summon the resident for the operation itself. A touch-and-go battle to save a man's life was something for which the refugee had no relish. Particularly if it seemed doomed to failure. When the case was recorded Tony would receive the credit for brilliant organization. Andy Gray might chalk up the loss of one more patient. The pathologist turned from these unworthy suspicions as Andy spoke at last.

"Radioactive's a big word, Dale."

"A word that covers a great deal of sinning," said the pathologist. "I can recall a radium case we treated here before the war. When the A-bomb, as we think we know it, was only a fever spot in some physicist's brain. Of course, *these* burns are far more profound, but——"

"But you're jumping to no conclusions yet," said Andy.

"Not until I've made my tests."

Andy nodded. "I remember reading about that case. Wasn't it a bit of grand larceny that backfired?"

"This one could be just as simple," said Dale. "No one will ever know how much of our stockpile—radioactive or otherwise—is being shipped out of this country every day. Or what syndicates control the traffic. Or how they punish their soldiers, when they step out of line——"

"Offhand, then, you'd say this was a killing that didn't quite come off?"

"It could be just that, Andy. But we aren't being paid for that sort of thinking, are we? Our job right now is to get this fellow conscious, so he'll talk to Inspector Hurlbut."

Andy raised his eyebrows. "If Hurlbut's on his way here, it must be important. What about Ash?"

"They reached his wife at the Waldorf. He's driving down."

"Isn't this one of Mrs. Ash's party nights?"

Dale shrugged. "Apparently he meant to be late at this one. He'd already left when we reached her."

`Andy twitched his fingers into pale yellow gloves and backed from the scrub room: the sterilized nurse enveloped him in an operating gown with one practised flip. The surgeon spoke quietly, his voice muffled in gauze.

"We'll proceed without Dr. Ash, gentlemen."

Tony had already come up briskly, his own voice muted. "The patient will be ready in a moment more, Dr. Gray. As you see, he's taking whole blood after the plasma. Dr. Easton authorized an injection of ACTH to minimize shock——"

Dale Easton stepped back a bit and surveyed the scene as a whole. The lights were dimmed down above the table, though the anæsthetist was already at work. In another room across the tiled floor the two scrub nurses were still preparing for their task, in that easy hospital rhythm that seemed so unhurried, yet never wasted a motion. In the penumbra an unsterilized probationer hovered like a frightened shadow, ready to press the electric button that would start the clock above the instrument case in the corner. In the ante-room, glimpsed through the wide glass windows in the double doors, a policeman dozed in an arm-chair—a bit of blue melodrama that would come alive when the patient was wheeled out after the operation.

The patient himself was remote from all this activity, a hump of flesh beneath a tented sheet, an effigy that already seemed resigned to the waxen pallor of death. . . . The flask of whole blood, tilted above the great vein at the victim's ankle, was part of the strangely inhuman aura that surrounded the table. Dale Easton pulled back from his musings. Life has grown too complex for my blood, he told himself sombrely: I'm far more at ease in my own haven—next door to the morgue. The world of death has its drawbacks, but its patterns are absolute. A scientist can set his course there and hold it to the end.

With a slight effort he forced himself to concentrate on the world of life—in this case the two scrub nurses, moving in the chiaroscuro just beyond the pale glow of the operating-room lights. Ryan and Talbot, he told himself, with that same mock solemnity that had always been his shield. Vicki and Julia. He wondered idly if Vicki Ryan was still Tony's diversion after hours. If Julia Talbot (for all the purity of her devotion to a nursing career) was still hopelessly in love with Andy Gray—whose own devotion had settled, long ago, into a mould that no woman under heaven could shatter.

IV

In the smaller scrub room the tall, boldly handsome girl took another brush from the basin and began to work the bristles beneath her nails. "It's the first time Dale Easton has stared at me in business hours," she said. "Maybe I don't know my own strength."

"Quiet, Vicki!"

"See for yourself. He's leering over that mask like a satyr. What *is* this strange power I have over men?"

Julia Talbot threw down her own brush and faced her room-mate. "If Dr. Easton happens to be looking your way, you can be sure he has something else on his mind."

"One can never be sure with men," said Vicki. "That's what makes the species interesting."

"How many scalps do you want, Vicki? Your record in this hospital must be complete."

"Not without Dale. *And* your idol, of course. But then no one can tag Andy Gray. Including you."

The argument, so far, had been routine—and the two girls had thrown their insults impromptu. Vicki Ryan, as opulent as a streamlined Venus (and almost as completely revealed in the thin gown all working nurses wore in the tropic climate of the operating room), answered her friend's last gibe with a flirt of her thighs, and returned to her scrubbing. Julia Talbot (whose figure was no less sweetly rounded) continued to stare through the door to the theatre, grateful for the chance to unmask, now her room-mate's back was turned.

It had been true last week, she thought. No one could tag Andy. He was mine to dream over then. Mine alone—until that creature moved to Schuyler Tower. 'Creature' was a term that Julia employed rarely. Somehow she could not dignify Pat Reed with human attributes. Especially when she pictured the past those two had shared.

How much of the gossip was real? There had been rumours of a flaming fortnight in Hawaii, just after Andy had returned from his last tour of duty in Asia. And some said that Pat had been his part-time girl on a recent vacation. But there had been no sign of the creature for months thereafter, and Julia had hoped against hope that Andy himself had put the affair behind him. Now, it seemed, Pat herself had returned for an encore. It was quite like her to call it a rest cure, on doctor's orders—to lurk- up there in her suite in Schuyler Tower, while she tried out her arsenal on the resident surgeon, one more time.

Grateful that Vicki had not tossed those facts into their lazy argument—and throbbing, even now, to the drama in the making just outside—Julia Talbot threw down her brush and began to soak her forearms in the basin the two nurses shared.

"Did Tony tell you what's up?"

"Only that it's a general débridement." Vicki tossed a careless glance at the table, where the three doctors were in conference with the anæsthetist. "I'm surprised that Andy is doing the cutting. Tony can handle burns: they've been his speciality ever since their spell in Japan."

"I'm told he has other specialities."

"I wouldn't know, dear. Or would I?"

Their laughter, too, was routine: it was no secret to Julia that Vicki was spending most of her dusk-to-dawn liberty in Tony's quarters, just off the same surgical unit where they were now preparing to robe. Even as she chuckled Julia found time to wonder at her own easy acceptance. A small-town girl, with a background as wholesome as a four-tone advertisement in any national weekly, she would once have bristled at such an innuendo. Two years on one's own as an O.R. special could do a great deal for one's tolerance. Or was it the constant battle of life and death that sharpened your

zest for living—even when you were too tired to see beyond
the grey-white blue of tomorrow?

"Tell me, Vicki, why you dislike Dr. Gray?"

Vicki Ryan shrugged. "Some men affect me one way, some
another. Occasionally a man turns up whom *I* don't really
happen to affect at all. According to the books, I should
make my real play for just that type. But I'm quite content
to leave Andy Gray to his career. Offhand, I'd advise you to
do the same."

Julia sighed inwardly, admitting the logic of her room-
mate's reasoning. Aloud she said, pertly enough, "Yesterday
he smiled at me, after that four-hour trephine. Who knows
what he'll do tomorrow?"

"I tell you he's married to his work," said Vicki. "That
kind is hopeless. And speaking of work, they're flagging
us now."

Robed and gowned, the two scrub nurses approached the
table, Julia a pace behind Vicki. Somehow it had always been
natural to let the tall girl lead the way at these moments:
Vicki had been her mentor since she had brought her brand-
new cap into the nurses' home. The best surgical special in the
hospital, Vicki had been a first-rate teacher, on more than one
front. Julia knew that it was only because of her skill that
Vicki had survived the aura of scandal that surrounded her—
an aura that was amply justified. Even Emily Sloane, the O.R.
supervisor (an acid spinster whose ideas of discipline brooked
no argument), was content to give Vicki the elbow room she
needed, after hours. . . .

Perhaps I should take a leaf from Vicki's book, thought
Julia. Certainly it's ridiculous to fasten all my longings on
one man—especially when he seldom realizes my existence.
Virginity could be a burden at times, as the first faint shadows
began to fall athwart one's twenties: what cynic had said
that the longer you have it the less it's worth? Perhaps *he'd*
notice me oftener, if he heard that other men were interested.
She banished the ignoble thought as her eyes met Andy's
across the table. He needs me tonight, she told herself firmly.
Even if that need is purely medical, it's enough for now.

For the tenth time that week she wished that Andy Gray

could have the rest he so badly needed. Of course it was impossible to picture the operating room without him, when an emergency was on the table. Sensitive, as always, to his moods—after their hours of shared tension—she looked deep into his eyes as she awaited her orders. Instinct told her that he was concerned tonight, not only with the job at hand, the welfare of the patient, but with something she could not name.

When Andy spoke his voice was quite contained. "Bad burns tonight, girls. We'll want to cut some thin grafts. If this fellow lives it will be immediate grafting and adreno-cortico that saves him."

"Plus the fact we have the first team tonight," said Tony Korff. "Don't leave *that* out, Doctor." Already at attention with a clamp between his gloved fingers, the senior intern bestowed a wink on Vicki Ryan.

"I'm always grateful for the first team," said Andy Gray. "They should know that by now." Julia could feel him draw farther away with each word—into the surgeon's citadel, where no man (or woman) dared to follow. She risked a question nonetheless.

"About this ACTH treatment of burns, Doctor. What do we have to go on?"

"Surgeons in Cleveland have been using it," said Andy. His eyes brushed hers for an instant, and she felt their faint warmth. Quite as though she were a student who had asked a reasonably intelligent question in some graduate seminar. "The adrenocorticotropic hormone—ACTH for short—is a true miracle worker: we've all known that for some time. Since it's derived from the pituitary, it controls the adrenals and thereby lessens shock. Out in Cleveland they've kept several cases alive that would have died otherwise."

Even now Tony refused to be academic. "Soon a doctor will be nothing but a technician with a hypo of ACTH," he said. "Would you advise me to seek other employment?"

"Not so long as your fellow-man is bent on self-destruction," said Andy dryly. He threw an inquiring glance at the anæsthetist, still intent on the needle taped to the patient's vein. "May we have him now?"

"I think he'll stand up, Doctor, if you make it fast."

"What's his condition?"

"Surprisingly good, since Dr. Easton made his last injection," said the anæsthetist. "There was no discernible blood pressure then: in fact I was positive you'd lost him. The count's above eighty now, and still rising."

"I shot some cortisone in there too," said Dale Easton. "His adrenals might be too knocked out to produce it right away."

Julia found that she was nodding in solemn agreement with the gauze-masked faces above the table. Her question about the miracle hormone had been strictly for the record. She knew as well as Andy himself that most of the miracle was due to its stimulation of the adrenals, those small glands lying above the kidneys. The powerful substance they produced was the real controlling hormone of the whole human system—particularly in shock such as followed severe burns.

"Prepare for a sight, everyone," said Andy. "Dr. Korff described this case as a dilly. He was guilty of understatement."

He twitched the sheet aside as he spoke. Julia's gasp was quite automatic. Two years as a special had inured her to human wreckage in all its forms—or so she had reasoned, until she found herself staring at the naked body on the table.

Tony had done his work well: the victim was ready for the healing knife. The real wonder was that he still breathed at all. At first glance the man seemed a mass of charred flesh from the waist up, the face burned beyond recognition, the chest and arms rowelled by a fire that could scarcely belong to this earth. Here, thought the scrub nurse, is a celestial rainbow gone berserk—as though some mad painter, dipping his brush in the aurora, had smeared this flesh at will. From chin to umbilicus the body was criss-crossed with giant welts. Without knowing why, Julia felt that this tortured skin had not really been burned at all. It was rather as though the ultimate cold of space had licked it—the absolute zero where stars exploded without sound and no life dwelt.

"These can't be acid burns——" She had spoken without thought, violating hospital protocol by offering an opinion when none was needed. Feeling Andy's eyes upon her, she coloured to the roots of her hair as she took her place beside the instrument table.

"We'll call them that for now," said Andy mildly. "Scalpel, please."

Julia slapped the knife into his hand. With that motion she felt the lights come alive on the table, as the probationer threw the switch: a faint whir from the facing wall told her that the O.R. clock had been set in motion, timing their work to the last second. Across the table, at her place beside the sponge bank, Vicki Ryan offered her the solace of a final wink before she, too, slipped into the rhythm of the task they were sharing.

Even Vicki looks a trifle shaken, thought Julia: this must be a novelty in her book as well. Then, as she joined the team in earnest, she forgot to think at all.

Expertly draped by Tony Korff, the wounded body yielded to the healing magic of the knife. Andy dissected the charred tissue away without wasting a stroke. Time was precious here, for the burned flesh could not be permitted to absorb, poisoning an already damaged body beyond repair. Dale Easton voiced the prevailing thought from his observer's post, the first word to be spoken since the operation began.

"Even with ACTH and cortisone, this hardly seems worth while. I don't see how he can live."

Andy spoke quietly, out of his rock-like concentration. "Fortunately we needn't make that decision. As long as he lives we work on him. When he dies he's your responsibility." A coagulum of skin and chemical, twisted as old leather that has rotted in the sun, dropped from table to basin as he spoke. "This much of him is all yours right now. You can run your chem tests later."

Working swiftly behind him, Tony and Vicki applied hot pads to the areas denuded of skin, controlling the small amount of bleeding. Already the anæsthetist had turned to his supply table to replace the flask of whole blood. Absolute quiet settled on the room, broken only by a faint, spine-tingling whisper as another strip of weirdly marked skin ripped free under the scalpel. A third flask replaced the second as the anæsthetist checked the patient's blood pressure one more time and answered Andy's wordless question with a nod. When Julia raised her eyes to the clock at long last, she was shocked—as always—to note that the operation was over an hour old.

Most of the burned area were now well denuded. Tony, working with a dermatome along the undamaged area of the back, had begun to shave away paper-thin sheets of fresh skin, which were laid precisely in place over the raw areas, almost before the surgeon's knife could move on. At a nod from Andy, Julia added her own hands to Vicki's, to bind down the pressure dressings that were beginning to give the victim's head and shoulders the appearance of an outsize mummy.

Once again she could only marvel at the constant tempo of their effort. Perhaps he'll live after all, she thought; perhaps he'll even tell us what strange hell he's visited. . . . Certainly there was no better dressing for this type of burn than the victim's own skin. Plastered down under pressure, living cells from the grafted sheet would begin to cement it to the raw flesh beneath, stopping the loss of vital fluids that so often wept a life away.

"We'll take the other side now," said Andy. "Fortunately the damage there isn't nearly so profound."

Julia's muscles were aching as she returned to the instrument table, but she was only vaguely conscious of that bone-deep weariness. Vicki, she saw, was even busier, her deft hands in constant movement as she flicked dressings through warm saline solutions, twisted them expertly, and passed them on to Tony. The whole left side of the patient was deeply swathed now, with the dark knob of a clamp showing here and there—mute evidence that Andy's knife had gone deep to free the tissue beneath from its potential danger.

The hands of the clock showed that the better part of two hours were behind them: the strain of the long ordeal had begun to press down on them all. Only Andy Gray seemed unmoved—an iron tower in the midst of the constant bustle, the soft-voiced orders. As always in such moments, he seemed to possess no nerves at all. Why, Julia wondered, must he be tense and irritable in other moments, when the average mortal could afford the luxury of calm?

Her eyes brushed Dale Easton's as she passed a fresh
clamp: the pathologist, immovable as Buddha at the table's
head, was studying her with a kind of detached interest—
almost as though he had read her unspoken question. Easton
and Gray, she thought. Twin icebergs, moved by the same
compulsions, to the same ends. Why, when she understood
Andy Gray so clearly, did she love him too?

"Fair enough, Tony. He's all yours."

Julia pulled back with a little start as Andy's voice cut
across her musings. Working with only the surface of her mind
engaged, she had not noticed that the last dressing had been
strapped home, the last clamp removed. The patient was a
true mummy now, with the mummy's ambiguous repose.
Not even the tip of his nose was visible in the cross-hatched
bandages: the very eyelids, packed deep in wet gauze, seemed
to rise like hillocks in a flat plain of white. But the deep,
snoring respiration was proof enough that their two hours
of travail had not been wasted. Andy stepped out of the
hard cone of light above the table and peeled off his gloves.

"Nice work, team," he said quietly. "I'll make no bets, but
he may have a chance to walk again. Or to talk, at least——"

He bit off the sentence in the middle, and grinned at Julia
as he stripped off his mask—as though they already shared
one secret, and might share another, in time. "Bed him down,
Tony, if you please. And make sure the infusions go on
through the night. We'll need a check on blood protein
levels, of course. And keep up the ACTH and cortisone.
I'll be in Dr. Ash's office. He may want you too, when you've
finished——"

It was over then, as quietly as it had begun. Julia stood
motionless beside the instrument table as Andy turned
towards the door—and pulled back to admit the orderlies
with their wheeled stretcher. No one stirred in the room as
the deep-snoring mummy was trundled into the lounge. The
patrolman in the arm-chair, rumbling to his feet with a
truncated snore of his own, trailed the stretcher into the
corridor. Tony, stripping off his mask, yawned openly and
cast a speculative eye at Vicki Ryan—who returned the glance
with interest

"I've nothing to add to my report, Doctor," said the intern. "Sure the Head will be needing me?"

"I'd stand by, just in case. The law will keep you company in the meantime."

Tony shrugged, and trailed the stretcher into the hall, with a parting wink for Vicki. If Andy noted the byplay he gave no sign. Instead he waved Dale Easton through the door, started to follow, then turned back once again, to lay a quick hand on Julia's arm.

"Chin up, Miss Talbot," he said. "You can't be as tired as you look."

I won't blush again, Julia told herself firmly. I won't let him see what it means, to have him notice me as a fellow human. It took real effort, but she kept her voice as impersonal as his own.

"I'm not a bit tired, Doctor. In fact I'll be on call tonight, if you need me."

"I'll always need you, Julia," he said. "That's one thing you can rely on." He was gone with the words, already stooped a little under his own fatigue.

Julia's chin lifted as she faced Vicki Ryan. "Well, dear? Is that the way to handle men?"

Vicki yawned, catlike. "You're learning," she said. "Wonder what he meant by *need*? A verb like that can be very active sometimes, you know——"

Julia found she could laugh after all, even as she faced the post-operative litter that seemed to choke the whole room. She could remember how she had once shuddered at that welter of sponges and blood-soaked dressings, mingled, as usual, with empty ampoules and red-stained blood-flasks. It would need two hours' hard labour to prepare the room for its next emergency. For once she felt an overwhelming urge to dodge this inevitable chore. She wanted to be alone on her cot at the nurses' home—to go over every syllable of Andy's brief farewell.

"Will Sloane let us off this time?"

"I'll have her wig if she doesn't," said Vicki. "She was a scrub herself once—even if it was twenty years ago. She knows what backache means." The tall nurse paused abruptly as the supervisor herself stalked in from the corridor.

At fifty, Emily Sloane was as astringent as her name. No field commander could have fitted his uniform more perfectly than Emily; no authority in the hospital (from Martin Ash down) was more thoroughly respected—and feared. Like most good supervisors, Emily had come up from the ranks, without favours. There was something ageless about her now, something withdrawn, as though she had put life behind her long ago. As usual, she had kept clear of the operation until the doctors had departed. Now, obeying a sixth sense that functioned automatically, she was on hand to take charge of the aftermaths.

"Talbot and Ryan, you can go off duty now." Her voice was part of her manner—low-pitched, with the whiplash of authority in scrupulous control. "Which of you is on call?"

"I am, Miss Sloane." Julia had spoken mechanically. She went on, ignoring the dig of Vicki's elbow. "I'll stay if you want me."

When Emily smiled Julia thought of many things. Her stint as a probationer, when she had observed her first autopsy, and fainted dead away; the consuming homesickness of that initial year of training—when she was still too young to understand how subtly the hospital routine would replace one's need for outside affection and too self-centred to understand that her chosen work could often transcend self; the slow understanding of the beauty that is healing.

Emily Sloane summed up those memories in her trim white person. At times it was difficult to remember that the supervisor was human, for Emily, like the hospital she served, seemed governed by her own laws, and bleakly unimpressed by the bustle of the world without. Her bitterest enemy could hardly deny that she was a symbol of the nurse at her finest— though it was rumoured that she had no reality outside the starched perfection of her uniforms, and stored an extra thermometer where her heart should have been.

"Like any good special," said Emily, "Ryan is warning you never to volunteer. Get back to your quarters, Talbot. You'll probably have enough work to satisfy you before morning."

The two girls went down the hall on quick tiptoe: there

was something about Emily that inspired hurry and quiet, in that order. "The spirit of East Side General," said Vicki Ryan, but even Vicki was speaking in a whisper now. "Honestly, would it surprise you to see her drift through a door some day without turning the knob?"

"I *wanted* to stay and help her," said Julia. "And there's nothing I wanted less than a clean up job—until she walked into the room. I don't think she's in the least spooky. If you ask me, she's just plain lonesome."

"Most nurses are, if they stay in nursing long enough," said Vicki. "It's a lonely trade—like religion, or lighthouse keeping."

"Speak for yourself, dear," said Julia, laughing. "You seldom seem lonely."

"That's because I don't give myself time," said Vicki. "Emily and I have different ways of keeping busy, that's all. So, I dare say, have you. Take it from one who knows, you'll end up in her shoes some day. If the work doesn't kill you first, or you don't corner the right man in between."

They walked out of the elevator as Vicki spoke and through the back corridor to the quadrangle of dusty city grass that separated the main bulk of East Side General from the nurses' home. For no reason she could name, Julia Talbot felt a chill that had nothing to do with the warm summer evening.

As always, she found herself blinking a little in the open air, a little frightened by its strangeness. It seemed for ever since they had crossed this same rectangle of withered grass in answer to the emergency call. She tucked an arm through Vicki's and forced a laugh she didn't feel. At this moment she would have given a great deal to turn back to the white, looming sanctuary they had just quitted. To remind herself, however briefly, that she mattered a little there—no matter how heedlessly the world itself might pass her by.

v

Emily Sloane surveyed the hectic disorder of the operating theatre and let out her breath in a contented sigh. Now that she was alone in her special domain she could even pretend that her sense of well-being was complete. There had been no real pain since morning—and, while she guessed the cause of that pain all too well, it was still easy to pretend that her fears were groundless. Tomorrow would be the time to face up to those fears, when the results of her test were in. Tonight it was more than enough to roll one's sleeves and attack the disorder of the operating room.

The surgical supervisor could have summoned any one of a dozen students to perform this task, merely by lifting a telephone: it pleased her to do this particular job alone— with a dispatch that would have left those same probationers dizzy with admiration. Somehow her mind was always freer while she worked: she could even afford to laugh at this strange compulsion that made neatness a virtue above rubies. Like her own small person, her operating rooms were always spotless. After all, she thought, it's no one's fault but my own if I sometimes forget where these impersonal things leave off and Emily Sloane begins.

She had never spared herself, from her first year of training, and her reason for this denial of self was her own. She had known, even then, that love (or even affection) would always elude her. Just as surely, she had found an acceptable sub- stitute in her work, almost from the beginning. It was only last year, when the pain began in earnest, that she had begun to question the wisdom of her self-immolation. It was only now (as her hands flew willingly to their task) that she dared to pause and ask herself if this long self-sacrifice had meaning.

As the oldest inhabitant of the nursing home, Emily was well aware of the worn small change of gossip that linked her name to scandals past and present. It was said that she cherished a secret passion for every doctor in the hospital— and most of the visiting specialists. That her martinet's manner was compensation for those unrequited, one-way romances.

That she made fetishes of her frustrations, cherishing them as only an old maid can, and sharpening her longings as avidly as an old-time surgeon.

Something's up tonight, she told herself as she cleared the floor of its last scrap. Something that goes deeper than this débridement—a threat far more sinister than the blue-coated watchdog she had passed in the corridor. Thanks to the adjacent slum area, the law was no stranger to East Side General: Emily herself had stood by the operating table more than once while big and little criminals had screamed their lives away. She could discount the grapevine rumours that had already reached her, the hint of doom, ticking visibly just outside these walls. And yet, when she thought of the conference now getting under way in Martin Ash's office, she was sure that the threat was genuine.

She felt no twinge of fear. The chaos that boiled and fretted outside the walls of East Side General had always seemed remote as a summer thunderstorm. The only times she had been really afraid were the times she was forced to doff her uniform and venture into that chaos—on her short, unwanted vacations, on the errands she must run in New York on behalf of her department. Once she was safe within these walls again she could laugh at her fears.

Why, when she carried the agent of her own doom within her, should she quail at the threat of doom outside? She would die as she had lived—if die she must—hard at the work she loved. To the end, she would rest secure in the knowledge that her own domain was neat as a new pin, that her control was absolute.

The operating room was almost tidy now, and she could feel the good, tired completion that came to her only at such moments, the sense of work well done, the anticipation of rest well earned. Perhaps I'll sleep on my own tonight, she thought, though it's too much to pray for slumber without dreams.

She felt the pain then—its soft, familiar pounce, like a cat that moved warily in the dark, so gently that one always forgot the rowelling of its claws. Pray God it leaves me in peace tonight, she thought. Pray God it's only my spinster's nerves, exacting their inevitable toll as I face another midnight and fight down the conviction that I've lived in vain.

VI

The private office of the hospital head, well insulated by an ante-room and a double door that opened only to the pressure of a button beneath the doctor's desk, seemed empty of life as the clock in Schuyler Tower boomed the hour of ten: the figure that stood in the shadows by the window was part of the stillness. Only the photograph on the wide desert of desk top seemed alive in its golden frame. Dr. Martin Ash, moving away from the ambush of his own *portières*, stared down for a long time at the laughing girl, haloed in the glow of the desk lamp, yet seeming to vibrate with a hidden glow all her own.

Catherine was lovely when she married me, he thought with all the shock of an original discovery. It's hardly fair that she should be even lovelier today—and just as certain of her place in the scheme of things. But that, too, was another enigma he would never solve. Nine days out of ten, he could accept Catherine at her face value and find the bargain good.

He had driven downtown for a ritual visit to his office before the owl shift took over; the problem that his senior intern had just dumped in his lap was still too brand-new to reach his brain. Now, awaiting the arrival of Inspector Hurlbut, he had permitted himself the luxury of solitude while he wrestled with a deeper, more personal problem.

He glanced resentfully at the single, typed sheet that contained Dr. Anton Korff's report of the strange accident he had brought to emergency. Try as he might, Ash could not force himself to worry in advance. He had stood at the window in the operating room door while Andy Gray worked over the patient, unseen by the group round the table. Viewed from that angle, the case had seemed merely the aftermath of the tooth-and-claw struggle that went on endlessly in any metropolitan underworld. Besides, Korff's penchant for dramatizing his accomplishments was well documented in the office files.

There were letters on his desk that cried for signatures, a whole stack of personal mail that had poured in during the afternoon, while the half dozen typewriters in his ante-room chattered frantically to keep up with that massive correspond-ence. The quarterly report of the hospital's finances (with its ominous red-ink entries) also awaited his inspection—and its eventual, half-apologetic transfer to Catherine. Or rather, to Catherine's competent tax lawyers, who would grant the hospital's book-keepers another lease of life, at a ninety-cent discount on the income-tax dollar.

Martin Ash forced himself to settle at the desk, though he could not bring himself to touch his mail or the light switch. Instead, he picked up his private phone and dialled his operator on the switchboard downstairs.

"Does Dr. Gray know I'm waiting, Ethel?"

"Indeed yes, sir. He's with the inspector now, I believe. Up in surgical. Shall I put out a tracer?"

"Never mind," said Ash heavily. "I'll wait here."

So Andy was putting Hurlburt through the usual paces before he brought him on the carpet for their conference. Trust Andy to cut all possible corners, to save him all the time he could. The head of East Side General teetered back in his overstuffed swivel chair and stared hard at his wife's pictured image. Once again he was positive that Catherine was laughing at him and pitying him in the same vibrant breath.

She wanted me twenty years ago, he thought—as definitely as another woman might want a foreign car or a blooded stallion. And, since Catherine Parry had never tolerated want in any form, she simply purchased me out of hand. It had happened as simply as that—with no more fanfare than Catherine might use today in writing his next cheque. The fact that it had been a good bargain could not alter the basic fact.

Put it down to chance that he had been interning here, after those hard-scrabble years at the third-rate medical school his parents could never afford. Put it down to chance that Catherine Parry had come to Schuyler Tower that very year, to enjoy a nervous breakdown. Their first meeting had exploded a spark that had never died, even when they were quarrelling most bitterly. Looking back on it now, he saw that it was her sublime assurance that had fascinated him, quite as much as the enticement of her body, the promise that was soon exceeded by the performance . . . and her conviction that nothing could prevent her marriage to a brilliant (if unknown) Jew who could never have clawed his way to a living without her.

Dr. Martin Ash teetered still farther in his swivel chair and studied his wife's smile through half-closed lids. Catherine had always had courage—he could grant her that. Even now he was not quite sure what strategy she had used to break her father's bitter opposition to the marriage or how she had forced that troglodyte to grant his only daughter unlimited funds in advance. In those days Dr. Martin Ash was still known to his familiars as Marty Aschoff, and the tenement smell had still clung to him, like mould but recently exposed to the healing sun. A product of the very slums that still sprawled at the gates of his hospital, he had always been too busy fulfilling his destiny to be ashamed of his origin. It had seemed natural that his parents should go on living here, in the block just behind Rilling's brewery—that they should refuse to move to the house Catherine had so often threatened to buy them in the suburbs, preferring to live out their lives in the only real home they had ever known.

Life with Catherine had rubbed away the last of the tenement blight and replaced it with a mahogany-brown Florida tan. It had been Catherine, and Catherine's millions, that had sent him to the Mayo Clinic to burnish his surgeon's skill. It had been his wife, and her influence, that had made his climb up the medical ladder so rapidly—and so preordained. Sometimes, when he tried to measure that climb, he felt his head spin a little, even now. From chief surgeon to board member, from vice-president to acting head—each step had been met with the full knowledge that he could not fail.

No one could say that either he or Catherine had sold the hospital a bill of goods. Catherine herself could not complain that he had shirked his part of the bargain. They might quarrel violently over ways and means: they were united in their devotion to East Side General, their determination to make it a model of its kind. With no false modesty, he could insist that no hospital in New York boasted two better surgeons than Dr. Andrew Gray and Dr. Martin Ash. No hospital gave more consistent service to the community— the red-ink entries in its ledgers were proof of that.

What had he given Catherine Parry in return for this largesse? From the first he had tried to give her love—and found that passion was, at best, a facile substitute. Too many of their differences (and some were, indeed, fundamental) had been settled on the altar of Eros—or referred to the future, in a kind of uneasy truce. It was grotesque that they should be existing on this same basis after twenty-odd years of married life. Or was "married" too solemn a word to dignify their union?

Martin frowned again at the portrait—and the pictured likeness of Catherine Ash continued to regard him with wide-open, trusting eyes. It was almost a relief to hear the boom of Hurlburt's voice in the ante-room, to rise and switch on lights, welcoming the Inspector and his doctors with the offhand ease that was now as natural as breathing. He noted, with a certain relief, that only Andy and Dale were in the Inspector's wake—and a bulky silhouette in tweed whom he recognized instantly.

"Hello, Pete," said Martin Ash, agreeably enough. "I was wondering when you'd turn up."

Pete Collins, reporter at large for the *Chronicle*, shambled into the office, for all the world like a St. Bernard on leash. Pete had the same careless bulk, the same deceptive friendliness. He had covered East Side General for his paper ever since Ash could remember. Even now (when he had improved in status) Pete still dropped in daily, in search of the elusive spark of human interest that could transmute bare fact to drama.

"Glad you don't mind, Doc," said Pete Collins. "The Inspector minds—plenty."

Ash kept his face intact: the professional smile he offered

his visitors was part of the armour. "When did *he* join the tour, Andy?"

"From the beginning," said Andy. He dropped his long-legged bulk in the most comfortable chair as he spoke; Dale Easton had already settled on the window seat. "Pete was having his first beer with Otto, in the morgue——"

Martin Ash spread his hands, soothing Hurlburt without words. "Say no more, Andy. I'd trust Pete in this as I'd trust myself, Inspector."

Hurlburt settled in the facing arm-chair. "How far is that, Dr. Ash?"

"Tell me what you know," said Martin. "We'll see how he reacts."

"Let me tell what *I* know, first," said Collins. "I doubt if the Inspector can top it at the moment. First off, Korff picks up his two dump cases on the warehouse platform. The CD squad comes into the picture—complete with Geiger counters and sluicers. Victims rushed to emergency—stripped down and, presumably, decontaminated. As of now, the D.O.A.'s on ice. The other one's upstairs, with a wire recorder and a cop—when and if he decides to stop snoring and start talking. Which, at time of writing, is a poor bet either way. Have I left anything out?"

Ash frowned and glanced at Andy. The resident surgeon tossed up his hands. "His injuries were extensive. Frankly, I don't understand why he's alive at all. Thanks to our injections, his endocrines are in gear—after a fashion. I hope to get him conscious, but I'm making no promises."

Pete Collins yawned and spread a wad of copy paper flat on one knee. "Take over if you like, Inspector," he said. "I'm all ears."

Martin Ash did his best to beam on this war in the making. Hurlbut, he reflected, resembled a discontented graduate student more than a specialist in the homicidal aberrations of man: from his horn rims to his neat grey striped linen suit, he was more student than sleuth—with a generous soupçon of cynicism under his easy manner, the cynicism of the man of the world, who has looked on most human activity and found it without coherence or inner meaning. By contrast,

Pete Collins seemed the eager second-year undergraduate, waiting expectant at the master's feet. Martin needed a second glance to note the tired sparrow pockets under the reporter's eyes, the sag of the body under those expensive tweeds. Hurlburt has kept his alertness, he thought. Pete is a full back gone to seed.

The Inspector spoke first, as Pete's eyes dropped to the copy paper on his knee. "Of course you heard they came from Brookhaven?"

"Since when would a couple of radioactive burn cases from Long Island turn up in a Manhattan warehouse?"

"Brookhaven's the word you're using in your story, Collins—and don't you forget it."

"Never mind my story for now, Inspector. I'm shooting for day after tomorrow, and the week after. Don't forget, the *Chronicle* has a man at Brookhaven too. They've reported no accidents over there."

"Maybe we'll play it even closer," said Hurlbut. "Those could have been fluoric acid burns, you know——"

"You'll never sell that one to the news agencies either."

"Why? No one but you knows that the cases were radioactive."

"Correction, Inspector. That CD foreman was a talker. He'd laid the whole story on the line before your boys could muzzle him——"

"We can muzzle the agencies," said Hurlbut quietly. "Just as we can muzzle you. Tomorrow the *Chronicle* runs a straightaway item about two workers from Brookhaven, overcome *en route* to their jobs and picked up on this doorstep. We'll mention that one is still living, and keep our fingers crossed. Maybe it'll bring the right man out of hiding. Maybe he's already skedaddled with his load of mischief. It's still worth the chance——"

"Give a little more," said the reporter. "Suppose you were stealing Grade A chemicals for a profit—what'd you go after first? They say the Russians have plenty of uranium. What about tritium? Or heavy water?"

Hurlbut sighed. "Come out of your daze, Collins. Heavy water couldn't burn a man to death."

"What about one of those top-secret compounds they haven't even dared to name?"

"Washington is worrying that angle right now," said Hurlbut. "I'd keep my nose clear of it, if I were you."

"You're among friends, Inspector. Why won't you admit that the stuff's been leaking out of every port on the Atlantic seaboard? Or would you say that they've got the whole shebang in a box right now—somewhere in mid-Manhattan?"

"That's nonsense, and you know it."

"Play it close, if you must," said Collins. "But you must admit that this hysteria about *bombing* New York is strictly for the comic books. One of those boxes could be ticking on Park Avenue right now—and we can both name the address. Any Oak Ridge student with the wrong kind of passport could put one together in his spare time—and buy his plane ticket just before he set the clock——"

"Maybe *you* should be writing those comic books, Collins."

Ash cut in quickly. "Even if all this is true," he said, "it's something we hardly want to face just now. Let's assume it's simply another case of thievery, until the Inspector proves otherwise. Above all, let's keep our suspicions to ourselves— along with what news we have."

"The only real news we have now is that breather upstairs," said Collins. "And he may stop breathing at any moment— as Dr. Gray just pointed out."

"We've a recorder at his bedside," said the Inspector. "You'll hear the first playback, if you'll take orders now."

Pete pulled down the corners of his mouth. "I'm on your team, Inspector. How often must I tell you?"

"Either he talks," said Hurlbut, "or he's a dead end. Unless we can name him from his dental work. From the outside, you can't be sure if he's a man or an orang-utang——"

"Does a query go on the teletype, just the same?"

"The query is out now. Not that we expect much. That neighbourhood is as deserted as a moon crater after dark. Maybe a hundred trucks an hour use it as a short cut to the midtown tunnel. Until we've had Dr. Easton's autopsy, we can't even be sure those tw fellows got their lumps in New York——"

Dale Easton lifted a detaining hand from the window seat. "Correction, Inspector. This isn't official yet, of course. But I'd stake my licence that those were fresh burns. And I think your medical examiner will agree."

"It's a six-State teletype just the same," said Hurlbut. "And of course we'll comb the district for witnesses. You can print that much, Collins—with the official statement about Brookhaven. And make sure you mention the one who's alive! That's most important——"

"Pardon me, if I sound dramatic," said the reporter, "but shouldn't you give that policeman at the bedside some support —at least, till morning?"

"There's a cordon round the hospital now, if anyone's interested," said Hurlbut. "That's something else you'll keep out of your story." He got up in earnest and pulled his hat over one eyebrow. Martin Ash just escaped smiling as he rose to extend his hand. With that flamboyant gesture Inspector John Hurlbut ceased to be a doctor of philosophy. Now he was on his feet, with his bald crown covered, he was every inch the detective who had come up from harness.

"I'll step in in the forenoon, Dr. Ash, with what news I have." The Inspector favoured Pete Collins with a parting scowl. "For your sake, I hope it *was* a falling out of thieves— if I make myself clear." He left the office with a curt nod for the two younger doctors—a poker face that had retained its composure to the end.

"I thought he'd ask for Korff," said Martin Ash. "Tony's feelings will be hurt."

"The sergeant who reported those cases was at Hiroshima, too," said Collins. "There wasn't much to add." He dropped his fold of copy paper in the waste-basket and followed the Inspector's trail with all the aplomb of a slightly weary bloodhound. He was humming as he paused in the doorway.

"In case you're wondering about the tune, gentlemen . . . ?"

"I recognize it," said Ash. "Gounod's 'Funeral March of a Marionette'."

"The theme song of our generation, Doctor," said the reporter. "Those who insist on humming 'God Bless America'

prove they have no ear for music. Hold everything, Inspector.
You can give me a lift uptown."

Ash rocked quietly in his swivel chair. "Does Hurlbut
know more than he's saying?"

Dale laughed outright. "Right now, sir, I'd say he knows
less. What about you, Andy?"

"I'll answer that question with another," said the surgeon.
"How many D.O.A.s have you autopsied this past month
without a tag? How many has the medical examiner named
afterwards?"

Ash nodded, out of his own memory book. He, too, had
ridden enough ambulances to endorse the cruel logic of his
resident surgeon's remark. The perfect crime, after all, was
a commonplace in any slum. The destroyer who struck by
night, and vanished without a trace, was as familiar as one's
next-door neighbour in these sunless canyons. Weighing this
truism, Ash could wonder at his opposition to Catherine's
ambitious plans for East Side General—to say nothing of his
own future. A threat like tonight's would be unthinkable,
once they had accepted their last glittering offer, sold out
in toto, and moved the whole hospital uptown. Far uptown—
where trees could spread their leaves in May, and sunlight
touched every window.

"I won't keep you, Andy," he said. "You should have
gone off duty hours ago. And I'm sure you've a job in the
morgue, Dale. Thanks again for not being alarmed——"

But he sat for a long time after his assistants had quitted
the office. Now, more than ever, he admitted he was powerless
to work tonight. Certainly he had no logical reason to be
afraid; he could feel nothing but contempt for this human
flotsam that had been tossed into his domain. Yet there was
no denying the chill that clutched his heart.

When he entered his office he had put a surgeon's long
coat over his evening clothes—his invariable custom when
he stole time to return to the hospital. The crisp white linen
never failed to restore his sense of belonging, the serenity
he lost (as inevitably as a swimmer who ventures beyond
his depth) whenever he stayed too long uptown. And yet, as
he stripped off the surgeon's office garb and donned his

London-tailored evening coat, he could find no real fault with the image reflected from the pier-glass in his wardrobe door.

A bit stocky for the diplomat, he thought—a little tired at the edges, like a Hollywood stand-in who has posed too often since the day's shooting began. But even Marty Aschoff could not deny that Martin Ash belonged to that tail coat. That he had earned the right to wear it—as surely as he deserved the rosette of the Legion of Honour in his buttonhole.

I'm an actor in two worlds, he thought, and I know my lines by heart. He left the thought at his desk and moved quickly among the hooded typewriters of his ante-room to the steps that wound down to the great, shadowed rotunda of the hospital proper.

Thanks to the hour, the entrance hall was quiet now, as the last stragglers from the private pavilions moved from elevator to taxi. The wards had sent their visitors downstairs a good hour ago. Sensitive, as always, to the changing moods of the hospital, his eyes moved automatically to the three constants—the rectangle of light that spilled from the central switchboard, the statue of Jesus that stood, with outspread hands, on the ramp that led to the nurses' chapel, and the figure in the wheel chair, just outside the operator's window.

He could not remember crossing that marble lobby without finding the hospital chaplain in his place. So long as there had been an East Side General Hospital there had been a Father O'Leary, ready to comfort the sick of every age or creed. Even when arthritis had crippled his joints at last the padre had insisted on visiting his charges in this same wheel chair. Now, thanks to the hormone that had just saved a criminal's life upstairs, Father O'Leary's pain had been eased—and all but cured.

Tonight the breath of summer moved softly through the great brass-bound doors that were never closed. The padre lay back in his wheel chair, apparently dozing at his post. Martin Ash, wise in the ways of the hospital chaplain, did not even trouble to approach on tiptoe. He could feel the lines of fatigue smooth away from his own tight clamped mouth, long before Father O'Leary spoke, in an easy whisper that was as familiar as the white forelock that lay across one temple.

"Good evening, Martin. Aren't you a bit late for Catherine's party?"

"Who told you this was a party night?"

The padre cocked one blue eye towards the telephone operator's window. "Who but Ethel? Your wife just called to ask when you'd be coming uptown. Ethel, like a good second in command, said you were on your way now."

Martin Ash sat down on the curve of the balustrade that separated Father O'Leary's vantage point from the wide marble desert of the rotunda proper. "So you still know what happens here before it happens?"

"Why not—when I'm at the nerve centre?"

"How many years has it been, Father—or is that question indiscreet?"

"Not at all," said the priest. "You know I was here when they brought Him in." He did not raise his eyes as he spoke— it was Ash who looked up at the benign, deep-shadowed statue in the recess above them. "Name the date if you must, Martin. You know your medical history."

"Our foundations were laid more than fifty years ago," said Ash. Humour the aged when you can, he thought; we've played this same scene, with the same lines, for a hundred midnights. "Isn't it a long time to stay in one parish?"

"Not when you need your parish—and it needs you."

The priest spread his hands above the rough hospital blanket that covered his frail body to the waist. With a real sense of shock Ash noticed their almost transparent thinness. Yet Father O'Leary's voice was robust enough when he spoke again, out of another tranquil silence.

"I can remember when they brought Him in for the first time, Martin. There was nothing here but the foundations. We kept the statue covered with tarpaulins while they built the hospital round it."

The hospital you're remembering, thought Ash, and the hospital we're in tonight are more than half a century apart. In your way, you're the only link between two eras. He tried to picture the old priest in Catherine's dream hospital uptown, and gave up the effort. He had tried before to explain Catherine's reasons for insisting that the move was overdue. Father O'Leary had always listened with the same patient smile. But Ash had felt sure his words were wasted.

"It would be like draining His lifeblood away," said the priest.

Martin Ash looked up from his musings. Had he voiced his indecision aloud? Or had Father O'Leary simply read his mind?

"Has Catherine discussed her plans with you, Padre?"

"No, Martin. I've only heard the rumours. Catherine has stayed away from us for a long time now. Will you tell her how much we miss her?"

You mean that, too, thought Ash. You're prepared to forgive the woman who plots your extinction. He had no illusions about Father O'Leary, if the move uptown was made. Like the Saviour who brooded above the rotunda, the priest's roots went deep. Far too deep to survive a transplanting.

"Catherine owns most of our outstanding bonds," he said. "Most of our board members are officers in her father's banking chain——"

"We all know that, Martin."

"Then you must know I've fought the idea. I've always felt that I belonged here——"

"East Side General belongs here, Martin. You and your hospital are one and the same. You can't divorce yourself from it—any more than you can divorce Catherine."

"You think I can have both, then?"

"You always have," said the old priest quietly. "Why shouldn't you go on loving your work—and your wife?"

Because I *can't* have both, thought Ash. Not on my terms. Never, in all my married years, have I felt free to give myself wholeheartedly to this hospital, without the risk of losing Catherine. How can I deny we've grown steadily farther apart, ever since she dreamed this idea of moving uptown? Or that I must give in soon or lose her completely?

Aloud he said only, "I can't fight her for ever."

"Of course you can't, Martin. That would be no marriage at all."

"Then you wouldn't hate me too much—if I agreed to the move?"

"You must do what you think best," said the old priest slowly. "I have no right at all to advise you." His chin dropped to his cupped hand: for a long time he stared straight ahead —so quietly that Ash was sure his presence was forgotten. "I'll say this much, Martin—don't attempt to force the issue. Time has its own way of settling quarrels. Often it's a way we least suspect."

How much, Martin wondered, did Father O'Leary know of the burn cases Korff had brought in tonight? Was he facing the threat squarely—and suggesting that some hidden engine of death (ticking inexorably just outside these white walls) might blow them skywards tomorrow?

It would be a solution of sorts, he admitted. Manhattan real estate would be no less valuable if its slums were levelled at a blast—along with the hospital that had served those slums so faithfully. Perhaps the only way to remake our jerry-built cosmos is to raze it and start anew. He put the insane picture behind him and laid a hand on the priest's shoulder.

"We must keep what we have, Padre. Somehow, we must stay where we belong."

Father O'Leary smiled but did not lift his head. "God bless you, Martin. God guide you both."

Dr. Martin Ash walked quickly across the rotunda. When he turned back in the entrance door a nurse was wheeling the chair along the ramp to the elevators and Father O'Leary's room in Schuyler Tower. The old priest sat quiet as a stone. His eyes seemed glazed—and as empty of life as the eyes of the figure that brooded in the shadows above him.

VII

Deep in the hospital mass, where a corridor branched east to the surgical wards and west to the staircase that led downwards to the morgue, two doctors paused by common consent, as though reluctant to part company.

"Be honest, Andy," said Dale Easton. "Admit you're scared blue. You've every right to be."

The resident surgeon kicked open a fire door and stepped out to the cool of evening—or what poor substitute an air shaft afforded. "I guess I can steal a minute for a cigarette," he said. "I haven't time to be afraid. Not with the life I'm leading these days."

Dale leaned in the open doorway and offered his friend a light. "Ash didn't seem in the least flummoxed. But of course it wouldn't show."

"Speak for yourself," said Andy.

"Personally, I'm buying the smuggling theory, along with Hurlbut. It's easier to sleep on than a time bomb."

"Don't tell me you're resigned to that sort of grand larceny," said the surgeon. "Give us a few more years of stockpiling, and we may accumulate the energy—atomic or otherwise—to save all our lives. And cure our ills in the bargain——"

"That I'm *not* buying," said Dale Easton. "No more are you. The last thing mankind needs nowadays is a cure-all."

"Aren't you getting pretty profound—considering the way we earn our living?"

The pathologist grinned above the steady spark of his cigarette. "A fellow still has time to think, down there with Otto and the stiffs. Too much time, I suppose. But I could tell you what's wrong with the world, if you pressed me a little."

Andy Gray did not smile. Dale Easton's opinions, like Dale's autopsies, were not to be taken lightly. "Just so long as it's a secret between us," he said.

"Point One, we've let the machine get away from us," said Dale. "Point Two, most of us don't give a damn if it has. Point Three, the machine is so completely in control of our lives today, we'd break our necks if we tried to get in the driver's seat again. Check, so far?"

"Are you asking the steel brute to do an about-face and worship man?"

"I'm saying it should knuckle down, at least, and take orders. But why should it listen? What's worse, why should my average fellow human *want* it to listen? From where he's sitting—if he happens to be on the right side of the Atlantic—life has never been easier, or more profitable——"

"In spite of the headlines?"

"Who gives a damn about news any more? Scaring headlines are commonplace nowadays. Most of us have lived with doom so long we don't believe in it, any more than in Santa Claus. Show the average American the front page today, and he'll turn to the baseball score. And I'm not belittling my fellow citizens. No one can live with doom indefinitely, without pretending it doesn't exist. Look at the way we reacted to Pete Collins's crack about a time bomb. For our sanity's sake, could we have reacted differently?"

"And you blame this on the machine?"

"Doesn't it deserve the blame—to say nothing of the grease monkeys who made it? Why should we sit back and let it work for us—yes, even think for us? And why can't we be ashamed of our surrender—until it's too late?"

"Just because they've invented a mechanical brain to do your income tax is no reason to stop working."

"I can't think of a better reason offhand. Thanks to cybernetics, the original menace of the steam engine and the mechanical reaper has been magnified to a surrealist nightmare. A jabberwock that Dali should immortalize on canvas——"

"You just said the jabberwocks were giving mankind more time to enjoy life."

"Mankind is hypnotized by the monster. He only *thinks* he's having fun. Inside himself, he's never been emptier. And never more afraid. Not since he's lifted his knuckles from the ground."

Andy looked hard at Dale. Behind the thick horn rims the pathologist's eyes were twinkling in the gloom of the air shaft.

"If humanity's case is that desperate, why are you so cheerful?"

"Personally, I'm an incurable optimist," said Dale. "It's only when I think of man in the mass that I start bellowing."

"Man has blundered through other crises and survived."

"Because he depended on his own strength. Not on a

self-starter he could spark with a button. Where's his pride in
being human, nowadays?"

"Are you saying that every time a machine does something that only men could do before, it takes something out
of men?"

"Shall I quote Thoreau's remark about railways—to
mention just one boon to humanity?"

"I read the Sage of Walden too, Dale. Wasn't it something
about looking behind the smoke—and finding that only a
few are riding, the rest run over?"

"Don't tell me you agree. I was expecting an argument."

"I'll go this far with you. Machinery by and large has
brought power and abundance rather than happiness. Too
often it's put the power in the wrong hands—and distributed
the abundance so badly that war has become all but inevitable.
Would the average Russian be growling in his throat today
if he ate as often as the average American? And would all this
talk of man's delf-destruction continue for one moment if the
average man could be sure he'd eat as well tomorrow?"

"You haven't given me an answer," said Dale.

Andy blew a smoke ring towards the Manhattan stars.
"I'll stay with you on one count. Man still wants a cure-all—
but it must come from within. Maybe he'll discover he must
go over the brink to find it. I agree that the average life must
contain more individual striving before the species can truly
improve—that we must rediscover our pride before we can
give the machine its orders. And I'll agree that discovery is
getting harder with each passing year——"

"You haven't lost faith?"

"Not for a moment. Have you?"

"Sometimes," admitted Easton. "My own profession
frightens me most of all. *We're* gadget-ridden, too, you
know. A few years ago the general practitioner would sweat
his heart out to save a single patient from pneumonia. Today
he orders penicillin and leaves his office on the dot——"

"There are still more patients than doctors."

"My point remains. A physician can't afford to lose his
pride, any more than John Doe. Look at the average intern
on the make today—like Tony Korff. From the start, he's

had his eye on a city practice. Usually it's a speciality within a speciality. His goal is a three-car garage and mink for his wife. Even with helicopters, the G.P. will be extinct in another generation——"

"Don't say that so hastily," murmured Andrew Gray, "you're looking at one now."

"You're a born surgeon. And if you weren't a throwback you'd be earning your fifty thousand uptown with the career boys."

"Surgery's my trade, I'll grant you. But I've kept up my *materia medica* too. I'll tell you more, Dale. The moment my shoulders stop itching from that Army tunic I'm heading for the sticks—without a helicopter." Even in the half-light of the hospital fire escape Andy's craggy profile seemed to soften with each word. "If you like, I'll take you with me. My guess is that you're a throwback, too."

"Don't tell me this tall timber is in Florida?"

"My home State—where else? I'm glad you remembered I'm a Florida Yankee." Hearing his voice go on, Andy Gray could feel the tension round his heart grow less with every syllable. "A town on the Gulf Coast you've never heard of. A turpentine-and-catfish town that's been self-contained since before the Civil War. My brother's the minister down there. We're going to build a cinder-block clinic, with a church attached. He'll treat souls there and I'll treat bodies. But we'll be working together—that's the important thing. My kids are going to grow up there on the water with real people."

"And starve in the bargain?"

"No one starves in that corner of Florida. Nature sees to that, right at your front door."

"I meant emotionally."

"Wrong again, Dale. You see, I've always wanted a cultural education. I didn't have time for it in college, as you did—I didn't even have parents to see me through so I took the shortest way. I fought for my M.D. and my internship. Eventually I hope to learn to be a man. A human being I'd be proud to know, not just a scientific instrument."

"Maybe you've just summed up our discussion, in yourself."

"Maybe. A man never knows what he's capable of, until he tries."

"You might even say that's the secret of happiness—to be proud of what you are, not of what you have." The pathologist flipped his cigarette into the dark. "Incidentally, is this dream on a full-time basis?"

"Far from it. I think this is the first time I've put it into words." Andy kicked the fire-door open and they entered the hospital once again, muting their voices from long habit. "Maybe I'll scuttle it day after tomorrow. I might even move uptown with the hospital, and join the Park Avenue Association."

"With or without Pat Reed?"

Andy scowled at his wrist watch. "So you've heard I had the backing—whenever I want it? I was wondering how fast that story had got round."

"Going to visit your beauteous patient now?"

"After I've made the rounds. As resident, I can hardly do less."

"And I must open that burn case," said Dale. "Want to look in later?"

"I'll stop for a beer, if I'm not side-tracked."

Hurrying towards the surgical wards with his nervous long-legged stride, Andy Gray fought down his rising discontent. Somehow, he had never intended to put his dream in words. Now that he had stated it precisely, he knew that he must sound mildly insane, even to Dale. A dedication to life above self, while it was applauded in the abstract, could never be explained in strictly practical terms to another human. The pursuit of wealth for wealth's sake had always been the American way, the three-car garage the culmination of the American dream. Even to hint that life might be more rewarding with no car at all was worse than un-American. Wondering what Pat Reed would say if he asked her to share that existence as his wife, he just escaped laughing outright.

But this was no time to remember Pat, or Pat's all too earthy lures. So far, he thought, I've held those lures at arm's length: if I can fight them down tonight it's unlikely that she'll keep up this huntress-and-quarry game much longer.

He felt his pulse settle into a familiar, trip-hammer beat as he pictured what was awaiting him, in the Tower suite.

Try as he might, he could not picture the Florida piny woods in detail now. The metallic whisper of palms in the wind, the hard, bright cobalts of the sea beyond his brother's veranda were stage props now for an impossible morality play—unreal as a painted plate in some encyclopædia.

But he forgot his bewilderments as he stepped under the drop-light at the entrance to the men's surgery ward and picked up his first chart. I'll go next year, he promised himself. Or the year after—even if I must go alone. In the meantime, who can deny that I'm needed here?

At first glance the huge, high-domed room seemed an abode of the dead, so quiet were the sleepers in their long rows of cots. He moved down the line with the nurse on duty, pausing at each bed to check the charts, listening with a practised ear to the soft-drawn breathing of a patient still too deep in post-operative anæsthesis to know if he lived or died. Carcinoma of the prostate, he noted mechanically. He'll live, thanks to our knowledge of the sex hormones. Because he came to us in time, he may even leave this bed with a complete cure.

The next bed (already screened away from the rest of the ward) told its own mute story. Pete Revelli, he thought absently—known to a generation of interns as Pete the Barber—who had started life as a hospital bootlegger and ended as the head waiter of a famous restaurant. Pete the good provider, who had been too busy seeing his three law-abiding sons through Columbia to notice the diseased gall bladder that had brought him, screaming, to the table that afternoon, too late for surgery. Andy breathed a prayer for an old friend as he covered Pete's face again and signed the death certificate on the nurse's clip board. At least *he* went out happy, he thought—a citizen and a model father, despite his bizarre start. He has left his world a better place than he found it. How many of us can say as much?

On his way to the private wing he paused in a small room at the end of the corridor to check on his own special patient. The small boy who lay in the hospital bed seemed even smaller against that sterile desert of white; the bluish skin tone was pronounced, in the glow of the bed lamp. The nurse spoke softly at his elbow.

"We just discontinued oxygen, Doctor. He's resting comfortably now."

Andy moved automatically to the oxygen tent that still stood in the corner. "Keep it handy, in case. And call me if there's any change before morning."

But he did not leave the boy's bedside for some moments. From birth, Jackie Simon had been what is known, in popular parlance, as a 'blue baby', and yet, like most infants with his particular affliction, he had somehow managed to survive. Now, at the age of six, he seemed too frail to be a tenant of earth. Andy continued to stare down at the bedside chart—the clinical picture was there, clear as a page from a surgeon's textbook. When Jackie had been only a bundle of cells in his mother's womb something had gone wrong with the cluster that eventually formed into heart and blood vessels. As a result Jackie had been left a heart cripple—victim of the developmental defect that doctors labelled the tetralogy of Fallot.

A child of the tenements, Jackie was unusual in other ways. His father was a musician of sorts, his mother a schoolteacher invalided before she could draw her pension. Even at this tender age the boy had shown signs of talent in his father's field: when disaster struck, both parents had been saving what they could to launch a possible career. Neither had realized Jackie's true difficulty, until he had almost died of pneumonia that spring. Dr. Andy Gray, noting that telltale blue tint from the boy's first days in the wards, had made the diagnosis—and offered the only possible way out. Thanks to the work of the pioneers at Hopkins University, Jackie's ailment could be cured by the knife, though it was an operation that few surgeons would risk, even now. Andy was risking it tomorrow, with the parents' consent.

It would be a ticklish job, of course—but those were the kind he loved. A gamble that was not a gamble, strictly speaking—for Jackie's life was already lost unless his heart could be restored to its normal function. Here, at least, the duel between life and death was clear-cut, with a reward worthy of the challenge.

He left the room with his calm restored. This was the part of his day he liked most—a panorama he could revel in alone, with no need to apologize for the emotion he felt as he looked upon his work and found it good. Even the girl in the GYN ward, whose life he had saved only yesterday, thanks to the hysterectomy that had removed the flaming infection of her abortion. Even the would-be suicide whose slashed wrist arteries he had tied off under a brachial nerve block. Yes, it was a strange, rich world whose interest was never-ending, for its canvas was broad as life itself. Like any man-made cosmos, it had its passions and its torpors, its unbearable happiness and sorrow. But the excitement never varied. It was part of its blood stream now—like the first night of a play endlessly repeated, a tragedy that had its echo of burlesque, a human comedy with a touch of the divine where he was at once author, *raisonneur*, and audience.

With no conscious sense of transition he found himself stepping out of an elevator on the top floor of Schuyler Tower, that region of individual suites with penthouse exposure and pastels to beguile every convalescent. Not that pastels and Pat Reed had any real affinity—even if Pat had had the slightest excuse for this prolonged stay on the outskirts of his domain. Knowing that his feet must carry him through her door eventually, he managed to linger a moment more in the all-glass solarium, with its breath-taking view of the East River and the grey city slumbering beneath.

He looked down for a while at the few lights that still showed among the huddled tenement blocks to the north and west—and pulled back by instinct when he heard the whisper of wheels in the corridor. Father O'Leary's chair glided into view, with the padre half dozing in the wicker depths. Andy needed only one glance to identify the white silhouette that supplied the motive power; after all, it was quite like Julia Talbot to make sure that the hospital chaplain went to his rest on schedule.

Even in the dark, he thought, there's no mistaking her purity—or her dedication. A stanza of poetry came into his

mind unbidden, and he spoke it in a whisper to the unheeding
gloom:

> *She walks in beauty, like the night*
> *Of cloudless climes and starry skies;*
> *And all that's best of dark and bright*
> *Meet in her aspect and her eyes. . . .*

He had known, without asking, that Julia Talbot came
from a land of wide horizons—a happy land, that she had
deserted of her own volition to seek a destiny of her own
choosing. From the first day their paths had crossed here,
he had sensed the depth of that dedication. A Nightingale
with the down still on her pinions, he had told himself.
Regardless of his own motives, no man had the right to
tamper with such innocence.

No man at all. He repeated the conviction now. It was odd
that every other man who had known Julia Talbot during
her years at the hospital followed the same instinct. The
nurses' home had always been a happy hunting-ground, for
staff and patient alike: by any usual yardstick, a girl as pretty
as Julia could have taken her pick of both doctors and
convalescents—matrimonially or otherwise. And yet she had
gone her own way serenely, before and after her capping.
Her future already seemed pre-ordained as Emily Sloane's.

Was this a logical fulfilment for a woman, after all?
Would it be too wrong of him to break through the girl's
wall of reserve, to make his own offer, before the hospital
claimed her?

With a companion like Julia at his side, he could go home
again without fear of failure. Somehow he knew that Julia
would understand that stubborn dream of life at the water's
edge, in a tranquil, sun-bitten land. She would see that this
scramble for position could break a man before his time, that
the driving pace could force him to other escapes . . . Pat
Reed, to name just one.

Julia could save him from Pat and all that a second, final
surrender to Pat implied. He had only to hold out his hand.

Knowing in advance that such capitulation was beyond
him, he lit a final cigarette and moved out to the shallow

balcony that dominated the river and the great bridges to the north. Heat haze pressed down on New York tonight—a heavy heat, pregnant with the promise of unfallen rain. The night was a beast, waiting to pounce, to tear his last scruple away.

At that moment he felt sure he could never retrace the dusty path he had followed. Like his generation, he would not go home how ever glibly he might plan that home-coming. Too much bitterness lay between—too many broken hopes. And (if the truth were faced squarely) too much ambition to raise himself above the poverty that had dogged his footsteps from the beginning.

Ten-thirty sounded from the clock tower just above his head, a muted bell that seemed part of the hospital's own heartbeat. A scant hundred feet down the hall, Pat Reed would be awake and waiting—curled in her high hospital bed, confident that he would arrive before drowsiness claimed her. Confident, too, that she could force him to an avowal from which there was no retreating.

Had he clung to this escape to Florida as an antidote to Pat's long-term lure? Had he invested Julia Talbot with qualities she did not possess, to create an alternative to Pat Reed and the Reed millions? His lips twisted in the smile that his friends knew too well, a grin that went deeper than cynicism, a wordless admission that man is frail and woman the vessel of that frailty. Julia Talbot would choose her own husband in time, when the feathers of the Nightingale had been replaced by the armour of maturity. He, praise Heaven, could keep his own integrity so long as his hand could wield a scalpel. As for the natives of his brother's parish—well, they would continue to die of hookworm and pellagra, as they were born to die.

Life is a weed, he thought. It will flourish without me, no matter what holocausts may sweep the world. In the meantime I am the resident surgeon of East Side General, and I've one more patient waiting.

His feet had already taken him down the corridor, past the respectful smile of the floor nurse, up to the heavy brass knob of Pat Reed's door. His eye dropped mechanically to the leather sleeve that kept the door from closing tightly, even now. It's all the insurance I need tonight, he told himself solemnly, hearing the faint purr of Pat's radio within.

He watched his hand lift slowly and fasten on that knob of brass. Then he went in swiftly, without pausing for the formality of a knock.

VIII

Dr. Martin Ash followed the curve of the hospital drive and slid under the wheel of his convertible. He had already noted the unfamiliar patrolman, chatting quietly with the watchman at the gate: now, as he let out his brake and coasted down the incline to the street, he could see other blue figures, pacing unobtrusively in the dark on both sides of the hospital entrance. For all the world as though we were entertaining a visiting celebrity, he thought testily. Celebrities are Catherine's field, not mine. Then he remembered that Hurlbut had promised them a cordon tonight, while the burn victim still lived. He just escaped snorting as he nudged his automatic starter.

As always, he felt his heart lift with the mighty purr of the engine. The Cadillac convertible (it had been Catherine's gift on his forty-fifth birthday) was a giant come to life, ready to grant his slightest whim without question. If he liked, he could cut across town to the Holland Tunnel, the New Jersey turnpike—and that pack trip through the Rockies he had promised himself since boyhood . . . never uptown to the Waldorf and the charity fête that his wife was sponsoring even now in the grand ballroom.

The temptation died as he coasted to a stop to say good night to the gateman. And yet, once he was on the road, he swung south instead of north, skirting the dank wall of the brewery, then turning south again, to enter a street of rotting brownstones. The block was half alley, half front yard for the teeming dwellings that opened on either side, spilling their young to the pavements in prodigal, raucous bursts, whining with pushcarts, hideous with this morning's

garbage pails and last week's bortsch. Despite the advanced
hour the whole area still pulsed with life—each house front
clotted with humanity, each window black with gossiping
heads. Parking the long, sleek car between two quarrelling
pushcarts, accepting the salutes of the vendors as his due,
Martin Ash stepped out to the pavement and mounted the
steps of the only home he had ever known.

"Hi, Doc! How goes it?"

He shouted a greeting to the tailor who peered up from
his basement lair—and wondered if Rifkin was calculating
the price of his tail coat. Not that the doctor and his evening
dress were strangers to this neighbourhood: Martin Ash
seldom quitted the hospital without stopping at his parents' for
a moment, regardless of the hour.

Childhood closed round him with its treacherous sounds
and odours as he mounted the creaking stair: the endless,
mingled cacophony of the tenement, like a giant heart that
never slept, the brown smell of poverty like a miasma that
claimed its own for evermore.

On the next landing he paused for breath, letting the
memory come back unbidden. The day long ago, when he
had run screaming up these same stairs, terrorized by the
warm taste of blood on his cut lip. Even now he could feel
the impact of the fist in his face and the warm, protecting
arms of his father, when he reached sanctuary at last.

"He called me a dirty kike, Papa!"

"Quiet, Marty! The whole house will hear you!"

But he had sobbed his heart out nonetheless, while his
mother applied cold cloths to his lip—and berated his assailant
in a tongue more natural to them all than the English he
brought home from the school playground.

"Who was it, Marty?"

"Pud Donegan. I knocked him down. And he's bigger'n
me, too——"

His father's voice had been calm and quiet. "You shouldn't
fight, son."

"But he called me a *kike*, Papa!"

"What is a kike, Marty? A name, that's all. Do you know
why he hit you? Why he used that name?"

"He hates me. They all hate me. I wish I hadn't been born a Jew."

Martin Aschoff, Sr., had shaken his head with all the deliberation of a prophet pronouncing judgment. "You do not mean that, son. You are scared and hurt, so? And when men are scared and hurt they say and do things they don't mean. That's why young Donegan hit you—why he used that name. He's afraid of something, so he takes it out on you——"

"He won't hit me again, Papa!" (Even now he could remember how magically the sobs had died away.)

"There will be other blows, Marty. You must learn to bear them. It will be easier if you put your own fears behind you. Above all, if you take pride in your race. Remember, the Most High made a covenant with your father Abraham—and He has never broken it. A Jew is always a Jew. No matter where he is, that covenant goes with him—as his shield and his pride——"

Now, as he climbed one more flight, Martin Ash could hear those words again. They had stayed with him since that day—through the City College of New York, through medical school and the snubs of his internship, through those first terrible days when Catherine's people had fought an underground battle to break the engagement, to spoil the marriage itself. But not once had he been ashamed of being a Jew. He felt no shame tonight as he opened his parents' door—only a quiet pride.

There was his father in his skull cap, a shawl over his shoulders despite the heat outside. As always, Martin Aschoff sat in his favourite chair, with the radio playing softly close to his ear. All but blinded by cataracts that were not quite ripe enough for surgery, the old man could barely distinguish dark from light, though his facile fingers could tune in his favourite symphonies by touch alone.

"Hello, Martin. You're late tonight."

"Hello, Papa." The director of East Side General bent above the arm-chair to kiss his father's wrinkled forehead. His mother had already bustled out of the small kitchen, with both arms held out in greeting. No matter how often her son might visit her, she offered the same welcome—the embrace for the wanderer returned from far places. Tonight, however, as she held him at arm's length to admire his evening clothes, Rebecca's face showed real concern.

"Already you are late at Catherine's party——"

"It's only a charity dance, Mother. It will go on without me."

"Catherine will not go on without you, my son. She needs you beside her, now."

"I'm on my way, Mother. I only stopped by for a moment —to see how you two were."

"Such nonsense! Would we, perhaps, fly away?" But his mother's tone had already betrayed her. So had the slow, groping pressure of his father's hand as it closed on his own. The Aschoffs had come to depend on these nightly visits as their only link with the bustling city without. They would have been hurt had he forgotten to stop tonight.

"What is the music, Papa?"

"Ach, Martin! With all I have told you, can you not recognize Beethoven?"

"Of course. The 'Moonlight'——"

"The 'Appassionata,' son. For shame!" Martin, Sr., was chuckling in his beard. It was a standing family joke that Martin, Jr., had no ear for music—and less memory. "Someday we will go over the symphonies together—when you have more time——"

"I wish we could, Papa. I don't seem to have time for anything these days—outside the hospital." Not even for Catherine, he thought—and admitted that he had come here deliberately, to postpone their meeting even longer. He sat at his father's side for awhile, listening to the composer's storm of bitter sweet passion.

"That man, too, has known despair," he said, all but unaware that he had spoken his thoughts aloud. Despair at mankind's capacity to ignore genius. Rage against that great blockhead, the world—translated into melody that would outlive the land that nurtured it. *My* rage, thought Martin Ash, can only beat out its strength against the stone walls that prison it. His mother's voice broke in on his musings.

"Come to the kitchen, Martin—and see what Catherine gave me. A *dishwasher* yet!"

The kitchen was fully modern—he had seen to that years ago. Tonight it still gleamed like new, from the electric range to the double porcelain sink. Beside the huge white rectangle of the refrigerator was an automatic dishwasher—Catherine's latest gift. Martin stared at it blankly, feeling a little of his resentment dissolve. It was no secret that Catherine was fond of his parents. Was this, perhaps, her latest bribe—her hope of lessening their unspoken objections to the hospital's move uptown?

"Have you used it yet, Mother?"

As they returned to the tiny parlour she looked at him with a laugh that was almost roguish. Both of them knew that the expensive machine would never be used—unless Catherine were present, and then only to keep from hurting her feelings. In Rebecca Aschoff's credo, food was part of the love you gave your family. Serving it was a privilege, never a chore. One didn't gather up the scraps and leavings of love and sluice them through a ravenous monster.

"Catherine was telling me how wonderful the new hospital will be when it is built," his mother said quietly. "It is a fine wife you have got, Martin——" But her voice had broken after all, and she did not quite meet his eyes. "We will miss you."

His father spoke above the dying strains of the music. "This is no longer the ghetto, Rebecca. In America there is no law to say the family must be close together. Martin has his life. He must live it—so."

"But if he goes uptown——"

"Always our boy will do what is best for him."

"But that's just it, Papa." Again Martin Ash was barely conscious that he had spoken aloud. "What is best?"

"What will make you happy is best, my son."

"But Catherine——" He let the thought take its own shape, knowing they would understand him without words. His wife had never hurt his parents consciously, either by word or deed. In her way, he knew, she loved them quite as much as he—even though she understood them not at all.

To her, they would always be an uninspiring old Jewish couple with their best years behind them—and no adventure before them but death. Try as she might, she could never see them with his eyes or understand their need for his nearness.

"Catherine is your wife," the old man said. "What she does, she thinks is best for you. But if she knows you will not be happy, she will do what you want."

"Ach, Martin," said his mother. "She is your wife indeed. And she gives tonight a ball—in your honour. You must go to her now."

On the stair again, he knew that he had not found the answer that he sought. The answer was waiting, deep in his own soul, and he was afraid to look there. Afraid to admit, even for an instant, that he sided with Catherine now. *She will do what you want, if she knows you will not be happy.* How could he put his unhappiness into words when Catherine had been his symbol of felicity for twenty years?

Working (like any honest wife) from the heart outwards, she had made him what he was. The Marty Aschoff he remembered was only a ghost, a figment of his parents' love who existed only in their stolen moments together. Martin Ash was his own man.—and he deserved the best, because he had earned the best.

He stumbled on the last step as he always did—and damned the soulless landlord who had neglected that last, loose board since time began. There was his Cadillac convertible, snugly parked between the two quarrelling pushcarts. Even tonight he could smile at the solemn ring of children that surrounded it, without daring to approach within touching distance of its glittering mudguards. Had a stranger dared to park here, the small fry from this block would have swarmed over his tonneau in an instant, to pry loose what souvenirs they could. Dr. Ash's Cadillac was something else again. Dr. Ash was a legend the slum dwellers respected instantly, regardless of age—and yearned with all their beings to emulate.

Perhaps Marty Aschoff was not a ghost, after all. Perhaps it was he who wanted desperately to sit in that skyscraper office, in the clean air of upper Manhattan. To read the word "Director" as if in a mirror through his ante-room door. To feel the respect and envy (particularly the envy) of the Park Avenue doctors who would still snub him if they dared. The doctors with their names in the Social Register and their ancestors safely deified in colonial churchyards.

He sighed—and the tenement street seemed to give back his sigh, like a tired body that knows it will never rest again. When he slid under the wheel of his car at last he remembered to lift his eyes to the miracle of Schuyler Tower, rising like a jet of white fire at the street's end. Dr. Ash felt a tear gather at the corner of one eyelid.

The car had already slipped into automatic gear. He did not lift his eyes from his driving as he skirted the hospital's back door. Then he turned down the private ramp and entered the traffic of the East River Drive, to keep his rendezvous with the woman he loved—in a world where he would be forever alien.

IX

The Beethoven hour on the radio, nearing its ending, had begun the last movement of the "Emperor". High in Schuyler Tower in the suite that Pat Reed had occupied for a week now, the music poured from the expensive portable set that Pat had brought here to solace her rest cure. The tall girl in the bed drank in the music with all her senses, savouring the last pounding rhythm as intently as she enjoyed the presence of Dr. Andrew Gray, now in the act of applying the cone of his stethoscope to the valley between her breasts. . . . He's remembering, too, she thought exultantly. That scowl doesn't fool me for a minute. Or the idiotic patter about charts and diets. He knows just why I'm here, and what medicine I really need. Why is he holding back, when he needs me just as badly?

The stethoscope was cold against her heart, but she ignored its persistent pressure, knowing that the beat had never been stronger. This late bed check was only routine. Andy had come here tonight for her sake, and his own. It was quite like him to bring in the floor nurse too—a line of communication, if he decided to retreat one more time.

"Continue medication, Miss Eccles. I think that's all."

Pat spoke sweetly, as the nurse moved out of the radius of her bed lamp. "Will I live, Doctor?"

"I think so, Miss Reed." He had always been careful to observe the formalities in the presence of the hospital staff. "Of course the final decision is Dr. Plant's, not mine." Plant was Pat Reed's personal physician, and one of the city's leading internists. It was Plant who had suggested that she come to Schuyler Towers for the "rest she so desperately needed". The phrase had been hers, not Plant's. Most humans in this century, she reflected, were desperately in need of rest. It was only the few who could enjoy it on their own terms.

She could afford to wait with lowered lids while Andy and his floor nurse conferred at the foot of her bed. It had been an amusing game so far—even if it was a trifle prolonged. Bed rest and a rigorous diet. Sedatives and an hour's exposure on the sun deck each afternoon. Exhaustive tests, to prove once again that Patricia Reed (like the grandfather who had founded the dynasty in Chicago beef) was a perfect physical specimen, ready and willing to outfight any man at his own game. An elaborate subterfuge, in short, while she waited for Andy Gray to admit that existence without her was unthinkable.

When you've had your own way from childhood, she reflected, waiting for anything can come hard. Especially a two-legged bundle of prejudices that calls himself a man. She had no doubt whatever of Andy's eventual capitulation. After all, no man who had enjoyed her favours once had failed to return.

Her heart pounded as the memories of those two wild weeks in Hawaii came surging back. She had been on one of her interminable, restless cruises then—with a second husband firmly dumped at Reno, and no new adventure in prospect. Andy had been fresh from service on the Asian mainland, a disillusioned veteran who had seemed, at first glance, unlikely material for a lover. Pat chuckled as she watched him covertly through lowered lashes. Herself an expert in such matters she had learned long ago not to judge a book by its cover.

Orders had called him to San Francisco (and his final discharge from the corps) long before she could tire of him as she had the others. In fact she was troubled by the nagging suspicion that he had been glad when the orders came. They had corresponded in the years that followed, while she had waited for him to give up this hospital job and return to her in earnest. Their shared passion had flamed briefly—when he had joined her for a winter carnival in Quebec, and again on a short holiday in Bermuda. But on these occasions he had shown no sign of making the job of entertaining Pat Reed a full-time career.

There had been other lovers in those years—even a near miss at a third husband, while she had sulked a summer away in France in the hope that Andy would join her. None of them had approached Andy in intensity. None had been more than a diversion, really, while she awaited the moment when she could brand him as her own.

'Brand' (she pursued) was a strong verb. Yet how else could she describe her effect on the men she had known? In Andy's case she would apply her trademark more gently —so carefully, in fact, that he would never feel its impact. Let him go on with his surgery, if he must. Thanks to her help, he might even have the recognition he deserved. Yes, no matter how she looked at it, marriage to Andy Gray was a desirable end. The culmination of twenty-nine years of hectic living, and its logical fulfilment.

She would be good for Andy, too. Her sophistication would be the perfect foil for his gaunt integrity. She could not help but enrich his outlook, even as she burnished him into a softer pattern. And of course her money would be there always, smoothing his path. . . . She opened her eyes wide. The nurse had just gone out on quiet tiptoe. Andy himself stood in the half-open door, with his lips twisted into a familiar smile. For one moment Pat was sure he would follow the nurse into the corridor. Then he came towards the bed and took one of her hands in his.

"It's about time," she said.

"I quite agree," he said. "What are you doing here?"

"Resting—on doctor's orders."

"What do we have here that you want?"

Pat offered her famous grin, the Gioconda smile that wilted most men in their tracks.

"I'm not buying now," she said.

"I'd say you were buying plenty: Eighty-nine a day for the suite alone——"

"I've made eighty-nine dollars while we've been talking."

"You—or your grandfather's stockyards?"

"Does it matter?"

"Not really," he said. "But don't you ever feel a twinge of remorse?"

"Why should I feel remorse?"

"Have you ever thought you're living on frozen power you didn't even create?"

"Are you trying to pick a fight about my grandfather, Andy? Couldn't we fight over something nearer home?" She was all but basking now, as he continued to keep his back turned. He wants to give in, she told herself. If he won't admit it now, that's pure masculine pride.

"Switch the radio, won't you, Andy? Wayne King is on N.B.C."

Andy went dutifully to the dial, tuning out the dying strains of Beethoven for the ultramodern rhythm of the dance band. But he stayed outside the circle of light round her bed: the craggy planes of his face were an enigma in the half-dark.

"From the 'Emperor' concerto to 'The Invitation Waltz'," he said. "That's a jump in any language."

"When I was a girl," said Pat smoothly, " 'The Invitation Waltz', as you call it, was known as 'The Blue Danube Waves'."

"It's still an invitation," he said dourly.

"And it's still our waltz," she said. "Or have you forgotten that, too?"

They both fell silent as the smooth minor rhythm filled the hospital bedroom. Pat closed her eyes, remembering a moon over Diamond Head, the whisper of palms above a terrace at the Royal Hawaiian—and two figures, clutched in a single silhouette as they swayed to waltz time. They had both come out of the surf, after a midnight swim. She could recall the phosphorous gleam in her unbound hair and the tang of salt on his lips as they met hers.

"Wayne King is playing at the Waldorf tonight," he said. "At Catherine Ash's charity ball."

"What's that got to do with you and me?"

"A parable, Pat," he said quietly. "Catherine, and Martin Ash. And you, and I. *Plus ça change, plus c'est la même chose.* Translate, please—your French is much better than mine."

"Why should we resemble Catherine and Martin?"

"At the moment," he said, "we're four of a kind. Which is why I keep my distance."

Pat stared up at him round-eyed—and, for the first time tonight, her wonder was genuine. She knew Catherine Ash well enough—a rather silly woman, with more kindness than judgment. A bitch, in fact, who felt she could buy prestige for her all-Jewish husband as casually as another woman might buy pearls. Not that she had any real prejudice against Martin, Pat added quickly—despite his Old Testament profile. But it *was* a little grotesque of Catherine, insisting that her money could open all doors.

"If you're comparing yourself, for one minute, to Martin Ash——"

"You want to marry me," he said dully. "Three days out of five I want you—on any terms you'd care to name. Doesn't that make us four of a kind? And would you say it's the sort of contract that tends to happiness?"

"I haven't offered you a contract yet, Andy."

"It's immodest of me, I know," he said. "But what else could bring you here?"

"Dr. Plant's orders," she said mockingly. "Or have you forgotten that he's my physician—and you're only the resident?"

He had remained at a safe distance from the bed; he spoke now as though he had not heard that last, teasing remark. "Of course they may be ideally happy: I wouldn't know——"

"Are you back to Catherine and Martin?"

"I suppose I'm old-fashioned," he said, "but I believe a man should earn his own happiness. All the way."

You'll earn yours when we're married, she promised him silently. I'll see to *that*, Dr. Gray, never you fear. Aloud she said only, "Tell me what you really want, Andy. Let me help you to achieve it. Isn't that what wives are for?"

"You made me happy once," he said. "Wildly, unreasonably happy. Naturally I'd like more of the same. What man wouldn't?"

"You made me happy, too," she whispered, and held out her arms. He took a quick step forward, and she felt triumph pulse in her throat like a roused beast of prey. Then she saw he was wary, even now, for he had paused at the bedside and lifted her hand to his lips. I must be careful, she told herself, and made her voice small as she clung to his hand and pressed it hard against her breast.

"It's true I've come back, Andy. Because I couldn't stay away. Isn't that why *you're* here tonight?"

"I think we should have this thing out," he said. "Naturally the orderlies are taking bets on the outcome."

Pat shrugged. "Naturally. What are the odds?"

"Everyone expects me to win you—or is it vice versa?"

"You might be a bit more gallant about it, Andy."

"Tell me this much, Pat," he said slowly. "What can I give you—besides what we've already had?"

She laughed in earnest then. An analyst had once told her that she dominated all her men (lovers and husbands alike) because of overcompensation. The hidden yearning, never confessed before, that she might find some man who would ravish her in turn. The analyst, as she discovered later, was a quack, with spectacular urges of his own. In fact they had enjoyed a whole week in a shuttered suite at the Hotel Carlton in Cannes, without taming her rampant pysche.

Would her life end on that note—at the doorstep of a luxury hotel, with a man whose face she could never quite remember? She put her arms swiftly round Andy's neck and kissed him. It was not a kiss of passion. Rather, it was her last good-will offering, with surrender at its heart.

"Of course you'll never believe I'm ready to settle down," she said.

He did not quite return her kiss, but it was a long time before he drew back into the shadows beyond the night table. He's half ready to believe me now, she told herself. Steady, Patricia—and don't overplay your tremolo.

"You asked me what you can give me," she said. "A *raison d'être*, first of all—the one thing my money hasn't bought me, so far. A home, instead of a world tour. A child, if you'd like one——"

"A *child*, Pat?"

"Motherhood must be a tremendous adventure." Her voice was vibrant with sincerity now: for the moment she had almost convinced herself that this synthetic domestic picture was really her heart's desire. She could see the nursery, down to the last detail: Mother Goose wallpaper (originals, of course, by a good modern); a whole wall devoted to television; a brace of nannies to ensure apple-pie order, always. . . . If the occupant of that Lilliputian heaven failed to come into focus, she could blame it on the company she had kept so far. With Andy at her side—and Andy's career as her star—she could be reborn again, along with their son.

She heard Andy's voice, through the fog of self-dedication that had all but obscured her original purpose. "Do you think I'd make a good father?"

"Would I be here if I didn't?" Instinct told her that she must play her part to the hilt now. She went on quickly, letting the words form *ad lib*. "Is there a greater thrill than making a family—or helping your husband to be what he ought to be?"

"Is it me you want—or my success?"

"Both," she said—and she was still improvising. "But I'm not sure that any woman can ever have you spiritually. You're too close to your surgery for a mistress to come between—or a wife." She let her voice fade to a vibrant whisper, while she weighed the import of her words. The truth, she reflected, is spoken all too often, out of the white heat of passion. She had just realized, with her impromptu avowal, the basis of Andy Grey's appeal. Or was challenge the proper word?

So far the men in her life had offered no challenge whatever. They had made love either to her bank account or to the well-tuned lute of Aphrodite that was Pat Reed, in essence. Andy, who had spurned the lure of her millions from the beginning, was a different breed. Always he had retained something of himself—the work she could never share, the dreams he had never even tried to put into words, even when they were closest. Until she broke down that final barrier, until she could really possess him, she knew that she would stop at nothing to make their marriage a reality.

I'll make him kiss me again, she told herself, obeying the instinct that had guided her in a dozen love duels. But I'll make it count, and I'll offer it on my terms.

"Dr. Plant is sending me home tomorrow," she said.

"Don't forget I read your chart, Pat," he told her, with a touch of the schoolmaster's tone. "If we prescribed a sedative tonight, it's only to prepare you for the life you'll be leading tomorrow."

"Never mind tomorrow." She was out of the bed before he could speak, tossing the sheet aside with one thrust. A bright ladder of moonlight entered the room from the balcony and she moved towards it on lazy tiptoe, letting it outline her figure completely, taking Andy's silence as a good augury.

She heard him take a step towards her and then another—and kept her eyes fixed on the moon-bathed tenements below her windows. She shivered as his hands found her at last. Then he was kissing her as though he had never been away.

"We're good for each other, Andy—won't you admit it?"

"Good at this, you mean," he said.

She closed her eyes, losing herself in the remembered scent of frangipani, the tom-tom of a dance drum that might have been the echo of her own heart. Only it wasn't a tom-tom, but a soft tapping on the outer door of her hospital suite.

Even in her rage she could admire Andy's aplomb. Without breaking stride, he lifted and deposited her on the bed; with that same forward motion his hand found the switch of the standing lamp beside the bed. The hands that folded the sheets about her were wise in their trade, but they were no longer the hands of desire.

"Lie back out of the light," he whispered. "Look innocent, if that's possible." Then he spoke to the outer door, just before the second discreet tap. "Come!"

It was a permission to enter as casual as his manner—or the stethoscope that he was balancing idly between his palms, like a badge of office. For an instant Pat was suspicious of this *savoir-faire*. Then her antic humour returned, and she found herself shaking with inward laughter. I've made my point, she told herself. The next move is his—and he'll make it on schedule.

The floor nurse came into the room with all the deference due the Reed millions—even as her eyes raked the resident surgeon for signs of lipstick.

"The operator wants you, Dr. Gray. Emergency on Medicine Three."

"Tell them I'm on my way." He turned to Pat, with his deference intact. "I'll run now, if you'll forgive me. Something's popping downstairs——"

But her eyes held him at the bedside until the floor nurse had vanished. "Be honest, Andy," she said. "Are you glad or sorry you were saved by the bell?"

"At this moment," he said, "I wouldn't risk an answer."

"That's all I need to know," she said. "I won't even ask you to come back later. Tomorrow will do nicely."

"You'll be out of here tomorrow."

"And so will you, if I have my way," she said. "Good night, darling. Go and save another life, if you must."

She watched him pause for an instant in the doorway to gather authority about him like invisible armour. He went out without speaking—and she knew he was deep in the problem that awaited him in the operating room, back again in the safe arcana of his profession, where temptation was unknown.

X

Tony Korff was deep in his recurrent dream, the dream whose essentials never varied, though the subconscious mind from which it was dredged added a colourful detail now and then. Basically, it was Hitler's own dream of world rule—and in this case the Fuehrer had triumphed. Sometimes Tony was the Leader's right-hand man, sometimes he became the Leader himself. Always brown-shirted legions marched triumphant from Washington to the Pacific, with only a few stubborn islands of resistance left to conquer. Always the panoply of war dissolved into a parade between two frenzied heart-beats.

Tonight he was alone in the reviewing stand, the Leader incarnate, accepting the victory shout with his right arm extended. The marching feet mingled with the beat of distant music; the adoration of a thousand lifted faces was for him alone. And yet something was wrong with the picture, a single, jarring note he could not define at first. When he understood at last his whole being recoiled in horror. The marching feet, which had thundered before in perfect rhythm to the distant band, only whispered tonight. When he dared to look down, at the neatly-booted feet of his legion, he saw that they were gliding, as one man, in mincing waltz time.

"The Blue Danube", he thought. Only it's a Red Danube today. All at once he was staring wide awake in the broom room that served as his bedroom. Sweating in the terror-ridden darkness, he groped for the bed lamp. The pillow was still fragrant with a haunting scent. Arpège, he thought bitterly—at thirty dollars the ounce. A gift from one of Vicki's richer patients. He cursed Vicki Ryan with all his heart. Women like her were, in reality, as unsubstantial as their perfumes.

He rose from the bed, still in the grip of that towering rage, and cut off his bedside radio—and the music of Wayne King. Knowing that sleep was beyond him now, he reached for a cigarette and fumbled for the gin bottle. There was still a good four fingers left. He bit out the cork and drank without flinching, to the last drop. Gin—the tipple for failures. At least he could carry his liquor like a man.

The alcohol did not numb his racing brain: in fact he could not remember when his thoughts had been clearer. It was quite true that the night brought counsel, he reflected. Too often, for those who could not sleep, it was only the counsel of despair, the sober case history of the doomed and damned.

Take *your* own case history, Tony Korff. Scion of the slums (and did it matter if the slum was located in Berlin or Moscow, Shanghai or Manhattan's East Side?), fathered by a naturalized Baltic Russian upon a fräulein of the streets, raised in an orphanage . . . naturally you'd hate the world with your first conscious breath. It could be truly said that the Tony Korffs of this world were fathered in corruption, nursed on hate, and raised to man's estate in the shadow of that same unreasoning hatred.

You, at least, escaped the shadows before it was too late. America has given you everything, before the Army and after. Why should you hate the smug, well-fed American world even more? Why should you feel only contempt for Andy Gray (who has been good to you, in his fashion)?

He abandoned the futile self-analysis and lifted the bottle to his lips again, forgetting that it was already empty. I'm as good as the best of them, he told himself, and to hell with these revaluations at midnight. At least he would have his medical degree in another month, his required years of internship behind him complete with the coveted seal of a New York hospital. One stroke of luck was all he needed now. The capital to buy himself a good practice. Or an appointment somewhere in America, where the pickings were at hand.

He ignored the still, small voice that reminded him an assistant residency was the best he could hope for anywhere. As for capital—well, that was a dream he had abandoned long ago, save in gin-fogged moments such as this. When the fog refused to descend, blotting out the hard pattern of reality, he could only writhe in a bath of sweat—and wish that he had died in his first Berlin street brawl.

Perhaps (since he would not sleep tonight) it would be well to visit the burn patient once again. The man had shown no real sign of reviving when he had left him a few hours ago, after making sure that the tape recorder, and its attendant minion in blue, were correctly placed at the bedside. And yet these moribund cases sometimes show a last, strange spark of vitality in the hours between midnight and dawn.

His mind turned to the conference that had been held in Ash's office. Fully expecting to be summoned to state his views, he had sulked for an hour in the corridors outside the director's ante-room while he damned them all for their obtuseness. Obviously the sergeant who had discovered the bodies (and guessed that the burns were radioactive) would snatch all the glory. He had already verified that much from the early editions of the tabloids, which had carried photographs of the scene—with Sergeant Donelly larger than life beside the sheeted figures. Dr. Anton Korff, the man of science who was really in charge at that very moment, had been dismissed (with a mis-spelled surname) far down in the story.

He began to ponder those burn cases in earnest as he felt his rage seep slowly away. No one would believe the solemn fiction that the trouble had begun at Brookhaven. And yet the police had shown a touch of genius in admitting that one victim was still breathing—and expected to make a statement. If the cold-blooded criminal responsible for this business had read the first editions (and it was reasonable to assume that he would be eager for the official version of his crime) the story might bring results after all.

Tony Korff stared through the windows of his room at the courtyard of the hospital—and the blue-coated figure that all but merged with the shadows between Schuyler Tower and the medical wing. During his internship he had handled his share of criminal cases: he had watched the police bungle their chances—or seize upon them brilliantly. Clearly the present case was a mystery wrapped in an enigma, unless the second victim revived enough to speak. Or unless the killer (Tony could hardly doubt that there was murder behind the affair) dared to show himself in an effort to choke that speech for ever.

The senior intern felt his scalp prickle as he weighed this final possibility. In a case like this, he reflected, a man could use a go-between. You might even say that inside help was imperative. Perhaps it was well that his name had been mentioned in the story—even with the mis-spelling. He had taken bribes before, when a man's life hung in the balance within these walls, and a name mentioned—even *in extremis*—could bring ruin in high places.

This time he was sure that the evil went deep—but, then, he had looked into the depths before, without flinching. Naturally he understood the capabilities of evil men better than these others, including Inspector Hurlbut. Had he not lived with evil and its aftermaths, from his beginning?

The phone burred softly at his bedside, and he just escaped growling aloud, like a hound on the scent. But it was only Andy Gray, after all—his voice oddly gay for the hour.

"This time I have the dilly," said Andy. "Get over to Medicine Three as fast as you can dress. And if you have company, send her about her business——"

"I am quite alone," said Tony stiffly—and his voice had translated from the German without his knowledge. Ordinarily he would have answered the resident's gibe in kind. "Who is it this time, Andy?"

"Believe it or not, it's Bert Rilling. Plant just brought him in personally. Seems he was working late at his office——" Andy, reflected Korff, might have been a schoolboy on a lark. "He thinks it's a femoral embolism. I'm inclined to agree, subject to inspection. George Plant isn't often wrong in his diagnosis."

No wonder you're so gay, thought Tony sourly: vascular surgery has always been Andy's speciality, and he had scored most of his personal triumphs in that field. It was Andy's uncanny luck to be on the spot tonight, when they brought in the brewer. The beer that poured through Rilling's warehouse doors in an unending stream was no more famous than Rilling's personal philanthropies and the political power he was said to wield in both New York and Washington.

If Andy had been absent tonight, thought Tony, I could have handled this case just as easily. *I* could have stood at the

grateful patient's bedside afterwards and accepted his thanks
for saving his life. *Bert Rilling.* He spoke the name aloud—
and knew he was still framing his thoughts in German. Why
should that name strike a dim chord? He put down his
schoolboyish daydreaming and assumed his professional
manner again, as deftly as he donned his short-sleeved coat.

"Where are you now, Andy?"

"On my way to Medical Three, but I've alerted the O.R.
already. Plant will assist, but I'll want you too. Julia Talbot
will pass——"

"Who's setting up?"

"Ramsey's the intern in charge."

"Ramsey's a *Dummkopf*. Send him about his business.
I'm on my way now."

XI

The grand ballroom of the Waldorf was draped with the
flags of the United Nations tonight (though the hammer and
sickle was conspicuous by its absence). The flags had been
Catherine Ash's inspiration—along with the famous orchestra
and the idea of making every third dance a waltz. The guests,
as usual, were something else again. Standing on the step-up
from the dance floor, Catherine herself felt almost calm. It
had been a good party from the start, even when you discounted the fact that foreigners, regardless of their background, were always hard to entertain.

In a way she was sorry that the United Nations had come
into fashion again (on a strictly limited plane) after its long
Korean eclipse. Too many languages, bombarding a hostess
in the same hour, could produce a headache all their own.
She could never understand why these Frenchmen and
Dutchmen and Slavs should parade their native tongues so
blatantly, when they were wined and dined at America's
expense. Or, to be exact, at the expense of the Committee to
Prevent Future Wars, which was Catherine's most military
charity at the moment.

Certainly these bilingual diplomats (if diplomat was not too strong a term for the dancers spinning at this moment to the lure of Wayne King's music) could afford to remember their Basic English. She looked over the sea of bobbing heads and found the picture good, on the surface. The women, if viewed from a slight distance, seemed quite as flawless as the men.

In a way, she thought, this was a tribute to New York— and to New York's well-known ability to civilize all comers, superficially. Even the Maharanee from India (with her caste mark like a blazon just beneath the looped pearls on her forehead) seemed a New Yorker tonight—above and beyond the perpetual famines and fratricides of her native land. Even the coal-black princess from Eritrea (whose invitation had been sent out by the committee after much soul-searching among its Southern members) was waltzing as though to manner born.

Catherine's eyes, still roving the harlequin pattern of the dance floor, had found Martin at last. She was glad that he was dancing with a reasonably safe Parisienne at this moment: Martin's French was almost as good as her own, thanks to those long holidays abroad—with two hours of Berlitz on the side, when he began to show his first hint of restlessness. She had never regretted those French lessons for a moment. Any more than she regretted her investment with the Mayos (when Martin's whole post-graduate future had been at stake), or the fortune she had poured into East Side General to keep its book-keepers sane. Martin had justified all her hopes, on every front.

Thanks to Arthur Murray, he could waltz as well as any man in that huge ballroom. Thanks to the tailors and tutors she had hired, he could appear in any capital of Europe as though he had lived there always. He could talk of the post-war poets and their clashing symbols, with all comers—and hold his own. He could flirt with pretty women without endangering his reputation, and argue with five-star generals on the make-up of a presidential policy without admitting whether he were Liberal or Tory. Thanks to me, she thought, he's a man of the world, and a model husband. How many wives can say as much?

A model husband, she amended instantly, for the fleeting hours they had together—and who was she to complain if their married life seemed to shrink with each passing year? She had built Martin according to a rigorous blueprint. If he had fulfilled that blueprint beyond her most optimistic dreams she could only rejoice in his success. If he was waltzing too well just now (and complimenting the French diplomat's wife just a bit too fluently), Catherine was the last wife under heaven to wonder if she had the right to be jealous.

We've outgrown jealousy long ago, she told herself. Martin has been all I hoped he'd be. Tender and understanding (when he's had time for me). A passionate lover even now (when he's been able to ignore his telephone). A *companion* (she underlined this word, a little impatiently) whom I'd be proud to introduce as my husband, no matter where. No one could say that her faith had not been justified. Not even her stiff-necked family, who still chuckled over their dreary anti-Semitic jokes in private, and still took malicious joy in excluding Martin from all their tribal functions.

Tonight she could even admit her father's ultimate sneer, the final judgment that intransigent patriarch had taken to his grave. "Come what may," Morton Parry had said, "he'll end up as your creation—never as his own man. Left to himself, he might end his days as a successful baby-snatcher in the Bronx; with the best will in the world, I can see no better future for this fellow you insist on loving." Tonight she would have given a great deal to bring her father alive— just for an instant. Even Mort Parry (who had once resigned from a New York club because it had admitted a registered Democrat to its roster) would be the first to admit that his daughter's husband wore his tail coat better than any other man in the room.

Granted, she had bought Martin his first tail coat—and his first teacher of French. She had paid for his first appointment at East Side General and used every lever to lift him to the top. The basic fact remained: Martin was the stuff of which leaders are made. The end product justified the means.

I've lifted him clean out of his alien background, she told herself. Once the new hospital is a reality, the break will be complete. For the first time tonight her eyes clouded with doubt. Why did Martin still refuse to discuss details of the transfer—even now, when the papers were all but drawn? Why (when he admitted all her arguments were just) did he withdraw deeper into himself, no matter how adroitly she brought up the question of their future?

Naturally Father and Mother Ash would object to the move (she never used the name they clung to in these silent dialogues). What if they did feel lonely in that unspeakable tenement, so far from their famous son? Mothers and fathers everywhere were facing up to the fact that children were people, with lives of their own. Besides, Catherine added virtuously, it was scarcely her fault that these strange old people chose to live in the slums.

In her secret heart she was glad they insisted on remaining downtown. When a man breaks with his past the break should be complete. And yet she could hardly deny that Martin himself shrank from that final break. It was almost as though the very concept had risen like a barrier between them.

But she could not afford to admit such thoughts beyond the threshold of her mind. This is my world, she concluded firmly—for. Catherine Ash was a sensible woman, after all, and never argued with herself for long. My world and his, one and inseparable. If her money had made that world—well, that was part of an eternal pattern. Money was only frozen power after all, and power had ruled the world since the days of tooth and claw. It was absurd to say that the power had begun to run amok, both here and abroad. People were always saying that the present could never survive the errors of the past, but the world ticked on, regardless.

Still, it would be well if she and Martin saw much more of one another in the future. Whatever had come between them could surely be dissipated if she could have him for herself alone, once again. She would begin by vetoing his plan to remain in town this week-end: it was really absurd that he refused to forget his hospital for an instant, with a man like Dr. Gray as his deputy. Martin had said often that he would trust Dr. Gray's judgment above his own. Yes,

there was no reason under heaven why he should not drive
her out to Parry Point tomorrow and stay until Monday.

Unless—and the thought chilled her to the marrow—there
was another woman. But Martin's work was his only other
love, and she would conquer that rival, too, in time.

She looked up sharply as the rhythm of the orchestra
changed; had she thought of it in advance, she would have
ordered them to play no rumbas tonight. Martin did not
always rumba well with a strange partner. But a quick,
anguished glance told her that her husband was no longer
on the floor. Had he disappeared with that hussy from the
boulevards? No; the woman was very much in evidence, and
flirting outrageously as she quivered in the grip of the
permanent United Nations delegate from Ecuador.

Certainly, after his tardy appearance, he would not dare
to return to the hospital without sending some word.
Catherine moved quickly from her place on the daïs, skirted
the sweep of dance floor, and hurried into the outer lobby—
all but deserted now, as her guests flocked back to the music's
lure. She saw her husband at once, just as he emerged from a
phone booth.

"*Martin!*"

He came to her at once with his hands held out, offering
the same well-remembered smile that always chided her for
her vehemence. "At your service, my dear—now and always."

Warmed by the pressure of his hands, she decided to be
light for once. "You were calling the hospital. I can always
tell——"

"My last call tonight, I assure you."

"May I count on that, really?"

He slipped an arm through hers; for a moment they stood
side by side on the steps to the dance floor, bowing like a pair
of sleek automatons as the faces of friends whirled by in the
crowd. "I told you about the burn cases we've been treating
with ACTH——"

"Yes, dear. I wish I understood better."

"I had to be sure there was no change. Andy had another
piece of news. We've bagged Bert Rilling at last."

Catherine kept her lightness with an effort. She was not

sure if Martin knew that this same Bert Rilling had already
agreed to defray most of the expense of their projected move
uptown. "Don't sound as though you hunted patients with
an elephant gun, dear."

"Plant brought him in a half hour ago. The kickback of
a mitral lesion, they think." As always, he was speaking his
strange jargon glibly, quite as though she could follow every
word. "They have him on the table right now. It's an operation
I'd give a great deal to perform myself—even if it is Andy's
preserve."

"You promised, Martin!"

He smiled down at her with the boyish droop to eyelids
and lips she had grown to love more with each passing year.
After all, it was the outer sign that he was prepared to obey
her in most things.

"I haven't forgotten this is our dance, Catherine."

He held out his arms as he spoke, and she moved into
his embrace without another word. For tonight, at least, he
was all hers: she knew she must be careful to keep the triumph
from her voice. But she could not resist a scornful glance to
left and right as he piloted her expertly into the stream of
dancers. We're the handsomest couple on the floor, she
informed the world at large, and her flashing eyes dared
the world to contradict her.

The handsomest and the happiest, she added quickly, and
smiled up at her husband for reassurance. Her triumph faded
instantly as she read the loneliness in his eyes—and knew that
his mind was far away. Pressed close in the sharp rhythm of
the dance, she begged him to come back to her. Begged
wordlessly and with all her heart, out of a loneliness that
matched his own.

XII

Watching Tony Korff scrub just outside the operating
suite, Andy Gray stole a final look at his instrument nurse,
already hard at work under the lights. He would never know

if the white shadow had been Julia—far back in the solarium of Schuyler Tower. He could never ask if she had noticed the faint trace of lipstick at the corner of his jaw, when he hurried to the medical wing and found her there, ready to take his orders. For no reason at all, he felt sure that Julia had known he was in Pat's suite all along. That she had sent the floor nurse to rout him out when the emergency call was first broadcast. Finally, that she had rescued him (from a fate once considered worse than death) for reasons of her own.

A fate worse than death. He chuckled inwardly at the phrase, for it fitted his dilemma perfectly. He had been within an ace of yielding to Pat—on a primitive level, granted, but a yielding nonetheless. If I'd gone through that business tonight, he thought, she'd own me tomorrow, or the day after. As irrevocably as Catherine owns Martin Ash.

He smiled at Julia through the glass wall of the scrub room and felt his heart give an unaccountable leap as the smile was returned. Perhaps she understands me better than I do myself, he thought. Perhaps it's fate that we should finish what's left of tonight together—and who cares if we must share most of that communion across the carcass of a millionaire brewer?

The orderlies had just wheeled in the patient. He glanced curiously at the sheet-draped figure as his trained ear caught an ominous tremolo note in Rilling's deep, snoring breath.

"How much have you picked up, Tony?"

"Rilling was working late at his office and passed out at his desk."

"In the brewery?"

"In the brewery." The senior intern leaned over the antiseptic and lifted his dripping arms from the solution. "It seems he got to a telephone just in time. Plant's coming in now—why not ask him yourself?"

Andy grinned as a nurse came forward to tie his mask. He had not missed the gin in Tony's breath—or Tony's sullen air of martyrdom. The aftermath of Eros, he thought, joined to a hangover in the making. Yet he had no fears as to Tony's ability to slide into harness. The intern had drunk

himself into stupors before, and risen to the emergency bell
as automatically as a fire horse.

"Come when you're ready," he said. "We'll give the
pre-op anæsthesia a chance to work a moment more."

Dr. George Plant stood above the table, chatting with
Julia. A successful internist, with a girth that matched his
affability, Plant had always been a favourite with the surgeons.
Tonight he offered Andy the tribute of a roly-poly bow. The
gesture, somehow, was not at all grotesque.

"The right man for the right job," he said. "I'm lucky to
find you here."

"You're sure it's a femoral embolism?"

"With a mitral valve lesion to spark it," said Plant. "See
for yourself, Doctor. I've known this fellow for years
now."

Andy looked down at the humped figure on the table.
Viewed from this angle, Bert Rilling seemed almost as
formidable as one of his beer barrels. A blond Teuton, with a
head like a swollen bullet, the skin tone already greying under
the oxygen mask the anæsthetist had just fitted above his
mouth and nose.

"There have been clots before, I gather?"

"A few small ones—but nothing like this."

Andy nodded. The picture was clear before he folded
back the sheet that covered the brewer's leg. A heart damaged
by rheumatism—with a leaky valve between the chambers
of the left side—could be a traitor to the body it served.
Thanks to the irritation of those chamber walls, the blood
had begun to clot there, instead of moving through the
circulation. Breaking loose at last, these clots had travelled
down the branching arterial system, jumping squirrel-like
from larger branches to smaller, until they reached a vessel
through which they could not pass.

So far, the backfire of the circulation had not been serious.
Tonight, when a larger clot had closed one of the great
trunk lines of the blood stream, only the scalpel could save
the patient from cyanosis and death. Amputation would have
been the solution a few years ago. Today, thanks to the miracles
of vascular surgery, it was sometimes possible to open the

blood vessel involved and remove the obstruction with no danger to adjacent tissue.

"Did he say anything when he regained consciousness?"

"He was too weak to be coherent. I needn't say I came prepared. He's already had adrenalin and intramuscular digitalis while we waited for the ambulance."

Andy murmured his approval as he began his examination. The brewer's respiration was laboured, and the oxygen had not improved his colour noticeably: the skin of his legs was already dusky blue, almost to the thighs. Andy's fingers followed the course of the arteries in either leg. They found what they sought quickly enough, as they moved from ankle bone and back again—the absence of pulsation at the posterior tibial was matched at the dorsalis pedis. Already the picture was ominous. A clot in the thigh, blocking the artery itself, inevitably slowed the whole blood current, building along its own length until the original obstruction was extended far back towards the heart, closing adjacent channels as it thickened.

"Can you localize the block, Dr. Gray?"

"Not precisely. But I'll bet on a saddle thrombus at the bifurcation of the aorta."

He heard Julia draw in her breath across the table, and smiled at her again, forgetting that his smile was now hidden in sterile gauze. He could see the picture building behind her wide, staring eyes. What he had called a "bifurcation" was the division of the great trunk artery that issued from the heart itself. A saddle thrombus would be merely a Y-shaped clot, riding at the point of division, with extensions down the large femoral arteries of each leg.

"That means an embolectomy, of course."

"Precisely," said Andy. "D'you think he'll stand it, Doctor?"

"He'll have to," said Plant.

"You've notified his relatives?"

"He hasn't any, so far as I know. Certainly there's no one in New York. I'll take the responsibility."

Andy nodded briskly. Already his mind was deep in the job ahead—too deep, in fact, to pause over externals. Later, he would remember Plant's wheeze of apprehension as he moved away from the table, and the strange, hard light in Tony Korff's eyes as he came out of the scrub room and bent to examine the patient in turn. For the present his vital forces were focused on the task at hand.

"If you'll come with me to the cabinet, Miss Talbot——"

Julia held the tray while he went down the shelves, selecting the special instruments he must use. Slender, flexible bougies from the GU section, tipped with delicate steel corkscrews, which were usually employed to dislodge stones from the ureters. Packs of gossamer-silk threads, streaming from needles that seemed mere flashes of light. Dura needles, used ordinarily to suture brain tissue. A Cameron light for abdominal surgery, that would be just as valuable for the job tonight. Finally a probationer was sent down to obstetrics, to fetch several rolls of umbilical tape, which would be used at the final stages of the operation—if and when they arrived at that stage with a living patient.

"We'll use local anæsthesia, with an injection of sodium pentothal," said Andy. "And don't let up on that oxygen for a minute, Dr. Evans." He paused beside the anæsthetist as he nodded to each of his team in turn—a captain who knew that his orders would be followed without question.

Tony Korff emerged from the scrub room, already masked and gowned. Andy noted with approval that the refugee's slight truculence had vanished, along with that air of hangover. Tony, he reflected, was a natural-born surgeon—even if his preoccupation with Tony Korff would keep him from the success he otherwise deserved.

"What approach will you use, Andy?"

"The right femoral, I think. We can open just below the inguinal ligament. I'm pretty sure there's an obstruction in the artery on that side."

"Can you reach the bifurcation?"

"It's possible—if the clot isn't riding too high."

"What if it is?"

"Then we must open the abdomen and expose the aorta itself."

Tony glanced down at the heavy-breathing patient, and

once again Andy noted how the intern's eyes had narrowed above the mask. "Are you hoping he'll live that long?"

"It's only a hope, I'll admit. But we've lost him anyway if we don't reach that clot."

When he, too, was scrubbed and gowned Andy paused just outside the circle of light to take in the scene again. Julia was still busy at the sterilizer, giving her own last instructions to the student nurse who would assist her. Dr. Plant had moved behind the glass window of the observer's gallery, surrendering the field to the surgeon in charge. Tony still hovered above the table, studying Rilling with that same curious intentness. The patient himself had been prepared expertly for the operation, his legs encased in sterile towels almost to the waist. The operative area was exposed in a long rectangle of thigh, groin, and abdomen—a humped plateau of fat and bulging muscle, brightly carmined by the antiseptic swab.

As he approached the table at last, on a nod from the anæsthetist, Andy noted that the cyanosis of the skin was even more pronounced—the fatal, dark blue tone that told of the oxygen absence beneath. Rilling was dying below the waist— dying by inches, now that the life-giving element could no longer reach his tissues via the blood stream. The plasma needle at the elbow vein of one arm could not remedy that lack, though it would help sustain the vital organs until the surgeon came to the rescue. For the present, the flow was cut down to a slow trickle, for it would have been fatal to overload the already weakened heart.

"How's the pressure, Dr. Evans?"

"Ninety over fifty," said the anæsthetist. "Pulse none too steady. You might as well begin. He's as good now as he'll ever be."

The instrument table moved closer as Andy squared off above the patient. As always he felt the familiar contraction of his heart, in the second before the first special tool came into his hand—in this case the syringe of novocain that would block off the field of surgery. His eyes met Julia's, but she was a girl no longer, not even the angel in white who had detoured him from Pat. Like Korff and the probationer, like the very instruments that waited in shining rows to obey his fingers, Julia Talbot was part of the complex mechanism he controlled—a machine that had already begun to function as smoothly as a car going into gear.

The slender novocain needle plunged, raising a curve of tiny weals, in a line one-third of the distance from the inner to the outer thigh. The line indicated precisely the location of the fossa ovalis, an opening in the tough sheath that covered the thigh muscles. It was here that a branch of the femoral vein emerged, the surgeon's obvious entry point. A second, larger needle, probing deeper, released a mixture of novocain and adrenalin—a measure designed to constrict blood vessels in the area and numb the surrounding tissue for a longer period. A final thrust drove the needle deep into the upper thigh, blocking the ilioinguinal and iliofemoral nerves.

"Local anæsthesia completed," said Andy. "Scalpel, please!"

But Julia had already slapped the knife into his palm. He watched it move swiftly, as though it possessed a life of its own, slashing a six-inch incision in the humped fat of the thigh.

"Skin towels, please."

Tony began to clamp the sterile towelling on the edges of the wound as the scalpel clattered into a waiting basin. That particular knife would not be used again. No matter how carefully the skin was treated with antiseptic, there was always danger of carrying bacteria downwards from the pores and hair follicles.

With the incision clamped wide and protected by its sterile dressing, Andy accepted a fresh scalpel from Julia and began to dissect in earnest. The knife went about its work in long, fluid strokes, opening the fatty layers that advertised the brewer's love of easy living. . . . In a matter of seconds, it seemed, a bluish structure came into view, running downwards and inwards towards the knee.

"The saphenous vein," said Andy. At moments such as this he found himself speaking like a lecturer on anatomy. No matter how often the miracle of the human organism was revealed to him under the knife, the exploration had an air

of high adventure. It was an emotion he never shared with
others. Outwardly he would always be the model surgeon,
ice-cold and aloof.

"We can trace it into the fossa ovalis and find the femoral
where it joins the large vein." He continued in rhythm with
the fast-moving knife, for the benefit of the probationer who
was staring round-eyed into the wound, from a vantage point
above Julia's shoulder. "That vein, as you know, returns
blood from foot and leg; the artery that is our objective
should lie beside it—unless this fellow is a museum piece."

He had already slipped a length of tape beneath the
saphenous vein. Now, lifting it gently, he began to dissect
along its length, going ever deeper as the vein seemed to
burrow downwards into its tight ambush of fat. So far there
had been virtually no bleeding. Normally, blood supply in
this region was profuse, and the control of vessels presented
a real problem for the surgeon's assistant. Tonight, thanks
to the circulation block above, the area seemed lifeless—
as though Bert Rilling were already a corpse, ready for the
autopsy table.

"Here's the fossa. I'd better infiltrate again."

Julia had already offered the syringe, its barrel angled
precisely, so that Andy's fingers could slip into the metal
rings that controlled the thrust. Moving carefully now, he
forced the needle point into the glistening white layer that
covered muscles and vein at this point. Then, as Tony grasped
the guiding tape beneath the vein, Andy lifted the tissue at
the edge of the fossa in a pair of forceps and, using small
dissecting scissors, slit it boldly, on the side towards the
foot. Again, he found, his anatomy was faultless. As the
tough white structure parted he looked down at artery and
vein, lying together in the same fibrous tube, between the
muscle layers deep in the wound.

"Cameron light, Miss Talbot."

A second probationer, outside the operative zone, took
Julia's nod and cut the overhead switch. At the same instant
the sterilized lamp carrier, moving swiftly above the incision,
bathed the wound in a penetrating glow—high-lighting the
dissected tissue clearly, exposing the deep structures beneath

with all the sharpness of a textbook plate. The scalpel
enlarged the slit in the fascia until there was room to slip
the light into the wound itself, directly beneath the femoral
artery. The picture completed itself, with every ominous
factor present. Towards the knee, the light glowed pinkly
through the artery wall—and its contents of liquid blood.
Above, towards the body trunk, the glow was masked entirely.
The dead-black silhouette told its own story, with no need
for words.

Andy spoke quietly. "I'll try to enlarge the incision before
opening the artery. Obviously we'll need room." The scalpel
was already at work, opening the trench where vein and
artery lay, until the great trunk vessels were exposed in an
eight-inch ditch. Even as he worked, he could not help but
note the strange inertness of those matching vessels.

"Tape, please."

The tough umbilical tape (used normally to seal off the
last tie that bound mother and child) slapped into his palm.
Inching it beneath the femoral artery, he worked slowly
upwards, as high as he could reach. This, as the whole team
knew, was the potential life-saver—if and when he could
dislodge the clot. Thanks to the tape, he could shut off the
resultant blood flow instantly, until he could suture the
incision he was about to make in the arterial wall.

"I'm going to open the femoral artery, Tony," he said.
"We'll put in the closing sutures first." Of course the normal
urge suggested that he open the vessel at once and investigate
the embolus beneath that straining wall. The prudent vascular
surgeon, thinking far ahead of the exploring knife, was always
ready for an emergency before it could develop. Andy himself
had worked in too many pools of fast-forming blood to
risk a similar recurrence now.

It took all the skill in his fingers to manipulate the tiny
curved needles, until the silken sutures had looped the portion
of the artery above and below the clot. It was a tedious job,
since it was impossible, at this point, to secure the strands
where they would be needed later, in event of a sudden,
uncontrollable hæmorrhage. The best he could do was
establish the area where he would exert pressure as needed.

He let out his breath in a sigh that was echoed round the table as the task was finished—and did not dare to check the clock on the facing wall.

Another scalpel came into his hand as he focused at last on the opaque barrel of the femoral artery—the battleground where he must win or lose a life in the next few moments. As he had expected, the wall of this vital vessel was tough, resisting the first slash of the knife. When it opened at last, for the classic two-inch incision, he knew that he had attained his first objective. Here, at least, was the terminus of the clot. The slow dark ooze that appeared under the steel (a graphic contrast to the instant bright red spout that would have issued from an unblocked artery) told its own story.

"As we thought, the obstruction is practically complete. Let's see how easily it dislodges."

The forceps had already moved into the opening of the arterial wall, fastening gingerly on the ragged end of the blackish, viscous clot that projected downwards, clear in the operative field. The obstruction came free with deceptive ease: this portion, as he knew only too well, could be delivered entire. The trick lay in the surgeon's fingers and their degree of pressure.

Two inches, then three. He dropped the dark, malignant structure in the waiting basin and probed further. As he had expected, the upper portion of the obstruction (extending into the patient's torso to a spot no surgeon could delimit) refused to budge. He lifted his eyes from the wound for the first time, permitting a wholehearted curse to escape his lips as his questing fingers emerged from the wound with a broken bit of clot, and nothing more.

"Steady all—this isn't easy."

It was part of his character that he refused to face the thought of failure, even now. Much later he would remember that Dr. George Plant had pressed his forehead hard above the glass of the observers' gallery, and that the glass was beaded with sweat, as Plant faced up to the loss of his most profitable patient. He would even retain a nightmare vignette of newshawk Pete Collins (and why was Collins roaming the halls at this hour?) side by side with Plant in that same

observation post. Nothing mattered now but the flickering
life under his hands—and the skill that could snatch life
from the void.

"Will you pass the corkscrew bougie, Miss Talbot?"

The special instrument (an *habitué* of the GU wing, but
a stranger here) was in his palm now. He eased it into the
artery opening, working it slowly upwards—and breathed
more easily when he felt resistance not too far above his
point of incision. The bougie turned slowly between his
fingers, working its way into the broken terminus of the clot,
much as a practised wine steward might manipulate a wine
cork, rotted beyond repair. A gentle tug and another tentative
turn convinced him that he had found purchase, of a sort.
And yet he drilled patiently on, inserting the bougie still
farther before he dared to pull back in earnest.

"Ready on the tape, Tony. It's now or never."

The whole table held its breath with the surgeon as the
bougie began to inch its way out of the wound. There was
the clot once again—a malignant Old Man of the Sea, clinging
stubbornly to the artery even now. For one sickening instant
Andy was sure that the bougie would emerge without its
anchor. . . . Then he let out his breath, along with the other
watchers, as clot and corkscrew twisted from the depths of
the incision, bit by bit. Even now he used all his iron technique to work slowly, letting the obstruction follow his
guiding fingers, with no persuasion from the instrument
that had anchored it and compelled it to yield.

Four inches were delivered now—then six—then eight.
A dark, irregular structure that seemed an organ in its own
right, pulsing with life like a near-ruptured appendix or an
incised intestine. Finally, when it seemed as though the clot
was never-ending, the elongated end appeared in the wound,
tapered smoothly where it had fitted into the artery of the
other leg. Even as Andy lifted it to the waiting basin the
embolus assumed its characteristic saddle shape—with one
leg shorter than the other, where he had broken off the first
portion of the clot.

"Tape—quickly!"

The red geyser that had spouted into the wound was both

a warning and an accolade. A twist of the tough umbilical tape, in Tony Korff's fingers, anchored the artery and the flow in a split second. Andy stood by for an instant as the senior intern sponged away the blood with his free hand. Then he began to work smoothly, all tension gone now that their objective had been attained. The sutures dropped easily into place, tightening the femoral artery above and below the point of entry. Stitch by stitch, like a cautious housewife, he brought the arterial wound into snug alignment, knitting the edges into an all but undamaged line that would heal smoothly, allowing no nucleus for another blood clot later.

Tony spoke for the first time since the operation began, as the surgeon stepped back at last.

"What about the other leg? Are you sure the whole clot is extracted?"

"The end looked smooth enough. We can be sure from the skin tone, when we've closed."

It was a routine matter to repair the incision and place the dressings. Results were instantly apparent when the towelling was folded back on the patient's other limb. Already a pinkish tinge was creeping into the skin as blood began to pour through the arteries once more.

"Will you step down to the floor, Dr. Plant," Andy asked, "and test his heart?"

The pudgy doctor moved quickly under the lights, with all his briskness restored. Andy could sense the beaming smile under Plant's mask as he lifted the stethoscope from Rilling's chest.

"He'll come out of this one, too, Andy—thanks to that knife of yours."

Andy smiled. "Thank the team, Doctor. I could never have done it alone."

"You saved his life, there's no doubt of that. My job is to slow him down in the future."

Pete Collins put a frowzy head through the operating room door—a bizarre intrusion into this world of medicine. "Can I say he passed a comfortable night, gentlemen—or is that premature?"

Andy allowed himself the luxury of a yawn. "Keep out of

my way, Pete. I'm sure Dr. Plant will give you the details."

"I've got the details now," said the journalist. "And I'm throwing the lead your way, Andy. On page one. Aren't you even grateful?"

"Right now," said Andy, "I'm too tired to know. All I want is coffee and sleep, in that order." He could feel the expected let-down—a blend of nervous exhaustion and plain, bone-deep weariness—invade his spirits as he stepped aside to let the interns wheel out the patient. And then, as he untied his mask and found himself facing Julia Talbot, weariness vanished abruptly, as though some magic hand had sponged it clean away.

It was a strange sensation, and he paused at the door to savour it fully. I might be coming out of ether myself, he thought. I might even be reborn in a finer mould. In a way it's like discovering your youth again. Or, better still, relearning how good it is to be alive. He put some of his exuberance into words, before the familiar wall of hospital protocol could settle between them.

"Will you join me in a cup, Miss Talbot? I think this will be our last drama tonight."

Even though she was standing in the half shadows, he could see that the girl had coloured faintly. But her voice was steady enough as she came forward.

"Of course, Doctor. We keep a pot boiling in the diet kitchen when we're operating."

"As though I didn't know," he said, smiling.

He stood aside to let her precede him down the corridor. The pink tinge in her cheeks was unmistakable, but he felt that she was pleased by his request. Too pleased for her own good, perhaps. He held the thought at arm's length as he followed her to the elevators. No one but a sentimental fool like himself (too busy to indulge that sentiment for most of his waking hours) could hope for Julia Talbot's love. Not when he considered the years, and the frustrations, that divided them. And yet he knew he had stirred her in some measure, that the moment was his, to handle as he saw fit.

This seems to be my night to conquer, he thought. In

fairness to her, I must give her the complete blueprint.
Including Pat Reed—and Pat's golden offer. Including the
fact that I've nothing to offer Julia herself but my disillusion,
the opportunities I've lost. And of course that crazy dream
of settling in practice beside the Gulf. A dream I'll probably
abandon tomorrow, when Pat repeats her offer.

Keep your own dedication inviolate, he told her wordlessly. Keep your dreams, and your youth: I have no right
to encroach on either. Even though you rescued me from
myself tonight, I've no right to ask you to be my full-time
saviour.

XIII

Julia emerged from the diet kitchen with a coffee mug in
each hand and smiled down at the tousled dark head that
rested against the back of the arm-chair. The ante-room where
Andy Gray was dozing, a kind of cubby-hole that gave access
to the corridor of the surgical ward, was hardly a trysting
place for lovers. And yet (for all its business-like bareness)
that room was rainbow-hued tonight.

Pausing just above the arm-chair, she made sure that he
was asleep. He looks ten years younger, she thought, now
he's found a corner to rest in. Younger and wiser, now that
his mask of cynicism has been put aside at last. It's almost
as though he'd gone back to another world—a simpler
existence, where ambition did not dog one's footsteps, where
life was its own reward. Where a man made his own luck
from the start, with no long-legged siren to confuse his
destiny.

Julia put down both cups and settled in the facing arm-
chair. Despite her best resolves, her heart was racing: a sixth
sense insisted that this moment would not come again. He's
brought me this far with a reason, she thought. Something
is preying on his mind—a trouble that we can share. A
dilemma that we might even solve together.

Probably I'm dreaming this, she concluded. Tomorrow,

in the clear light of day, I'll see him in his true perspective, admit (once and for all) that I can never share his future. Yet even as common sense moved into the debate she needed all her self-control to keep her place, a safe two yards' distance from that tired head. Had she obeyed her deepest instinct, she would have cradled him on her breast and lulled him to the repose he deserved.

Andy opened his eyes and met her questioning look head-on. She knew that his defences were down, in that fleeting instant between sleep and wakening. I can ask you what I like, she thought, and you'll answer truthfully.

"Have I been dozing long?"

"A half-hour, perhaps."

"And you kept the coffee warm," he said. "You're a girl after my own heart."

"Tell me this much, Andy," she said. "When have you last felt rested?" She wondered, fleetingly, if she had ever used his first name before.

"I can answer that by the book," he said. "On my last vacation in Florida. Two years ago, to be exact—when I visited my brother down on the Gulf."

"You look rested now," she said. "I wonder why?"

"Now that you mention it," he said, "I was wondering myself. D'you know what I was dreaming?"

"Tell me, if it bears repeating."

"I dreamt I was home again," he said. "Odd, isn't it—when I never really had a home?"

"Are you asking me to be sorry?"

"Don't be anything but yourself,". he said. "Tell me what you're after here."

"Nothing I haven't got," she said quickly. "I just happen to be a nurse who enjoys nursing."

Andy Gray yawned widely, and grinned at her round the yawn. "No lingering homesickness? No yearnings for a husband—a career—or both?"

"I'm quite happy," she told him, steadily enough. "Sorry if that sounds boring——"

"I don't believe a word," he said. "You don't believe yourself."

"Have it your way," she said. "I *would* like a place of my own some day. Not just a home, either. A clinic somewhere —a thousand miles from here. A place where you could really heal the sick, without thinking of the fee—or the publicity——" She broke off suddenly as she read the light in his eyes and wondered if she had already stumbled on forbidden ground.

"You should meet my brother," he said. "Timmie would give you a job tomorrow."

"I've always wanted to go to Florida," she said. "Is he a doctor, too?" The light had gone out of his glance, as though he had extinguished a lamp far back in his brain. Julia watched him narrowly as she measured the depth of his withdrawal.

"Timmie's a doctor of souls," said Andy. She saw that he was careful of his words now, as though he were speaking of a stranger he had no right to describe too intimately. "I should say, the Reverend Timothy Gray. Degrees from both sides of the Atlantic. Enough big-parish offers to make him famous. And he's chosen to set up his altar in a Florida county—where half his parishioners are Greek fishermen. Can you picture him at all?"

"Very clearly," said Julia. "He's the man who brought you peace. I'd like to know him better."

"Timmie could use a district nurse," he said. "Not that he could pay a salary. Would you give up this life to help him?"

"Won't you go back—eventually?"

"Don't answer my question with another."

"I don't want to be rich, Andy," she said. "I don't even want to be famous. And don't say it's un-American, please."

"You still haven't answered."

She spoke quickly, before she lost her courage. "I'll be your assistant," she said. "If you'll offer me the job."

"Just like that?"

"Why not? I've seen you work. I know you'd make a success of it."

"I won't deny I've dreamed of going back," he said slowly. "I've even drawn plans for the hospital I'd build next door to Timmie's hurricane-proof church. It's an innocent enough dream, as dreams go. Too bad it isn't for either of us——"

"Give me one reason why."

"Because what you just said simply isn't true. Because we mean to succeed here."

"Isn't your brother an even greater success?"

"By his yardstick, yes. It isn't mine."

"You said you were happy there. Here at East Side you're too tired to know if you're even alive——" She broke off on that, a little startled by her own daring. "Maybe I'll still take that job. Even if you don't show me the way."

He stared at her for a moment of silence, and she felt the hostility in his eyes. He's trying to drive me away, she thought. He's trying to be something he's not.

"So you'd like to return to the simple life," he said at last.

"Isn't it what we all want, in this century?"

"It isn't that easy, Julia."

"You said I'd be useful. That's what really matters."

"Most of us want to be useful. The big question is where and when."

"You'll go back some day," she said. "I'm sure of that now."

"But I won't. I'll only talk of going, in my weaker moments. I'm Martin Ash's boy—and I'm going to outlast him. And you'll probably succeed Emily Sloane. If you don't use your wits and marry one of your wealthier patients——"

"Do you want to be Martin Ash? Do you really envy him?"

"What doctor wouldn't?"

Again she felt sure that he had said one thing and meant quite another. She pursued her advantage quickly. "So you look forward to playing God some day in the director's office? I'd say your brother was wiser."

"Because he's content to bring God to his fellow men?"

"Because he has faith," she said. "Where have you lost yours?"

She watched him spread his hands and knew that she had touched him at last. "Now it's my turn to answer a question with another. Do you honestly believe that *homo sapiens* has justified his existence?"

"I'm a nurse," she said. "You're a doctor. We've pledged ourselves to keep him alive. Why should we be such fools, if he isn't worth saving?"

"Because we enjoy our work. Because we'd both be lost if we thought of our patients as human."

"You've no right to be so bitter," she said. "No matter what life has done to you, it's still worth living."

"It might be at that," he admitted, "if there were more people like you and Timmie. Unfortunately you're both too good to be true——"

"Just because we've no thirst for glory?"

He looked up sharply. "What made you use that phrase?"

"I'm glad you recognized it," she said. "Shall I give you the rest?"

"If you can remember it," he said—and he was staring into the void again. Julia quoted softly, as though the magic of the words could bring him back again:

" 'May the love for my art actuate me at all times; may neither avarice, nor miserliness, nor the thirst for glory, nor for a great reputation engage my mind; for the enemies of Truth and Philanthropy could easily deceive me and make me forgetful of my lofty aim of doing good to Thy children.' "

"The Prayer of Maimonides," he said. "I haven't heard it since medical school——"

"But you *remembered* it, Andy. You wouldn't remember if you didn't believe."

"Of course I believe it should be part of every doctor's creed. I'll go further—a doctor should be dedicated, like a priest. The fact remains that most of us are business men first and healers second. God knows I'm not immune to that thirst you just mentioned. I've been poor and friendless all my life. Do you expect me to be poor for ever—if I can go Ash one better?"

"Are you arguing with me or with yourself?"

She watched him come back from the void and felt the unspoken yearning in his eyes. "Did you know that Pat Reed and I were thinking of marriage?"

He wants to hurt me, she told herself. He wants to drive me from his life for ever—and he's pulling me closer with every move. "I heard rumours on the grapevine," she said. "No one mentioned you were engaged."

She watched him brace his shoulders for all the world like a condemned criminal about to walk his last long mile. "I can marry her when I like," he said.

"You might be a little more gallant about it."

"One doesn't have to be gallant with Pat Reed. She's above gallantry."

Julia hugged her knees and looked up at him, unsmiling. I can play this straight if you like, she told him wordlessly. If you insist, I can even pretend you mean what you're saying.

"Tell me one thing, Andy. Why does she still use her maiden name?"

"Dislike her if you must," he said. "She's still quite a girl."

"Would she still be Pat Reed if she married you?"

"She'll always be Pat Reed," he said. "That's something no man could change."

"Would you take her down to Florida?"

"She'd take me," he said. "To Palm Beach. Never to my brother's side of the peninsula."

"You'd keep up your practice here?"

"Naturally. I might even let her buy me a hospital. Catherine Ash is doing as much for her husband——" He got up with the words, like an actor who has all but forgotten his exit cue.

Julia sat on unstirring—still holding him with her eyes. She had never felt closer to Andy Gray, now that his absurd play acting was ended.

"Tell me one thing more, Dr. Gray. Do you expect to be happy in this marriage?"

"I expect to be busy," he said. "So busy I won't have time to ask myself."

"You could be happy in Florida. I'm sure of that now."

"Maybe a doctor has no right to happiness. Not if he loves his work enough. Have you ever thought of that?"

I could make you happy, she thought. With no effort at all, I could lead you out of this dead-end street you inhabit, away from your compulsion to destroy yourself. But she kept her voice calm as she got to her feet. Calm and remote as a nun who has renounced life for ever.

"You haven't forgotten the Prayer of Maimonides," she said. "That's all I really need to know."

Their eyes held and his were the first to drop. "If you'll stop by the wards with me for a moment," he said, "I'll see you safely to the nurses' home."

They did not speak again as they walked side by side through the ghastly blue lighting of the corridors and across the white desert of the surgical ward, silent as a tomb in the last hours before dawn. In the detention room at the far end of the wing they paused for an instant beside the bed where the burn case lay. The man's breathing was stertorous—and it was obvious to Julia that he was dying. She looked questioningly at Andy, but he made no comment as he checked the bed chart and the switch of the wire recorder.

In the corner, hunched like a waxwork effigy, the policeman on guard stared back at them with unwinking eyes. Like others in the hospital, Julia had heard and discounted the rumours that surrounded this strange case. Now it seemed all too likely that this patient, at least, would carry his mystery to the grave. But she made no attempt to break through Andy's reserve as they moved on. She had had enough unanswered questions tonight.

In the spacious private room where Bert Rilling lay in state, with a special nurse at his elbow, their score as a surgical team was redeemed again. The brewer was sleeping peacefully, after a final injection of heparin and dicoumarin, a medication that decreased the clotting ability of the blood and lessened the chances of further complications. Dr. Plant's own medication—digitalis and other heart stimulants—had been administered an hour ago. There was nothing to do but wait and trust that Rilling's ailing heart would resume its normal function.

The clock on Schuyler Tower was a dim moon, riding high above their heads as they crossed the sere rectangle of grass that separated the medical wing from the nurses' home. Julia did not dare glance at the hands; tomorrow was another day—and, as usual, tomorrow was already here. She paused on the bottom step and held out her hand.

"You'll go to Florida yet," she said. "To the right side of the peninsula. I'll take odds on that."

"Thanks for your faith," he said. "I wish I could share it."

"Don't you believe in yourself at all, Andy?"

"Only in my work, I'm afraid."

"I haven't heard a word you've said tonight," she whispered. "Not a single word."

"Don't try to make me into something I'm not, Julia."

"Why shouldn't I? Isn't that why women were invented?"

Her hand was still in his as she stepped down to the walk again. When their lips met, she did not know if he had drawn her closer or if she had walked into his arms of her own accord. She knew only that their kiss was spontaneous, that it was part of the challenge she had just offered. For that moment, at least (like the other lost moment when he had wakened with his defences down), he was willing to share all his loneliness, his hurt pride—and his conviction that life was meaningless without love.

And yet, even as she felt the hunger of his lips and his hard, angry arms, she knew that she could do nothing but wait. He would come to her in his own way or not at all. Perhaps he would really go to Pat Reed instead, and destroy his last hope of survival. In either event, she was powerless to sway that tortured indecision.

"That was for believing in me," he said. "Don't make the mistake again."

She had felt him draw back, even before he left her arms. Now, as he turned on his heel and strode back towards the looming shadow of the hospital, she could almost hear him curse beneath his breath. He needs me, she thought. His heart knows that no man under heaven has a chance alone. Yet he's too hard-headed to admit that ancient wisdom of the earth.

She stood on the steps of the nurses' home until the clock on Schuyler Tower brought her back to reality. When she climbed the stairs to her room she was fighting back the urge to tears. Or was it an even crazier urge to laugh aloud?

XIV

Four miles uptown, in a penthouse above the East River, Martin Ash sat bolt upright in bed and knew he would sleep no more. The room was grey with dying moonlight—a cold promise of the dawn that was still hours away. In the twin bed at his side Catherine was sleeping as peacefully as a child, with a child's dream-smile on her lips. Guessing what that dream would be (and hating and loving her in the same breath), he bent to smooth her pillow before he left the room on tiptoe.

They had argued before bed tonight—and settled the argument by time-honoured means. As always, he was not quite sure who had emerged the victor. True, he had won his immediate point—the necessity of his presence at the hospital this week-end. Catherine would go out to Long Island alone, for once. Not that Catherine was ever really alone for long: there would be a dozen house guests to amuse her. Important people he would have enjoyed meeting not too many years ago. Gay people, who could stir her to laughter that never found an echo in his own heart. People who were merely rich—so rich, in fact, that they would be more than willing to underwrite the last lap of Catherine's fund-raising for the new hospital uptown.

Yes, she would leave him alone for once, and, though she had complained bitterly of his neglect before she dropped into that long, dream-filled slumber, she would forgive him in the morning. Catherine always forgave him gracefully for his devotion to his work: understanding the work itself was something beyond her power. His wife, he reflected, was the sort of woman who could give everything to her husband's future without realizing that there were areas where she had no right to trespass.

Catherine's planning had always been as flawless as her company manners. The new hospital would be as neat as the architect's blueprint. The life he would lead there (as the august and somewhat aloof director) would be blueprinted just as rigorously. He stumbled into his living-room and

switched on the light in protest against the ghostly moon-
beams that lay across the terrace outside the french window.
Like everything that Catherine owned, that formal salon was
a thing of beauty—pure Louis Quinze, from the petit-point
cushions on the love seats to the panelled overmantel that
had been transported, in all its rosewood splendour, from a
château in Tours. Only one thing is lacking, he thought—the
touch of a human hand.

He thought of the scores of rooms they had shared, of the
homes that had never been home. Their bridal suite on the
old *Majestic*, when that Cunarder was queen of the Atlantic.
The castle in the Apennines that Catherine had rented for
their first long summer abroad, and the gaunt house in
Mayfair where he had met his first royal duke. Hotel rooms
from Hong Kong to Cairo—breathless with the heat of
desert noons, cool with the blue shimmer of the sea. This,
too, could be a hotel suite: the penthouse had been their
New York headquarters for years, but there was no trace of
himself within its walls.

I could pack and go tonight, he thought, and nothing of
myself would remain. All this is Catherine's, and she loves
every expensive piece, because it's her collective symbol of
security.

His mind went back to the burn case at the hospital, and
the threat it posed. What if their worst fears were true—and
a time bomb was ticking somewhere in the heart of Manhattan? When their hour came, Catherine Ash and the
humblest slum dweller would be equally helpless; his wife's
plans would be destroyed in a twinkling, as completely as
this home that was not a home. Try as he might, he could not
picture Catherine shorn of her possessions and still enduring.
The slum dweller, who lived by his own wits, would be made
of tougher fibre.

Then he remembered that Catherine would be driving to
Long Island tomorrow, a whole world removed from this
unsolved mystery. It would be quite in the pattern of their
lives that she should escape the threat, while he and his parents
waited stolidly in its shadow. Quite in character that *he* could
face death without even warning Papa and Mama Aschoff of

the possible danger. He knew in advance what their answer would be.

There was a faint rustle in the hall that led to the bedroom. Catherine was moving into the glow of the lights, her eyes still heavy with sleep. Waking and finding the bed empty beside her, she had sought him instantly—not through fear, but because her need of him would not be denied. Looking back, he could not remember a night they had passed apart. Even when he was working late downtown she would wait wide-eyed for his return, refusing to relax in sleep until he was at her side. By the same token, he knew that he must go out to the island tomorrow—or face the possibility of her return to claim him once again.

"Why can't you sleep, Martin?"

Now, of course, was the time to speak, in this clear-headed hour before dawn. To insist, once and for all, that his roots were too deep for transplanting, that the Marty Aschoff she had married was the only reality, never the too smooth caricature she had superimposed. He opened his mouth to release the bitter words, and found he could not hurt her after all. Martin Ash was her lifework. He could not destroy that creation without destroying Catherine as well.

"Get your own rest, darling," he said. "I'll come back in a while."

"Is it something we should talk over, Martin? Something I've done—or left undone?"

"It's only that I can't sleep, Catherine. Believe me, I wish I knew the reason."

"If you'd leave things to Andy Gray tomorrow. Two days on the island are just what you need——"

"I don't deny that, my dear. It just happens the hospital needs me more."

"Are you in trouble down there, Martin? Please tell me if you are——"

"Have I ever been in real trouble without telling you?"

Of course I haven't, he added wordlessly. Thanks to your money, my path has been satin-smooth from the start. Thanks to your friends in high places, I'm one of those envied healers who saves every patient.

"I've told you the facts," he said. "We've a burn case I want to check on personally, just for my private book. And I must see how Andy made out with Rilling——"

"If you like, I'll stay in town, too."

"I wouldn't hear of it, Catherine. No more would your guests."

"Promise me this much, Martin. Will you try to come out when the day's over?"

"I'll do my best," he said. He kissed her gently as he spoke—careful, even now, lest he stir the embers of the ardours they had shared an hour ago. Not that his interest in that slender, passionately cared-for body had lessened with the years: the act of love as distinguished from love itself was the one dynamic in their life together that had direction and meaning. And yet, much as he might want her (if only to cheat his loneliness), he wanted to face up to that loneliness even more. If I can sit here quietly and await the dawn, he told himself, I may see my future clear at last. I may even understand the reason I was born.

"Go to bed, Catherine," he said. "We've fought this out for now."

"Were we fighting, Martin? I didn't realize it."

"You haven't gone to bed," he said coldly. "You know I'll belong to you by daylight. Can't you rest on your laurels?"

He knew that he had hurt her at last—and took a twisted pleasure in the pain he was inflicting. At that same moment he remembered the nightmare from which he had wakened. It was a familiar, recurring dream that had plagued his midnights for a long time now. Catherine, on a deep satin divan that rose up to engulf them both. But this was a dream of hate, never of love. Its ending was invariable. Suddenly, between kisses, he would fling her from him—so violently that she had no time to cry out. Then, with exquisite savour, he would watch his fingers fasten on her throat, choking the cry at her lips until her eyes grew rich as purple grapes, with blood at her lips like wine.

He needed no memory of his student psychiatry to diagnose that vision. Men had always dreamed this of the women they possessed—or who possessed them. Sometimes the dream burst the bounds of the super-ego, dredging the whole screaming torment to the surface of one's brain. Then, as the nightmare and reality merged, men had often killed the thing they loved most—because, in loving, they were losing the pride in their maleness, the right to be a free agent which is the heritage of all men.

"Good night, Martin. Just remember I love you. No matter what you do——"

He did not look up as she vanished into the bedroom. He knew she would lie awake for a while, hoping that he would come to her one more time before their long, white night had ended. Eventually she would sleep the sleep of the just—the good woman, certain of her possessions, including the husband she had all but tamed at last.

He glanced at the Sèveres clock on the overmantel. Still a good two hours to dawn. He could sleep here with his unsolved problem—if he yielded to temptation and swallowed one of the tablets in the pocket of his robe. It would not be the first time he had dropped off on the love seat, with his limbs cramped into the cushions like a tired child's.

The pellet lay in his palm, while he weighed the price of forgetfulness. This sleep, at least, would be free of nightmares. Phenobarbital—the old man's friend, the exile's solace. I, too, am an exile, he told himself as he gulped it down.

xv

Nelson, the night watchman at East Side General, quickened his pace as the clock on Schuyler Tower chimed the hour of four. Deep in the tunnel that led from surgery to pathology, the sound was muted to the vanishing point: the watchman's ear, tuned to the hospital's changing rhythms, counted the dull beats by rote. Four a.m.—the hour when life hovered on the brink, half willing to take the final plunge. East Side General had never seemed quieter, never more at peace.

On the landing, where a light bulb glowed like a murky

star, Nelson stopped before his station and lifted the key from the hook. Inserting it into the slot on his time clock, he clicked the imprint of the hour on the record dial. At the sound, a heavy steel door inched open a cautious crack, letting a shaft of light into the half gloom of the stairway.

"That you, Sam?" It was Otto, the night keeper of the dead-house.

"Last call tonight," said Nelson. This, too, was part of their routine. Hours after the regular conference of the pathology staff, the night watchman and the custodian of the dead had fallen into the habit of meeting for a visit of their own. Somehow (and Nelson had often wondered why) the morgue seemed almost friendly at this hour. And business-like, too, he added instantly, letting his eyes rove down the gleaming files of iceboxes, like coffins in some arctic igloo, the deep-grooved marble tables in the autopsy room beyond. Death was all round you, yet death was not an enemy at this hour.

"I've got beer," said Otto.

This, too, was expected on Nelson's final round. Beer was brought in from the Greek wagon down the block after the doctors' meeting adjourned. Otto always put aside a few bottles for himself and Nelson—and for Dale Easton, too, when the head pathologist was working late.

Nelson slung the leather-stitched clock from his shoulder and settled into a chair. Restored after a long sip, he permitted himself a yawn. Man, he reflected, is not a nocturnal animal, no matter how hard he strives to change his habits.

"The doctor is working in autopsy?"

"He's finishing a dissection, Sam. Stay where you are, please. You are old friends——"

"I remember Dale Easton when he came on the staff," said the watchman. "I knew even then he was one of us, Otto. One of the men who prefer to sleep by day."

"Says he enjoys his work too much to leave it. That is simpler. We are not vampires, afraid of the first cock-crow——"

"But you live for the night, Otto. Even when it is long——"

The custodian of the morgue drank deep and wiped his lips with the back of one massive hand. For all his bulk, Otto seemed powerful as some benign Cerberus. Thanks to his bald head and the series of chins that descended to meet the collar of his immaculate smock, he might have passed for an outsize baby—until one noted the crow's-feet round his calm blue eyes, the wisdom of the tired mouth.

"Not even the night is long," he said. "Not when a man has made peace with himself."

"You can say that easily. You, too, enjoy your work."

"It keeps me busy," said Otto. "People are always dying."

The watchman glanced at the neat row of iceboxes. "Are these your friends, then?"

"They are better friends than you think."

"What good are the dead? They can't talk."

"They tell me things just the same."

"And the women? Do you find them beautiful now, as well?"

"No, Sam. The dead are never beautiful. It is only an invention of the romantics—this idea that man dies in peace. Man fights for life, to the end. Even when the end has been easy——"

"And when it is hard—what then?"

"Go into the autopsy room. Look at the cadaver the doctor works on now. You will see a hell that Doré could not invent."

"The case from Brookhaven, eh?"

They exchanged knowing glances. The story of the burn case had been down the grapevine hours ago: it was stale gossip now. "Death was pure terror for that one," said Otto.

"Does this story frighten you?"

"I gave up fear long ago. No city is immortal. New York will crumble like the others, when God wills it. If I am to die in the rubble, why should I picture death before it comes?"

"Maybe New York will last for ever," said the watchman. "This time, even God may be kinder. I cannot believe that it will be destroyed. But, then, I refuse to believe that we are moving uptown. Perhaps I have no gift for prophecy."

"Ash will fight the move," said Otto. "Perhaps he will win after all."

"You can't fight money for ever," said Nelson. "Money outlasts us all."

"You will go uptown with the others, then?"

"What choice will I have? To you, it makes no difference. Your cellar will be the same. But me, I shall spend an hour on the subway each way. So will most of the staff. And what of the people who come to our clinics? Even if they could find us uptown, we will frighten them away. We will be too clean—with our new-found wealth. No, Otto. This hospital is part of its neighbourhood. It will be a sin to move it."

"The slums must go. We all know that. Someone must let in the sun. If *we* don't let it in, as good Americans, the bombs will do the job——"

"Destroy the slums, by all means," said Nelson. "But do not destroy a hospital to make way for tomorrow. There can never be too many hospitals—or too many doctors like Ash and young Andy Gray. Or Dr. Easton," he added, with a glance at the half-open door where the pathologist's night lamp blazed above an autopsy table.

"Or Tony Korff?" asked Otto with a crooked grin.

"There have been too many Tony Korffs since the days of Hippocrates," said the watchman. "Too many doctors who were bloodsuckers first and healers second——" He bit off his words precisely and put down the empty beer bottle. The buzzer had just sounded at the steel door that stood between the land of the living and the dead.

Otto sighed at his feet and moved from light to shadow, releasing the spring lock as he went. Nelson got up, too, with his clock slung at his shoulder, when the stretcher trundled in on noiseless wheels.

"Another friend to cheat your loneliness," said the watchman. "I'll be on my way."

He stepped back to let the orderly wheel the stretcher under the droplights—and smiled as he noted that its sheet was hardly less pale than the cheeks of the probationer who trotted beside it. Hospital regulation demanded that this girl, who had probably seen the patient die, accompany him on his last dark journey. Nelson could guess that it was the first death she had witnessed as an active assistant. At least, the first after dark.

"I'm going up to the wards, Nurse," he said. "Would you like me to walk part way with you?"

"Thank you, watchman." The girl was standing on her dignity, he saw, but she was no less grateful. They moved down the long reach of the underground tunnel side by side. Watching them go, with the bored orderly bringing up the rear of the procession, Otto closed his door against the world without. He had seen many nurses cringe when the death cart passed. Perhaps it's their youth, he thought; it's only natural that the young should dread the reality of death. The old, of course, are wiser—if you can call their disillusion wisdom. The dead could hurt no one, not even themselves.

He stared down at the form outlined by the loose draping of the sheet. The man rested on his back on the flat metal tray, poised now, with grotesque finality, before the row of iceboxes. Otto flicked back the sheet and stared down at the grey empty face. A man like myself, he thought. A bit older, perhaps; a good deal thinner. Certainly a good deal unhappier, though it's beyond my power now to read the life story on the brain behind that twisted forehead. A ward patient, the chart says, a vagrant from the Bowery kerb, gone to a land where no promises are broken.

Otto sighed and rubbed his bald forehead, as though he could rub the image away. Nelson's right, he thought. This night *has* been longer than usual. Even if you have turned sixty-five, it's too late for philosophy. He sighed again, and chuckled at his own flash of sentiment. Then he moved quietly to the half-open door to the autopsy room.

Dale Easton was still at work above the table, and still wearing the apron the X-ray technicians used to protect themselves from radiation. The massive gloves that came halfway to his elbows made his work with the scalpel awkward, but he was still dissecting painstakingly, with the infinite reluctance in each stroke that only the pathologist knows. The cadaver under his hands was now more a grinning skeleton than a man. Accustomed as he was to such techniques, Otto found his eyes had strayed to the far wall before he spoke.

"We just got a patient, Doctor." The joke was worn wafer-thin with age, but it came to his lips mechanically.

Dale snipped a strip of tissue from an exposed rib and

dropped it into a small box on the side table. A larger box had already been filled and sealed: this, Otto knew, was destined for the laboratory at Brookhaven. The smaller receptacle (lead-lined, like the pathologist's garb, and borrowed from X-ray) was for the hospital's own use. Dale Easton was too practical a scientist to overlook this opportunity to study an acute radiation burn on his own.

"A new patient, Otto?"

"Fresh off the wards, Doctor."

"What's the diagnosis this time? Too much Bowery?"

"Too much Bowery," said Otto. "The chart gives the cause of death as syphilitic heart disease. He's one of our repeaters."

"Old or young?"

"They all look old, Doctor. But this one is seventy-nine."

Dale nodded; he had not yet looked up from his dissection. "Put him on ice. We'll do him in the morning." Both of them knew that the case was worth nothing more than the routine autopsy the records demanded.

The pathologist worked on for a moment more after Otto had padded out. Part of his mind was asking why Otto had troubled to come in after all. Was it possible that the old fellow was lonely, after these years with the dead? Or did he feel that Dale himself needed the solace of a human voice between dusk and dawn?

He stripped off his gloves at last and went to scrub away the last memory of the long task. There would be time enough tomorrow for the laborious classification of the effects of radiation on that dead tissue. Time enough to correlate his findings with the lab at Brookhaven. It had been his idea to suggest the two-way analysis, and Inspector Hurlbut had endorsed it instantly. Perhaps they might even be able to identify the actual chemical involved and, with this solid fact to guide them, trace the thefts to their source.

But he had put off all thought of such matters until another working day. Holding that resolve before him, he went out to the refrigerator room and stood thoughtfully in the shadows while he watched Otto slide the newly arrived cadaver into its icy bed. There was unopened beer on the table across the room, and he went to pour himself a glass.

For the first time he realized that the night had passed without Andy Gray's half-promised visit. Not that he had really expected the resident to join them here, though he could remember a time, not too long ago, when Andy had been only too glad to drop into the morgue to debate the verities.

Watching the collar of foam seethe into a compact mass at the rim of his glass, Dale wondered if Andy was still with Pat Reed—if the bargain now pending there had been sealed in earnest. The whole hospital knew that she meant to tie Andy down to marriage, with no holds barred. How ever it might bet, the hospital had agreed that no one but a fool would turn down those millions—if they were offered without too many strings.

Even with strings attached (and most bargain packages turned into snares in the end), he could not blame Andy for capitulating. Surgeons, Dale recognized, were seldom touched with the pure flame of science. Skilled technicians, with all the compulsions of their trade, they carried their talents close to the surface—and, like bravura performers in every profession, their emotional conflicts were never-ending. There might even be truth in the Freudian suggestion that men chose surgery because of an innate sadistic urge. Hearing the slam of the icebox drawer, Dale looked up and laughed at his own musings.

"Would you agree that most surgeons are sadists, Otto?"

The custodian of the death house pursed his lips. At that moment he resembled an outsize baby more than ever. A strangely robust baby who has lived down most human appetites long ago, without losing his zest for life itself.

"I once heard Dr. Freud say as much," said Otto slowly.

"Then you and I are advanced psychotics, too," said Dale. "Necrophiles, who find pleasure in the dead."

"It is evident, Doctor," said Otto. "It is also sensible. At least they can't talk back."

They chuckled together at the joke. Perhaps it was all the funnier because they both recognized its hidden truth.

II—MORNING

I

THREE times daily, as regularly as the ebb and flow of the tide below its windows, a surge of humanity passed the marble Christ in the lobby of East Side General Hospital. This morning, when the first stiff-capped nurse came briskly through the great brass doors that were never closed, the lobby still gleamed with soap-suds as it awaited its morning bath and polish. Corded mountains of newsprint towered beside the service lifts for distribution in Schuyler Tower and the other private wings. Probationers were stirring in the corridors that fanned out from the central rotunda, their blue linen uniforms immaculate still, their stocking seams at military perfection. Interns yawned towards their morning rounds, still heavy-eyed from last night's wrestle with death, or last night's poker game. The surgeons, here for early operations before going on to their uptown surgeries, were marked by their quiet absorption, by the satchels that were their passports. Once the first arrival had checked in with the receptionist, they seemed to come in swarms—followed by the caps of a dozen hospitals as the specials appeared for their morning shifts.

Moving in the heart of this steady stream, Dr. Martin Ash could feel routine descend upon his spirit like balm. An hour's hard grind awaited him in his office, and his first operation in the clinic was scheduled for nine. When he doffed his surgeon's gown at noon he could count on his staff to keep up the pressure until his long day ended. At this moment he felt no twinge of envy for anyone in his orbit—and this included Andy Gray, his titular assistant, fast asleep at this moment, because he wasn't operating early.

En route to his office, he nodded pleasantly (if somewhat absent-mindedly) to his doorman and his receptionist, to the switchboard operators just off the rotunda—and, finally, to the battalion of typists who were already hard at work in his ante-room. He was not too preoccupied to notice that all of them stared a little, before they resumed their professional masks. The director of East Side General seldom arrived at this early hour, especially when his wife had been entertaining the night before. He could hardly pause to explain that he had spent most of the night on the couch in his living-room, or that he had left home in a kind of half daze, because he refused to continue an argument that could have but one ending.

The trip down the East River Drive had restored his spirits magically; the mere sight of these towering white walls had lifted him into a calm that seemed destined to endure for ever. As a doctor, he knew it was euphoria pure and simple, a natural reaction from his black melancholia of the night. Yet he had ridden other waves of renewal and stayed clear of that pit of despond. Perhaps he would do as well today—if Catherine kept her distance.

Behind his desk at last, he attacked his mail with real zest, driving two secretaries at top speed until even the most difficult items were conquered. Save for a familiar nagging pain behind his eyes, he still felt rested and all but renewed when he turned to last night's admissions list and read Andy's report on Bert Rilling. He found that he was chuckling as he read: only Andy could have saved that porker from the death he so richly deserved. Of course, if Rilling lived, he would be one more enemy to fight, when the question of moving the hospital could no longer be side-tracked.

"Pardon me, Doctor——"

He glanced up quickly. Miss Steele, his chief secretary, a ramrod-stiff girl as coldly efficient as her name, was studying him through her horn rims.

"What is it, Agnes?"

"There's a police Inspector outside—and a man from the F.B.I. They say they have an appointment."

Hurlbut again. Martin Ash frowned at his empty desk. He would have preferred to put off this conference until noon, but he had no excuse for refusing to see the Inspector now.

"Are they in the reception room?"

"Of course, Doctor."

"Tell them I'll be in at once."

Before he rose from his desk Ash dialled the surgical ward for a last-minute report on the burn case. As he had expected, the situation had worsened. He was still frowning as he opened the door that gave access to the small consulting room where he received his more distinguished patients—and others who had good reason to come and go quietly.

Despite his secretary's warning, he could feel himself recoil a step as his eyes met the probing glance of Don Saunders, the man from the F.B.I. Here, thought Ash, is a bloodhound whose face is as well known as any movie star's. If *he's* on the case it must be really hot. And yet no voice could have been milder than Saunders's, when he rose and held out his hand.

"I know you're busy, Doctor. We'll try to make this short——"

"You've found your man, then?"

"Far from it. Can you help us there?"

"No, Mr. Saunders. The patient we brought in last night hasn't regained consciousness. And I'm afraid he's sinking fast."

When the F.B.I. man smiled there was no effect of mirth. Watching that compact bulk settle in an arm-chair, Ash was reminded of a boxer who can anticipate his opponent's feints. "The inspector and I have already looked in on the fellow. I'd say he was a dead pigeon—wouldn't you, Hurlbut?"

The Inspector sighed—and settled deeper in his own arm-chair. Hurlbut seemed unusually quiet today. The sort of numbed acquiescence that often follows a severe beating from higher up.

"Why he's alive at all is beyond me."

Ash took back his authority with a shrug. "Blame that on our new wonder drugs, gentlemen. I'm still afraid you'll get nothing of value from that source."

"He may still be useful, if we play him right." Saunders leaned forward sharply. "That's why we're asking your help."

"I'm afraid I don't follow."

"You've seen the morning papers, of course?"

"Only the headlines."

"As you know, Hurlbut gave out the story that these two cases were from Brookhaven. Collins's paper played it straight, for once. I can't say as much for the tabloids. One columnist is already screaming that an atomic killer is loose in Manhattan——"

"Do you believe that for a moment?"

The mask of the federal man was bland as cream: only the hard eyes betrayed him. "My beliefs aren't important. In a way I'm sorry that Hurlbut let the cat escape this far. Still, it may serve its purpose. Obviously a killer of some kind is at large. If he's read those stories, and pondered them, he may over-reach himself, even now, to silence that man upstairs."

Hurlbut cut in heavily. "Every paper said that we were expecting a lead at any time. They made it sound real, too: I almost believed it myself——"

Again the director of East Side General held up his hand for silence. "You set a neat trap, Inspector. I can't see that I'm part of the bait——"

"You aren't, Doctor," said Hurlbut dourly. "But East Side General is still the trap. The cordon's still out, you understand. And we're combing the neighbourhood with everything we have. We're still hoping our man will panic and break from cover. Suppose he does, and gets clear. Suppose he leaves his clock behind——"

"You mean he'd blow up a corner of New York, just to silence that patient upstairs?"

"He might think it was worth while. None of us can be sure he wouldn't."

"What are you suggesting?"

Saunders cut in swiftly. "We're asking if you'd like us to kill the story. Tell the papers the man died without saying a word. At least that would take the danger away from your doorstep."

Ash sat quietly for a moment, while the implications of the offer sank home. "I wish you'd tell me all you know before I answer," he said.

Inspector and federal man exchanged glances: it was
Saunders who spread his hands, like a gambler exposing a
pair of deuces. "It won't help you much in your decision,
Doctor—but you've the right to know. First off, the chemical
was stolen from Oak Ridge——"

"So it *was* a chemical?"

"I can't label it," said Saunders. "Not even for you. I can
say it's liquid, volatile—and radioactive. Violent enough to
be shipped in lead cylinders. Several of them have been
pinched recently. Apparently the thieves have been running
them East by van. We found one of those vans last midnight.
In a boat slip downtown. Its tailboard looked as though it
had been toasted in a blast furnace, then chewed up by a
dinosaur."

"So it was a chemical that caused the trouble? It wasn't
an after-effect of a bomb blast?"

"I think we can infer as much, Doctor."

Ash met the visitor's eyes. "It wasn't uranium hexa-
fluoride?"

"No, Doctor," said Saunders patiently. "And we won't
play guessing games, if you please. Maybe we're scaring
ourselves—imagining this is part of a bomb, and that it's
being assembled right under our noses. But it's a possibility
we can't overlook. Of course, it's more likely that the stuff
is simply being exported, illegally: we know that a syndicate
has been running similar kinds of contraband out of New
York for a long time. Eventually we'll break the case. We
might crack it now, if you'll assist."

"Can you be more precise about what happened in that
van, before it was abandoned?"

"We can assume the stuff leaked *en route*. Or when it was
being unloaded. I've told you it's volatile, in its present form.
If a seal broke on one of those containers, it'd spout death
like a flame thrower. Let's say the driver and his helper were
roasted alive, while they were making delivery. Whoever is
at the receiving end in New York knew he could never call
a doctor. So he dumped the bodies, and then the van
itself——"

"And the chemical, too?"

"That's still under cover, worse luck. Unless it's already out of the country—which doesn't seem likely. The whole timing indicates that the receiver was his own shipper—that he worked out of this neighbourhood—and that he'd stop at nothing to cover his tracks. It isn't within reason that he can get away free, especially if we can scare him while he's lying low."

Martin Ash got to his feet. "Thank you, gentlemen," he said. "I can understand my part clearly now."

"Then you'll go on pretending that fellow upstairs is about to talk at any moment?"

Ash went to the window of his office and stared across the hospital esplanade at the tall iron gates of the outer entrance, and the tenements across the way. Somehow they had never seemed so richly alive; try as he might, he could not summon up a picture of dissolution.

"You're asking a great deal, Mr. Saunders," he said at last.

"There's a great deal at stake, Doctor."

The federal man was right, of course: there was no longer any choice. The enemy (and it hardly mattered if he was nameless, so far) must be outfought, and outwitted, on every front. The safety of his hospital personnel—like the safety of those tenement dwellers outside—was something beyond his control. The director of East Side General nodded slowly.

"We'll work with you, of course."

Saunders held out his hand. "Thank you, Doctor. It takes courage to make this kind of decision."

"You'll be here, too, remember."

"Danger is our business. It isn't yours."

"What if there's a panic, before the event?"

Both Hurlbut and Saunders smiled wearily. "You'd be surprised how well people can live under the shadow of their own doom," said the federal man. "Everyone in New York will read that columnist's scaring headline. Naturally they'll hang on their radios and jam all the bars for the next television programme. But I don't foresee any panic—not until there's something real to panic over——"

"I must alert my staff, of course."

"Naturally. I'll see to it that neighbour hospitals are ready to help—if you need help later." Saunders got briskly to his feet, with the air of a man who has just had a weight shifted from his shoulders. "I'll be in touch through Hurlbut's office. Will you show me the back door again, Inspector?"

Ash continued to stand in his window after the visitors had gone. Saunders was right: a man could live just so long under the threat of his own dissolution. Eventually he went mad—or, following the tough instinct of *homo sapiens* for self-preservation, he ceased to heed all prophets, good or bad. I don't believe a word of this myself, thought Ash. Simply as a prudent routine, I'll order a state of siege at the staff meeting: we'll be ready, if this man-made lightning strikes.

And then he thought of his wife, and laughed aloud. At least he couldn't share her week-end now. What was worse, he could never tell her why. Perhaps I'm playing down my danger with a purpose, he thought. Is it the old death wish coming to the fore again? Is *that* why I'm refusing to move from the shadow while there's still time?

There was no crying need of his presence here, if disaster struck: in fact he would do well to delegate all real decisions to Andy Gray, whose wartime experience far transcended his own. Emergency services were as well organized as a boat drill on an Atlantic liner; thanks to Andy, they could go into gear at a moment's notice, without the slightest hitch. No one could censure Dr. Martin Ash for taking his regular week-end off at this time. No one but Ash would know that it took greater courage to return to the gold-plated prison he shared with Catherine than to linger here—and await the release that might come with extinction.

II

En route to the surgical ward and morning bed check, Tony Korff ducked into a diet kitchen and poured himself a cup of coffee, hot and black. He drank it down in swift gulps as he stood in the open door to the fire escape. Far below him New York shimmered in the haze. The blocks of skyscrapers to north and south, the proud cliffs of flats far uptown, were mirage-like in the heat. Another scorcher, he thought absently: another round of drudgery. Then, as his head cleared under that scalding draught, his mind came awake in earnest. He had not slept a wink since he had assisted at the operation that had saved Bert Rilling's life: he had needed all his will power to keep clear of the brewer's room until he could stop there as a matter of hospital routine. Even now he was half afraid to verify the discovery he had made under the operating-room lights.

A second cup, and a few pieces of toast filched from a special's tray, were all the breakfast he needed. He was ready to take the plunge now, to risk everything on the conviction that Bert Rilling and he were anything but strangers. Without knowing why, he glanced quickly to left and right as he left the diet kitchen—a habit that clung from his days in the Berlin ghetto, when enemies were everywhere. Then he moved cautiously forward, clinging to the wall and moving swiftly, with a rodent-like hunch to his shoulders.

As he had expected, there was a "No Visitors" sign on the door. The two men on a bench outside (he knew instinctively that they would be vice-presidents of the Silver Cap Brewery Rilling had owned so long) rose at the sight of the white uniform that meant a doctor. Tony shook off their half-spoken questions and pushed on importantly into the sick man's room, closing the door carefully behind him. The special at the bedside was already on her feet, offering him the chart. He put on his professional manner, studying the record even as one hand darted under the flap of the oxygen tent to measure the brewer's pulse.

He forced himself to concentrate on details, and kept his eyes away from the patient's dim profile, half glimpsed through the plastic wall of the tent. The pulse beat was irregular and hurried—that meant auricular fibrillation, a sure sign of the gradual breakdown of the heart itself. The chart showed that leg circulation still held up, thanks to Andy's daring surgery—but this was only a partial victory. A diseased heart had propelled those clots into the blood stream in the first place. That same heart was gradually losing its function now. Almost surely it would kill the brewer before Rilling could rise from this bed again.

You can't die until I'm sure of you, thought Tony Korff. Damn you, I won't *let* you die. He came back, with a start, to what the nurse was saying. Remember your dignity, he warned himself. Remember this is a routine visit, nothing more.

"Will you examine those spots on his fingers, Doctor? I noticed them just now when I came on duty. The night special says they were even more visible when he came back from the O.R.——"

Tony lifted the beefy hand (even that insensate member seemed familiar) and cursed the headache that still kept his mind from focusing. Only three fingers were involved, but the spots were clearly visible. Incipient skin gangrene, he thought, and put on his professional manner with a vengeance.

"Localized emboli, nothing more," he said severely. "These cases always shoot a volley of small clots into the system. One must have blocked the artery to the finger ends. Circulation out there isn't too good anyway——" Instinctively he let his hand close on Rilling's, to test the skin tone. The brewer moaned, through the fog of opiates, and jerked back his hand.

"*Mein Gott!*"

Tony felt his heart leap wildly. The voice cut across the years, with all its guttural fury intact. A scene unfolded in his mind, like a crazy cinema run backwards. A slimy alley, deep in East Berlin. His own face, twisted in fear and rage, as he stood with his back to the wall and fought with the courage of desperation to throw aside the hands that strove to drag him to the miry kerb. The explosion of two beefy fists, scattering the gang to right and left. The broad-shouldered bully (bigger and angrier than the smaller thugs who had cornered him), saving his skin in a matter of seconds, even as he sent the whole gang scurrying for cover.

"*Mein Gott! Was ist das hier?*"

Tony Korff knitted the fingers of both hands to stop their

trembling. "Give me that flashlight, Nurse," he said quietly. "I want to check his colour."

There was no sound in the room but the whine of the motor outside the oxygen tent. The beam of the flash, cutting through the plastic wall, haloed Bert Rilling's head in a kind of grotesque nimbus. Forehead and jowls seemed to gleam with a bluish light of their own, mute advertisement of a failing heart. A silhouette out of my past, thought Tony He's dying, and I mustn't let him die. . . . And then, as though answering the unspoken thought, Bert Rilling opened his eyes. For a moment the sleepy gaze seemed to light with recognition as he focused on the intent, dark profile just outside the window of the tent.

Tony held his breath until the brewer subsided into coma again. He was sure now—so sure that he scarcely dared draw breath. *Kurt Schilling*, he thought. Only you're Bert Rilling now. After all, it was an easy change to make when you crossed the Atlantic. Even when we first met I knew that you'd not be content to rule a Berlin slum for ever. That you'd smell out Hitler's sickness and change sides in time. . . .

He broke off the soundless monologue and pulled back from the window before the half-attentive nurse had time to grow suspicious. From that chance encounter in the alley (when Kurt had taken him under his wing and trained him to become a kind of minor henchman) he had feared and respected Schilling, in equal measure—and obeyed his orders without question. It was Kurt who had taught him to stop cringing, to face his enemies unafraid. Thanks to Kurt, he had discovered that there is no substitute for intelligence and no tyranny like the tyranny of the mind.

When he heard that Schilling had vanished into the great mill-race of America he had borne no ill will towards his protector. After all, he had grown up without friendship or love. He had expected nothing from Schilling, beyond the fact that the two-fisted bully would use him so long as he was of value. Besides, he was already planning his own escape from Germany. He was not too startled now (once he had survived that first shock of discovery) to find that their paths had crossed again.

Why shouldn't his companion of the slums be an American millionaire today? Why, above all else, should he grudge Rilling-Schilling his rise to fame? It was inevitable that Kurt should make his fortune as an American businessman turned politician. There were still corners in New York where the Nazi fires were firmly banked, needing only a strong breath to flame again.

Kurt had used him once—and Kurt must find use for him again. After all, he had no choice, providing he lived long enough to understand that Tony Korff was a threat to his new position. That Tony had every right to demand some provision for his future, in return for keeping his mouth shut.

He turned again to the chart—a quick-witted doctor, intent on saving a life, if not for the reason he had sworn to the day he received his diploma. Auricular fibrillation meant quinidine, of course. Sometimes the drug could perform a miracle of its own—and Tony Korff was badly in need of a miracle this morning. . . . He picked up the phone on Rilling's bed table and dialled the office number of Dr. George Plant, praying that the fat fool would be at work on time for once.

When the internist's sandpapered voice purred out of the receiver, Tony almost shouted his relief.

"How's your star boarder this morning, Korff?"

"Still viable, sir. I wish I could say more."

"Circulation still holding up?"

Plant, reflected Tony, would be just as breezily confident on the day of his own funeral. "The skin tone is excellent below the waist," he said crisply. "There's no sign of a fresh complication. But the pulse is something else again. I'd diagnose an auricular fibrillation in the making——" He grinned at the suddenly silent receiver, then nodded briskly as Plant gave the order he was hoping for. "Quinidine? An excellent suggestion, Doctor. I'll order it right away."

Back at the oxygen tent after he had telephoned the pharmacy, feeling the respectful eyes of the special nurse upon him, he knew that he could not linger. Now that the drug was ordered he could do no more than wait—and pray. He stole a final glance at the profile of the brewer, so like a death mask as it sagged in narcotic slumber. Old Kurt should be grateful for this help, even if he would pay well for it later.

The nurse was at his elbow now. He cursed her silently and drew back at last.

"Is there anything I can do, Doctor?"

"Make sure he gets that quinidine, the moment it arrives. And call me immediately if there's the slightest change——"

In the hall his wrist watch told him that he still had time to spare before he inspected his ward. I must keep busy, he told himself. At any cost I must slow down the part of my brain that works for Tony Korff—until I'm sure of Rilling, and Rilling's gratitude. Obeying a quick impulse, he turned down the corridor that led to the detention room where the burn patient lay. As an annex to the ward itself, this, too, was part of his bailiwick.

He saw at a glance that the man was *in extremis* now—dying, in fact. The nurse at the bedside (and this, thank God, was one of his ward girls, who took orders without question) got up gratefully as he strode to the bedside.

"I'm so glad you're here, Doctor. I was about to ask for a stimulant order."

His eye noted the covered tray at the bedside. Probably the poor devil was beyond stimulation now—but he'd be criticized later if he didn't make the attempt.

"I'll shoot in an ampoule of coramine," he said. "Have you a syringe?"

While the nurse was passing the instrument he picked up the ampoule from the tray and discarded it in favour of one marked metrazol—the second was by far the more powerful stimulant. Drawing the contents into the syringe, he snapped an elastic tourniquet in place on the dying man's arm, twisting it viciously to bring up a vein already turgid with failing circulation. From far away he watched his thumb depress the needle, transferring the drug to the blood stream. I can keep my hands at work for East Side General, he thought. My brain belongs to Tony Korff this morning—and to Korff's glittering future.

"We're almost out of oxygen, Doctor," said the nurse. "Could you watch him while I order another tank?"

Tony nodded absently. Since his boyhood, death had been only an incident in his day. Still, it seemed odd that this fellow must die incognito, without mourners.

"Is the law still outside?"

"Not any longer, Doctor. They must have given up hope that he'd ever talk again."

The nurse had hurried out as she spoke. Tony continued to study the moribund burn victim, without really seeing him at all. His eye noted that the colour had improved a bit, round those mummy-like bandages; the pulse under his finger had grown stronger, as the potent stimulant jolted at brain centres depressed by shock. Abruptly the half-hidden face muscles twitched, as though the man were about to speak. Tony came back sharply from his wool-gathering— a doctor once again, with a job to do.

This time he siphoned two full ampoules of pentalene into the syringe. If the fellow were going to talk, it must be now or never: since he must die in all events, it would do no harm to jolt him once more, as he stood with one foot across the border. The needle sank home, plunging until the contents of the syringe had started towards the fast-fading brain. Only then did Tony lift his eyes, to make sure the nurse had not returned. There was no sound from the hall as he pocketed the empty ampoules and moved closer to the bed.

It'll need a moment more, he thought, hearing the girl's step at last. He took the oxygen from her hands, even as he was barking an order for an adrenalin needle. When the door had sighed shut a second time he knew he was in possession here. He, and he alone, would hear the message that would issue from those blistered lips. . . . The police would be grateful to anyone who took down that dying statement. It did no harm to have the police on your side, when you were about to purchase a practice in a city like New York.

The face muscles were beginning to twitch violently under the sterile bandage packs. Tony watching the legs go into a spasm—like giant jack-knives twisted in the confining sheet. Only a doctor would know that this was the convulsion that preceded death, an automatic response to those extra shots of pentalene.

A groan escaped the puffed lips. A groan, and a single word Tony, with one ear hard against the bandaged cheek, heard it clearly.

"*Silver——*"

"Go on, *Dummkopf!*" Tony all but shouted, hoping that the sound would reach the damaged brain.

"*Silver—Silver Cap——*"

Tony scowled down at the feebly jerking body, unable to translate what he was hearing. Once again he bent above the man's ear and barked an order—unaware that he was speaking in German in the excitement that gripped him. But he knew, even now, that this spurt of consciousness had been a synthetic response, beginning and ending in the jolt of three pentalene ampoules. He felt the pulse flutter one more time and then taper into silence. A strange immobility that was shattered by the death rattle that burst from collapsing lungs.

The nurse was in the doorway before he could step back from the bedside. Obeying another instinct, he whirled towards her with outstretched hand.

"Give me that adrenalin—quickly!"

The chest bandages ripped under his hand. He hesitated for an instant—shocked, even now, by the nightmare pattern of the burn tissue beneath. But his mind did not slacken in its headlong pace: now that he had begun this dramatic fight for life, he must play his part to the end—if only for the record.

Thanks to the adrenalin needle, he could keep that record straight. No one need know of those extra ampoules of pentalene in the pocket of his surgeon's smock. When he made his report later he would say merely that he had dared to inject adrenalin direct.

He plunged the needle twice before he was sure of his objective. At the first attempt the steel grated on a rib: then the dark blood that spurted into the barrel of the syringe told him that the needle itself was deep in the heart cavity. Actually, of course, this new injection would have been useless, even were the patient still living. But it would make a good story in the interns' room tonight.

"Was I too late, Doctor?"

"Stand back—I'm not sure——"

He dropped the needle in the tray and took up an already lifeless pulse. His mind was free now, racing round the reflex he had just witnessed, the final gasp from the threshold of death. *Silver Cap* . . . Would that be Silver Cap Beer and Ale, the brew that had bought Bert Rilling his share of metropolitan political loot and all its perquisites? Fantastic as it seemed at first view, there must be some connection between the friend of his youth and this charred lump.

His eyes were on the ripped bandages, on the segment of chemical-gutted flesh he had just exposed to plunge the needle. There was something familiar about that grey-white eschar—a parallel that his memory could pounce on instantly, and treasure as its own. In that flash he knew that the gangrene-like spots on Rilling's fingers, and the burn scars he was observing now, had been caused by the same agent. In that burst of perception the whole picture came clear.

Bert Rilling had somehow come in contact with the chemical that had burned two men—killing one and eventually the other. No one but he—who knew the Berlin thug of yesterday—could picture that chain of events more graphically. It was Rilling—or his agents—who had dumped those bodies on the platform of the warehouse. Somewhere along the route Rilling had come in contact with the chemical that had caused their deaths.

He followed the mechanical routine of listening to the burned man's heart and, hearing nothing, pronouncing him dead. The formal gestures seemed never-ending: he ached to get free of this room, to pace the corridor outside and revel in his knowledge. There would be no time for conscious planning before noon—not with his ward still to check, and a long stint in the operating room to follow. But the whole afternoon was his own, and he knew just how to employ it now.

Quite logically, he had already decided that this information was his personal gift. He did not dream of sharing it with anyone—least of all, with the police. The same instinct that had kept his hand from the switch of the wire recorder warned him to say nothing now. Time, and the state of Bert Rilling's health, would dictate his next move—but it would be the move of a hunter who is sure of his quarry, and wise enough to hunt alone.

"Bring me the death certificate later, Nurse—I'm behind schedule now."

He was free from the cadaver now. Free to roam the hospital a moment more before the treadmill claimed him. It needed all his self-control to escape a shout of joy as he rounded a corner—and collided with a fellow intern deep in a newspaper.

"Heads up, Korff!"

"Watch where you're going, can't you?"

He had just time to glimpse the story that young Wilson was reading. The daily blathering of a famous columnist— a once brilliant reporter who had learned, long ago, that screams of doom, delivered with a flavouring of venom, bring more readers than the clear light of truth. The headline today was in the best shocker style, a blob of fat red type that smeared the page like blood.

ATOMIC KILLER RUMOURED
AT LARGE IN MANHATTAN

HOSPITAL GUARDS ONE VICTIM,
WAITS FOR OTHERS

It took an instant for the words to make a pattern. And then Tony Korff began to laugh despite himself—a rocking, almost hysterical mirth that sent him reeling down the corridor like a man far gone in drink. He felt Wilson's eyes follow him, and shrugged off the youngster's curiosity. In his heart Wilson had always considered Tony Korff a squarehead—and at this moment it hardly mattered to Tony if Wilson was right.

"Atomic Killer Rumoured at Large in Manhattan." American humour, thought Tony, has always been the art of exaggeration; American journalism, too, was beginning to slip down to the grotesque levels of its own comic sections. Bert Rilling had begun his days as a thug to the manner born; with luck, he would end them as a respected citizen. Never, in his long journey to fame, had Bert killed without a reason.

Even now Tony could not believe that crazy splash of ink was justified.

As always, there must be a simpler explanation below the surface. Bert must tell him everything when he emerged from his narcotic coma; if Bert was reluctant to speak, there were ways of forcing him. In the meantime he could afford to laugh in earnest, as he pictured the vast police drag-net spread over the city, and the strange haul it would dredge from the depths.

He remembered the cordon of bluecoats that still ringed the hospital—determined, even now, to keep the killer from reaching his dying victim, unaware that the menace had already cancelled out. He thought, with brief contempt, of the bustling Inspector, who had been too busy to question a mere intern last night. In a way it would be fitting now to make the same Inspector pay dearly for his error—if he were not positive that Bert Rilling would pay far more.

He was humming a wordless tune as he entered the surgical ward, unaware that it was the music for an obscene marching song that Hitler's Brown Shirts had once bellowed in the teeth of a stunned world. His head was high as he walked, and his white-clad legs seemed almost to strut. The world was his oyster this morning. He could afford to extract the pearl in his own way, at his own time.

III

At that moment (a full city block distant, though they were under the same roof) Bert Rilling's mind was wrestling with realities, in a cloud of pain and opiates. It began with a cautious backtrack—not too far for safety. Back to the sudden lance of agony that might have been death in tangible form. He could even remember the bitter smile as he reeled under that stab of pain and admitted his case-hardened body was not immortal after all. Soft living had done it, the easy wealth that America had bestowed on him from the beginning. He

knew he was suet-fat today—an old man at fifty, in fact, a
stubborn old man who refused to take his doctor's orders.

Yet he had faced death in his brewery office as arrogantly
as he had faced his other enemies. He had noted the failure
of his leg muscles as incuriously as though he were already
outside his own body. Sprawled face down on his office
carpet, he had inched his way to the phone by using the full
strength of his massive arms and shoulders. Not one man
in a hundred could have lifted that porcine carcass to the
phone. But he had had minutes to spare, after he had dialled
Plant's number, before he tumbled into oblivion. A whole
aeon, in fact, when he could have repented his sins. He had
wept instead—as the old have always wept, when they admit,
at long last, that they will die alone.

Only he hadn't died. He had been conscious, after a
fashion, when Plant burst into his office. He remembered the
clang of the bell as the ambulance backed up to the loading
platform just outside his door. The procession of men in white
that seemed never-ending. The hovering archangel who
brought the life-giving oxygen tent, the tall, lean surgeon who
had examined him so competently. He could even recall the
operating room. The pale green walls had reminded him,
oddly enough, of the Grotto, a night club he had owned in
Munich long ago.

There was nothing remotely familiar about the monsters
of modern surgery that moved in upon him, one by one.
He had tried to scream—but no sound would come. He had
tried to rise against the gloved hands that held him there,
against his will. But the needle was already in his arm, bringing
its own surcease. He had smiled drowsily, resigning himself
to this death that was not death, quite certain he would live
again.

Now as his eyes, small-pupilled from the narcotic, adjusted
themselves to his shuttered hospital room he saw that his
optimism was justified. They had brought him back from
death with their miracles, saved him from his own folly: his
stubborn refusal to admit that his best days were behind him,
the greater folly of lingering in his office after hours, when a
van was due from the West. Not that he could regret that

lingering now, when he thought of the ruin his presence had averted.

But he was too tired to let his mind wander that far afield. For the present he preferred to concentrate on that hospital room. The plastic tent that covered him, and the bath of oxygen that flowed over his head and shoulders like life itself, giving him the heady illusion of youth and strength, even as he admitted he could not raise his head from the pillow. The respectful silhouette of the nurse just outside, ready to spring up at an instant's notice and do his bidding. Perhaps I'm not really alive, he thought. Perhaps this is a station on the way to Heaven, and you're my attending angel. But that was impossible: even in his near delirium he admitted that he had resigned his hope of Heaven long ago. Besides, Tony Korff would never be waiting on the threshold. Like himself, Tony belonged to the blackest pit.

It had seemed quite natural to come out of his coma and find Tony's face within a few inches of his own. Even the flashlight and the sharp-nosed stare were part of the gutter rat he remembered. His mind stumbled on the epithet, insisting that it was not too harsh. The ghetto that had spawned them both was a natural background for a rat: in the life they had shared once, the rat was often king. It was strange that Tony had always wanted to be a doctor. Stranger still that he should steal and kill to earn his way to a university. Strangest of all that he should have the wisdom to escape the general collapse of Europe before it was too late.

America (and the providential explosion of the second world conflict) had given Tony just the impetus he needed. When Kurt Schilling had become Bert Rilling he had made it his business to check on Tony's progress. Often he had all but yielded to temptation, and revealed his identity to his former ally, with the suggestion they join forces again. As Bert Rilling's second in command, Tony could still go far. As a practising surgeon in New York, Rilling felt sure, the boy would never be better than second-rate.

But he had never quite brought himself to make the first move towards that reunion. On the contrary (knowing that Tony was interning at the hospital across the way from the brewery), he had been at some pains to make sure their paths did not cross. He had known from the start that time would only whet Tony's appetites. Remembering the gutter rat he had befriended long ago, he might only discover a full-grown jackal, eager for his life-blood. Now, when he was quite sure that Tony had recognized him, he was neither glad nor afraid. For the moment he had the queer, fatalistic feeling that this meeting had been ordained long ago, by a fate he was powerless to change.

Certainly he had no fear that Tony would betray him. He had left Kurt Schilling behind in East Berlin, for good and all. Tony would be the first to understand that, to protect his secret, at a price. Bert Rilling was sure that the price would be high, but Tony would be worth the cost. It would be recompense enough to have a friend from the old days, someone to whom a man could open his heart without restraint. Rilling was not the first refugee to learn how cold New York could be to a visitor—even a visitor who had made his fortune there.

As to the source of that fortune—well, he would keep that secret to himself for a while, until he tested Tony's mettle. But it was comforting to know that he had a messenger at his bedside, when a messenger was really needed. A courier who would stop at nothing to reach his destination. In short, a friend he could trust implicitly—providing the bargain was to the friend's advantage.

He let his mind back-track a bit further, testing his present dilemma from all angles. He was safe for today, at least—he felt positive of that. Tonight and tomorrow might prove another story, if Tony was stubborn about the bargain. But he would not let Tony be stubborn too long. In fact, now he had begun to weigh things in earnest, it seemed clear that he could no longer do without Tony Korff.

What had happened last night at the brewery could have happened to anyone forced to depend upon others than himself. He had always chosen his agents with care. He had paid them far more than their market value, if the truth were known, to ensure loyalty in advance. The driver who had backed the huge beer dray into the landing stage was one of his oldest employees. It was not the first time he had finished their round trip thus—using the last hour of his shift to unload the truck himself. Of course he had known in advance that the night watchman would be gone at this hour (being a trusted employee, he had his own key to unlock the gate). Normally he would have delivered the sample sack to Rilling's office, ready for inspection in the morning, before the load itself was transferred to the vats.

Yes, it had been just as routine as that—and just as foolproof. Ordinarily Rilling would not even have been present to check the delivery of that innocent grain sack. Over the years, he had found it simpler to delegate a certain authority, even a certain elementary trust. Yet he had lingered after hours in his office because he was at home there—far more at ease in his shirt sleeves than in evening clothes in a restaurant uptown.

He remembered that he had scarcely troubled to glance outside when he heard the dray rumble to a stop a few feet beyond his door. After all, the stuff had been arriving from Tennessee for months now, without a hitch. No transport inspector under Heaven would have dreamed of stopping a load of beer kegs as they rumbled south—or the tight-packed hop bags that those same lorries brought into New York on the return journey. No one would guess that a small bottle was deep in that sample bag—a lead-cased bottle containing a chemical that was, quite literally, worth its weight in diamonds. Thanks to the smoothness of his arrangements, he had been taking those deliveries for granted. Had he remained uptown, he would have turned in with a clear conscience, sure that the sample bag would be locked away in his office when he arrived in the morning.

He would never know what might have happened if he had continued to pore over his ledgers in the office—if he had not yearned for the sound of a human voice and strolled out to the platform to superintend the unloading. He was in time to note that the driver's helper was a new man, one he had never seen before, though he could trust his agents in Tennessee to screen each newcomer carefully. He would never know whether the man had been nervous, careless—or both. Or whether it was sweat-grimed hands or a guilty conscience that made him drop that sample hop sack as he lifted it from lorry to platform.

There had been two explosions, hideously blended. The first had been harmless enough—a prodigal cascade of hops trickling from the split gunny sacking at the tailboard of the lorry. He had had a glimpse of the bottle, a squat lead rectangle that had been safely bedded in hops a second before and now rolled free, to crack its seal against the iron studding of the tailboard. The second explosion had come at that precise instant—a prismatic flare, as though a volcano had spouted alive in the depths of the lorry, as though some evil djinn had burst from the dawn of time to remake the world in his image.

At first he was certain that the flare had dissolved both driver and helper in their tracks. Later he knew that the fire had done no more than sear their life away, while he stood helpless on the platform. Only one thing had saved him from destruction, too—the lead jacket of the bottle had melted and run together, closing the mouth for a few precious moments. He had had time to scurry into the toolroom and don the asbestos suit that always hung in readiness there, in case a vat exploded. Time to clamp a wrench on the bottle and hammer the molten lead across the mouth. His right hand still tingled faintly as he recalled the pain in his finger tips, when some of the deadly fluid had burned through his gloves.

Once the bottle was locked away in his office safe, his mind had spun back to sanity again. After all, he had dumped incriminating evidence before, and lived to remember all the details. Last night's disposal had been simple enough, thanks to the pitch-black streets that fanned out from the brewery. Looking back on it now, he admitted that he might have been a trifle hasty when he spilled the two charred bodies at the first convenient moment. Certainly the spot he had chosen was too close to the brewery. Had he known, at the time, how easily he was to abandon the lorry he would have sent car and cadavers alike into the same watery grave.

He had stripped off the asbestos suit he had not dared to discard, and sent it swirling towards the sea from the quay beside the brewery in the suction of the outgoing tide. Dishevelled as he was, and soaked in the sweat of terror, he had not dared to make his way to a lighted thoroughfare and hail a taxi. Instead, he had followed the instincts he had transported from his childhood, and hugged the slimy walls of a dozen warehouses, the blind alleys that he had memorized long after the need for such concealment had vanished from the life of Bert Rilling.

Stumbling through the brewery gates at last, he had felt a presage of what was to come. He had ignored the first lancing pains while he fumbled his way to the loading platform to sweep away the last scrap of evidence that might advertise the night's near debacle. He had hoped to reach his office desk in time, to swallow one of the tablets he kept there always. But he had been far beyond such elementary aid when he gained the office with his last hard-won breath, only to stumble full-length on the carpet.

All in all, he thought, I've handled things well enough. The lorry plates are locked in my safe, along with the bottle. Even if the police can trace it they'll never connect me with the owner. He had always transferred contraband with the utmost care: an international operator couldn't be too careful these days, no matter how well he selected his subordinates.

Bert Rilling felt his spine curl as he faced up to the complete blueprint of his dilemma. Both fists closed on his covers, as though he possessed the strength to toss the hospital bedding aside and return to his office unaided. It was true that lone wolves lived longer than those who ran with the pack. He had kept his name clean of petty thievery; the very men who had lost their lives on his loading platform had been paid off a thousand miles away. And yet he had never trusted the delivery of this deadly contraband, or the collection of his fees, to another hand.

The system had paid handsomely in the past. One might almost say that it had been a series of deals among friends— the same friends who had broken heads under his tutelage in Germany, not too many years ago. It hardly mattered if those same friends were spatted diplomats now, on the fringes of the Iron Curtain, or the captains of freighters

waiting in Brooklyn for the tide. Up to now he had always
gone aboard with his loot—whether the rendezvous was a
first-class cabin on a luxury liner or the tobacco-fouled chart-
room of a tanker bound for such home ports as Stockholm
or Trieste, Istanbul or Bangkok.

The beauty of such deliveries was their absolute safety.
Bert Rilling, after all, was a true citizen of the world. Thanks
to the friends he had made in high places, and the actual,
cheque-book proof of his sterling citizenship, he was beyond
suspicion on this side of the Atlantic. Goodwill at his ports of
destination was something else again. He knew only too well
that it took but a single slip, a rendezvous missed at a Brooklyn
pier or a shipment delayed in transit, to dry up the income
that was his lifeblood nowadays. Smugglers were legion,
after all, in these parlous times: the powers abroad, who
devoted millions to siphoning American abundance into their
own arsenals, would replace him in a moment, if he failed
them tonight.

The *Baltic Prince* was his present contact. A freighter out
of Oslo, with ports of call that did not appear on the innocent
bill of lading that would clear the Barge Office this noon.
The *Baltic Prince*. His drug-numbed train echoed with the
name, a bell tower whence even the bats had fled. Captain Falk
commanding. Captain Falk was an old friend. A philosopher
after his own heart, who knew that most men were apes—and
the earth a dying cinder.

If Falk sailed without that lead-covered bottle tonight his
empire here in New York would crumble as though it had
never been.

Of course there was still Tony Korff. He had trusted Tony
in the past with missions far more hazardous than this. From
his present vantage point it seemed that he would be forced
to trust Tony one more time. After all, it would be simple
enough to bring him in line—when he was on his feet
again.

Bert Rilling's eyes moved to the half-drawn blinds on the
window. Even now, as his senses swam back towards the
tropic languor of sleep, he was aware of the early sunlight
on the window sill. Thank God for the hour, he murmured,

forgetting, in that sudden prayer, that he had renounced
God years ago. Thank God for the off-centre providence that
brought Tony to my bedside when I needed him most.

Later, when his head had cleared in earnest, they must
have a long visit, for old times' sake. He could rely on Tony
to arrange that meeting, just as he could rely on instinct to
stage-manage the reunion. Bert Rilling closed his eyes and
dismissed the threat of Tony Korff from his mind. It would
not be the first time that he had turned a potential menace
to his advantage.

IV

Catherine Ash, wakening in her bedroom far uptown,
smiled a lazy welcome at her image reflected in the huge
circular mirror above her dressing table. Despite the early
hour, she was not surprised to find herself alone. Remembering
last night's quarrel—and the passionate aftermath—she let
her whole body relax in a long, contented sigh.

The fact that she was alone set the seal on her victory. She
knew, only too well, that Martin had spent the last hours of
the night on the love seat just outside her door. That he had
risen with the dawn and slipped out quietly, rather than
resume a discussion that could only prove how right she was.
She glanced at the bedroom clock, glad that she had wakened
in time to phone the hospital before Martin began his first
operation. There was no need to think what she would say:
that, too, was part of the game they played.

In a way, thought Catherine, a quarrel now and then is a
good thing for one's marriage. The wounds healed quickly,
especially when you had been married a long time and knew
what the other would say in advance; the emotional relief
was only a prelude to the renewed ardour that came with
reconciliation . . . . If you like, Martin (she was already
rehearsing her lines, as though she held him firmly at the far
end of a telephone), you may work this week end. Perhaps

I'll drive in and surprise you before it's over—how would you like that, darling? Perhaps I'll even drive down to the hospital and bring you back with me.

She flung back the bedclothes on that half-formed plan—a gesture of sudden abandon, as though her dream picture had brought him into this very room. Standing before her mirror, framed from head to foot in its huge golden circle, she dropped her lace nightgown to her feet. Not bad for a woman of forty, she told herself with narrowed eyes: take me point by point, and I've more to offer than half the girls I know. Of course, if we'd had children . . .

If we'd had children. . . . The thought lay like a reproach on the threshold of her mind, and she turned her back on it impatiently as she continued the lynx-eyed survey of her body. Were her hips a shade too opulent—and did the tiny crow's-feet below her eyes show clearly by daylight? She was certain that Martin liked her a little on the buxom side—and that tiny worry wrinkle between her brows wasn't the sort of thing the average husband would notice. Still, it would do no harm to spend most of Monday at the beauty salon. Madame Annette had promised to slim two pounds from her midriff in a single treatment; and a mud pack would do wonders for any wrinkle. Even one that was etched by a too active brain, a too demanding love.

If we'd had children, she thought, none of this would seem half so important. Martin was cut out to be a family man—it's part of his racial birthright, just as it's natural for him to want a wife who'll grant his every whim. Had it been too wrong of her to deny him the sons and daughters he'd longed for? Had it been fear of a mixed heritage that had made her hold back from the dedication of motherhood? Or was it a selfishness that went even deeper?

Again she turned away from a question she did not dare answer. It was a relief to sit at her dressing table and shake out her thick blonde hair, to laugh back at her image as she began the ritualistic hundred strokes of the brush. Some marriages, she told herself, are too perfect as they stand to need hostages to fortune. She could even ignore her father's voice, though the words echoed clearly in her ears. As clearly as though that inflexible Brahmin had been standing at her shoulder.

"Marry him if you must, Catherine. Since you're my daughter, I know when you've made up your mind. But I still say you'll give him everything but yourself——"

I loved Martin then, she insisted wildly. I love him now, more than I'll ever say. What if the marriage has been childless? It's been a perfect thing—despite his crazy moods. But her father's voice persisted, grim as any prophet's.

"You're starting on the wrong foot, Catherine. You want this fellow more than he'll ever want you—and in your heart you'll always be a little ashamed of wanting him. So you'll try to possess him, which means you'll break him of his manhood, or lose him outright. And because you love him you'll want nothing to come between you. Because you're ashamed of his background you'll never give him children —or even a home he can be proud of——"

Catherine got to her feet and flung her quilted bathrobe about her shoulders, as though that long-dead father were really in her bedroom and about to reproach her for her nakedness. She was still trembling a little, long after her maid had brought breakfast and the morning papers. Sipping her coffee without tasting it at all, forcing herself to scan the news with a mind that scarcely registered the familiar headlines of doom, she wondered if it were too late for children, even now. Surely there was no better way to drive her father's ghost back to its uneasy grave.

After all, she reminded herself, women have had children at forty—or even older. Her friends would laugh, of course, but she could endure their laughter, for Martin's sake. A mother at forty-one, say . . . But she would be over sixty when her son was still at college. And Catherine Ash would never consent to be sixty, not if she lived to be a hundred.

Rising from her breakfast tray at last, she put out her hand to ring again for her maid, and remembered it was high time to phone the hospital. As she lifted the receiver her chin went up firmly. Her father would have recognized that gesture of defiance and applauded it.

"Is that you, Martin? Am I disturbing you?"

"Not at all, darling." His voice was quiet and far-off.

"I've ordered the car for ten. Sure you won't change your mind and join me?"

"Haven't you seen the papers, Catherine?"

"We could leave the chauffeur," she said coaxingly. "It always soothes your nerves to take the wheel. And we might even stop for lunch on the way. Let my house party shift for itself."

"Read the headline on Jack Carter's column," he said. "You'll see why it's impossible."

Her mind went back to the paper on her dressing table and the half-registered headline she had glanced at a moment ago. "Don't tell me you believe such nonsense, Martin."

"The chief of the FBI was in my office an hour ago," he said. "He's asked that I alert the hospital for any eventuality."

"I must say you don't sound alarmed."

"I won't have time to be alarmed today, in any case. But the threat remains. I must stay and meet it."

Catherine caught her breath sharply—a gasp of incredulity that just escaped being an outright laugh. "Husbands have used strange excuses to dodge parties before, dear. Yours is something of a classic——"

"I assure you it isn't an excuse. And I must ask you to hold what I've said in strictest confidence."

"Of course, dear," she said brightly. "And you're *still* sure you won't come out to the island?"

"Good God, Catherine! Haven't you heard a word I've been saying?"

When she had soothed away his flare of temper at last, she hung up slowly, knowing, without troubling to glance at the mirror, that the worry line had never been deeper. Not that she was afraid for Martin—not even if the hospital was swarming with police at this very moment. Things like that simply didn't happen in America. Men, she told herself firmly, were like little boys: there was nothing they enjoyed more than their own imagination, a threat to their safety where no threat existed.

Even if that absurd news story were true she refused to

consider it a personal menace. Maniacs were always breaking free, only to be tracked to earth again. It might be true that this particular case involved the hospital in some bizarre fashion: she would never permit it to trouble the future of Martin Ash—who was her chef-d'oeuvre, her husband and her lover, all in one perfect package. And yet in a way it was a shame that she had thirty-odd guests awaiting her on the island. It was really too romantic, that Martin should be working with the FBI, after all these treadmill years. It would have been fun to linger in town today and take a hand in the game.

She shrugged off the temptation as she walked out to the sunny penthouse terrace and stared down at the river far below. Save for a slow-moving file of barges and a lean black freighter hugging the island shore, it was strangely empty at this early hour. She watched absently for a moment while a dozen half-formed revolts flashed through her mind, as insubstantial as the sun motes that danced in the oily rush of the tide.

The freighter was flying the Norwegian flag; Catherine narrowed her eyes to spell out the lettering on the stern. The *Baltic Prince*, out of Oslo. She followed its progress, until it vanished in the heat haze down-river. It looked lonely and a trifle lost, against the towering cliffs of Manhattan. Yet she was sure the *Baltic Prince* knew just where it was bound, and why.

Perhaps she and Martin should plan a long sea voyage in the near future. Not another luxury liner this time, but a simple banana boat. One where you sat at the captain's table as a matter of course, and might even be allowed to steer awhile, in good weather.

Havana and Barbados and Port-of-Spain. Exotic ports in the deep Latin south, where tourists never went. It was just the change Martin needed.

V

His wall clock reminded him that it was well after eight,
but Martin Ash did not go to the operating wing when he
had hung up on Catherine. Instead, he moved down the bank
of elevators in the lobby and took the first lift to Schuyler
Tower. Father O'Leary would have been up and about
hours ago: he hoped to catch the padre in his room, before
he began to visit in the wards. This was not the first time he
had gone to the priest, as humbly as any communicant, with
a problem too heavy to solve.

Father O'Leary, as he had hoped, was still seated in his
wheel-chair on the small balcony outside his quarters, luring
a circling gull to the rail with scraps from his breakfast tray.
Martin Ash sat down quietly in a deck-chair and smiled a
wordless greeting. He knew that the old priest would take
this visit as a matter of course. He had made it a habit lately
to stop by this room for a few moments before his morning
clinic.

"Don't tell me you've been quarrelling with Catherine,"
said the old man. "I refuse to believe it."

The director of East Side General smiled naturally for the
first time today—and felt his nerve ends loosen behind that
smile. "We always quarrel after one of those gala evenings.
If you can call it quarrelling. But I haven't come to you in a
domestic mood this morning, Father."

"I know, Martin."

Ash looked hard at the silvered profile in the wheel chair.
So far the padre had not lifted his eyes from the business of
coaxing the gull to a safe landing. "So you know why I'm
here—before I say it?"

"Don't call me clairvoyant. It's just that I've been under
this roof a long time. It's about those burn cases, isn't it?"

Martin nodded mutely. The hospital grapevine had done
itself proud today. Thanks to that alarmist columnist and the
glimpses of patrolmen at every entrance, it had not been
difficult for his staff to draw conclusions. At least they need
not know the whole truth now. He could save that for his own

conscience—and the benign father confessor in the wheel-chair.

"Had you heard the second victim died half an hour ago?"

Father O'Leary sighed. "Perhaps I'm getting old, Martin. That bit of news hadn't reached me so far."

"With good reason. I ordered Korff to keep it dark when he reported to me. And we're holding up the death certificate, of course, until we hear from Inspector Hurlbut. After all, this business is police routine now. A kind of solemn masquerade that may bring results——" He drew a deep breath on that, and plunged in earnest, until he had given the padre a transcript of his interview with Hurlbut and the man from the FBI. "Do you think I was wise to—agree to all they asked?"

Father O'Leary did not speak for a moment. The gull, its suspicions soothed away at last, had settled on the railing and was pecking bits of toast from the breakfast tray.

"What else could you have done, Martin?"

"Every life in this hospital is my responsibility. What right have I to endanger my staff—to say nothing of the cases that can't be moved? Take that boy Andy's doing a Blalock on this morning——"

"The congenital heart," said Father O'Leary, and though his voice echoed Martin Ash's own thought his thoughts seemed far away. "If Andy saves Jackie it'll be a real miracle. It's hard to think that a miracle might be wasted——"

"Exactly. That poor kid was doomed, until surgical knowledge came along to give him a chance. How can I let Andy operate, with this business hanging over us? Shouldn't I at least move Jackie to another hospital?"

"You could hardly risk that without alarming everyone here."

"Perhaps that's just what I should be doing, Padre."

"Don't you see? The one thing that none of us can afford today is panic. We've made our choice long ago—a way of life that's worth dying for, if need be. Whether we like it or not, we're all in the front line for this war—and the battle is already under way."

"I know people who would disagree."

"Balance things up, Martin. The police have a trap baited: they think it's worth the trial. You must take their orders— as you already have."

"Even if it blows us all to kingdom come?"

"Suppose this is the last link they need for the hydrogen bomb. What would Jackie's life be worth then?"

Martin struck fist to palm. "And who are *they*, Padre?"

"The godless who'd remake the world in their image. Not the Russian people, heaven forbid. Not *people* anywhere. Only the madmen who'd lead them to their doom——"

"Are *they* doomed, then, Padre? Or are we?"

"The godless are always doomed, Martin."

"I wish my philosophy were as comforting."

"You believe that, too, in your heart. You know you've done right."

"I'm a doctor, not a world citizen——"

"All of us are world citizens today, Martin. That's another thing we must learn, or perish."

"It's still a heavy choice, making the hospital a potential target. You'll grant me that?"

"God puts responsibility where He thinks it can be borne," said the priest. "Sometimes the burden is too heavy. I'm sure it isn't in your case."

"I'm glad you think I did right."

"No one would want you to act differently."

"Not even Catherine?"

"Look at me, Martin. I knew your father before you were born. I watched you grow up and find yourself. You've done what you knew was right from the beginning—you couldn't help yourself. Take this quarrel with Catherine. Wasn't it because you felt you must stay on here for the week-end— and share the common danger?"

"Partly. There were other things."

"Like moving the hospital." Father O'Leary lay back in the wheel-chair and closed his eyes. "I can't believe that project will go through, somehow. Doesn't a great deal of the financing depend on Bert Rilling?"

"He's promised to put up forty per cent of the cash. More, if need be——"

"Is he going to live?"

Martin Ash looked up sharply. "He was marked critical on the morning report. Andy did an amazing job on the thrombus, it seems. But I'm afraid that's only a stopgap——"

Father O'Leary's voice was a bare whisper. "Understand me, Martin, I pray for Rilling's soul as sincerely as I do for yours. But I hardly think that his heirs share his passion for philanthropy and headlines——"

"His only heirs are a bank or two——"

"Isn't that what I said? We're still where we belong. Let's pray that we stay here—no matter what evil is loose in the world."

"Catherine could put up the whole sum herself."

"Catherine is a shrewd business woman, despite the blueprints she draws. I'm convinced it's a risk she'd never take alone. Without Rilling, the move will soon be just another project. Women like Catherine have many projects, Martin."

"I wish I had your detachment," said Ash. In his gentle yet forthright fashion Father O'Leary had just summed up Catherine's emotional pattern—and the peculiar frustration that seemed to plague rich women everywhere. It was quite true that Catherine must have a project, lest she perish. And yet, no matter what paths she followed, she always returned in the end. His welfare was her reason for living, his success her only real triumph. Even when she all but smothered him he could not doubt that shining loyalty.

"Does it disturb you, Martin, that Catherine must constantly be in action—constantly driving herself, and those about her?"

It was true, of course. Catherine was never still because she could not afford to pause and think. If she refused to leave him alone for more than a few hours, if she insisted that he accompany her everywhere, that, too, was part of her malaise. The Catherines of this world must always turn to others, lest they discover their own emptiness. If the Martin Ash that she had built over the years, with such loving care, was a different being from the man he had meant to be, he had no right to blame his wife.

"She's a good woman, Padre," he said.

"And a fine woman, my son. Look a long way, you won't find better."

"I mustn't interfere, then—if she insists on moving us all uptown?"

"Do what you can to dissuade her, my boy—and leave the rest to God. I still say He picked the right man for the job."

Ash got up heavily. "I'm operating in five minutes, Padre. Thanks for the advice."

The blue Irish eyes opened wide. "I gave you no advice, Martin. I only confirmed the voice of your conscience."

Martin Ash let his hand rest on the old man's shoulder— a familiar gesture of good-bye, a gratitude that went deeper than words. He had risen with leaden limbs from the deck-chair, but he could feel his step grow lighter as he moved down the corridor and rang for the elevator that would return him to his familiar sphere.

The wall at the corridor's end was a turret of clear glass, framing the East River far below and the bustle of traffic just upstream from the first of its three great bridges. While he waited for his elevator he watched the dark silhouette of a freighter, angling expertly with the tide to warp into a berth on the Brooklyn side, almost directly across the river from the dank, fortress-like rectangle of the Rilling brewery.

Five minutes before, the sight would have brought up his familiar dream picture of flight. He would have pictured himself seeking out that Brooklyn pier, slipping away from Cathetine and career to walk up that gangplank and buy a ticket to nowhere. He might even have stepped out to the first balcony of Schuyler Tower for a nearer view of that rusty tramp—transformed, by a magic all his own, into an argosy bound for adventures he had never known. But Father O'Leary had just confirmed the voice of his conscience. That stern daughter of God was at his elbow now, reminding him that his day was only beginning.

One more memory came out of the past, unbidden. The picture of a tortured young man, still in his white uniform, though he had been off duty long ago that day, pacing the waterfront and reading the names on a dozen rusty bows. That had been Dr. Martin Ash in the final hours before his

wedding—yielding, even then, to man's ancient instinct to
fly from the compulsions of life shared with another.

Eventually, of course, he had returned to his quarters at
the hospital and put on his dark wedding suit to join Catherine
at the licence bureau. What if he had gone aboard one of
those freighters and left all this behind? It was hard to picture
any existence from the one in which he was presently
embarked. Harder still to picture Martin Ash going to the
devil on well-greased skids. A ship's doctor, perhaps, with
hands that had begun to tremble in the morning, and a gin-
blurred brain. Or an island king in some nameless archipelago,
with six honey-coloured offspring. . . .

Probably he'd have been just as dead inside on Pago Pago
as he was today on the island of Manhattan. At least there
was work waiting in his clinic—the famous Ash Clinic which
Catherine had endowed in his name, to mark their twentieth
anniversary. There was always work to dull his unhappiness,
the only solace to remind him that he was a man of affairs
and not a walking zombie.

The elevator light blinked red, and he went down to the
surgical wing, to scrub for his first operation of the morning.

VI

Andy Gray opened a cautious eye and glared at the alarm
clock at his bedside—a faithful servant who had forgotten he
could sleep an extra hour today. His tiny bedroom, in the
staff quarters of the surgical wing, was bare as some anchorite's
cell and, at the moment, stuffy as a broom cupboard. He
stared resentfully at the window, remembering how he had
tumbled into this bed on the right side of dawn, without even
pausing to let in the last cool breath of the summer night. At
least he had plummeted into a sleep without dreams. Perhaps
it had been nature's instinctive protest—lifting his mind from
the treadmill where it had spun so long.

Nine sharp—and, like the faithful fire horse who answers

all bells, he was already on his feet and ready for another day. With luck, he might keep out of the treadmill a while longer, if he focused on externals. An ice-cold shower first, to drum new life into your blood stream. Once over lightly with a razor—and decide to do without a haircut another week. Cram last night's whites into an overflowing laundry bag and take your next-to-last change from the linen press you shared with Tony Korff. He went through those rituals like a man in a not too unpleasant dream. At any time, now, he would wake up completely—and face the fact that he was in love with one woman and all but branded by another. It was a dilemma he was in no hurry to untangle. Assuming that it could ever be untangled to his satisfaction, to say nothing of the ladies involved.

As usual, his freshly laundered whites resisted him like armour. He shrugged his shoulders to open the starched sleeves, and performed a deep knee bend to unlimber the trousers. Surveying his face once again in his mirror, he admitted that his too long hair made him look more like Lincoln than ever. That, too, was in the books: the Great Emancipator had had his troubles; most of them were unresolved to this day.

Perhaps it was the nature of man to resist emancipation to the end. Perhaps he was happy only when he was slaving for something greater than himself—a monolithic state, a killing hospital routine, the creation of a perfect skyscraper or poem. Or the pursuit of such elusive Utopias as world government or ideal love. So we're back again at love, he told himself savagely—back to the greatest tyrant of them all. It was bad enough when a man desired one woman with all his heart and soul. When he wanted two of the species— for entirely different reasons—decision could be hell on earth.

He stood quietly in his cell while he assembled the tools of his trade: his stethoscope and clip book, the morning report that one of the orderlies had left on his night table. Outwardly he was the model resident, checking his day's routine for a last time before he stepped on the treadmill. Inwardly he was assailed by memories that set his pulses racing.

Pat Reed's body, as she stood in her balcony window, bathed in moonlight. . . . He knew what it meant to hold that body in his arms, knew the savage bliss she could bring. That craving would return, like an addict's desire for a narcotic that could block thought and flood a man's whole being with an exultation that did not belong to this world. Yet she had offered him far more than an antidote for desire, while they stood face to face in her room. The vistas she had opened for him were limitless. After all was said and done, money was a kind of sixth sense, whose lack made it impossible to enjoy the other five. The tyranny of an endless love duel (strictly out of business hours) might be worth while—if he could buy the career he yearned for.

The memory of Julia Talbot was equally bright—the eager innocence of a body that had never yielded itself before, the ardour of lips that brought back other, no less disturbing, memories. Thank Heaven he had retreated from that trap without betraying his inner turmoil. Trap is the right word, he told himself doggedly, a snare no less beguiling than Pat's silken lure. To the dark-haired surgical nurse, love and marriage were synonyms. With Julia it was all or nothing— an excellent reason for his quick retreat.

It was no accident that she had reacted so quickly to the picture of Timmie's Florida parish and the work they might accomplish there. Herself a small-town girl, Julia was born to be a small-town doctor's wife. Andy Gray, as the record proved, was destined for better things.

Or so he had insisted in the small hours before dawn, on the steps of the nurses' home. A cynical withdrawal had been an essential part of his role—the big moment in the scene of renunciation he had planned so carefully. Come what might, he could never involve Julia in the burning fire of his ambition—or permit Julia to lure him back to Timmie's level of selfless mediocrity.

Yes, it was as simple as that, and as heartbreakingly complex. If he did not love Julia with all his heart it would be easy enough to renounce her now. If he had not desired Pat Reed with all his being (to say nothing of the career she could open before him) it would have been even simpler to possess her one more time and turn his back on passion once and for all.

He had chosen Pat, as he stood with Julia on the steps of the nurses' home. The fact that he had put the choice in words, for Julia's benefit, only made the choice inevitable. Obviously he should go to Schuyler Tower at once and clinch the bargain, before Pat escaped him. With one hand on the knob, he noticed the envelope on the carpet for the first time: a squarish, expensive envelope with his name slashed across the front in a hand he recognized instantly.

For all his firm resolves, his hands were trembling a little as he broke the seal. The note was short and to the point—like Pat herself:

Darling,

I think we understand each other quite well—don't you? Anyhow, I've had my rest cure, and I hope you've decided you deserve yours.

My night special will leave this at your door. Just to tell you that I've checked out when you read it. As you already know, I'll be at the Plaza most of the day. Certainly after five, when I'd adore to pour you a cocktail and hear your plans.

The note was unsigned, and that, too, was quite in character. For all its polite phrasing, it was a command, not a social summons. Pat's cards are on the table, he thought. She's daring me to show mine and learn who's the loser.

He did not believe for a moment that she had left the hospital. Pat seldom rose before noon, even on the last lap of a pretended rest cure. Besides, he was sure that she would wait for Dr. Plant's morning visit, if only for the sake of appearances. Weighing her note between his hands, he toyed with the impulse to go straight to her room—and decided that this was exactly what she expected, as final proof of her victory.

Not that she needs proof after last night, he thought bitterly. The huntress is sure of her quarry. The woman of many loves will await her chosen mate over the martinis, at five sharp. . . . He glanced automatically at his alarm clock

Thanks to this brooding, he had all but outstayed his hour of grace.

He tore the note into small pieces and flung them into the first wastebasket as he went through the orderly room. There, just outside the entrance to the surgical ward, was the familiar glass door of the diet kitchen where he had played a part so carefully with Julia, only a few hours ago. Yielding to another impulse, he pushed his way in. Jackie, the crippled heart case, was on the books for nine-thirty sharp. He would need coffee, at least, before he faced that ordeal.

Vicki Ryan was seated on a high stool before the model range, buttering toast and presiding over the coffee pot that was never allowed to cool. The tall surgical nurse looked fresh as the morning. Meeting her eyes as he mumbled a greeting, Andy pulled back sharply from her animal magnetism, even as he chuckled inwardly at his own caution. Here, at least, was love in the clinical sense of a misused word—love with no aftermaths. More than once (and with no need for diagrams) Vicki had told him that she was his for the taking. He wondered briefly if Tony Korff, whom he always considered a born neurotic, were wiser than he—and accepted a cup of coffee with his scowl intact.

"Julia's gone to steal eggs," said Vicki. "Why not break down and have breakfast, just once?"

"I'm afraid I haven't time."

"Of course you have, Doctor. They haven't set up for Jackie yet, if that's what's bothering you. We've had a busy morning in this corner of the factory——"

"You seem cool and collected."

"I've kept free of it so far. But I'm on my way now to scrub for Dr. Ash. I'm on instruments at the clinic until noon." Vicki regarded him quizzically—an impudent lift of the eyebrow that had charmed more than one intern to indiscretion. "And now that we're being personal—you look like the last man to leave the party."

"We had Bert Rilling on our hands about three."

"So I'm told. I've also heard you covered yourself with glory. But of course that's routine——"

She bent forward as she spoke, to pour him a second cup:

her large, grave eyes, sleepy for all their freshness, dared him
to move into her orbit, however briefly. Perhaps I'm going
quietly mad, he thought; it isn't within reason that every
woman here should fall swooning at my feet. He sat on a
facing stool and fought for calm.

"It was a routine job," he said. "Besides, I had Julia.
That's half the battle in advance."

"Shall I tell her you said that—or would you rather
not?"

"Much rather not," he said, and studied her with composure across the steam from his coffee. The moment of
desire had passed, like a summer squall. He saw now that
Vicki Ryan was a nice girl, despite her habits. A girl whose
only real fault was a somewhat unselective yearning to be
friends with all the world.

It takes all kinds, he reflected. Especially in a hospital.
And yet, in her way, Vicki is the nurse incarnate—even more
than Julia. A woman, in short, whose urge to give is greater
than her common sense. Brooding over that discovery as he
sipped his coffee, he concluded that it was girls like Vicki
who gave the profession a bad name at times, in spite of their
good intentions. She's no more a nymphomaniac than Julia,
he insisted. She just wants people to like her. It doesn't
matter if it's a beaten surgeon like myself or an opportunist
like Tony. He came back with an effort to what Vicki was
saying.

"You're looking rather pale, Doctor. Could it be we're
worrying about the same thing?"

"It could indeed," he said.

"It's too bad he died, isn't it? Or will it be better for us
all, when the news gets out?"

Despite his control, he just missed laughing aloud. "So
you were thinking about that burn case all the time?"

"Certainly. Weren't you?"

"It was on my morning report," he said. "Along with
Dr. Korff's final notes. I might add that it's supposed to be
a secret that goes no farther than surgical. Dr. Ash was
particularly anxious to keep that fellow alive. And he *is* alive
still, so far as the world outside knows——"

"I'll offer a small bet that Pete Collins has already broken the story."

"Hurlbut would have his hide, if he dared."

"Still," said Vicki, "I'd breathe easier if the facts were on the noon broadcast. Wouldn't you?" She got down from the facing stool and laid a hand on his arm. For an instant he saw a gleam in her eye that reminded him, all too forcibly, of Pat Reed. "Frankly, I'd hate to be blown to bits, and never know——"

"Is there something you don't know?" he asked with an impudence he didn't feel.

"Think it over, Doctor," she said. "If you can't follow me this far I won't translate."

"Perhaps I follow you all too well."

"I wouldn't put it past you," she said, gaily enough. "What's more, I see Julia coming down the corridor, so I'm sure I'm wasting my time. Good luck with that crippled heart." She was gone as she spoke, smiling broadly at Julia as they passed in the half-open door.

The dark-haired nurse came into the kitchen with two eggs balanced on her palms and offered him a good morning as tranquilly as though they had known each other for ever. If she remembers that kiss last night, he thought, she's taking the memory in her stride. If she's admitting the fact that I'm labelled for delivery to Pat Reed, her defences are in perfect order.

"One of these was for Vicki," she said as she broke both eggs into a pan. "But I'm afraid we both overslept this morning. Won't you join me?"

"Vicki's loss is my gain," said Andy, and he was pleased by his own steadiness. "But you've no right to be up so early."

"I'm scrubbing for the crippled heart," said Julia. "Emily Sloane's request, no less. All the regulars are busy this morning, it seems——"

"That's no reason to drag you on duty——"

"Emily knows I love it," said the dark girl serenely. "Of course, if you'd rather look round for someone else——"

"You know there's no one I'd rather have."

"Then we're back where we started, aren't we?"

"Back to last night, you mean?"

He watched her colour, ever so slightly, as she salted the eggs. "Sunny side up, Andy?"

"Please—if it's not a play on words."

"You've every right to be sunny this morning," said Julia. "You're marrying the tenth richest girl in America, and buying your own hospital the day after tomorrow. At least, that was the note on which we parted——"

"So it was. And you're going down to Florida, to be Timmie's district nurse. My memory's as good as yours."

"Have you any objections?"

When he did not answer she bent above the skillet and devoted her whole attention to their breakfast. Andy noted, with a perverse pleasure, that the spots of colour at her cheek were crimson now.

He did not speak again until she had set out the two platters of eggs and toast on the sideboard of the diet kitchen. He had expected the silence to strain his nerves: oddly enough he could not remember when he had felt more peaceful— even though he was quite certain that his next move would be the wrong one.

"Would you like me to write Timmie a letter of introduction?"

"I'd rather introduce myself," said Julia. "After all, I'm sure that Dr. Ash will give me a recommendation."

"Of course you aren't really serious."

He watched her take a letter from one starched pocket. "I wrote this last night, before I turned in," she said. "Would you like to read it?"

"On the contrary. All that matters is you haven't mailed it, so far."

"But I shall, Andy. Even if I can't take you with me."

"Why, Julia—why? I've told you the life isn't for you——"

"And suppose I insisted that everything you said about your brother was an inspiration?"

He devoted himself to his breakfast. Have the last word if you must, he told her silently. I'm old enough to know it's useless to combat idealism in the young. Once again, he was sure that his refusal to argue had put her on the defensive. So sure, in fact, that he was silent until the last morsel of food was gone.

"We've time for a smoke before we start on Jackie." He lighted her cigarette and then his own—and held out his cup for still more coffee. "You've no right to do this, you know. It isn't fair to either of us."

"Tell me more, Andy——"

"I can give you a real hand up in New York. And you must know by this time that I'll never be able to operate without this sort of breakfast——"

"That's no way to insult your fiancée."

"I doubt if Pat can boil water. And you know very well what I mean."

Julia gathered the plates demurely. "I understand you perfectly, And it's quite true I haven't sent the letter——"

"What's more, you'll never send it. I won't let you throw your talents away."

The nurse spoke with her back turned: the fact that she was rinsing the dishes in scalding water, with an aureole of steam about her dark hair, did nothing to detract from her slender beauty. "You've guessed a great deal about me, Andy. May I risk one guess about you?"

"I wouldn't. It might boomerang——"

"You haven't asked her yet, have you? Not really?"

Of course I haven't, he thought, with a flush of annoyance. It was Pat who asked me to marry her. In fact she's been the aggressor from the start. Aloud he said only, "Our engagement is official, Julia. Whenever she cares to announce it."

"Then I'll send this letter to Timmie the day I read the story on the society page."

Julia turned from the sink and dried her hands on a towel. He watched the movement of her hands, admiring their precision with a part of his mind that had no connection with this near quarrel. Only a surgical nurse could do so much with so few lost motions, he thought. Only a woman you love could come fresh from dish-water and make your heart turn over.

"Is that a challenge, Julia—or a bargain?"

"Call it both," she said. "Until I read it in the papers I'll insist you still belong to us. Never to her. And don't tell me I've misplaced my faith again—I won't listen."

"Can't I belong to both?"

"Answer that yourself," she said. "I must scrub for your operation—if you still want me."

I'll always want you, he told her wordlessly, letting her leave the field with her own small triumph. It was a relief to sit here quietly and alone—the last quiet moment he would know until his working day ended. At least I've made my point, he thought: she knows I'm as good as sold to Pat.

Ten minutes later, when he entered the anæsthetic room, next to the theatre where he would begin today's work, he was as calm as an acolyte. The science of medicine, he reflected, was a blessed escape for all those who could not make up their minds.

VII

Jackie was still sleeping under the pre-operative medication. Andy reviewed the case swiftly in his mind, feeling that usually reliable organ mesh into gear as smoothly as his surgical team was massing to back his assault on life's very citadel. Operations on the heart were easy to over-dramatize: that tough and beautifully articulated mechanism was often stronger than the truant body it served. It was not this small patient's fault that something had gone awry, months before his birth, perhaps at the very moment of his creation.

Science, for all its wizardry, had yet to explain why Jackie's life cycle had failed to follow the normal graph set down by numberless centuries of human evolution. It was a miracle that had given man a heart of four chambers, two auricles and two thick-walled ventricles, the right side receiving blood from the great veins that returned it from torso, limbs, and brain, the left side receiving the blood from the lungs to send it pulsing down the arteries to every body cell. Somehow Jackie had been denied this miracle.

For a reason that medicine was still unable to explain, this simple division of the vital pump had not been accomplished. The artery to the lungs was constricted, until only a thin stream of blood could be pumped through to them. At the same time the partition called the septum, which divided right and left ventricles, had failed to form properly. Blood, weak in oxygen and held back by the barrier of the constricted vessels, escaped into the left side of the heart—and thence into the body—without receiving its necessary oxygen. During his short span on earth Jackie's activities had been cruelly limited by this lack. Unable to play at will, or even to exercise moderately without consuming his pitifully short supply of oxygen, he had existed so far in a kind of limbo, neither living nor dead.

Until recently there had been no hope for children like Jackie: few heart cripples could hope to exist beyond the play-pen stage, and these, too, were pathetic prey for every disease from which the young must suffer. Now, thanks to the wonder workers at Johns Hopkins, who had studied the plight of such doomed children for years, an operation had been devised to solve the problem—a daring, almost virtuoso feat of surgery. When successful, it shunted blood round the constricted lung artery into the oxygen-rich bed of the lung capillaries themselves, where the vital supply could be restored.

Extended bed rest and a build-up diet had done wonders for Jackie during his sojourn at East Side General. Today he was as ready for surgery as he would ever be. From his side, Andy knew that his own tired body would never be fresher. As for the turmoil in his mind, he could rely on the iron compulsions of his craft to banish his last self-doubt, once he picked up the scalpel.

In the dressing-room he slipped into a one-piece coverall that is the surgeon's battle dress, and looked into the scrub room. Julia, already busy at the side table, spoke to him in her normal, impersonal tone, the sexless, uninflected voice they always used from the moment they entered their workroom.

"One of the students is sick this morning, Dr. Gray. I'm afraid we're a little short-handed: we may not be ready by the time you finish scrubbing."

"I'll get ready just the same," he said. "Then I might step into the clinic and see how Dr. Ash is doing."

"He's taking longer than he expected. I think he found some complications."

Andy nodded. Martin's first case this morning was a gall bladder, and they could be the very devil, especially when the stones were deep in the common duct. Perhaps he could give his senior a hand one more time: he had long ago lost count of the operations he had finished in the clinic when Martin Ash had a truly busy morning. He picked up a brush at the sink, just as the loudspeaker overhead uttered his name, with its familiar, wheedling tone intact. Andy cursed adequately behind his mask as he picked up the phone.

"You haven't started, Andy?" It was Tony Korff, drawing his own conclusions from the fact that the resident himself had answered the phone. "Can you come down to emergency?"

"What is it this time?" For one crazy instant Andy was sure that this meant some new development in the burn cases. But Tony's chuckle banished that hope instantly.

"This one is quite respectable. A crushed chest from that highway job—when a crane went berserk. Probably a goner, but I want you to certify it——"

That, too, was quite like Tony, and Andy damned him in turn as he sped for the elevator. Usually the refugee considered himself self-sufficient—unless a sixth sense warned him that his patient was probably beyond all hope.

In the corridor he just escaped a head-on collision with Emily Sloane. Even in this preoccupied moment he could not help noticing that the supervisor's face was drawn with weariness—and a fear that went beyond tired nerves. A clinical picture of pain ignored, he thought, complete to the last detail. I must check up on Emily. Working by the clock for too many years, these O.R. specials can drive themselves to the brink before their time.

"Easy does it, Emily. How's Dr. Ash progressing."

"He'll be busy for another hour, Doctor." The supervisor's tone, as usual, was as dehydrated as her manner. "Could you delay starting in this theatre for a while?"

"I not only can but I must. I'm due in emergency now. We'll hold everything until Dr. Ash is ready to close."

He stepped into the elevator, frowning over the image of that white, too slender figure. He must call Emily to his office this afternoon.

In the observation room just off the emergency ward he found Tony Korff and a junior intern working over a stretcher obviously fresh from the ambulance. The patient under their hands was fighting for each painful breath, as a collapsed chest wall failed to yield under the straining lungs. A plasma flask waited on a high tripod above the stretcher, its needle poised. For all his skill, Tony was unable to find a point of entry. Andy came forward quickly as he sensed the refugee's dilemma.

"Thanks for coming so soon, Andy. His circulation is in collapse from shock."

"Looks like lung damage from here," said Andy tersely. "Let's try the ankle vein. And get me a cut-down set to be sure."

He tested the thready pulse while he waited, making no attempt to remove the temporary dressing that covered the damaged lung box. The pulse and skin tone underlined the picture ominously enough. As the instruments came into his hands he wondered how Tony—always so steady in emergencies of this sort—could have wasted time jabbing for a flattened vein.

The cut-down set, as it was called in hospital argot, was kept constantly sterile for crises such as this—a scalpel, forceps, and a hollow metal needle known as a cannula, along with the necessary sutures to anchor it firmly. Andy scrubbed quickly at the wall basin while Tony worked at the ankle—there was no time for complete asepsis now. Watching the intern work, he saw that Tony was in the groove, painting the skin expertly round the point of puncture with long, sure strokes, tenting the area in a bandage ready-made for transfusions. No matter what was troubling him, he thought,

Tony's in the team again. The moods of the exile, like the exile's loneliness, were something he would never understand fully.

Then, with no sense of transition, he was beside the stretcher, slashing an inch-long incision down the bone groove in front of the ankle bone. Dropping the scalpel in favour of the small curved forceps, he separated tissues with quick, probing strokes, until a dark blue structure appeared in the depths of the parted tissue—the vein he was seeking, though it seemed all but lifeless under his hand.

The forceps, thanks to its peculiar structure, glided under the vessel with no lost motion, lifting it into clear view; twin loops of tough silken thread slipped into place above and below the firm arc of steel—one loop to tie off behind the cannula, the other to anchor the tube in the vein itself.

"Ready with plasma?"

"Ready, Doctor."

The scalpel moved instantly to open the vein. The hollow metal tube followed the knife as though it were part of that fluent, downward swoop—and entered the vein for a good portion of its length. Secured, in one quick twist, by the loop of silk, it held firm. Andy let his fingers glide back along the vessel until he had found the second thread, and pulled it tight in turn, preventing any real leakage from the opening he had made; Tony had already sponged away the ooze, dark red from oxygen lack.

Moving back from the stretcher, Andy saw that their junior intern knew his job as well. The plasma tube was already locked into place in the cannula, without making direct contact with the surgeon's hands or the wound itself. Already the level in the flask above their heads was dropping steadily, as the vital fluid found its way into a fast-fading circulation.

Andy whipped in his sutures and tied a loose dressing, above the emergency puncture. When he peeled off his gloves he saw by the wall-clock that the whole procedure had used no more than three precious minutes.

"Is the blood-call out?"

"On its way now, Dr. Gray."

Andy turned to Tony Korff. "We'll take him to Theatre C. Ash is operating in the main drag at the moment."

The refugee nodded. "I phoned the scrub room while you were tying off. The set-up is being transferred now."

They followed the emergency into the long rectangle of the hospital elevator. Andy had already begun his preliminary examination, percussing the chest area on the damaged right side with light strokes. As he had expected, the percussion note was booming, with an odd, drum-like sound. Breath sound, heard through the stethoscope, was faint, high-pitched—and too distant for comfort.

"The picture's not too robust, Tony."

"I thought I'd found a pneumothorax," said the senior intern.

"It's getting sizable now. But if it's a true laceration of the lung air pressure should control the bleeding at this stage. And that's just what isn't happening." They stepped out to the operating-room floor and followed their patient towards the nearest doorway. "Do we have permission to work on him, by the way?"

"His wife's in the ante-room now. Will you talk to her or shall I?"

"Leave her to me," said Andy. His younger, too intense colleague was apt to be brusque on such occasions. "Stay with him, and watch for a possible accumulation of air. If that lung's as badly damaged as I fear, we can't afford a shut-down in respiration."

The patient struggled momentarily as they paused to manœuvre the stretcher through the swinging doors, and a rattling cough came from the straining ruin of the chest. Andy watched the gush of the small but definite hæmorrhage, and frowned in earnest.

"See if you can get Evans for the anæsthetic—he understands this type of trouble. The sooner we get a tracheal tube in place, the better I'll like it." There was no need to say more as Tony shepherded the stretcher into the still half-ready theatre. Wounds like this were none too common, but the danger was obvious. Already it was evident that the blow on the chest wall had torn into the spongy lung tissue beneath.

Probably it was not damaged beyond repair; but, thanks to
the high blood content of the area, a mixture of air and blood
had already escaped into the chest cavity itself, compressing
the injured lung with every breath. As the pressure built up,
both good and bad lung would be constricted more and more.
Eventually, if no relief came, there would no longer be
enough functioning lung left to maintain life.

It took only a few moments to persuade the pale, dis-
traught girl in the ante-room that immediate surgery was her
husband's only chance. Tony was at the phone when Andy
returned to the operating theatre, giving orders to the blood
bank downstairs. Emily Sloane, Andy noted with approval,
was herding a squad of student nurses with her usual speed—
and her usual acid tongue. Well or ailing, Emily would have
his operating room in readiness before he slipped into his
gown. He followed Tony into the scrub room as the senior
intern banged up the phone.

"What did you order—type O?"

"A thousand cc.," said the refugee. "There's no time for
matching."

"Where's Miss Talbot?"

"Making sure that Jackie goes back to the ward. You're
postponing the Blalock, I take it?"

Andy nodded as he began to scrub in earnest. Jackie's
crippled heart could wait a little longer, with no added danger.
A life was ebbing on the table just outside that steam-misted
door. Emily Sloane's head had already thrust into the opening.

"Any new instruments, Dr. Gray?"

"Nothing except a lung-root tourniquet. We're set up for
chest work now."

"Nurse Talbot brought one on her special tray."

Andy grinned under his mask. He could trust Julia to
remember most things—whether it was the last word in an
argument or the last item on a surgical tray that would make
the most delicate operation foolproof.

While he scrubbed he watched the preliminaries in the
operating room. The anæsthetist (he judged, by his bulk, that
it was Dr. Evans) had already joined the group, with an
intern at his side. While his assistant lifted the patient's head

clear of the table and cradled it in his hands, the anæsthetist
began the methodical insertion of a laryngoscope—a long
metal instrument with an electric bulb inside the panel. Thanks
to this illumination, a tube resembling an enterprising snake
was next worked gently down the windpipe. The tube would
supply oxygen to the straining lungs while they worked. An
ingenious double balloon near its end would permit oxygen
and anæsthetic gases to enter the lungs under pressure during
the critical period when the chest wall must be kept
open.

Julia walked under the operating lights, scrubbed and
ready, as always, a good three minutes before her surgeon.
He watched her come across the white-tiled room and felt
his heart miss a beat, even now.

"Will we be doing Jackie after this, Doctor?"

"I think not, Miss Talbot," he answered, just as formally.
"The team should be rested for a Blalock. Suppose we try to
fit him into the late afternoon, when we've all caught our
breath?"

Tony had already accepted his gown from one of the
student nurses and hurried to prepare the patient. With Julia's
aid he turned back the sheets that swathed the victim to the
chin, exposing the pitiful wreckage of the rib cage—the
danger zone where the unwary surgeon ventured at his peril.
Even from that slight distance Andy saw that the physical
damage was not as extensive as he had feared.

When Julia slapped the knife into his hand there was no
hesitation as he drew an operative line along the course of
the rib he planned to resect, no lost motion as he helped
Tony to clamp the long fringe of towels along the lips of the
wound. Automatically he noted the almost total absence of
bleeding, and sought the anæsthetist's eye—not at all reassured
by Evans's dubious shrug. The flask of whole blood was
already flowing into the ankle vein: the best they could do
for the next half-hour was move fast, and hope.

The periosteum, the tough covering above the rib cage,
opened under the slash of a new knife for a full ten-inch
incision. A periosteal elevator came into his hand, a curved
instrument with fairly sharp edges. He worked the blade

beneath the rib, until the end showed clearly on the other side,
then shoved it forcibly down the whole length of the bone—
a manœuvre which stripped away the periosteum in one long,
fluent stroke. This was an essential bit of surgery, so that the
tough sheath could later form a base from which new bone
would be laid down and a new rib could grow.

"Costatome, please." But Julia had already slapped the
instrument into his palm—from here on, he knew, she would
be part of his body, her muscles under control from his brain.
The costatome, a guillotine in miniature, bit through the rib
at each end, permitting him to lift it easily from its bed.
Below the incision the remaining periosteum formed a
relatively bloodless barrier, through which the chest cavity
itself could be entered with ease.

Allis forceps came into his hand—slender-toothed instruments which facilitated the tenting of the periosteum for the
next long incision. There was an audible hiss as the space
round the lungs, the pleural cavity, opened under his hands.
The sound resembled the spurt of air from a punctured tyre,
so great was the pressure from the lacerated lung.

"Respiration's improving," said Evans, from the head of
the table.

Andy looked up and nodded. "You can see how the
pressure of that pneumothorax was interfering with the
expansion of the lung—and how it was hampering the heart."
He had spoken formally and lifted his voice a trifle, for the
benefit of the overhead microphone. He knew, without
glancing beyond the lights, that the glass-enclosed observation
gallery had been crowded with students and interns, ever since
word had gone out on the emergency. He had spoken aloud
from a sense of duty only. Deep in his work, he was unaware
of an audience and careless of their approval.

Surgical scissors completed the opening of the periosteal
bed for its entire length. The anæsthetist adjusted his dials
in rhythm with Andy's motions, decreasing the pressure of
the gases flowing into the patient's lungs now that the
obstructing accumulation of air was relieved step by step. As
Andy inserted his hand to raise the lung there was a gush of
blood mixed with air. Tony Korff sponged rapidly, clearing

the incipient hæmorrhage and giving the surgeon a clear view at last.

"Just as we expected. A laceration caused by the broken rib."

The focal point of the danger was now in the operative field, near the top of the lower lobe—a jagged tear in the spongy lung tissue, resembling nothing more than the rupture in an orange skin after it had spilled to the pavement. A red, pulpy mass bulged through the tear—and from this mass blood oozed redly. The pulsation was rhythmic, as though controlled by some invisible metronome. Even when Andy squeezed the living sponge with one hand the flow was retarded rather than stopped.

"The pulmonary artery must be torn. Or one of its main branches inside the lung."

"Looks like the end, doesn't it?" Tony Korff said.

Andy shook his head sharply. That was the one weakness he could never forgive, Korff's tendency to quit when the going got really hard and success seemed beyond him. "Has he lost much ground, Dr. Evans?"

"He's better, if anything, since you relieved that pressure," said the anæsthetist. "The blood is going in nicely now. We can replace faster than it's being lost."

"We'll take a chance then," said Andy. "The lobe must come out."

Even in his fog of concentration he could feel the watchers stir in their glass cage. An emergency lobectomy was hardly an ordinary procedure: in this case it was the only surgery that could save the patient. Deep within the lung tissue (as that pulsing ooze showed only too graphically) the thin-walled pulmonary artery had been ruptured, an injury impossible to repair. He had no choice but to remove the damaged portion. Fortunately man could survive with only one-sixth of his normal lung tissue intact. There would be no permanent damage from removal of half the organ now exposed in the wound.

"We've no time to dissect the lung root and isolate the vessels," said Andy. "Not with the patient in a deep shock. Lung tourniquet, Miss Talbot, if you please."

The tourniquet was a simple device, somewhat like the wire snare used by throat surgeons to remove tonsils. It carried a strand of heavy braided silk, which Andy now looped round the root of the lung—where artery joined vein, at the joining of bronchial tube and trachea. As he drew the loop tight the flow of blood under his free hand slowed down and then stopped. A second braid of silk, and a third, tightened beyond the tourniquet, were placed for added precaution. He fitted the loops carefully, relying on the feel of his fingers rather than on direct vision.

Julia began to pass lung clamps across the table— prehensile steel instruments, capable of crushing the lung and anchoring it while he cut and sutured. He placed one clamp with its jaws across the lung root itself, just above the emergency sutures, and another a quarter inch farther up the stalk. The scalpel flashed in a quick, sure arc, biting cleanly. The lobe of the damaged organ lifted from the wound, leaving the stump triply held by tourniquet, suture and clamp.

"We'll ligate the pedicle," said Andy quietly, not even hearing the deep sigh that ran down the observers' benches. The needle darted precisely to its task, carrying the tough fibres-in small, careful stitches, until the whole base of the root was engaged. It was a laborious business, but a necessary one. Many surgeons considered ligatures superfluous, after such elaborate precautions had already been taken. Experience had taught him that one could not be too careful in a lung case. Until the stump had healed completely the danger of hæmorrhage was ever present—and hæmorrhage at this point in a patient's anatomy could bring death in a few moments' time.

When he looked up at last he saw that hardly half of the flask of whole blood had flowed into the circulation. Evidently the whole operation had been carried through in close to record time. He glanced at the head of the table, taking the anæsthetist's nod as his accolade. Already the improvement in the patient's condition was obvious, even from the gallery. The throb of the heart (visible through the membrane of the mediastinum, which formed the central partition of the chest cavity) was stronger, and perceptibly slower.

"How's pressure, Dr. Evans?"

"Rising steadily, Doctor."

"Fair enough. I'm going to close."

Evans nodded and moved a dial on the machine, lifting the pressure of the air flow. Immediately the remaining portion of lung visible through the still open chest wall inflated to perhaps twice its former size. Julia had already slapped a catgut needle into Andy's palm. The wound was closed with care: incisions of this type must be airtight, for even the youngest intern in the gallery knew that nothing must disturb the normal pressure in the undamaged lobe.

When he had finished at last, and the skin was sutured as well, Andy surrendered his place to Tony, who whipped the last of the towel clamps aside and strapped a dressing in place above the wound. "Sorry I appeared to give up so easily, Doctor," said the refugee. "Your audience will never forgive me."

Andy blinked, and looked up at the gallery, as though he was only now conscious of its silent applause. "He'll want another flask of blood," he said evenly. Now that he was in contact with externals again, he could recognize a definite lack in Tony—a withdrawal of thought and energy to some field of his own, a far remove from East Side General. "Penicillin, of course. And an oxygen tent until he's out of danger. Will you inform the wife that he came through it well, or shall I?"

"The pleasure's mine, Doctor," said Tony. "May I congratulate you on another brilliant job?"

He went out after the high-wheeled stretcher without waiting for a reply. Andy watched him narrowly, almost hoping he could detect an unsteady gait: it would not be the first time that the brilliant but unstable refugee had come to the operating room a little the worse for alcohol. But Tony Korff had never walked a straighter line—nor walked it with greater arrogance.

Martin Ash came into the scrub room as Andy was peeling off his gloves. The older surgeon looked tired and drawn, but there was a quiet light of satisfaction in his eyes. So the gall bladder was a success, thought Andy. He did not make the mistake of asking that question. For all the work they shared, Ash had never quite put their relationship on a personal basis. Andy was not quite sure, even now, whether the head of East Side General disliked him or regarded him as a potential rival.

"I heard you'd be doing the heart case, Andy. Too bad you got side-tracked."

Andy grinned above the sting of the antiseptic. "This one was worth saving, too."

"You did a fine job—but that goes without saying."

"Thank you, sir. Will you expect me at the noon conference?"

Martin Ash leaned against the door-jamb and fumbled for a cigarette. Andy studied him guardedly as the expensive platinum lighter flared. Rumpled though he was—and blood-stained from a hard morning in the clinic—Ash seemed vibrantly alive. I've never seen a handsomer face, thought Andy. Or a sadder one. The lovely Catherine must lead him quite a life.

"We'll meet as usual," said Ash. "Not that I've a great deal to report: I'm sure the grapevine has done my work in advance——"

"I've been too busy to listen."

"You heard that the second burn victim died, of course."

"It was confidential on the morning report." He watched Ash remove the cigarette from his lips, wondering why the older man's whole body should relax so abruptly as he expelled a cloud of tobacco smoke.

"The police asked me to give them that fellow as a decoy," said Ash slowly. "God knows why, but they believed they could frighten their quarry out of hiding—if we pretended he was about to name names——"

"I see."

"Do you see what might have happened, if the plan had worked?"

Andy grinned. "I've been under fire in other languages. I'll admit it's a novelty in one's own country, but——"

"The fire has eased a trifle," said Ash abruptly.

"I'm afraid I don't follow."

"Hurlbut phoned me between operations. I've already

released the news of the second death to the afternoon papers."

"Did he tell you why?"

"A directive from higher up. Someone in Washington got skittish at the breakfast table when he saw the morning news from New York. It seems we mustn't offend a former ally overseas—even if he is our undeclared Nemesis today——"

"I still don't follow."

"It's simple enough, Andy. At this moment we mustn't say that our enemies are shipping radioactive chemicals abroad—with help on this side. We mustn't even imply that one of those enemies might blow up a metropolitan hospital, rather than reveal his identity."

"So we inform him, via the public print, that he can stop worrying?"

"Precisely. We say he's in no danger whatever, so far as *we* are concerned. Which, of course, is nothing less than the truth. I still wish that burn case had spoken up before he died."

"Does Hurlbut think he's an outside chance to corner his man?"

"He still insists the job was done in this neighbourhood. He even believes that he'll make an arrest by tomorrow morning." Ash sighed again. "We've both interned in this district, Andy. And we both know that's what a policeman always says—when he's at the end of his rope."

"Will you tell the conference this much, Doctor, or is it *entre nous*?"

"I don't think I can do less. I haven't had time to check the hospital's temperature. Have you noticed any sign of nerves?"

Andy met his superior's eyes. "Most of us have been under fire, sir—in odd corners of the world. I'd say that those who haven't are ready for baptism."

"We're still on emergency, you understand. Even if we're no longer a direct target——"

"We're ready now, sir. I can answer for that."

Ash dropped a hand on the younger man's shoulder:

Andy could feel the chill in the finger ends. "You're a comfort, as usual," he said. "I wish I had your staying power."

"Call it habit," said Andy. "I've never been noted for my courage. Or say I fell into the right job. That's even simpler. When I'm working I don't notice the world outside——"

"Speaking of work, when will you take that heart case?"

"Not before five."

"Five will do nicely," said Martin Ash. "If I can, I'll be in the gallery."

Andy dropped his eyes to hide his confusion at the compliment. When he looked up again Ash had vanished.

The operating theatre was empty when he crossed it, *en route* to the next demanding chore of a day that now seemed endless. He had hoped, vaguely, that Julia would linger—but that, too, was only wishful thinking. Julia had offered her friendship and her loyalty; she had outlined the path she would follow. Whether he would join her on that journey was for him to decide, and him alone.

It was only when he turned into the surgical ward that he remembered his date with Pat Reed. Tentative though it was on paper, he knew that she would expect him not later than five—and knew, just as surely, that she would not wait for him for ever. A girl like Pat had playmates everywhere: in New York she had only to lift a phone to summon them by the dozen. And yet he had posted Jackie for that same hour: he could hardly change the time again, after telling Ash.

He wondered if he had chosen the hour instinctively, if only to put off his decision a little longer. In the same breath he hoped that some force beyond himself would make decision inevitable.

VIII

Dr. Dale Easton emerged from the noon conference in the director's office with an inward sigh. As he had expected, the meeting of the hospital department heads had accomplished nothing—or everything, depending on one's view-point. The solidarity of the staff (no matter what emergency might arise) had been established beyond dispute. But then, Martin Ash had had no reason to doubt anyone's loyalty, even before this bizarre threat arose. Or so Dale brooded, as he moved down the hall, and waited for Andy Gray at the stairway that led to his own domain.

Isolated as he was from the rumours that had filled East Side General that morning, Dale had felt no real sense of relief when he heard of the burn victim's death—just as he had refused to consider the crazy headlines that Otto had brought to the laboratory that morning. The cold light of truth was all that really mattered in Dale Easton's world: there was little discernible light in the news these days, and no pattern that a trained observer could follow.

Life, from the pathologist's view-point, had a definite beginning, a growth (the inevitable consequence of that beginning), and a foredoomed end—usually by violent means. A close reading of today's news could only convince him that humanity at large was repeating the same cycle, on a global scale. For this cogent reason Dale Easton avoided newspaper and radio alike.

There was Andy Gray, looking quite as gaunt as usual, and quite as preoccupied. Watching his friend emerge from the director's ante-room, Dale all but yielded to the impulse to descend the stairway and let the surgeon follow his own obscure path alone. Then their eyes met—and he saw that Andy's frown, and Andy's need for a moment's respite, quite matched his own.

"Lunch, Andy?"

"I'm afraid not, Dale. I've an appendectomy in the clinic in fifteen minutes—with a kidney to follow."

"How do they feed you—intravenously, while you're operating?"

Andy chuckled as they fell into step together, turning down the stair to pathology, as though by common consent. "It's an idea, now you mention it. Did you have something to show me?"

"It won't come as a surprise," said Dale. "But it's worth a second glance."

They entered the laboratory by the side door. The pathologist took a slide from his drying rack and fitted it methodically under the large microscope that stood beside the window.

"Burn tissue, I take it," said Andy.

"A bit I didn't send to Brookhaven."

Dale watched carefully as his friend fitted one eye to the lens. The pattern of the slide was already etched on his own brain—so accurately that he could have sketched the damaged tissue without a second glance. When Andy raised his eyes they did not speak at once. The pathologist replaced the slide on the rack—and perched on his high work stool. He permitted himself the ghost of a grin as he voiced the thought they were sharing.

"As you've seen, it's a chemical burn of some kind. It isn't the result of an atomic blast—though it does have a surface resemblance."

"Enough to fool me last night," said Andy. "I'm sure it fooled Tony—and our friends on Civil Defence."

"It's harder to fool a microscope," said Dale. "The fact they were *fresh* injuries gave me my first clue. As you've seen, the eschar is formidable. But there's none of the gangrene-like breakdown they had at Hiroshima—what we've come to call the peculiar aftermath of atomic radiation. Granted, there's a degree of radiation present: the C.D. counter shows that clearly——"

"Can you name the chemical, Dale?"

The pathologist shook his head. "Brookhaven can, I imagine," he said. "Naturally, they aren't talking out there."

"Would you say this chemical could be an ingredient of an atomic bomb—past or future?"

"Hasn't Brookhaven said just that—by saying nothing? Our time clock may still be ticking round the corner. It may still strike—even though we've eased the enemy's mind by admitting both burn victims are gone."

"Death is always ticking round the corner," said Andy. "We must still be prepared, until we've pinned it down." He paced the length of the autopsy room, and banged a fist on the dissection table. "And I'm not just talking of this threat to New York. Even if Pandora's box is open—there must be some way to clamp down the lid."

Dale Easton kept his rueful grin intact. "World government with teeth might do the trick. Plus a genuine return to God."

"Fair enough. Who'll lead the way? Congress—or the Federated Churches of America?"

"You're rather bitter today, Andy."

"Far from it. I'm just startled by this switch of credo. I always thought you were a fatalist. Now it seems you're a Christian."

"I believe man is immortal, at least," said the pathologist. He jerked a thumb towards the open door of the autopsy room, where the body of the second burn victim, shrouded in white, awaited his attention. "Including that bit of debris —and never mind the sort of life he led. Man must lose his life to find it—and I'll name the author of that philosophy, if your religion's a bit rusty."

"I can quote the New Testament as well as the next," said Andy, and Dale wondered why his voice had suddenly grown almost testy. "Has it stopped our playmates across the Atlantic from stockpiling for death? Will it stop *our* master minds from dumping the first load—if there's no simpler way out?"

"You *are* bitter, my friend," said the pathologist. "Can it mean you've decided to marry that uptown bank after all?"

Andy Gray moved back from the microscope. "Go to hell, will you? I've decided nothing."

"Then you're writhing in limbo, which is far worse. Just as we're all counting our pulses here—and getting religion pronto, before we vanish in a puff of smoke."

"Put it that way, if you must," said Andy gloomily. "The fact remains, I can't keep up this pace for ever. Maybe I'd even welcome a quick dissolution——"

"You won't reach out in the meantime and take a pinch of faith?"

"Thanks, Dale. You don't take faith like snuff. And I, for one, refuse to get religion—just because I may be dissolved in the next few hours. No more will you——"

"I happen to think we've always had religion."

"Haven't you heard that all doctors are atheists—especially lab doctors?"

Again Dale Easton glanced at the motionless shape in the autopsy room. "I believe in a force outside myself. The force that permits me to think—and invented love—and sparked that poor lump of clay under Otto's winding sheet. So, Dr. Gray, do you. If you didn't, you'd never have scheduled that heart surgery for five o'clock this afternoon."

"Come again, please?"

"You're officially off duty at five—with a good week of overtime you've every right to use. Outside the hospital, mind you. At a double feature cinema—or making time with your heiress. Or even under a wineglass elm, studying your soul. Instead, you throw in your lot with the rest of us. Shall I tell you why?"

"How can you—when I don't know myself?"

"Of course you know. You're staying here tonight because you believe in God. We're down in the books to handle this show as best we can. You know that none of us will come out of it the same whether hell explodes over New York today or next year. And you realize that any change in your outlook will be an improvement."

"Go and climb a tree, will you?"

"You said that once," said Dale mildly.

"It bears repeating," said Andy, and stalked out of the lab. Dale Easton grinned—and let the door slam without comment. After all, Andy had told him all he wished to know.

It was time for his own lunch, but the staff conference had spoiled his appetite today. Instead, he pulled off his coat and reached for the apron that was the uniform of his trade. Old Otto had already thrust his head in the door, as he heard footsteps cross the passage to the autopsy room.

"Ready for your new patient, Doctor?"

"Bring him to the table, Otto. We'll get this over."

When the second burn victim lay on the marble slab he worked for a long time without speaking, breaking this structure that had once been a man into its complex parts and reducing those parts in turn. Otto, as was his habit, pottered happily about the room, dropping the cross sections

into his neatly labelled jars of formalin and stacking the jars
according to a system all his own. Later these jars would go
to the laboratory for sectioning. Later still (when the tissues
had been set in paraffin blocks and shaved down in fragments
less than a cell in thickness) they would return to his microscope, as yet another exhibit in the endless victory of death
over life.

Was death always the final conqueror? Father O'Leary
thought differently, of course—but that was the padre's
special department, and the vessel of the padre's faith had
been forged in special fires. Not even the padre denied the
body's death and dissolution. Faced with this picture of
profound shock, and its inevitable aftermath, even the layman
must understand that the balance on which life hung was
precarious indeed. Medicine had worked its own magic to
steady that balance, to protect it against all comers. Until the
release of atomic energy (and the tragic demonstrations of
its power), man had taken his first long stride towards a truly
better existence—some had said, towards a working substitute for immortality.

Was the bomb only God's way of striking back at the
scientists? Or had an all-wise Creator withdrawn from this
earthly bustle, leaving man free to teach himself humility
one more time?

There was a knock on the outer door, and Pete Collins
strolled in behind a cigar, without waiting for an invitation.
Dale offered the reporter an absent-minded grin as he nodded
at a vacant stool. Pete was a frequent visitor, especially when
an unusual autopsy was in progress.

"You're just in time," said the pathologist. "I've a problem
on my hands today. How would the *Chronicle* define life?"

Pete raised his eyebrows. "On or off the record?"

"For the record, of course. I know just how this poor
fellow died. What was his life—and why?"

The reporter pursed his lips, as though Dale's question
was the most natural in the world. "We all know that life
is a series of mistakes, leading to a fatal one. Isn't he the
perfect illustration?"

"Too perfect for comfort. Maybe we've shared in his

mistakes. If we have—isn't it just that we should share his end as well?"

"But he's dead, Doctor. Dead as a mackerel. And he turned in his checks without talking. That means he bought us all a chance to live."

"I see you've kept your ear to the grapevine," said Dale Easton caustically.

"I'll tell you what I think," said the reporter. "Never for one minute did I believe that our Nemesis—rather loosely described as an atomic killer—would dare attack this hospital, with or without his atom buster. But I do believe that Hurlbut's right when he says he's lurking in the vicinity. And I think we've a fair chance to corner him—if he doesn't scare himself and pull the switch."

"So we're still in danger, of a sort?"

"Like everyone else in New York—or the world."

"Suppose the switch is pulled tonight—or tomorrow. Suppose it gets us all. One minute we're alive, the next, we're dead. What would be the real difference?"

"The soul leaves the body and goes to its reward. How long since you've attended church?"

"Do you believe in the soul, Pete?"

"Naturally," said the reporter, with a side glance at Otto. "Don't you?"

"I didn't, in my schooldays," said Dale. "I could dissect a cutaneous nerve and trace its function, right back to the brain. I could prove to myself that everything started in that master clock—from greed to God, and including love, friendship, and the ability to play Chopin from memory. When *that* clock stopped ticking I was willing to call it a day. Remember that story you ran a few years ago about the synthetic cell that lived on electric potential? I once believed there was no other real difference between life and death. Many of my friends still do."

"What made you change?"

"Fear, of course," said Dale—and he had not yet raised his eyes from his grisly task. "The fear that is breeding faith all over the world. The same fear our friend Andy Gray is too tough to admit, so far."

"So you've taken time off to be afraid?" said the reporter. "That really pleases me, Dale. It shows you're human after all. What about you, Otto? Or have you outlived fear, along with lechery?"

The keeper of the deadhouse considered his reply. "You are not really asking if I am afraid, Mr. Collins. You wonder if I know the difference between life and death. And I say it is an answer each man must find for himself. Perhaps we would fear death less if more of us had learned to live. I think as much each time I hear a sermon."

Pete chuckled, and his eye sought Dale's. "Don't tell me you come above ground long enough for church."

"There is a radio here," said Otto. "I listen in comfort. And I wonder at these preachers. Be good, they say—then you go to Heaven and live for ever. And yet, when these preachers come to the hospital too, they fear death as much as anyone. If life is but a stepping stone to better things, why do they shrink from the step?"

"Are you arguing against Christian living, Otto?" asked Dale.

"No, Doctor. I believe in doing right with everybody. But not because it earns me a passport to Heaven. Because it makes me happy here."

"Otto has something there," said the reporter. "Do right because it improves your disposition. And never mind what happens when you're gone."

"But where do you go?" asked the pathologist. "That's what nobody's told me yet."

Otto shrugged. "Does it so much matter, Doctor? Take yourself. I like you—and you like me, I guess. Years from now, when all that's left of me is up on that shelf in a jar, you may still remember. If I'm lucky, you may bring your little boy here for a visit—and show him what's left of me. You may even say, 'This was an old fellow named Otto. He worked here long ago. Sometimes he bored me with his foolish talk. But he was a good man who knew the secret of happiness: he proved to himself that goodness is its own reward.' That way, I'll live again in you and your boy. Isn't it the only sort of immortality that matters?"

"How about an old skunk like me?" said Pete. "Nobody would want to imitate Pete Collins. An unrepentant drunk who runs after women when he's able——"

"You don't tell lies when you write your news stories, Mr. Collins," said Otto. "And I still remember how you gave your pint to the blood bank last year—and the feature piece you wrote that made hundreds of others give, too. And your stories on the children's clinic when it needed more money and beds——"

"Don't put a lily in my hand, Otto," said the reporter. "Not after all the beer we've drunk together."

"You are a good man just the same. Maybe you will never reach Heaven, but you know about living——"

"What about me?" Dale Easton asked. "Do I have points, too?"

Otto grinned. "If I say no, maybe you will shove me in the refrigerator. Instead, I will ask one question. What do you look for in these cross sections of the dead?"

"For ways to combat disease, I suppose."

"But you turned down an offer from Dr. Plant to go into his uptown surgery," said Pete Collins. "A job that would have earned you more than any hospital could pay. Don't hide behind that apron, Doc. You're a do-gooder, too, just like the rest of us."

"All the same, I don't want to get knocked off tonight—or the day after tomorrow."

"Then why not pretend an illness in your family and get clear until this fellow's cornered? They can close ranks without you."

"What do you take me for?"

"Like Mr. Collins said." Otto chuckled and moved to the last icebox. "You're a do-gooder, too, Doctor. And it is time for a beer, before Mr. Collins goes to his office. There is nothing better for do-gooders who insist on being philosophers."

IX

Tony Korff strode through the great brass doors of East Side General and ran rather than walked towards the bus station outside the main gate. He was still damning the prosy routine of the wards that had pinned him to his job all the morning, the rush and bustle of the clinic, where he had been obliged to linger while he supervised the preparations for the afternoon session. Thank God he was free of that responsibility now—and his own man until five. There was little enough time for what he had to do.

"Looking for a lift, Doctor?"

He pulled back to the kerb and stared into the tonneau of the town car as though he could not quite believe his eyes. Pat Reed was laughing back at him over her chauffeur's shoulder. Though he had dared to flirt with her mildly during her stay at Schuyler Tower, Tony had never hoped for an opportunity there. The whole hospital knew that this stream-lined siren was on the trail of Andy Gray.

"If you're going uptown," he said formally, and offered her his most stylized bow. He was glad that his chalk-stripe blue gabardine (borrowed from a fellow intern's locker without his knowledge) was a perfect fit, that the pale blue foulard tie he was wearing was a genuine Charvet.

"Where can I drop you, Dr. Korff?"

"The Chronicle Building will do," he said casually, and wished for a fleeting moment that the ride could be longer. So far he had not quite dared to look at her direct. The replica in the vanity mirror above the chauffeur's head was exciting enough—a snug-fitted tailleur that would have cost him a year's pay, a fortune in stone martens bunched care-lessly at one shoulder. . . . Her legs were exciting, too, for all their slimness—honey-coloured from Southern beaches, too satin-smooth to need the added allure of nylons.

"Is it pleasant to be cured?" he asked.

"I wasn't really ill. You must have known that."

"Rest cures have their points, too," he said, watching her face carefully in the overhead mirror. But Pat Reed had already leaned forward as the car coasted to a stop at the gatehouse. A policeman stepped out briefly, nodded at the sight of Tony Korff, and waved them on.

"What was the meaning of that?"

"Apparently there's a killer on the loose in the neighbourhood," he said, and smiled at his own humour. "They thought he might be hiding under your lap robe. When they recognized me they gave up the idea."

"Then there's an advantage in being escorted home by a physician."

"It's unfortunate I can't go all the way," he said. There was a quality in her laughter that encouraged him to face her directly at last. Instantly he felt his heart turn over at the gleam in her half-closed eyes. He had read that same message before, in other eyes, in the back alleys of the world.

"Just how far can you go, Doctor?"

"I've an errand in mid-town, then I must hurry back." He had made his voice dry and deliberate, withdrawing in the hope that she would follow. That, too, was a tactic that had brought results before, in many languages.

"And here I was, thinking you were off for the day. Doesn't an intern have any rights at all?"

"No rights at all in business hours."

"When are you really off duty?"

His mind was racing, but he forced it to throttle down. Either she's fought with Andy, he concluded, or she's hell-bent to teach him a lesson. And I've blundered into the picture at the very moment she needs an extra man. Just as I blundered on the burn case.

"Two evenings and a full afternoon each week," he said. "Would you like the dates?"

Her eyes still brooded on him from a slight distance: he read the portents there and found them good. He wondered if Pat had instructed her chauffeur to lurk in the parking space beside the main gate, until the precise moment of his exit from the hospital. With a woman like Pat, all subterfuges were possible when she was really on the prowl.

"I know the dates," she said.

As their eyes met and locked he felt her sudden, animal magnetism—and relished it with all his senses. But his voice was still clipped and hard. Throw down the challenge if you must, he told her wordlessly. You'll find me a different antagonist from Andy Gray.

"May I ask why the sudden interest in my welfare?"

"I'm a woman alone in the world," she said. Even as his pulses hammered he could not help admiring the parody of innocence in her downcast eyes. "A renovated widow, if you insist, who loves to give parties. I can always use bachelors on their evenings off."

"Singular or plural?" he asked.

"Singular—if they're agreeable."

"I'd be only too happy to prove myself," he said, and bent forward to light her cigarette.

"You've proved yourself already, Doctor," said Pat Reed, and settled in her corner of the limousine with the air of a woman who has marked up yet another victory. "I've enjoyed our talks in the hospital a great deal. I'd adore to hear more of your work and your plans. This Tuesday I'm having a few people in for cocktails—at my suite in the Plaza. If you'd care to join us——"

"Will Andy Gray be there?"

"I haven't the slightest idea."

His hand fastened on her wrist. He gave her no time to be startled, and still less to protest, as he bent to kiss her hand. "I think you've told me all I've a right to hear," he said quietly. "Don't you agree?"

"Quite," she said. "Here's your destination—since I can't take you farther uptown today."

He never remembered descending to the hot bustle of the pavement outside the Chronicle Building. The limousine had whisked into the midtown traffic before he could speak again, leaving him nothing but the memory of that mocking smile. His brain still spun with vertigo as he turned into the old-fashioned marble lobby of the newspaper building, with its antediluvian cigar stand and its brass elevator cages like upended rat runs in Brobdingnag. Once he had stepped into a lift and asked for the city room, he felt his brain clear magically. Pat Reed might have her uses later: he was after larger game today.

An office boy led him to a hallway that opened to the file room—the newspaper morgue that treasured its dead news as carefully as old Otto at his best. Glancing about him, Tony noted that the wilderness of steel filing cabinets abutted directly on the city room itself—a deserted beehive at this hour, save for a few re-write men pounding routine stories, a pair of day editors hunched over a chessboard. He had not counted on this proximity, for he wished to come and go unobserved while he carried through this special job of research. Yet he had no other source, with the time at his disposal. The *Chronicle* was world-famous for its complete coverage: he could not move another step without having the essential facts at his finger ends.

"I'm Dr. Korff from East Side General," he told the attendant who emerged, mole-like, from the shadows of the filing cases and barred his path.

"Got your card, Doctor?"

Tony displayed his credentials with a flourish. "I'm here to check on a case I'm reporting. It won't take long."

The attendant led the way to a desk and an open register. "Sign here—and take that desk by the window. You'll find copy paper there, if you want to make notes. Nothing goes out, you understand——"

"Of course. I've been here before." It wasn't true, of course, but his fingers were itching for a pencil. "May I see all you have on Bert Rilling, the brewer?"

"I think his cuttings are in use. Someone was doing a story on his illness this morning."

Tony felt his heart sink. He heard the snarl in his voice, as though someone were speaking outside his control. "I'm the attending physician, and this is fairly important. Will you try to dig them up for me?"

The man turned with a shrug, then brightened visibly as his eye lit on a wire basket on his worktable, heaped high with fat manila folders. "You're in luck, Doctor—they've just been returned from the city desk. Make yourself com-

fortable, and take all the notes you want. Just so long as you
don't take any clippings——"

Tony sat down with the file on Bert Rilling and ordered
his hands to cease their trembling. Pretending to make busy
notes while he felt the morgue keeper's eyes upon him, he
saw that his former mentor was an important American
indeed—if one could judge importance by the volume of a
man's personal publicity.

The folders were neatly numbered. Significantly, the oldest
entry dated from Rilling's arrival in New York—or shortly
thereafter. There was a sketch folder crammed with feature
stories, including a number of magazine articles from other
publications. Tony glanced at these briefly before he passed
on to the news articles themselves. This afternoon he was
eager for facts, not pious embroidery of the success theme.

It was evident at once that Rilling-Schilling had lost no
time in pushing his way to prominence after his departure
from Hitler's shadow. The first important entry told of his
election to the Yorkville section of a German-American
society whose motto seemed to be patriotism plus. Already,
Tony gathered, Bert had purchased a major interest in the
Silver Cap Brewery; thanks to his enterprise, he had lifted
that mouldy ruin from the doldrums and pushed its product
into competition with the best American brands.

Tony smiled thinly and opened a new folder. So far the
picture was classic in its simplicity. Rilling had brought
money from abroad, more than enough to feather any nest.
That it was Nazi money he had no doubt. Even in those
remote days the big-wigs were placing their loot with care,
ensuring their continued financial status, no matter how the
next war might go.

The clippings showed a definite change in the career of
Bert Rilling as his adopted country rumbled down the road
to World War II. There had been a pattern in Bert's own
actions: the same instinct that had caused him to leave
Germany had placed him on the winning side, years before
the United States of America had realized it must fight for
its own survival. Headline after headline celebrated his
crusading leadership on war-bond drives, especially among

Americans of German descent. Long before Pearl Harbour
he had invested millions in the manufacture of aeroplane
parts; he had even figured in a much-publicized operation
whereby German technicians had been smuggled out of
Europe.

The halo of the good citizen was balanced firmly above
the émigré's bullet skull when the war ended—and Tony
admitted that the halo had been earned. His thin-lipped sneer
broadened as he read of his old friend's rise to political power:
that, too, was part of the pattern, part of the slow accretion
of wealth and influence that Rilling now accepted as his due.
Early in '52 there had even been a faint breath of scandal,
when a rampaging congressional committee investigating the
drug traffic in metropolitan New York, had proved that three
of the brewer's Democratic protégés were leaders of the ring.
Rilling himself had been exonerated, of course, when the three
unwary politicos were branded as tools of Moscow.

Rilling's pious acceptance of his whitewash, and his
appearance with the mayor on Central Park Mall as one of
the principal speakers in New York's annual I Am An American
Day celebration, were the last entries in the final, dated
folder. A supplementary folder, stamped 'current', contained
today's news story of the brewer's collapse and the daring
surgery that had saved his life. The clipping bore Pete Collins's
name, and Tony scanned it carefully, wondering if he would
find his own name mentioned. Perhaps, after all, it was better
that Collins had left him out: strict anonymity from now on
(in the light of his immediate plans) was essential.

Stapled to the current folder was a long galley proof,
with a numbered tab marked 'obit'. Tony could still smell
the acrid odour of printer's ink: he guessed that the obituary
had been set in type this morning, ready for instant use in
event of the brewer's death. He commended the *Chronicle* on
its efficiency and began to doodle rapidly on the sheaf of
copy paper before him. . . . Bert Rilling, with a swastika banner
in one fist and a Stars and Stripes in the other, throned on a
mountain of moneybags. Bert tumbling into a bottomless pit,
with his smug, porcine grimace unchanged. After all, no one
had the right to live for ever.

The picture was complete now; he could have drawn most of it from memory. Given his drive to power, his magnificent lack of scruples, and Kurt Schilling could have reached no other end. One thing was certain: though Kurt had changed his name and his citizenship, he had kept his European connections intact. The story of the drug ring was all the off-stage colour that Tony needed. He knew, from the letters he occasionally received, that much of the Nazi movement had gone underground in Germany, while it waited for a change in the political wind. Many of the moving spirits had merely crossed the line to work for the Russians, as Bert himself would surely have done, had he been trapped in Berlin.

Even if those contacts had been lost in the war years, Bert must have re-established them now. Once the Russian drive towards world conquest was really under way, he stood ready to supply his share of motive power. Perhaps Rilling had planned it this way, from the moment he set foot on American soil. Certainly he would feel no disloyalty towards the country that had made him rich and secure. Loyalty, in Rilling's dictionary, was directed towards himself alone.

Tony stared down at his sketch of Rilling, tumbled head first into the last circle of hell: there had been no need to draw the hand that had supplied the deciding shove. Rilling must renew their alliance: that much was self-evident. Once they had sealed that bargain, it would be Tony Korff who led. He had always known that his mind was far keener than Kurt's could ever be. It was high time he put that knowledge to the test.

Lifting the wire basket of clippings at last, he returned them to the custodian's desk with a few quick words of thanks. Now that he had made his decision, he was eager to reach the hospital again with the least delay. He skirted the reporters' desks, aware that a few more typewriters were chattering now in the great, dim cave of the city room—aware, with a sickening burst of rage, that someone had called his name. He pulled up sharply, a dozen strides from the elevator and freedom—and found himself facing Pete Collins.

"Isn't this a bit far north for you, Doc?" The reporter

was affable enough, but Tony, who had felt Pete's gimlet glance before, braced himself instinctively.

"What about *you*, Collins? I thought you were still at the hospital."

"So I was, until an hour ago. Matter of fact, I followed you down the steps. I saw you get in a lady's limousine and whisk away in style. Now I find you digging in *our* morgue for a change."

Tony did not hesitate for a fraction. Even if his reason for stopping at the *Chronicle* had been less ticklish, he could hardly afford to alienate Pete Collins. The right kind of publicity never hurt a doctor—even a doctor with plans that must never see the light of day.

"I was looking up a file on an old patient," he said. "Part of a case report."

Pete's eyebrows lifted. "I never knew you fellows went to such lengths with your history-taking. What's wrong with the hospital records?"

The refugee matched the reporter's smile perfectly. "Nothing. They're just a bit dry at times. And even interns like a change of air. Can I buy you a drink?"

"Believe it or not, I never drink while I'm working."

"Then you'll excuse me if I run? I should be at the hospital now. This isn't my afternoon off——"

Tony felt the reporter's eyes follow him to the elevator, and hoped he had not been too abrupt in his leave-taking. At least Collins was a veteran of the hospital beat: he could understand a doctor's need to watch the clock. He had forgotten the encounter long before the old-fashioned lift could deposit him in the lobby. His agile brain, meshing firmly with the problem at hand, began to grind madly as he hurried from lobby to pavement and stopped a taxi. Not that an intern could afford a taxi—but, then, he had no intention of remaining an intern much longer.

"Hurry, will you, driver? I'm a doctor on emergency."

The taxi driver slapped down his flag. "Where to, Doc?"

"East Side General, please." Tony settled in the corner of the cab and damned his fast-dancing mind. Above all, he must not seem eager, from this point on. When he faced

Rilling again he must pretend that collaboration—like their meeting—was inevitable. And yet he could feel his neck swell above the expensive tie he had filched from a forgotten patient's room. Try as he might, he could not loosen his tight-clenched fists or stop the pump of blood at his temples. He came back with difficulty to what the driver was saying.

"Still a lot of excitement down your way, Doc?"

"Not particularly. Why d'you ask?"

"No news on the killer, then?"

Today of all days, thought Tony Korff, I deserve a deaf mute at the wheel. He resisted the impulse to order the oaf to hold his tongue. Once again he remembered that he had every need to be inconspicuous.

"Sorry, I'm from out of town. What's this about a killer?"

"Didn't you see the papers? Fellow's supposed to be loose on the East Side with a blockbuster in his satchel. An A-bomb, no less. Me, I think it's a lot of hokum to take the people's mind off the mistakes the Government's makin'——"

"It could be," said Tony sagely. But crazy laughter had begun to bubble within him. It was quite true that a killer was at large in Manhattan. But his weapons were far less spectacular than atomic energy. A quiet murderer, he could afford to move softly now and pick his time. Why was the urge to reach Bert Rilling's bedside almost more than he could bear?

x

Pete Collins turned away from the window of his city room and scratched the stubble of beard he always wore for luck when a story was in the making. Though he seemed friendly enough on the surface, Tony Korff was a cold fish beneath: Pete had sensed as much from their first meeting. A queer, too wise fish, accustomed to navigate in murky waters. Too many foreign doctors who had found a toehold here since the war were of Tony's breed, it seemed. Brilliant technicians, in their way, without the human touch. Tony had illustrated all that, much too neatly, in their brief encounter.

Pete had watched the refugee bolt from the *Chronicle* lobby and leap into a taxi. Tony, as Pete knew all too well, was far too poor to afford a taxi. Also, he was reasonably sure that the intern was free until five. Why should he hurry back to the hospital, to an existence he obviously felt was far beneath his dignity? And why, of all places, should he be rummaging in the *Chronicle* morgue?

Remembering Pat Reed's limousine and the confident way Korff had settled beside that long-legged charmer, Pete wondered if the refugee was about to promote a bit of blackmail. Obeying an instinct that seldom failed him, he turned back among the stacks of the file room and glanced at the visitors' book. There was Korff's bold signature—and beside it, in the morgue keeper's neat script, the name of Bert Rilling, brewer.

Pete frowned and shouted down the dim aisle of filing cabinets. "Hey, Joe! Will you dig out Rilling's clippings for me?"

"Looking right at you, Pete," said the custodian. "In that wire basket."

Pete settled at the work table and yawned as he opened the first bulging folder. Somehow he always felt sleepy in the morgue, relaxed and yet oddly alert, as though these stacks of dead newsprint could lull his everyday senses, even as the acrid odour stirred a usually dormant corner of his mind. Tony, he observed, had whipped through Rilling's file at high speed, leaving the clippings in disorder. Yet there was no evidence that he had stolen anything. Tony was a German-Balt, like the millionaire brewer: both of them had left Germany not too long ago. What old memories was the younger refugee bringing up to date in this dusty corner?

The reporter continued to turn over the neatly stapled bunches of clippings, while a tantalizing pattern began to form in his brain. A plot with a solid beginning, and no discernible climax. Rilling had come from Germany almost twenty years ago—ostensibly a wealthy *émigré* who had abjured Hitler and all his works. Yet his Yorkville welcome had been waiting. His rise to power thereafter had been meteoric, when measured by ordinary yardsticks.

Here was an interview Pete himself had written, at the height of Rilling's wartime fame. He remembered the man perfectly—a bull-necked Teuton who could have posed for an anti-German cartoon without make-up. And yet a sterling citizen of his adopted land, for all that porcine exterior. Pete had given the devil his due and written a straightaway news story with no reservations. But he had refused to like Bert Rilling. There was something behind those eyes that advertised the eternal barbarian—something a mere news report could never hope to define.

Korff, he thought, could explain Rilling to his fellow citizens far more accurately than I. The refugee from Hitler, who had blundered upon a fellow refugee last night in an emergency operating room. Something had brought Tony Korff to the files to refresh his memory. A shared past, in Germany, when both Korff and Rilling were planning their escape? Or did Tony's visit to the *Chronicle* have a more immediate motivation?

Pete closed the file on Bert Rilling and stared down at the basket of clippings without seeing it at all. It was fantastic, of course—too fantastic to be true. There was no provable connection between Korff's strange visit to the file room, Bert Rilling's collapse at the brewery, and the wild story that had mushroomed out of those burn cases. And yet the whole thing could be just fantastic enough to be true.

Rilling was out of the picture—*pro tem*, and in all probability for ever. Pete Collins was always careful to check important admissions at East Side General, and Dr. George Plant had admitted (off the record, of course) that Rilling's chance of survival was slim. That left Tony Korff as the key— and whatever information Tony might be withholding at the moment.

It was an off-chance, as always—but such chances had paid well before, in the reporter's book. He strolled through the chattering aisles of the city room and settled at his desk, careful to make moves deliberate, as he dialled Inspector Hurlbut's private number. If Hurlbut picks up the phone, he told himself, I'll play it straight. If he's out I'll skip the whole business—and chalk it up as another brainstorm. Despite that pious resolve, he felt his heart leap when Hurlbut's familiar, weary baritone snarled at the far end of the connection.

"Collins talking, Inspector. Can we make a deal?"

"I doubt it." Hurlbut, he perceived, was in a bad mood—the end product of a blind-alley day. He made his voice casual, forcing himself to space each word.

"I won't say I have your boy on ice. But I can give you a lead."

"Where are you now, Collins?"

"At the office, turning over my thoughts. Does it matter?"

"Talk—I'm listening."

"I mentioned a deal, remember?"

"Have I ever let you down?"

"Frequently. I want this one on the line."

"Go on," said Hurlbut. "I'm still listening—not too carefully."

"You want a lead—I can tell by that rasp in your voice. And I want a story——"

"Are you playing this *ad lib*, Pete, or have you something solid?"

"Buy my idea and give me a half-hour's start if it pays. That's all I ask."

"Talk," said Hurlbut. Pete, who knew that martinet bark from his cub-reporter days, cleared his throat and responded in earnest. Even with his strange detachment he could almost hear the inspector's brain click into action as he gave a terse but graphic account of his meeting with Tony Korff in the corridors of the *Chronicle.*

"Is that all, Collins?"

"Quite all. Aren't you buying?"

"Maybe you should go back to your comic books."

"Maybe—but will you put a watch on Korff, just the same?"

"If I do I'll let you know."

Pete Collins smiled as he hung up the receiver on a dead

line. It was a gamble, of course—and, like all long shots, the dividends could be astounding. Come what may, he thought, I've pinned that refugee down. He glanced at the clock above the city editor's desk: Tony's taxi would be rolling into the esplanade of East Side General by now and the senior intern would be rattling up the steps, ready to make his next move. But his days as a free agent were over. When he emerged from the hospital again the Homicide Bureau (and, by extension, the *Chronicle*) would be privy to his every move.

The *Chronicle's* star reporter sighed, loosed his belt over his bulging midriff, and began to type painfully at his typewriter. A feature story, based on the recent exposé of corruption in high places. A story as old as the first parliament and as new as tomorrow's gang killing. A story he would abandon in a twinkling if his hunch on Korff should be as profitable as he hoped.

XI

Andy Gray leaned back in the swivel chair and lifted both feet to the corner of his desk. The cubicle that served as his office had never seemed more peaceful. Andy felt his eyelids droop and knew he would be sleeping in another moment if he dared relax.

There was no reason at all for this unheard-of pause in the midst of a busy day. Martin Ash, who seemed to have a passion for work this afternoon, had taken on the spleenectomy Andy had originally scheduled at four-thirty. Incredibly, he had nothing at all to occupy his time until Jackie's heart, which had now been moved up to six-thirty, because of congestion in surgery. He risked a glance at his watch and realized he had two solid hours to himself. Time to call Pat Reed, if he liked, and transpose that cocktail date into a supper *à deux*. Time to review his whole life pattern and banish Pat for ever.

Perhaps it would be best to yield to the compulsions of

a tired body and doze those two hours away. When he wakened he might even find that his subconscious mind (where duty and desire so often fight a drawn battle) had resolved his problem once and for all. His eyelids drooped in earnest just as someone tapped on the door. Andy's feet hit the floor with a guilty start. He had forgotten his appointment with Emily Sloane at four-thirty. He had even forgotten the sudden stab of foreboding when she had asked for this meeting, after he'd finished his lung-injury case this morning.

"Come in, Miss Sloane!" To his own ears his voice sounded casually hearty, but he felt its falseness as the door opened slowly and Emily stood on the threshold.

She's almost too immaculate, he thought, too wise and withdrawn from our worldly cares. It was simply incredible that she was here of her own volition, to seek professional advice. Like every other surgeon in the hospital, Andy had taken it for granted that Emily was immortal. Even that flash of concern, when he had noticed her tiredness this morning, had been forgotten in the driving tempo of his day.

"Well, Emily, what seems to be the matter?" It was grotesque, of course. As bizarre a question as though he had asked a mathematician to recite the multiplication table. And yet he felt that he must speak, if only to break her glacial calm. Probably she's overworked and wants a few days off, he thought. Or it's a personal problem outside the hospital— if one could picture Emily with personal problems. And then, still without speaking, she came forward and laid a card on his desk.

He saw at a glance that it was one of the standard forms from pathology. "Sandra Smith, surgical O.P.D.," he read aloud. The notation was in Dale Easton's hand. "Smears studied with Papanicolaou technique show definitely malignant cells. Suggest immediate examination and treatment."

Emily spoke at last and her cool, detached voice matched her manner. "I know this is routine, Dr. Gray. I'm sorry to bother you——"

He tossed the card on the desk. "Can't you call me Andy, after all these years? And who is Sandra Smith?"

"I am."

Andy felt his sudden upsurge of relief ebb from his mind. In that flash he knew just why he had stared so intently at Emily that morning. His surgeon's instinct had registered its premonition. Here, too soon for comfort, was the proof.

"Say that again, Emily."

"I took those smears myself and slipped them into a batch going to lab. The report came back this morning." Emily could not have been more impersonal if she were addressing a patient. "Now that I'm sure—I think I must have known long ago. One often does—even without special knowledge."

"Why did you put off coming to see me?"

Emily Sloane opened both hands and spread them palm downwards in a sudden, helpless gesture. He understood fully then—with no need of words. No woman could say that she was right about her own condition, that things had been hopeless from the beginning. What really mattered was the fact that Emily herself had abandoned hope long ago. She had every right to be calm at this strange, climatic moment, when despair and resignation met and merged. Why should she cringe at death, when she had never really lived?

He put on his professional mask, knowing that it would not deceive Emily for a moment. "Come into the consulting room, won't you? There may be some mistake about this."

She followed him dutifully to the door, pausing, as hospital usage demanded, so that the doctor might precede the supervisor. "I want you to examine me, Doctor. But there's no mistake."

Ten minutes later he was forced to agree with her completely, though he had really endorsed her diagnosis from his first exploration. That rocklike induration of the pelvic organs meant nothing less than a far advanced cancer of the uterus. He saw now that the malignant growth had already invaded the walls of the pelvis itself, had even begun its expansion towards the organs above. 'Frozen pelvis' was the clinical term for Emily's condition—an evil beyond medical aid.

There was no real need of a biopsy. He took one nonetheless, if only to delay the inevitable—slipping a Novak curette into the uterine cavity and detaching several bits of whitish, almost jelly-like tissue. He could diagnose under direct vision. There, as he had expected, was the wild cell growth, obeying none of the bodily laws that kept tissue intact. The invader that science had yet to tame had had its way, respecting no anatomical barrier as it laid down its deadly train.

Back in his office he waited tensely while Emily Sloane resumed her immaculate uniform. When she emerged at last, and sat down quietly in the consultant's chair, he was struck by the compassion in her eyes. She's sorry for *me* at this moment, he thought; she knows, all too well, that there can be no subterfuge between us now. Yet his first words were an automatic evasion—the instinctive effort any doctor would make to avoid sealing a fellow creature's doom.

"We won't have a report on that biopsy for several days, Emily. Suppose I call you when I hear from pathology?"

"You don't need it to make a diagnosis, I'm sure."

For the last time he marvelled at her calm. When he forced himself to speak again his voice broke, for all his care. "We always take a biopsy to check ourselves——"

"Tell me the truth, Andy." It was the first time she had used his Christian name. For one dreadful moment her thin hand darted across the desk blotter and covered his own. Then she sat back resolutely and folded both hands in her lap. "I came to you because I knew you would. It's carcinoma, isn't it?"

"It's carcinoma, Emily." Most doctors argued that one should never tell a patient of a hopeless condition. What could he do for a patient who had signed her death warrant in advance?

"And it's too far advanced to be cured. I know that, too——"

"It's far advanced, I'm afraid. But not necessarily hopeless. Radiation can do wonders with these cases."

"Palliative radiation." For the first time she sounded bitter. "That's what you'd give me, isn't it? When you know it can't possibly help——"

"We can't just quit, Emily."

"Why can't we—when the time comes?" She got up

quickly as she spoke, and offered him the ghost of a smile.
"I'm sorry, Doctor—you've been very kind."

He reached for a memorandum. "Let me give you a note
to Röntgen therapy. They can start treatments at once."

She waited while he wrote out the note and ripped it
from his daybook. He could feel her white shadow above
him, and kept his eyes on the desk. What if he raised them
and found that he was already facing a ghost?

"Thank you, Doctor. Thank you for everything."

Andy opened his mouth to speak, but no words came.
After she had gone he stared at the door she had closed so
quietly behind her. This was a time when a man felt utterly
helpless, when he regretted that he'd ever set out to be a
doctor. No one, he thought resentfully, should be forced into
this situation: it did something to one's professional pride,
one's self-respect.

He struck his fist hard on the desk blotter and bounced
up from his chair, as he realized that he had not offered Emily
a single word of comfort. Then he pulled up sharply on the
threshold of his office. Emily had come to him for facts, not
for human warmth—and there was no way to follow her now.

XII

Downstairs the clock above the soda fountain hung on
the stroke of five. Vicki Ryan, sipping the last of a chocolate
soda, surveyed her image in the rectangle of glass behind the
siphons and beamed approval at what she saw. You're a
strumpet, Ryan, she told herself contentedly. A strumpet to
the manner born. What excuses you is the fact you love your
work even more than your playtime. How many girls would
take an extra shift on surgical to fill a vacation absence,
without a word of complaint? How many would come up
smiling after the day she'd put in—to say nothing of last
night with Tony Korff?

In a way she would be sorry to miss Andy Gray's Blalock

—along with the whole hospital, she had been rooting for Jackie's recovery ever since the boy's admission as a charity patient. On the other hand she was glad to leave the field to Julia. Not that she expected her dark-haired room-mate to utilize her opportunity fully. Julia was irrevocably in love with Andy. Women in love, as Vicki knew only too well, are in the habit of over-playing their hands.

She glanced longingly at the soda siphon and turned away from the temptation to order another double chocolate. Her figure could stand it, of course: only last night Korff had said he preferred a woman he couldn't quite surround. So, for that matter, did Andy Gray. She had not missed the resident surgeon's appraisal as they sat over coffee in the diet kitchen. So (to round off the team) did the director himself. She just escaped shouting with laughter as she pictured herself in amorous dalliance with Martin Ash—and yet, was the picture so fantastic after all? Men of his race made excellent lovers. Perhaps they had not been friends too long to establish a more intimate relationship.

In her way Vicki was fond of Martin Ash—as fond as a woman of her kind could be of the opposite number. Frank as she had always been with the men in her life (when complete candour did not spoil her game), she was even franker with herself. She admitted that her zest for lovemaking was more practical than romantic—the joy of conquest for conquest's sake. Her image in the mirror smiled inscrutably, and she knew the reason for that smile, right down to her toes.

Yet I'm not a nympho, she insisted stoutly: the nymphomaniac is, by her nature, doomed to howl on the trail of the ideal mate, to try and discard a thousand lovers because she is for ever unsatisfied. *I'm* cut from brighter cloth. In my book, love-making is the friendliest thing two people can do together.

I'd be fun for Martin if he'd have me, she told herself. If I do say it as shouldn't, I'd do him good. She reviewed their last few times alone, remembering the warmth of his compliments at her skill, an occasional gleam that seemed to go beyond the camaraderie of the operating room. Rumours came and went here, but she was positive that the director's marriage was foundering. Perhaps this was the very time he would begin to seek solace elsewhere. Once he had discovered just how relaxing his senior surgical nurse could be, he could be counted on to be generous—generosity to women, whether wife or mistress, was another trait of Martin's forebears. It might be pleasant to be kept for awhile. Nursing was hard work, and it grew harder as one turned the thirty-year milestone. Unless, of course, you were dedicated like Julia—or Emily Sloane.

A picture of Emily rose in her mind unbidden, and she felt a nameless chill. Emily Sloane had never had a man, she would take odds on that. But did that make much real difference when your charms had faded, if you couldn't keep one? This time she got up from the soda fountain and paraded boldly to the juke box in the corner, the better to study the undulations of her figure. The lift of a chin that was still pleasingly plump (and no more). The curve of calves that were enticing even in hospital white. . . . Once again, self-confidence, and the long tally of her conquests, bathed her in a reassuring glow. What if she had discarded those part-time lovers, one by one? She could make the next conquest permanent, the moment she chose.

And then another, even more unwelcome, thought rose in her mind. When Emily retired she would almost certainly inherit the supervisor's job and her responsibilities. Hospital protocol demanded it, and there was no doubt of her fitness for the position. What if she were dedicated to the profession without her knowledge, beyond the power of her will to change? In eleven years she would be forty—and no matter how she managed her diet, she'd be plump as a tabby-cat. Plump and grizzled (her hair was the shade that would never respond to dye). In all probability, coy with residents and patients alike, in the hope of an honest proposal that would never come.

My ego is out of joint today, she told herself. None of this will make sense tomorrow—and I can still marry whom I like. She turned in relief as Julia Talbot came into the fountain and sat down at the far end. Here, at least, was a neophyte who could benefit from her wisdom. She pressed

the juke-box button for a waltz and sat down beside her
room-mate.

"Name your snake juice, partner. I'm buying."

"Coke with lemon, please," said Julia. Studying the dark-
haired nurse narrowly, Vicki noted a suspicious redness about
her lids. She's been crying to herself this afternoon, she
thought, and I don't have to ask her why.

"I guess I'll have a second soda after all," she said. "Why
are you in uniform so early, dear?"

"I'm going to Theatre C for a check-up."

"I know—to lay out the instruments with your own
loving hands."

Julia smiled down at her glass: there was a confidence in
that smile that disturbed Vicki, though she could not have
said why. "Put it that way if you like," said Julia. "If it's
wrong of me to love my work, I'm sorry——"

"I wasn't thinking of your work——"

"Andy, then, since you insist."

"Is that why you've been bawling in your room?"

"Are you my friend, Vicki?"

"I'm everyone's friend. Cry on my shoulder now, if you
like."

"Have you ever heard of a person crying because she's
happy?"

Vicki blinked in earnest. Julia had been cryptic enough
lately, but this was something of a record. "What happened
last night? Did he kiss you behind the scrub-room door?"

"If you must know, it happened on the steps of the
nurses' home." The dark-haired nurse finished her drink
with complete self-possession. "I'll tell you more. He's in
love with me—and he's too dense to admit it——"

"Come off it, sweet," said Vicki. "Even if he *was* absent-
minded enough to kiss you. That's nothing against his record.
I could make him kiss me, too, any time I liked——"

"Go right ahead, dear," said Julia serenely. "I won't mind,
if he enjoys it."

"Are you trying to say you're engaged?"

"Far from it, but——"

"Then listen to me. I've poured coffee after hours for a

dozen Andy Grays—and I've watched 'em go outside for
their wives. Men don't marry a gown and gloves and a well-
threaded suture. If you want him that badly you must make
your play for him in another language—without the old
antiseptic stink. Has he ever taken you out in the two years
you've known him?"

"You know he hasn't. What of it?"

"I'm being hard on purpose, Julia. When he takes off that
white coat and goes out it's the Reed filly he takes. What's
more, he's ready to marry her the minute she'll close the
deal."

"Not if I get there first," said Julia.

Vicki rose from the fountain. "Have it your own way,
darling," she said. "But don't say I didn't warn you. No one
man is worth that concentration—it only sours you on the
species. I'll grant you they're not much, but they have their
uses."

"I'll agree with you there," said Julia. "I plan to use
mine in a different way, that's all. And one of the species
is all I'll need."

"In that case I can only say, 'Happy scrubbing'."

As she rode up to the surgical ward Vicki was not at all
sure she had left with the last word. Julia had been increasingly
independent lately—ever since her relations with Andy had
evolved into a personal liaison. But of course liaison was
too strong a word. Julia Talbot was not the sort to have an
affair, even with the man she hoped to marry. Vicki sighed
deeply. The more she thought of her own sex, the simpler
men seemed. Simpler—and far easier to handle.

In the office just outside the ward Vicki accepted the
report from the floor supervisor going off duty. She was still
bringing the list up to date when Tony Korff strolled into
the office, looking handsomer than usual in his freshly starched
whites. Vicki promptly rose from the supervisor's desk and
stood behind the chair—a model of correctness, while he
checked the ward list in turn.

"Aren't you early tonight, Doctor?"

"I've a few specials to check on, if you've no objections."

His voice, she noted, was as starched as his manner: only

his fever-bright eyes betrayed him. Guessing at the cause of that fever, she moved even closer until one elbow brushed his shoulder, ready to tease him into a caress. It was the move of an expert, made without haste. He avoided the invitation just as expertly, bending his handsome blond head above the list so that his shoulder disengaged gently from the lure.

"Shall we do the ward together, Miss Ryan?"

"As you wish, Doctor."

He got up briskly, snapping the evening report into a clip board. She followed him, a correct pace in the rear, as he emerged from the office and turned down the first long file of beds. For the next half hour she was outwardly the efficient ward nurse, giving the senior intern the benefit of her special knowledge. Inwardly she was seething with anger. First Julia spurns my advice, she thought. Now this damned refugee spurns my body. Is it because he's had enough of me?

Vicki was still regretting her own eagerness when they moved into the men's division of the surgical ward. Here the openly admiring smiles of the patients reassured her somewhat as she checked the bed charts one by one. After all, she had never depended on interns for solace. There were plenty of staffers with frigid wives (and it was odd, in a way, how many doctors seemed to be unhappily married). Patients, too, in the rich private wards, who had been eager to show their gratitude. No, there was nothing quite like the lift in her heart when she moved through this world of males and felt it come alive and press about her with its unspoken desire.

Tony left her in the private wing at long last, to enter the big corner room reserved for Bert Rilling. She turned back to her office, dismissing him from her mind with a shrug; already it seemed grotesque that his withdrawal could have caused her a moment's pain. Someone was moving inside the office: she saw the thin shadow on the ground-glass partition, and could have sworn that her visitor had just emerged from the padlocked door that opened into the narcotic cabinet. Then, as the outer door swung wide, she saw that it was only Emily Sloane.

"Good evening, Miss Ryan." The voice of the O.R. supervisor was strained, almost as though she could not focus her mind on externals. Had Emily been a stranger, Vicki would have said she was too drunk to stand. "What brings you here tonight?"

"Miss Rensselaer is on vacation. As usual, I'm the sub——"

"I'm glad you don't say that bitterly, my dear. Really, I don't know what the hospital would do without you——"

"Or you, Miss Sloane," said Vicki dutifully.

"We're two of a kind, aren't we? Married to our work from the start——" The supervisor broke the sentence abruptly, and offered Vicki a faraway smile.

"Are you quite sure you're well, Miss Sloane?"

"Quite—except for a raging headache. I stopped at your cabinet for aspirin. Good night, Miss Ryan—and good luck."

Emily Sloane was gone with the words, as quickly as she had come. Once again Vicki found herself blinking—if only to convince herself that this was really Emily, and not her wraith.

So we're two of a kind, she thought. Has the old hag been drinking, after all these years—or is she a drug addict without our knowledge? She put down an urge to check the medicine chest and laughed at her own melodrama. Like all old maids, Emily was probably suffering from the vapours—and no thwarted virgin, regardless of her vintage, was responsible for her remarks at such a moment.

And yet (her mind stuttered helplessly and tumbled towards fear again) Emily was right, for all her near hysteria. We *are* alike, and it hardly matters that she's a burnt-out ghost and I'm still pulsing with more life than I'll ever share. Basically, we are both unwanted and unloved—and our work is our only reality.

Can I change all that overnight? she wondered. Can I make my next man permanent, and forget the others I could conquer later? Perhaps a new beginning would do the trick. If I left East Side General, found a job uptown, played my game straight, with matrimony the only stake. . . .

The buzzer sounded on the call board. She noted the bed number automatically as she flipped the metal arrow back into position. Rededicated—and reformed in the twinkling of an eye—she marched out of her office and down the long, sterile file of the ward. And then, as a low whistle ran down the room, she began to smile naturally again.

After all, she'd been a fool to let that old maid perplex her. There were lots of good years left. She'd play the field a while longer and ignore tomorrow.

XIII

Emily Sloane leaned against the door of her room in the operating suite and waited for her heart to resume its normal beat. That had been a near thing in surgical—Ryan had just missed catching her in the act. Her fingers relaxed their grip on the vial in her uniform pocket. Three grains of morphine from the ward medicine cabinet: it would have been impossible to explain that theft to anyone. Even now, when it was no longer necessary to explain, she could feel her face crimson as she recalled her long series of thefts. Of course this was the first time she had robbed the narcotic room of three full grains.

She lifted the tube from her pocket—a slender container just large enough to hold the tiny white tablets—and studied it for a moment before she placed it on the table beside her bed. The syringe was locked in the drawer of her dresser; she opened the drawer with the key she always carried, and placed the instrument on the table, along with the kit that general practitioners used to prepare hypodermics in the home—a rack with a metal spoon, and a small alcohol lamp to sterilize the needle. Emily made these moves with no real orders from her brain. It was not the first time the syringe and its needle had served her. The small, puckered craters that starred her thighs from pelvis to knee were mute evidence in this long, losing battle against pain.

Now that she was prepared, she could afford to be deliberate. Methodically she filled the spoon with water and drew up alcohol into the barrel of the syringe—leaving it

there for the time required to sterilize the instrument. Even
now, when it no longer mattered if the syringe was sterile,
she still repeated the formula—standing back a step from her
night table while the water came to a boil over the spirit
lamp, and catching her breath, as always, when the needle
hissed at its first contact with the bubbling water. It was a
routine she had repeated oftener than she could remember,
as she had eased the suffering of a generation of patients.
This afternoon she could afford to savour it to the last detail.

When the needle was thoroughly boiled she picked it up
deftly by inserting the tip of the syringe and lifting it bodily
from the spoon—a technique which permitted the assembly
of the syringe without making the needle itself unsterile.
The water had boiled down, so she added more, for it would
take the full two cubic centimetres of the syringe to dissolve
the dose she was about to prepare. As it came to a boil she
dropped in the tablets one by one, noting how quickly they
dissolved in the boiling water. At this moment she was
enraptured by her task—a chef who is also a gourmet,
lovingly preparing a dish she would presently enjoy with all
her senses.

She noted that the water was milky when she had added
the last tablet and began to draw the solution into the barrel
of the syringe. For a moment she felt her mind dissolve in
panic, lest this viscous white brew clog the needle before the
full dose could be injected. Emily Sloane had never bungled
a hypo in her life—she did not mean to bungle this one.

The syringe filled at last, and she sighed as she watched
air bubble in the barrel, a sure sign that the plunger was
clear. As methodically as she had prepared the injection she
rolled her sleeve shoulder-high and sponged the skin in the
curve of her elbow joint. The vein, she noted, stood out
cruelly, for she had been losing weight steadily all this last
long year. Could she risk a main-line dose, after all? She had
not meant to inject direct into the circulation—that, after all,
was something only the hardened drug-fiend could afford to
risk, and she hadn't sunk to that level yet. Only once, ages
ago, when the pain had been more than she could bear.
She could still find the small crater, a bluish speck where

vein and skin tone merged, in the hollow of the elbow joint. In a way it would be an adventure to release this massive dose into her blood stream.

She watched her hands fumble in the drawer of the night table—and she smiled to herself. After all, this was Emily Sloane's night for adventuring. The rubber tourniquet whipped round her upper arm, tensing under her expert fingers as she made a fist of her free hand to distend the vein still further. The syringe sank home, deep in the pulsing vessel: blood spurted up to mingle with the milk-white solution in the barrel as she released the plunger.

With no hand free to release the tourniquet, she injected directly into the distended vein itself—and, while the decision was still hers, noted solemnly how the vessel turned blue under that added pressure. Instinctively, obeying the discipline of twenty years' training, she quickly washed out both barrel and needle, and replaced them carefully in their case.

The skin of her arm was an angry blue-red now, as the blood backed against the tourniquet. Some of the circulation was seeping into the nearby capillaries—she recognized the languor, a sweet preview of what was to come. But there was no time to waste if her plan was to be carried through. Her bed was waiting, she saw—the covers drawn back with geometric precision, the single pillow plumped and ready. For all her iron will, she staggered just a little as she moved towards it at last.

The familiar half coma had reached her muscles now. She could hardly summon the will power to release the tourniquet. There was a final jab of pain as the blood, dammed in the veins and suddenly freed, surged through in its journey towards her heart.

Lying at ease on her pillow, she could trace that inexorable flow. Already it had entered the subclavian vein that carried the blood from arm to heart. Now it was pouring into the right auricle, distending it against the closed pressure of the tricuspid valve, until the thrust of blood in that chamber exceeded the pressure of its opposite number and opened the valve wide. She could almost feel the quick surge, as the tide carried its burden of narcotic to the very centre of her being.

There was a fractional pause (was it one or two tenths of a second—it had been so long since she had studied physiology?) while the ventricle filled. She could feel the individual throb of her heart, so different from any other heart in the world. Or so she imagined, as she felt the blood course through her lungs and back again to the faithful pump that had never forgotten its function. The next beat would carry the blood through the pulsing carotids to the brain itself.

Time seemed to have no end while she waited: that fragment of a second, while her heart performed its function, was an eternity—and she would have liked to prolong it to the judgment knell. Never had she felt more at peace—or more dynamic. She had dwelt in this nirvana before, and lived to regret the aftermaths. It was a comfort to know that aftermaths were behind her.

For a moment, as the full impact of three grains of morphine smote her brain, Emily Sloane clutched at the dregs of consciousness. Then she felt the room, the hospital, the world blend and fade, like a trick movie shot, a measureless instant that held its own ultimate meaning. It was both the beginning and the end of wisdom.

For a while longer the body on the neat hospital bed continued to breathe, with a rhythm that grew steadily fainter, like a gramophone that has repeated a familiar melody once too often. Then the breathing ceased. The heart, preserving an inherent rhythm of its own, continued its function for a little time—even when the delicate controls of the brain were silenced for ever. Then it, too, slowed and stopped.

Emily Sloane had no consciousness to savour her one real triumph. For now, at last, the evil thing which was growing wildly in her vitals, the thing which no medical skill could control, was powerless. The flow of blood from the body it was bent on destroying was shut off at the source—and, with its ceasing, those maverick cells gradually ran down and stopped their living process.

Death had done what life had been powerless to do. It had conquered the wild lawless thing which had brought it about.

XIV

Descending the bright green slope of her seaward-facing terrace, Catherine Ash drew her terry-cloth robe about the two wisps of silk that served as her bathing costume. It was actually cool, here at the eastern tip of Long Island; the city seemed unreal as a half-remembered mirage. This, after all, was the corner of her universe she liked best—the home of her youth, where Martin Ash had courted her, where she had won her first great victory over her father, and where she had ruled as queen for more years than she cared to remember.

As usual she saw that her week-end party was a smooth-running success. The shouts from the courts told her that, as well as the laughter of the hardier swimmers who cavorted in the heavy surf that pounded on her private beach. But the routine triumph was empty without Martin's presence. And this, too, was a let-down too routine to be ignored.

She hugged her dressing-gown even closer as she hesitated of the top step of the terrace—not because of the fresh off-shore breeze but from a sudden feeling of loneliness and need. When she was at the estate she was never really afraid of losing Martin—these rococo walls enclosed too many shared memories. She could not even be angry at his neglect, here in this sea-washed peace. And yet she continued to linger on the outskirts of her house party while she fought her nameless dread.

In an effort to calm herself she let her eyes rove down the lawn to the outward proofs of security that surrounded her. The estate had been built by her grandfather: today it resembled a Victorian wedding cake forgotten in the sun, rather than the abode of living mortals. But it was magnificent nonetheless, from the scrollwork of its endless verandas to the last foot of velvet greensward, brought to the very edge of the beach and worked over lovingly by a corps of gardeners. The great windbreak of cedars and Norway spruce, standing in a solid wall above the stone and concrete breakwater that divided her acres from the open dunelands just beyond, was assurance enough that no one could molest her privacy

This was her realm, sun-drenched and wind-cooled. But how could a queen take pleasure in her domain when the king was absent?

It was absurd, of course, but she wanted the reassurance of his voice to prove that he was still alive. When she had driven down the green parkways this morning she had sworn that she would not call him again—but the temptation was too strong to resist, now that the long day was waning. Somehow she missed him most of all at this perfect hour, when sea and sky were a haze of bluish gold and the air above her lawn was a warring symphony of gulls. Why, when all this beauty was his for the asking, did he cling to that slum-girdled hospital, as a baron to his donjon?

Ignoring a shouted invitation from the surf, Catherine turned back to the house, at a pace that resembled a run. Wide, striped awnings welcomed her gaily to her veranda. The tall, grave hallway, where her father's portrait, done in Sargent's best flamboyant style, frowned at her above his riding-stock, muffled the laughter from the tennis courts and the cries of the wave-harried swimmers. She was alone again—forsaken in the midst of plenty, with only an aged butler to welcome her.

"No New York calls, Burke?"

"No, Mrs. Ash. Were you expecting one?"

"Not really, I suppose. Will you see if anyone wants cocktails?"

She waited until the butler had gone before she opened the library door and picked up the telephone. Her fingers trembled as she dialled the East Hampton operator and asked for Martin's private number at the hospital. Thanks to her taut nerves, it seemed a long time before her call broke through the circuits to New York. Like the condemned felon who stands with one foot on the gallows trap, she saw her whole life in this too large, too comfortable mansion course before her eyes while she waited. Catherine Parry as a girl of six, standing at the same teakwood table to open her mountain of birthday gifts. The same Catherine, at sixteen, calling yet another number to ask why a long-forgotten beau was late for their dance date at the club. . . .

The phone began to ring at last in the shuttered office of the director of East Side General—even at this distance it seemed to resound against empty silence. Had he been pretending when he said that his presence at the hospital was essential? Was he lying on some uptown divan at this very moment, deep in dalliance with one of his own nurses?

Of course she was a fool to neglect her guests for this fruitless call. Even if he answered he would refuse to join her. Far back in her brain she heard the echo of her father's voice—as sharp, in its clipped wisdom, as the vibration of the telephone bell, a hundred miles distant in New York:

"Every doctor's wife feels neglected, Catherine. I suppose you're prepared for *that*, too?"

"I'm prepared for anything. Nothing matters now but Martin—and Martin's success."

"A noble sentiment, my dear. It does you great credit. Has it occurred to you that your Jewish suitor might do with a bit more rope—and a good deal less nobility?"

"You needn't be cynical, Father——"

"Cynicism is the name young people always give to common sense. I've told you before that you love him more than he loves you. That means you'll never be done pestering him. Coming between him and his work. Calling him when he wants to be alone——"

The ghostly dialogue died in her memory as the telephone bell beat against her ear. Her mind ranged over the immediate past, testing each moment they had shared together. What tell-tale signs had she overlooked in her complacence? She could not deny that they had quarrelled more often of late. Or that there had been too many nights when he had left her side to sleep alone. . . . A year ago she would have laughed at any hint of infidelity on Martin's part, in word or deed. The phone was ringing furiously now, as though the operator shared her impatience. Where were his secretaries, even though his own private office was empty?

Then she recalled that this was the tag end of a Saturday afternoon and that the crowd of stenographers would have left the ante-room long ago. Even Martin's personal watchdog (who resembled a filing cabinet more than a woman) would have quitted the office to enjoy what was left of the week-end elsewhere. Only Martin remained, driving himself at tasks a hundred hands could have performed as well as he.

No matter what threat might hang over the hospital tonight, it was monstrous that they should be apart. When she hung up at last she stood staring at the book-lined wall, wondering if she could bring herself to ring the hospital direct and force the switchboard operator to track her husband down. But even in her present mood such an admission of failure was beneath her.

When she walked out to her terrace again the voices of her guests seemed to come from far away, like echoes in a dream. The voice of her father, dead these many years, was clear above the babble. She made no effort to shut out its bitter wisdom. *I love him more than he loves me,* she thought. Why can't I give him a moment's freedom, a chance at real happiness?

"I say, Mrs. Ash? Aren't you coming for a dip?"

She looked up gratefully at the laughing boy who stood on the last broad step that led from lawn to surf. For that instant, at least, she wasn't quite sure of his name, or why she had invited him to the island—but the candid admiration in his eyes was enough for now. Forcing a laugh, she tossed aside her beach robe and ran down to take his extended hand. She was glad, at least, that her honey-brown tan more than matched his own, that her figure (revealed, for all the world to see, by those two wisps of silk) was lithe as any girl's on the beach.

"There's a heavy surf running," said the boy as they waded into the foam-curled shallows. "Don't go too deep, if it frightens you——"

She remembered him now, with a sudden, grateful lift to her heart—the young Englishman (a delegate at the United Nations) who had paid her such extravagant compliments at last night's dance at the Waldorf. Even his name came back. Stanley Potter, an Oxford blue who had chosen diplomacy as his career, rather then the bar. She laughed back at him as she plunged through the first towering breaker and struck out for deep water.

"Why should I be afraid? I was born on this beach!"

He followed her in a long, running dive that brought him abreast of her as the next wave crashed on their heads. Feeling his arms close about her to lift her through the sun-shot foam, she knew that he had planned this moment deliberately. Let him make love if he insists, she thought, and made no effort to free herself when they broke surface together.

"So sorry, Mrs. Ash," he said, and released her at last. "I had to be sure."

"Sure of what, Sir Stanley?"

"That you could swim as well as I. Wouldn't do to let one's hostess drown, you know."

"Does it look as though I'm drowning?"

"On the contrary, Catherine. May I call you that?"

"Why not—since you saved me from a watery grave?"

She spurned him as she spoke—with a heel at his midriff. Swimming the hard, eight-beat crawl that Martin had taught her one summer, she set her course for Spain.

"I say, Catherine! Don't drown a man before his time——"

But she did not slow her pace until she had cleared the ground swell and floated at ease in calm water, far beyond the last ripple of surf. It was amusing, in a way, to wait serenely as Sir Stanley Potter churned up at long last. Even more amusing to note the light in his eyes as he admired the slow thrash of her legs in the Atlantic ground swell.

"Thanks for staying in the race," she said. "I'm most grateful——"

"Don't be, please," he said. "So far I haven't been permitted to save you from drowning. Offhand, I don't think I've saved you from anything."

XV

Martin Ash climbed the tenement stairs that led to his parents' apartment—climbed them slowly, without quite facing the impulse that had brought him here. When a man is approaching fifty, he thought, he finds it difficult to face up to his childhood needs—the instinctive search for reassurance that has been the heritage of every child since Adam. In his case the need was complicated by a deeper reverence for the father, for this, too, was part of his blood, an instinct which no departure from his birthways could erase.

Now as he turned the knob of his father's door, knowing that it would be unlocked against his coming, he heard the throb of the radio just inside. The swelling notes of an aria building to its climax. For a second Martin Ash hesitated on the threshold. When he opened the door a cautious crack he saw that the tiny living-room was darkened as always— illuminated only by the green arc of the radio dial. There was his father, crouched against the machine, with the same prayer shawl about his shoulders, despite the heat. It was too late for withdrawal now. Martin Aschoff, Sr., had already turned towards the whisper of the opening door.

"Come in, son. I thought you were on Long Island——"

"Catherine went out to join her guests, Papa. I was detained at the hospital."

"Yes, Martin. When I heard the news I hoped you would stay."

"What news, Father?"

The old man touched the radio gently, a movement that was both caress and reproof. "Most often, this magic box gives me back my dreams. Sometimes it speaks of reality as well—and I feel it is only fair- to listen. I know the threat you are facing across the street, Martin. Did you come to tell me more?"

"There's no more to tell, Papa. In fact, I'm sure there's no more real danger for the hospital——"

"Did you come to reassure us, then? Did you think we would be afraid?"

"Of course not." I came to renew myself, thought Martin: but you know that as well as I. Aloud he said only, "Where is Mama?"

"Mrs. Hefner from next door is bringing back her daughter's baby. From a nursing home in the Bronx. Mama went to help her."

"Then it's well I came. I'll phone the hospital and tell them to send over a supper tray."

Martin Aschoff, Sr., lifted his eyes in mild reproof. "You should know your mama better, Martin. When has she left me without my supper? There are sandwiches and beer in the icebox. I can see well enough to find them."

The head of East Side General dropped into his usual arm-chair and lit a cigarette. Now that he was here he felt no need to explain why he had come. He watched the old man carefully, knowing that he would never question this extra visit. But his father was already speaking, as though he knew the danger of silence.

"Will you go to Catherine tonight, son?"

"I don't think so. Not until this danger is really behind us. She has more than twenty guests—she won't be lonesome."

"I still say that Catherine needs you, Martin. Remember, you have your work when loneliness comes. Your wife has nothing but you—and her hopes for you———"

"Catherine has her friends, Papa. And more interests than she can name———"

"Look at those friends closely—and those interests. You will find they are only pastimes, while she waits for your return." Martin Aschoff spread his hands above the glow of the radio dial, as though he could warm them in the flood of music that poured into the room. "Remember the words of Nietzsche—*Man says 'I will', woman says 'he will'*. It is the wisdom that all wives learn with time."

"I'm with her almost constantly, Papa." The younger Martin, puzzled by this oblique attack, watched his father warily through the smoke of his cigarette. "It isn't my fault I can't be with her now."

"It is quite impossible, then, that you go to Long Island tonight?"

"How can I leave the hospital, with this threat still hanging over us all?"

"You are right, of course. Your rightness does not make Catherine less lonely."

"A man can share just so much, Papa."

"And yet a man must share everything with his wife to

make a true marriage. It is a dilemma no man can solve completely."

"What would you have me do?"

"Share your work with her, Martin. Share your hopes and fears. Not just your love. There are other things in marriage besides love."

Share my work, thought Martin. That's easy enough to say, from your high plane of serenity. And then he remembered how often he had looked up into the observers' gallery at the clinic, while he was finishing a difficult operation, and found Catherine's intent face among the students. How often she had sat quietly at his side as he shouted his hatred of the world that had snubbed him, and gloried in his triumphs over others. It was true that there were vast areas of his past she would never understand fully, just as she would never grasp his desire to keep the hospital here, where it belonged. Yet her failures did not come from lack of trying.

Had he tried half as hard to span the gulf that sunders men from women—to touch her hand in comfort, how ever briefly?

"You should listen oftener to music, Martin."

He looked up at the old man's dim profile, startled again by his penetration. It was quite true that the music, poured so prodigally from the mahogany throat of the radio, had soothed the last of his doubts away. He remembered how often Catherine had begged him to go with her to the Philharmonic or the opera, and how patiently he had taken refuge in his work. It was strange that he must return to his father's house to rediscover the release that great music could bring. Stranger still that he should be unconscious of this abiding content until his father had put the reason into words.

"What are they playing now?"

"Handel's *Messiah*," said his father. "There is no greater beauty in the world."

"I wish I could come oftener, Papa. I'd give a great deal to listen more and think less——"

"You need give only your time, Martin. How long since you have entered a theatre or a concert hall?"

"Longer than I care to say——"

"And has it been longer still since you sat quietly—and listened to another voice but your own ambition?"

Dr. Martin Ash bowed his head and made no attempt to answer. His father smiled and drew back into his own arm-chair, as though the question had been addressed to himself alone. For a long time they sat there side by side in the cramped, heat-drugged room, while the dusk came down on the mean street outside and the music soared to heights few mortals would dare to scale.

"Am I too ambitious, Papa? Have I forgotten how to live?"

"Ask Catherine, my son."

Martin Ash stretched his limbs in the deep arm-chair and made no attempt to reply. At another time this would have been a perfect springboard for argument. Somehow he felt no need to argue now.

"Life is so simple here," he said at last. "Why must it be so difficult when I step outside this door?"

"Perhaps, like all Americans, you ask too much from life," said his father. "Here we ask for little, and are happy with what we receive."

"Why can't I be happy, too?"

"Because you know your wife is unfulfilled, Martin."

"What would you have me do? Move the hospital uptown?"

"Take her to the next symphony, for a start. Show her that you love her for herself alone—not for the power she has brought you. Perhaps that is all your marriage needs——"

Another long silence fastened on the room, broken only by the symphony that was building now to its climax. "Perhaps I could believe in my marriage if I could trust mankind," said Martin. He spoke with difficulty, as though his mind were stumbling behind his eager tongue. Now he broke off in the midst of his diatribe and shook his fist at the radio. "How can anyone believe, when the same brain that creates such magic can plot to destroy the human race?"

"Listen, Martin. Listen, and try not to question too much. This is the voice of man's soul. It helps you to know and understand your own. It brings you closer to God."

"A God who lets men destroy one another?"

"Never forget that these evil things are fashioned because men misuse the laws of the Most High. The same God put music in men's souls—and helped them to put their dreams in poetry, on canvas, in stone. The same God gave you the healing skill you use each day——"

"Father O'Leary has used that argument often. It is not God who does wrong, but those who misuse His powers."

"Can you deny it for a moment? Look at history before you answer. How long did the great empires endure when they turned aside from God? Can you doubt for a moment that this country and its allies will outlast the evil men who rule Russia now? The power remains. It needs only a few wise hands to bring back the kingdom of Jehovah——"

"The Kremlin has more hands at the moment——"

"The evil flourish for a time: only the good are eternal. You are speaking as a child, Martin." Papa Aschoff held up a soothing palm as Martin began to speak. "And why not? It is good for a man to speak sometimes as a child—even to think as a child. There is too much hate abroad today—and too much greed: we must all return to childish things, if only to find the pathway we have lost. If only to remember that God is love."

"Have we that much love to spare among ourselves?"

"You have left your old way of worship, my son. Today you are a Christian like your wife. You should remember the teachings of the man you worship as the Son of God."

Martin opened his eyes wide. "Do you know them, too? I thought you had always been orthodox."

"I follow the teachings of the God who spoke to Abraham and to Jacob," said his father. "But there are many great teachers in the history of Judaism—and Jesus who was called Christ is one of the greatest. It was He who said we must all become as little children, before we could enter the kingdom of Heaven. I could even say that it was He who kept you at your place tonight——"

"As the director of a city hospital? I would have been happier as a slum doctor, with my surgery in this tenement basement——"

"You did what God intended, Martin. You will obey His will tonight. He is speaking to you now. Open your heart and listen."

Father and son fell silent, as the dying chords of the *Messiah* filled the room. When the music ended, Martin did not stir for a long time. When he got to his feet at last he bent above his father's chair and kissed the old man on the forehead.

"Thank you, Papa. I think I can go on now."

He never remembered weaving his way among the pushcarts outside the tenement stoop. The benign shadow of Jesus fell across his path as he crossed the hospital lobby and pushed open the door of his office—the empty, week-end office that had been so lonely an hour ago. For an instant he stood in the door, sure that he had caught the echo of a telephone bell.

Crossing to the desk to open the blotter that enclosed his unanswered mail, he wondered if he should call Long Island —if only to see how Catherine was faring. But he was deep in his work almost before he could switch on his desk lamp. Besides, it was the dinner hour, and Catherine would be fully occupied as the hostess of twenty glittering guests. She would hardly understand the peace he had discovered in that shabby tenement, at his father's side.

XVI

The reflected sunset still glowed on the East River—a clear blue light that beat hard against the drawn blinds of Bert Rilling's room. Tony Korff, pausing at the crack of the hall door, checked the picture carefully before he dared to enter a second time. Without glancing at the bed, he knew that the patient only pretended to be asleep, there in the shelter of the oxygen tent. Bert Rilling was an expert at playing possum when he was not quite sure of his next move.

Tony braced his shoulders and walked in briskly—the

model intern, completing his day's rounds, a little impatient over the last private patient whose report was not yet complete. The afternoon special, idling over a novel by the window as her patient continued to doze, rose instantly and put down her book. I've made my point, thought Tony. The wards first—in case Ryan noticed I'd come back to work early. The first ritual visit here, just to give the old gorilla a chance to hear my voice, to make up his mind about me. From this point on I'll play the scene my way.

"How's our patient doing?"

"He's had a wonderful day, Dr. Korff. I'm sure he's on the mend."

"The last hypo should have worn off by now. I think I'll examine him."

He moved towards the bed as he spoke—slowly, to give Rilling all the time he needed. The bullet-bald head inside the isinglass window turned slowly on the pillow as the brewer's eyes opened slowly—an excellent imitation of a man rousing from a long slumber. The skin stretched tight across that gleaming skull was now a healthy pink. Even with that jumpy heart, thought Tony, you're too tough to die.

"If you please, Nurse. . . ." The voice was muffled, but clear enough. Rilling gestured lightly with his fingers, indicating that he wished the tent to be removed. The special glanced at Tony, who nodded benignly—still the model intern, who understood that a man of Rilling's status must be deferred to in all things.

"Raise his head a little, will you?"

He stood back from the bed while the nurse complied with his order, and looked down at Rilling with no outward show of recognition. The brewer returned his glance under half-closed lids, the stare of a sick man who knows he will live again, and is uncertain whom to thank. Tony took a step forward and picked up the brewer's wrist, to test the pulse. "You're looking wonderful, sir. How are you feeling?"

"I'm not quite sure, Doctor. Rested, but weak——" The brewer's voice was low and throaty, and this, Tony knew, was real enough, the after-effects of last night's opiates.

"Has Dr. Plant seen you today?"

Rilling nodded, as though the effort at speech had exhausted him. Tony smiled as he felt the hot probe of his old friends' eyes. Play it slowly, he warned himself. You can afford to take your time with him. No matter how he bellows when you're alone, remember that you're on your feet and he is helpless.

"Dr. Plant was most encouraging," said the nurse. "He ordered that we discontinue oxygen at increasing intervals——"

"He examined Mr. Rilling, of course?"

"I have the notes here, Doctor."

"Never mind them now. I'll check him again, just for our own records." Tony studied the girl narrowly as he spoke, and wondered if she, too, realized that such procedure was superfluous. It was still worth the risk, if only to keep Rilling on tenterhooks a while longer.

With the nurse's aid, he spun out his examination as long as he dared, punctuating it with frequent questions. Blood pressure and temperature, he noted, were both close to normal. The patient still complained of slight pain in his legs, but this, too, was to be expected. Andy Gray, it seemed, had done his usual masterly job on another ailing carcass. Tony folded the covers neatly into place again, and thanked his colleague from the bottom of his heart. Bert Rilling was ready for the grill now—as ready as he would ever be.

"Why don't you go out and have a smoke, Miss Lambert?" he said. "I've finished my wards now, so I've plenty of time to get Mr. Rilling's history. He wasn't in much shape for it last night, you know——"

"That's very kind of you, Doctor. I'll be in the solarium if you want me."

He closed the door carefully behind her, but his heart was pounding as he turned back towards the bed. Rilling had not stirred from his pillow, and his torpid lids all but masked his eyes. When he spoke his voice was casually friendly, as though they had parted only yesterday.

"You took a long time, Tony——"

"I wanted you to get used to me gradually, Kurt—or do you prefer Bert, these days?"

"I recognized you this morning, you know——"

"I hoped you would. You aren't too proud, then, to remember old friends?"

Tony had spoken in German, as naturally as the man on the bed. He moved forward and held out his hand. Knowing Rilling as he did, he could only admire the other's aplomb. The years between, and last night's brush with death, had scarcely touched that iron strength.

"I haven't forgotten, Tony. In fact I wondered when you'd turn up again. It's too bad we must meet like this——"

Too bad for *you*, thought Tony. In the past you've been the user—and I the tool you discarded at will. The roles are reversed today—and you're well aware of that reversal.

"Does it surprise you to find me a doctor, Bert?"

The hand still held Tony prisoner. "By no means. I once offered to buy you a medical degree—remember?"

What Rilling had just said was true enough. In the old days, when he was at the apex of his power in Berlin, Kurt had been prodigal of his favours. Tony could even remember why he had refused the offer. Help of that sort, once it was granted, could put him in Rilling's power for ever.

"I settled for America instead," he said quietly. "So far, I haven't regretted it."

"You were wise to leave the Party when you did, Tony."

"So were you. I can see you've gone a bit farther than I."

"Little good it's done me. Your future is before you. I've used up my life—or most of it——"

It's coming now, thought Tony. His lips curled in an involuntary sneer. He had not expected Rilling to make his moves so crudely.

"Don't say that, Bert. You had a close call—but we pulled you out of it."

"Did you take part in the operation?"

"I was Dr. Gray's assistant."

"I've heard great things of you, here at East Side General. Will you let me help you, when you're qualified?"

"I've never refused your help before, Bert."

"You wouldn't let me make you a German doctor."

"And you know the reason why. I didn't want to join the battalion of death. This is different."

Rilling smiled for the first time, and Tony noted instantly how that wolfish grin transformed his face. In repose, the brewer's moon-like countenance was an ideal advertisement for his product—a good man's visage, shining and benign. Now, as his thick lips drew back in that familiar grimace, he looked what he really was.

"So we are model Americans together, Tony?"

"Ready to help each other," said Tony. "I'd say that completes the picture, wouldn't you? There's only one thing I can't understand. If you admired my career so much, why didn't you get in touch with me sooner? One might almost think you'd been avoiding me——"

"So we are honest with one another now," said Rilling. "I *have* avoided you. Somehow I felt you might not approve of me, now you have turned respectable. It is good to find I was mistaken."

It's coming faster than I dared hope, thought Tony. Aloud he said only, "I couldn't let you do me favours for nothing——"

"We could have gone far together, if we'd stayed in Berlin," said the brewer. "But that is nothing, when one measures his chances here. Will you set up your practice in New York?"

"That was my plan from the start."

"I have connections here, you know. Very good connections. You'll live to bless the day you found me, Tony——"

"Is that all you do? Make beer and the right connections?"

Tony had put the whiplash in his voice deliberately. He matched Rilling's grin now, as the brewer winced slightly under the blow—then shrugged, in an excellent imitation of acceptance. At least we've stopped fencing, he thought. From here on we'll hit each other openly, without pulling a punch.

"Beer can make a man rich, Tony."

"Smuggling can make him richer," said the intern. "And the profits don't show on his tax return."

"Are you calling me a smuggler to my face?"

"I called you worse names in Berlin. Don't tell me you're getting soft."

"Try me, Tony." The brewer's lips were tight now. "Just don't try me too far."

"I'll go on guessing until you stop me. Just tell me how right I am. For a start, you brought your money out of Germany—and your address book. You've been shipping everything that could fly or float, from enemy aliens to heroin. You're a smooth operator, Bert. So smooth that you didn't slip once—until yesterday——"

The brewer's lips had begun to show blue against his pallor. Wondering how this soft tirade had affected his patient's heart, Tony sampled the pulse by instinct, even as his voice purred on. "Right so far, eh? That pile of rotten bricks across the way is only a blind—even if you do manage to show a profit on your books. A perfect blind for the sort of work you do after hours——"

Rilling broke in at last. "It's fortunate you can't prove a word of this, Tony."

"Old friends don't need proof, Bert. Not if they understand one another truly. Remember, I *am* your friend—and you never had too many."

Tony paused, but the rotund body on the hospital bed did not stir. When Rilling spoke at last his voice was calm enough. "Go on, *mein Schatz*—I am still attentive."

"Whatever you were handling last night, it was too hot for anyone but you to touch. And that was just as well, because something went wrong *en route*. I'm really guessing now, but I'd say it happened in the brewery—and that you're the only living witness——"

The pulse under his hand fluttered like a dying bird. If my finger were the antenna of a lie detector, thought Tony, I couldn't measure your panic more accurately. But he kept his voice as mild as Rilling's. "Try to be calm, Bert," he said. "Remember, I'm your doctor as well as your friend. Your heart kicked back on you last night, I gather——"

"*Jawohl*, Tony——"

"Because the job was left unfinished?"

"Put it so, if you like. It saves us time."

"Does that mean you need me? It's more than I dared to hope."

"Don't be too clever, Tony."

"But I'm eager to help you, Bert. How can you doubt that for a moment?"

"On your terms, *nein*?" The brewer's accent seemed to grow thicker with each laboured breath. Inured as he was to his old friend's gutter patois, Tony found himself straining for the words.

"Doctors must live, Bert, as well as brewers. I've finished other jobs for you, at your price."

"Perhaps I will not need you after all."

"Would I be here if you could do without me?"

"Still the same old Tony, aren't we? As smart as ever——"

Tony turned away from the bed. Now that he had made his point, he could feel his heart swell with triumph. But it was too soon to permit Bert Rilling to read the exultation in his eyes.

"Tell it your way, Bert. I'm tired of guessing."

He listened impassively while the brewer's tired voice purred on. From what he knew of Rilling, and what he had pieced together at the *Chronicle*, he was sure that his former associate was telling the truth—or, at least, enough of the truth to serve his purpose now. So the stuff was locked in the brewery safe, whatever it was. Delivery was due at midnight, aboard a freighter across the river. All he need do for Rilling was open that safe, extract a heavily sealed bottle, show a light in the doorway that faced the river, and wait for the scrape of a boat-hook on the quay just below. Captain Falk of the *Baltic Prince* would take care of everything thereafter. The story has a classic simplicity, thought Tony wryly. In three minutes more it will seem even simpler.

"What's in the bottle, Bert?"

"It is better that you do not know."

"I suppose you're right, for now." Tony smiled at his own secret, and did not turn from the window. "Won't Falk be surprised when you don't appear in person?"

"I have delivered other shipments by other hands than mine."

Tony paused, while he weighed that barefaced falsehood. "What if the night passes without a signal of any kind?"

"The freighter is already cleared by Customs. She will leave with the tide."

"And your business goes down-river with her, if you fail to make this delivery."

"By no means. But it is simpler for all concerned if these shipments leave on schedule."

"There is still time to send the captain a note. You must tell him that I, and I alone, will be on the quay tonight."

"It is better that he does not know your name, Tony."

"Much better. You need say only that a man in a surgeon's white coat will be waiting with the package—and that he is authorized to take the usual fee."

"I am far to weak to write, Tony."

"Let me write the note. You can still sign your name."

He was doubly positive of his control when Rilling offered no protest after he had settled at the writing-table. Words came easily to the sheet of hospital note paper under his hand. Habit, he reflected, died hard. He would never have expected Kurt Schilling to sign without protest, when the instructions to Captain Falk were down in black and white: Bert Rilling's name, slashed across the bottom of the page, was only a logical aftermath.

"Shall I read it aloud?"

"Never mind, Tony. I'll trust you that far."

"What shall I do with his cash payment?"

"You can bring it here tomorrow." The brewer's voice still seemed an echo beyond the tomb. "We can divide it down the middle—if that's agreeable."

Tony permitted his wolf grin to expand in earnest. Back in Berlin, he had never expected more than a straight payment for services rendered. "What's the usual fee for this shipment?"

"The cash will be in a plain envelope. You can count it later, if you insist."

"Don't keep me in suspense, Bert——"

"The usual fee is fifty thousand, for this kind of shipment."

Tony stifled his gasp of surprise, just in time. He had not permitted his mind to dwell on the financial return for tonight's work. Now that it was within his grasp he felt no particular emotion—only a deep sense of relief that this favour he would do Bert Rilling was both a beginning and an end.

"You'd divide fifty thousand down the middle, Bert?"

"Why not—since I've no choice?"

No choice indeed, thought Tony. What happens tomorrow is something else again. You're protecting your contact abroad tonight—and damn the cost. Tomorrow it will be a simple matter to eliminate me, as a threat to your future.

"Tell me one thing," he said. "Isn't it risky, playing a lone hand for ever?"

"We were both born to take risks, Tony."

"Isn't there a single Yankee you can trust for this job? Suppose I hadn't turned up?"

"Maybe I've been saving you for just such a moment. Had you thought of that?"

"Put it another way. Maybe you're at the end of your rope, and God sent me. Or was it the devil—since neither of us believes in miracles any more?"

He watched the brewer rear up feebly in his nest of pillows and then subside: the hands that soothed Bert Rilling could not have been wiser or more impersonal. "Sorry, my friend," he murmured. "Don't mind that rough edge to my tongue. You should be used to it by now."

"Could I—have some water, Tony?"

The glass straw and the lily cup were already in his hand. He watched them from a great distance, while Bert drank thirstily. Part of his mind was fastened on that bird-like pulse, the unmistakable cyanosis that had begun to invade the porcine jowls. Another part (in its way, the most active) was measuring the power of fifty thousand tax-free dollars in the life of a freshly graduated intern, about to carve out a practice in the cliffs of Manhattan.

"The combination for your safe, Bert. Where is it?"

"In my brief case over there along with the keys. You—go in by the side door—between the nurses' home and that block of tenements——"

Tony picked up the bedside chart with a small flourish. He had learned all he needed to know: the rest was routine.

"Things will look better in the morning, Bert. You won't regret trusting me."

"I'm sure of that, *mein Schatz*——"

"I see that Dr. Plant has prescribed a sedative. Would you like to drop off now—and wake up tomorrow with your job done?"

He did not quite wait for the brewer's reply: the syringe was already in his hand, masked by the towel on the night table, before his mind registered Bert's feeble nod. "Heparin," he said smoothly. "Just to guard against another clot. Not that we expect a recurrence, of course." Once again he blessed the easy hospital patter that disguised his real thoughts—to say nothing of the tremor in his fingers as he tested the plunger of the syringe.

"Sure you want it now, Bert? You can wait for your own doctor, if you prefer."

"I want to sleep tonight. The sooner the better." The brewer's voice was only a hoarse whisper, the whining eagerness for the needle that every intern knows.

Tony's hands were still shaking as he lifted the syringe and drew the barrel full of air. Nobody knew just how large an air embolism was needed to kill—but fifty cc. should do the job nicely. He glanced quickly at the door. Rilling's afternoon special had seemed well trained. He could hardly believe that she would burst in without knocking.

"The shot, Tony! For God's sake, the shot!"

So you're really suffering, thought Tony, letting his eyes trail down the purple silhouette of face and jowl on the hospital pillow. In a way, it might be simpler to leave Bert's future to the devil after all—but fifty thousand was fifty thousand, no matter how one measured his chances. He moved swiftly to the bed, his free hand already closed round the tourniquet.

"Make a fist, Bert. This won't take a moment."

The tube of the tourniquet bit firmly into the pneumatic flesh of the brewer's arm: the veins swelled out instantly as Rilling clenched his fingers. With a flick of his right wrist

Tony dropped the towel that had covered the huge syringe. Masking his move with a downthrust shoulder, he smashed the needle home into the first vessel. As the point sank in he wondered if Rilling had noticed that he had failed to swab the skin with alcohol. Germs would do the brewer no harm on the journey he would commence in a moment more.

Blood spurted back into the empty syringe before he could jam down the plunger. This was no time to risk a clot in the needle, blocking the lethal injection into the vein. His skilled fingers told him that air had already begun to bubble into the blood stream—and he let the plunger rise slowly under his detaining thumb. The pulse of power in his throat threatened to choke his own life away. For the first time, he thought, I'm both doctor and executioner. No one under Heaven would dream of questioning the death certificate I'll be signing in the next half-hour: a post-operative embolus, produced by a fibrillated heart. The one nemesis that medicine can never hope to conquer. Even Andy Gray will endorse my report.

"Is that morphine you're giving me, Tony?"

His hand soothed Rilling back to the pillow. "The best medicine in the world. A medicine that cures all diseases."

"It doesn't feel like a shot——"

"Why should it, my friend? It's only air."

"*Air?* But won't that——"

He felt the plunger jab his thumb, and knew that the syringe had emptied itself into the vein. In one deft motion he flicked the needle from the doomed man's flesh, dropped it on the night table, and fastened both fists on Bert's shoulders, holding him hard against the pillows.

"It already has, Bert. Can't you tell?"

The brewer opened his bluish lips to howl, but no words came. Tony's fists were firm as two steel claws, pinioning the feebly writhing body to the bed. He watched the left arm jerk and go limp, sure evidence that the air was reaching the victim's brain.

"Good-bye, Kurt. Just remember what you'd have done to me tomorrow——"

The body jerked one more time, as the victim's eyes seemed

about to pop from their sockets in the immensity of that final struggle for life. A trickle of blood appeared at the side of Rilling's mouth, where he had bitten his lip in that final convulsion—and then the lips, too, went slack.

Tony Korff stepped back from the bed, snatching the syringe as he moved. Rinsing it carefully, he covered it as before with the sterile towel. The room was still quiet as the tomb, and there was no sound from the hall outside. Tony breathed deep and choked down a howl of triumph as he pressed the buzzer. Once more he had gambled and won.

XVII

Stained by a half century of grime, the window of the Greek's offered, at best, a dim view of the esplanade and the doors of East Side General. Tonight, as the last sun faded on the walls of the facing tenements, Julia Talbot was not quite sure whether the soaring white flanks of the hospital were real or a mere afterpiece to her day-dream. She sat at ease in the wall booth of the dingy restaurant that served the hospital staff at all hours, knowing that Andy would emerge from that tall white prison in time.

The telegram in her purse crackled under her hands as she bent forward to sugar lukewarm coffee. She opened the worn handbag and spread Timmie Gray's message on the unhygienic marble table. There was no need to read a wire she already knew by heart—but she wanted it ready for Andy's eye, when he sat down beside her. Not that she expected him to be too surprised: once she had made up her mind, she had felt peace descend on her shoulders like a visible cloak. If Andy refused to share that peace, so much the worse. She could only make the offer.

"Have you been waiting long?"

Now that he stood above the table at last, she looked up at him with startled eyes, as though a stranger had addressed her. Though she had seen him only a few hours before, he seemed older—and far more tired than she remembered. The white surgeon's tunic under the rough tweed knockabout was his uniform even here. With no sense of volition, Julia put out one fist and struck softly against the starched armour— as though she still hoped to touch the man beneath.

"Won't you sit down for a moment, Andy?"

"If it's only a moment," he said, and his voice was as haggard as his manner. "Of course, your note said it was urgent——"

"Urgent to me, at least," she said, forcing a smile. "Why did you insist on meeting here?"

"I thought it was time we had an appointment outside. Will you forgive me if that's sentimental?"

She watched his hand pass over his eyes and linger there. "I'll forgive you anything, Julia," he said. "It's just that I've had a long day. It was a shock to lose Rilling, you know. Of course I was afraid all along that an embolus would finish the job. So for that matter, was Korff——"

Julia did not answer. She knew that she should resent his indifference to her nearness—to say nothing of the way she had summoned him here. It was enough to have him at her side, even if his mind was far away.

"I hope *you* aren't too tired to do Jackie with me tonight," he said. "I've already excused Korff as my assistant. He seemed a bit under the weather. Dr. Easton is coming up from pathology to take his place——"

"You know I wouldn't miss Jackie for the world."

"You can have Miss Ryan to help, if you like," he said. "I've already put her on call, if we need her——"

"Must we talk about the hospital now, Andy?"

"Habit dies hard," he said, and managed a grin of sorts. "I know I should be polite and ask why you summoned me so abruptly. But I'm sure you'll tell me in your own way."

"I want to say good-bye." Her voice trembled a little but her eyes did not waver. "Somehow, I wanted to say it outside the hospital."

"So you're leaving nursing while there's time?"

"Not nursing, Andy. Just East Side General." She handed him the telegram and waited quietly while his eye ran over

the words. "As you see, I didn't send that letter after all.
This is a confirmation of a telephone talk I had with your
brother in Florida. He told me to choose my own time of
arrival. My resignation is on Dr. Ash's desk right now.
Jackie will be the last scrub I'll do for you——"

"Unless I come to Florida, too?"

The violence of his interruption startled her, but she kept
her aplomb. "You think I'm quite mad, of course. Well, I
return the compliment, with interest. You're killing yourself
here in New York. Killing yourself deliberately, because you
can't conquer the itch to be another Martin Ash. In Florida
you could wake up some morning and discover you're
alive——" Her voice broke at last, and she covered her face
with her hands to hide the tears. "But of course that's too
much to ask of any man. Especially when someone's waiting
to buy him everything——"

She felt his fingers close on her wrist, and stared at him
out of tear-dimmed eyes as he took her hands away. "Is
that why you're running away? Because the spectacle is more
than you can bear?"

"Call it one of my reasons, if you like," she said hotly.
"But I'm not running away. I'm going where I'm really
needed——"

"I won't ask you to reconsider," he said gravely. "I'll
just tell you why I was late. Then we can go back and finish
our last job together——"

"I can guess why you were late, Andy. You were talking
to Pat Reed, weren't you? Making an appointment for
tonight, after Jackie's operation?"

"Pat did ask me to drop in on her later," he said with
that same maddening calm. "But I only talked with her a
moment on the phone—*that* isn't what delayed me. Emily
Sloane was found dead in her room a half-hour ago. I had to
certify the death as suicide."

Julia stared at him blankly, feeling the tears dry on her
cheek. Somehow the news did not really startle her. It was
almost as though she had guessed at Emily's unhappiness long
ago—as well as its probable cause.

"Don't you want me to tell you why she died, Julia? It

was carcinoma first, of course—you must have had some
inkling of that. But Emily was suffering from slow death
in another form. Loneliness killed her, too. The sort of
loneliness that only a busy woman knows, if she happens to
be unwanted——"

"Why are you telling me this, Andy?"

"Isn't the moral obvious? Let Timmie find himself another
Nightingale. Get out of nursing while you have your looks,
and catch yourself a man." He dropped her hands abruptly,
as though he already regretted his outburst. "Of course you
haven't heard a word I've said. In your way you're just as
mulish as I——"

"Just as mulish, Andy," she agreed. "Shall we get back
to work?"

They rose together and walked through the lunch-room,
into the cloying heat of evening. Neither of them spoke as
they crossed the esplanade and entered the long white
shadow of the hospital. It *is* a white shadow, thought Julia.
A shadow pale as death—and pure as an angel's robe.

"Do you feel you're coming home again, Andy?"

"I'm going back to work. Isn't that enough, in our
time?"

Back to work, thought Julia. And he means every word.
His work and his life have always been synonyms. He's much
too wise to separate them now, to ask for different meanings.

"It's the only home we'll ever have," she said. "I suppose
I'm a fool to hope for more."

"It feeds and shelters us," he said. "On occasion, it makes
us feel like God. Win, lose, or draw, it's something to belong
to——"

"East Side General—or the whole cult of healing?"

"Does it matter too much?"

As though by common accord they paused just outside the
wide-open doors that opened on to the great lobby—and
the statue of Christ that dominated the stair-well beyond.
Without pausing to look into that benign shadow Julia knew
that Father O'Leary would be waiting there, serene as time,
and just as certain that man's future, like man's past, was in
good hands.

"Let's go in by the nurses' entrance, Andy. I couldn't face the padre tonight."

"Why? Are you ashamed to be running out?"

"It isn't I who's running out," she said, and marched down the long curve of walk to enter the hospital from the rear.

He did not speak again until they were in the familiar shadow of Schuyler Tower. "Try not to hate me, Julia. I belong here, even if you don't——"

You and Martin Ash, she thought swiftly. Her eye had already caught the steady glow of light from the director's office window. She knew without asking that Dr. Ash was seated there, in the precise centre of his air-conditioned haven —with his day's work behind him, and no more destination than the whisky-rotted tramps who were howling at this same moment in the alcoholic ward. East Side General was a haven for everyone, she thought. An impregnable breakwater to life's gales—a shelter for all comers, regardless of age, race, or creed.

"Tell me one thing, Andy," she said. "When were you last outside?"

She felt the probe of his glance and knew that he had grasped her meaning before he spoke. "Is that a leading question?"

"Try to answer truthfully. It's really important."

"Why should I go out at all? I belong here, like an abbot in his monastery——"

"Somehow I can't picture Pat Reed married to an abbot," she said.

"You needn't be catty, just because you've found your own escape."

"Sure you won't risk an escape, too?"

"Come along, Julia," he said. "That's quite enough satire for one evening. They're setting up now for Jackie——"

"We're still outside the door. It isn't too late to run for our lives——"

"Never mind our lives," he said. "We were created to save other lives. With no thirst for glory in between. Or have you forgotten that?"

Even as he spoke his hands fastened on her shoulders. He

turned her slowly, giving her every chance to draw away before he pulled her into his arms, for another of those kisses that seemed to have no ending. "Be happy in Florida, Julia," he said when he released her at last. "You deserve happiness, more than most of us——"

Her eyes dared him to say more, but he had already stepped back to let her precede him. They did not speak again as they crossed the dusk-dimmed court of the nurses' home and entered the elevator that would take them direct to the surgical ward. Our private war, thought Julia, has been fought to a finish. Whether you surrender your sword in the next few hours is your decision, not mine.

III—NIGHT

I

THE clock above the door of the operating suite in East Side General Hospital pointed to half-past seven when Dr. Andrew Gray walked in at last. In the familiar tiled hall that led to the theatre itself he paused a moment more, if only to remind himself that this was his last Rubicon. Now that Julia was behind him, he had regained some measure of calm. After all, if she persisted in her insane resolve to leave the hospital he was the last man to stop her. Time, that miracle among healers, would mend her illusions—including the belief that her happiness and his were hopelessly twined.

I can walk up to that table when I like, he told himself: there's no need to say another word. Once she's put a thousand miles between us, she'll forget me fast enough.

In the past hour he had briefed Dr. Ash on the operation he was about to perform. In the tiny ante-room he had just quitted, Jackie's parents would wait with renewed assurance, thanks to the words he had just spoken. But this was no time to think of parents as people. Jackie himself was only a problem now—a stubborn enigma that would need all his skill. He walked resolutely into the operating room—and cursed inwardly as the lights above the table began to blur. He had told himself that Julia would be on hand as always, getting ready the last of his instruments. He had not expected his eyes to mist at the thought of losing her.

The door to the scrub room opened to receive him, before Julia could lift her eyes from her work: he felt sure that she had kept her glance lowered deliberately. Once the door had closed, he knew that he was safe. It did not matter that Dale Easton was already scrubbing at the long basin—and regarding him with a meditative eye. From the moment he dropped his elbows into the antiseptic he was his own man again.

"Sure this isn't too much for you, Dale?"

"On the contrary." The pathologist chuckled as he reached for a nail-brush. "I'll admit I'm as nervous as a junior nurse. But I'm an old enough bird to know it'll pass. Providing I get the proper briefing now."

"Surely you've seen enough of these cases in autopsy?"

"Too many, Andy. What are the chances of saving the boy, really?"

"Better than fifty-fifty—and I'm not being immodest." Andy could feel his nerves steady with each word he spoke. Already I'm more machine than man, he thought. When I face Julia across the table she'll be part of the machine, with no human emotion involved. He thanked God for that self-imposed detachment. Long ago he had learned that he must hold aloof from the tug of life, in order to save life. He would need that aloofness tonight.

"The clinical picture is clear, of course," said Dale Easton. "A block in the blood flow to the lungs, plus a defect in the partitions of the heart itself. You propose to create a connection with the arterial system, via the pulmonary artery——"

Andy heard his friend's voice purr on from a great distance. The healing knife, he thought, can do wonders: it can even create a new heart, if the hand that guides it is expert enough. I could have made my own heart whole by speaking a dozen words tonight—and I held my tongue instead. The accusing voice faltered and died, far back in his brain. He forced himself to match the pathologist's tone. The gallery would be crowded tonight, he knew: in his way, he needed a warm-up quite as much as Dale.

"Call it a sport of nature, if you like," he said. "In the developing child there is normally a connection between the pulmonary arteries and the aorta, so that blood need not be pumped through lungs that are not functioning. Unless it closes properly after birth, you must operate and tie off that connection. In Jackie's case the reverse is true: you must create a similar opening artificially. The same condition can either save life or threaten life."

"The philosophy of the scalpel, eh?"

"Exactly. In the hands of a bandit the knife can kill. Properly used, it can bring life."

"So could atomic energy. I doubt if we'll see the day."

"Don't despair so easily of the human race. It's a slur on the way you earn your living. Remember, when we were interns the only treatment for hyperthyroidism was surgery. Nowadays the patient merely swallows a dose of radioactive iodine and becomes a human isotope. In a week or two the iodine concentrates in the thyroid, radiates the diseased gland, and delivers a cure."

"Not always."

"The average is considerably over eighty per cent. A higher figure than we could ever hit with surgery, and a lot safer. Who can say the same weapon can't be aimed at cancer some day? If poor Emily had been born a half-century later she might be alive and well."

Dale Easton finished scrubbing and began the meticulous technique of drying hands and arms. "Don't climb out of your own century so fast. The human race may never survive it—even though iodine *is* now radioactive."

"Don't tell me you were resigned to being atomized an hour ago?"

"Prepared is a better word, Andy. Do you think that fellow bolted for cover, whoever he was?"

"That's my guess right now—even if the police won't admit it. These foreign agents are glamour boys only until they're cornered." Andy broke off to smile at Vicki Ryan as the tall nurse half-opened the scrub-room door. It had not surprised him when she had surrendered her ward tonight to assist at Jackie's ordeal. He knew that the news of Emily Sloane's suicide had shaken Vicki to the roots of her being—even as she realized that the mantle of supervisor would almost surely fall about her shoulders.

"Give us two minutes, Miss Ryan, and we'll start prepping."

Vicki's voice was an adequate shield for inner turmoil. "Isn't Dr. Korff scrubbing for this one? I already have his gloves out."

"Tony's a bit under the weather. I think we can manage with Dr. Easton, don't you?"

Vicki raised her brows at this unfamiliar attempt at levity. She knows why I'm making bad jokes, thought Andy. East Side General has marked her for its own tonight, and it'll take her a while to adjust herself to that bitter knowledge. He glanced over Vicki's shoulder at the bustle in the room beyond. At the moment he could rejoice with all his heart that Julia had chosen to escape.

"Isn't this quite a change for Dr. Easton?" The tall nurse was still impersonal as ice—her usual manner in the shadow of the operating table. "What size gloves does the doctor wear?"

"Seven and a half will do," said Dale. He sighed as he watched Vicki's trim body flick from view. "Poor Ryan," he said softly. "I suppose it's quite a shock to admit she's ending up respectable."

"Quite," said Andy—and turned to his work in earnest as the probationer entered with his gown on her stiffly extended forearms. The priest's white robe, he thought, the sterile garb of the healer, shutting me away, for a while, from the woes of mortal man.

Gowned and gloved at last, he walked into his domain with his hands folded in a towel. He saw at a glance that all was in readiness. Jackie's body seemed very small, in that high-domed room, under the merciless white bath of the lights. Dale had finished the elaborate prepping: their young patient lay on his back, with the right side of the chest slightly elevated and the whole operative field swabbed a bright carmine. The tiny intratracheal tube was in place, feeding its steady mixture of oxygen and cyclopropane into the lungs, along with a slight amount of ether. Jackie's breathing, Andy noted, was regular and quiet. As always, there was a slight bluish tinge at lips and ear lobes, owing to the boy's faulty heart. Actually he was receiving more oxygen than usual. Thanks to the cyclopropane, it was possible to administer an even higher concentration of that precious element than was normally present in the atmosphere.

"You haven't lost your touch, I see, Dr. Easton. Will you attach the oximeter?"

He stood back while the pathologist fastened the precision instrument to Jackie's ear lobe before changing his gloves. The oximeter was another of those modern barometers that gave a wealth of information to any surgeon during a long-drawn major operation. Constantly recording the colour of the patient's blood, it could sound a warning of its own: increasing redness indicated richer oxygen levels, decreasing redness a lowering of blood oxygen. In Jackie's case the initial reading would be well below normal: Andy did not wait for it now.

He met Julia's eyes just once, while she was arranging the square-windowed sheet about the patient's body. It was a glance that told him nothing. He gave himself a moment more, moving deliberately to inspect the items in his steel arsenal, one by one. There were his scalpels, their blades protected by gauze pads. The gleaming clamps that would secure the first small bleeders. The periosteal elevators and costatome, in case it became necessary to remove a rib. The strong-jawed rib spreader, ready to separate the rib cage, once the pleural cavity was entered, and open a space where the surgeon could work in safety.

On the larger table beyond, ranged in precise ranks, were the delicate rubber-shod clamps that would be used to stem the flow of blood in the vessels where the actual short-circuiting operation would be performed. Beside them were the delicate needles to carry gossamer-slender silk through the walls of those same vessels, establishing the vital anastomosis which would shunt the blood towards the oxygen-rich bed of the lungs.

"We're ready when you are, Doctor."

He knew it was Julia who had spoken, and inclined his head gravely as he walked back to the table. Violating the principle that a good actor never looks at his audience, he raised his eyes to the glass wall of the observation gallery. He had expected a crowd tonight, for this was a rare operation, and the very nature of its delicate anastomosis between major channels of the circulation made it of particular interest. But he was unprepared for the jam-packed gallery, the triple file of faces hanging like disembodied moons above the floodlit universe where he reigned supreme. He dropped his eyes to his work and spoke for the microphone just over his head.

"This is a classic case of the tetralogy of Fallot. We have already determined that the aorta lies in its normal position, on the left side—and, therefore, will make our incision at the right side of the chest, entering the pleural cavity through the second interspace if possible——"

He heard his voice drone on, and hoped that his hand would be as steady when the steel made its first stroke. Across the table he met Vicki's eyes, blue as winter ice in the bath of incandescent light. Julia, waiting at the instrument table in the penumbra, was only a vague white blur, and he would keep her in that same focus until the operation ended. Julia's behind me now, he thought, a might-have-been I'll regret all my days. Julia has escaped, but I am trapped—and docile, in my way, as Vicki Ryan.

"As you will observe, we are using the Blalock technique. Maximum exposure will be attempted, between the second and third ribs. Our object is to anastomose the subclavian branch of the innominate artery to the right pulmonary——"

From the corner of one eye he caught the wink of steel. Julia had already picked up the first scalpel and stood ready to slap it into his gloved hand. He gave the room a final evaluating glance, much as a general might survey a battle field selected long ago. Instruments in place, to the last suture needle; dressings prepared, including the large, moist pads which controlled bleeding and retained body heat as well. . . . For an instant he recalled his R.O.T.C. days in medical school—when the students had learned to raise hospital tents by crawling under the spread canvas and seizing the poles. He could even hear the muffled chant again, and smell the sere aroma of crushed grass.

"One ready, two ready, three ready, four ready——"

The wall clock hung on the stroke of eight. He turned to the anæsthetist and received his nod before he spread his hand across the table, palm up. The scalpel slapped hard against the glove. He did not look at Julia as he bent above the patient and the square of carmine-tinted skin that would be his

universe for the next few hours. The blade touched that square
of skin, hesitated a moment, then cut through in a smooth,
sure stroke.

II

Tony Korff paced his carpet for the hundreth time, and
forced himself not to glance at the clock on the dresser.
His pulse had outraced that timepiece for the last hour: he
knew that another eternity must pass before he dared to
venture out, though it was quite dark in the air shaft now.
I'm rusty at my old trade, he told himself—and settled at his
desk to fumble at a cigarette. Ten years ago I'd have taken
this job in my stride—even though my own future hangs on
its success. Why can't I be calm tonight, when it's sure to
go like clockwork?

When eight-thirty struck in Schuyler Tower he would
take up his medical bag, if only to complete his masquerade.
Following the corridor to the fire-escape, he would quit the
hospital by the nurses' garden, to make sure that he was
unobserved in the main halls. It was an escape he could have
followed blindfolded, thanks to his rendezvous, in that same
garden, with a generation of probationers. Once he was clear
of the surgical wing, it would be easy enough to enter the
maze of streets that bordered the hospital to the west. Even
if the police cordon was still enforced, the black bag would be
his passport.

In his mind's eye he could pace out his progress from that
point on. It was better to sit here quietly with his head in his
hands and review each hazard that awaited him. Far better
than to stagger to his feet again and wear out another strip
of carpet, while his nerves cried for action. Straight down the
squalid tenement block that housed the Aschoffs. Turn sharp
right, into the alley that cut back towards the brewery, and
the sweep of cobbles that led to the landing platform. The
door to Rilling's private office was just inside that rusted
iron cave—deep in shadows, no matter what the hour

Rilling had said there would be no watchman tonight. His fingers dropped to the pocket of his jacket, to finger the key to the outer door, and the matching key that would give him access to the office. The combination to the safe was in his pocket, too, but he did not need those figures now: the last turn of the tumblers was blazoned in his mind for all time. With an eight-thirty start, he could swing the safe door wide long before the stroke of nine. It was only a few steps across the brewery floor to the door that opened from the inside, direct to the quay. No one would notice his flashlight as it winked in the crack of that half-opened portal—no one, that is, but Captain Boris Falk, waiting across the river.

Tony Korff raised his head from his hands and studied the afterglow that lingered on the hospital ramparts. Then, with no real knowledge that he had risen, he was on his feet again, pacing the room like a baulked tiger. Somehow, he told himself, I must find a way to pass this next half-hour or go mad. I can't show my face in the building, now I'm officially on the sick list. I can't plan the spending of that fifty thousand again, without screaming aloud. . . .

In a way, now that Rilling was safe on a slab in Otto's morgue, he could regret the impulse that had made him snuff out the broker's life. Fifty thousand was pin money, after all, when he compared it to the vast sums that his former mentor had milked out of America—and America's enemies overseas. And yet it stood to reason that Rilling's days were numbered. It was safer, by far, to take this quick bundle of cash and let the profits of tomorrow go on glimmering.

Fifty thousand would buy him the practice he had yearned for since he had first set foot in New York. A maisonette surgery on Park Avenue, a receptionist-nurse handsome as a magazine cover, and a list of patients straight from the Social Register. With skill at his finger-ends, he knew success would be assured, once that long first step was achieved. In three years' time he could meet Martin Ash and Andy Gray on their own battlefield and fight them for patients. Celebrities from two continents would be numbered among his intimates. His private phone list would include the great beauties of the world. When Pat Reed was in town he would have a latch-key to her back door, where he would come and go at will. . . .

Pat Reed. His hand closed on the throat of his telephone, as he recalled that encounter on the hospital esplanade—and the challenge she had offered. The purr of that siren voice was just what he needed to ease his racing heart—or rather, to re-route its hammer blows into another, more familiar rhythm. Yes, he would call her now—and pray that she was home and unoccupied. He would meet her this very night— the moment this business at the brewery was ended, never mind the hour. With luck and a little audacity, he could beat Andy at his own game.

His voice shook after he had dialled the switchboard and asked the operator for Pat's New York number. But his purpose, and his tone, were both firm as steel when he heard her low, provocative murmur on the wire. In your way, he thought, you're my hope of Heaven—and my eventual reward. What's more, I'll have you in the next two hours.

III

In the office downstairs Martin Ash tossed aside his medical journal. It was time to face up to the fact that he had no business lingering here, with Catherine waiting on Long Island. High time to admit he was on his way—that love (to put things bluntly) was stronger than duty tonight. Yet he made no motion to pick up the phone as he swivelled back in his desk chair. It was one thing to admit his desire for a woman, even if that woman happened to be a wife of long standing. Quite another to acknowledge that he must come back to her on his knees or not at all.

It is not good for man to rest on his knees, he thought— save in his adoration of the one, the living God. He broke his wordless tirade in the middle and walked to his office window, avoiding the phone as though it were a coiled cobra. Even in the closing darkness the esplanade outside the hospital seemed to vibrate with heat waves. Sealed off as he was by the miracle of air conditioning, he stared back dully at the summer night, as though he could not quite believe in its existence. It's cool on the island now, he thought. A bracing coolness, fragrant with the breath of the sea. The bedroom windows will be open to that salt-sweet air. She's waiting for me there at this very moment—waiting and confident that I can no longer resist her.

Tonight Catherine would expect more than an apology for his day-long absence. And yet their quarrel (if one could call it that) would end on the same ritualistic note—with her sweet acceptance of his submission, the understanding that she had won the point at issue. Martin Ash banged a fist against the heavy thermal glass that insulated him from the hot breath of the slums outside. Of course it was his own fault, for daring to fight a woman. It was like hitting a pillow, he reasoned. All of a man's power was eventually swallowed by that terrible softness. Sometimes he suspected his wife of planning their quarrels deliberately—if only to be sure he would give in later.

In the same breath he admitted that his malaise tonight went deeper. He was afraid to go to the island tonight: surrender at this time would mean that her domination was complete. The projected move uptown, which he had opposed so long and so valiantly, would be the visible token of that surrender. He felt his fist close on the telephone—even as he fought down the urge to dial long distance, and called his father's number instead. It was a needless call, he knew, but it would hold temptation at arm's length a moment more.

The old man's voice came quietly into the room. It was easy to picture him, a mere hundred yards away, crouched above the radio that murmured faintly in the background.

"What is it, Martin?"

"You're all right, Papa?"

The question was part of his mood, and he regretted it at once—before his father's chuckle offered its own gentle rebuke. "Like your mother you are, Martin. Of course I am all right."

"You've had your supper, then?"

"An hour ago. You saw how Mama fixed me a nice sandwich of salami and a bottle of beer."

"Then Mama hasn't returned yet?"

"Why should I need Mama here? I have my music. All I need is within reach. And I can find my way about the place without bumping into furniture—you both know that."

"When did she say she'd return?"

"About nine o'clock. She phoned just now to say she would be on time."

"Shall I send someone over to read to you?"

"I need no readers, Martin. I have Beethoven with me now——"

"Shall I come myself, then?"

"Go to Long Island, my boy. What is keeping you here?"

Martin Ash felt the breath choke in his throat: somehow he had not expected his father to supply his final shove to serfdom. "Nothing, I suppose. If *you* don't need me——"

"It is your wife who needs you. How often must I tell you that?"

"I'll leave in a few minutes, then. If you're sure Mama will be there by nine——"

Again the quiet chuckle soothed him, despite his near panic. "You know Mama, boy. If she says nine o'clock, then nine o'clock it is."

Martin Ash did not signal the operator when his father broke the connection across the way. Now that his mind was made up, he felt oddly resigned—quite as though his surrender had been on the books from the beginning. First, of course, he must call in Andy Gray and turn over the reins of command until Monday. Then he would drop under the steering-wheel of his convertible and refuse to think at all until the sick heat pall of New York was behind him. He had all but begun to dial surgery when he remembered Jackie—and the operation that would seal Andy off from interruption.

Normally he would have called the surgical supervisor and left his message—but Emily, too, had gone to a place where no telephone could menace her tranquillity. He sat back in his chair and thought hard about Emily Sloane for a while—wishing, with all his heart, that he could feel a more personal grief for her suicide. Somehow he could hardly summon her image, though they had worked side by side for years. In its way that was the most frightening discovery of all—the grudging admission that Emily had been more machine than woman.

Perhaps he, too, was admired rather than loved. A machine that did its work perfectly, and closed off all contact when the long day ended. He took a final turn in his office, pausing to glare at the square of notepaper on his blotter. Julia Talbot's formal resignation from his staff, effective immediately. Not that it had come as any great surprise. He had studied the girl carefully of late and guessed at her deep unhappiness. The hospital needed Julia, he told himself with a small inward pang: she needed Andy Gray even more. And yet, how could a machine like himself deflect Julia from her objective?

Martin Ash shrugged off the last frustration of the evening and called his Long Island home at long last—wondering, while he heard the phone ringing in his library, why he felt no shame in his surrender.

When Burke answered after the tenth ring he kept his voice steady. This was no time to quarrel with servants, simply because he had resolved to cease quarrelling with Catherine.

"Mrs. Ash is not here, sir."

"She must be, Burke. She's expecting me."

"She left two hours ago, Doctor. By car, I believe——"

"Left her house-party?"

There was a small pause at the other end of the wire: he could picture the butler's look of triumph. "Most of our guests dined alfresco tonight, sir—if you'll pardon the expression——"

So they haven't missed her yet, thought Ash. It's her dinners they come to enjoy. Never the poor-rich girl with the lonely heart. He put the absurd image aside firmly.

"Did she go alone, Burke?"

"Indeed no, Doctor. Sir Stanley was with her."

Stanley Potter. A picture of the fair, slender Englishman came into his mind unbidden—a lover from any woman's dream book. But that picture was even more unreal. A woman of Catherine's age and habits simply did not take a lover so openly. Not even to spite a hesitant husband.

"Are you there, Doctor?"

"Yes, Burke?" If his mind had not been jumping so madly he would have enjoyed the picture of Catherine's butler, trying hard to be diplomatic—and failing.

"If Mrs. Ash calls back shall I say you're on the way out?"

"Tell her to call me at the hospital. I'm not sure of my commitments." He had not meant to be so formal with Burke, but he could not regret the icy tone when he had hung up. Sir Stanley can have his innings now, he thought—I'll have mine later. For the present, it's enough to learn that my wife is *incommunicado* with the man of her choice. Catherine will never know how narrowly I escaped complete surrender.

He sat quietly in his office, uncertain of his next move. If Catherine was really on the loose with a lover, he was the last man on earth to interfere. The reason for that passive resistance dawned on him gradually—and the wisdom he garnered was bitter, so bitter that his mind rejected it automatically, without pausing to wonder. Catherine is unhappy, he thought. Catherine is alone. Being alone, she has sought the first, facile substitute for love—an Oxford blue, from the U.N. team, a boy who could pass for Rupert Brooke in the proper lighting.

He rose at last from his swivel chair and moved down the gloomy hall that led to the rotunda. Father O'Leary still waited in the shadow of the Redeemer's statue—but Marty Aschoff was in no mood for redemption tonight.

Instead, he moved quickly to the left and stepped into the first elevator to surgery. Andy Gray was his second in command, and Andy would be busy for the next two hours. He would find a seat among the observers and watch Andy at work—until the cloud lifted from his brain.

IV

Andy Gray, lifting his eyes for a fraction, saw the shadow move and settle in the students' gallery. Martin Ash had joined his own interns at the observers' post. At the moment

Andy could not be sure whether he was flattered. The director's moves, in the past month, had been too puzzling to chart.

He spoke for the microphone, ignoring the late arrival. Ash would have approved the impersonal tone, he knew.

"You can see the exposure of the right lung hilus, and the great vessels." Puzzled though he was by the presence of his chief, he could still permit himself a small grin. The lay-out, so far, was as plain as a textbook drawing.

"It is usually best to inject novocain into the hilus at this time," he said—and he was addressing his assistant now, as usage demanded. "It blocks some of the sympathetic supply to the vessels of the heart and cuts down spasm of the vascular tissues."

"What about the pericardial sac?" asked Dale. "Isn't novocain indicated there as well?"

"Occasionally. It doesn't seem necessary here. The heart is regular and quiet——"

He swept the gallery with his eyes—and tried hard not to over-dramatize the gesture. Then he took the syringe and the long, slender needle from Julia's outstretched palm and injected a small amount of the anæsthetic solution round the tissues of the lung root. It was a touch-and-go technique, and he was careful not to enter the arteries or the thin-walled veins which passed into the lung tissue at this point. A delicate, even a tedious, step in the operation that was not yet launched, in the true sense.

Ten minutes later he stepped back from the table and permitted the sterilized probationer to mop his brow. From this point, at least, he was certain that enough of the solution had been injected to block the nerves in this vital area.

Throughout, the lung continued to function as regularly as a metronome. Andy noted that the pulsation had lessened, ever since he had opened the chest. The anæsthetist had once more lowered the gas pressure, varying the function of the organ to the convenience of the operator.

"You may inflate when you like, Dr. Evans," he said. "We'll wait a few seconds."

When he glanced up again at the gallery he saw that Ash had vanished from the phalanx of students. For no reason he could name, he was relieved that his chief had come and gone so quickly.

Under the revelation of the lights their small patient seemed more than ever inhuman. Thanks to careful surgery, the whole chest cavity lay exposed at last: rib spreader and costatome had done their work well. But the textbook image persisted, even now—when the operation for which they had prepared so meticulously would be launched in earnest. Andy's brain insisted that this exposed lung, and the complex network of vessels that embraced it, were living tissue, as sturdy as time and as delicate as a flower. Yet he recoiled from the next, inevitable knife stroke. Here, after all, was a supreme work of art, created by an immortal hand. It seemed a sacrilege to touch it.

"I can deflate the lung now," said the anæsthetist. "Oxygen tension is well maintained."

Andy nodded soberly: Evans's quiet voice had brought him back to realities without a jolt. A long forceps came into his hand, with a sponge held firm in its jaws. The steel probe moved deep into the wide red rectangle where the throbbing lung had already quieted. Using the sponge as a cushion, he pulled the lung root aside. The vessel came into view, precisely where he had expected to find it. A vein the size of a man's finger, arching over the lung root and lying against the thin pleura covering the back wall of the rib cage.

"The azygous vein. We must cut through it to immobilize the vena cava. It lies just above and partially covers the right pulmonary artery—which we will use in the anastomosis."

Again he had spoken by the book: even the newest intern could see that much of the picture. The vena cava, the great vein that brought blood from the head and upper extremities on its return journey to the heart, lay fully visible in the operative field, swelling and emptying with the pulsations of the heart itself, and the changes in pressure of respiration. An injury to this key vessel would have been irreparable.

At Andy's nod, Dale Easton took over the sponge-tipped forceps and held the vein in place while Andy slit the pleura with a pair of long, curved scissors and freed the vena cava for several inches. A pair of forceps clamped the azygous vein securely for the ligatures that were already waiting in Julia's outstretched palms. It was a simple matter to cut the vein and secure the severed ends with those tough strands of silk. Thanks to this partial immobilization, Dale was able to retract the vena cava well upwards, exposing still more of the area where Andy would fight his climactic battle.

A whitish, slender filament had now come into the operative picture, just above the hilus of the lung—the vagus nerve, lying close to the right main bronchus. The knife, skirting the filament as it went about its work, was careful to avoid direct contact. Vagotomy, the deliberate severing of the vagus nerve, was used in treating difficult cases of stomach ulcer, for the nerve seemed to control acid formation in the gastric areas. In Jackie's case it was better left alone. The vagus (Andy admitted once again that the name of wanderer was well earned) also exercised an important influence in the nervous control of the heart. Tonight he could not afford to interfere with the function of that already abnormal organ.

With the azygous cut and the vena cava retracted inwards, the scalpel was free to discharge its first real task, the freeing of a bluish structure that formed part of the lung root, beside the great branch of the bronchial tree. Andy spoke for the microphone again, but he was hardly conscious of his voice. His whole being was centred on the throbbing vessel under his fingers, the slow, careful progress of the knife.

"I am dissecting the right pulmonary artery free at this point. Just below where I am working, nearer the heart, is the block which interferes with the flow of blood to the lungs. Since we do not dare enter the heart itself we must ignore this constriction. Instead, we are about to make an abnormal opening, surgically, between a major branch of the aorta and the pulmonary artery which I am now exposing. Thus blood will be forced back through the lungs, thanks to the high pressure which occurs in the aorta. The fault will be by-passed, and the blood will be oxygenated at a normal rate."

For an instant his mind came back to the textbook patter he was offering so glibly. Admittedly it was a too simple summary of a difficult and delicate procedure—a master-stroke of surgery that had needed years of study and research. And yet this very operation was already saving hundreds of children from a special doom. So far he had every reason to hope it would save Jackie, too.

The knife continued its meticulous dissection along the root of the right lung, tracing the soft-walled pulmonary channel nearer the heart—and moving outwards as well, into the border of the lung tissue, where the vessel divided to send branches into each lobe of the lung itself. It was vital to free enough of the lung artery to make the anastomosis without tension—and even more vital to proceed without hurry. Ten minutes later he stepped back from the table and rinsed his gloves in the sterile basin just outside the heat of the lights. He had completed the first part of the exposure in record time. The next step would be far more delicate, since it involved freeing yet another vessel—which he would use to shunt blood from aorta to lung.

He addressed the microphone crisply, ignoring the tug of his own excitement. "As you will all remember from your anatomy, the aorta rises from the left side of the heart and curves normally to the left, as it does here. The left carotid artery, which takes blood to the left side of head and brain, comes directly off the aorta on the left side. So does the sub-clavian, which carries blood to the left arm. On the right side, both these arteries originate in a single vessel, the innominate, which later divides into carotid and subclavian. If our plans work out we will use the right subclavian artery to make our join."

Working as he spoke, Andy had already eased the vena cava aside, towards the centre of the chest and the curving outline of the aorta just beneath it. As the vein moved inwards another artery became visible, originating from the side of the aorta and running outwards and upwards.

"Here is the innominate," he told the gallery. "I will now free it partially, so we can get a tape beneath it."

The scalpel dissected the innominate away from its anchorage for perhaps half an inch. A blunt, curved forceps, slipped cautiously beneath the vessel, opened its jaws to receive a moistened piece of cotton tape from Dale Easton. This in turn was drawn snugly under the artery, forming a

sling. Cradled thus, the innominate could now be drawn
upwards or downwards, as later exposure dictated.

"You can all see where the recurrent branch of the vagus
comes off here," said Andy. "If we injure it, the right vocal
cord will be paralysed, so we avoid it at all times. The branching of the innominate should take place right where the
recurrent laryngeal divides." The knife had moved with his
words, dissecting along the throbbing vessel. Now he lifted
it away with the tape, to investigate the area beneath. A small
branch appeared just under the main vessel. This he secured
with a straight Halsted clamp, before cutting through and
tying each end securely.

"What's that one?" asked Dale Easton.

Andy felt his lips relax in a grin under the mask. When he
spoke he knew that his words relaxed some of the all but
unendurable tension in the room.

"Have you forgotten the *thyroidea ima*, Doctor? Where's
your anatomy?" He turned again to the microphone, knowing
that the pathologist had returned his grin, under the mask.
"Here's what we're looking for, I think." His fingers had
already moved the vagus nerve aside and continued down the
lowermost of the two branches of the innominate artery, the
subclavian—until he had exposed more than an inch.

"As you will see," he continued, "it is important to free
as much of the subclavian as possible at this point. Otherwise, we would have a drag on the anastomosis which might
interfere with the flow of blood, or even impair the joining."

Stroke by careful stroke, he continued to use the scalpel to
free the artery from its bed, as it travelled upwards and
outwards towards the arm. When it was unattached to the
point of its own first division he stopped the long-drawn
dissection at last, and took the first small clamp from Julia's
waiting palm. This important instrument had pads of rubber
on each jaw, to protect the delicate artery walls. He placed
the clamp with infinite care before he permitted the spring
to shut its jaws, closing the subclavian just beyond its inner
end. Then, as an added precaution, he gripped the ends of the
rubber padding that projected from the steel pincers and tied
them securely together. With this technique it was impossible

for the clamp to slip later—an oversight which could loose a fatal hæmorrhage into the operative field.

"What about the circulation in the arm?" asked Dale. "You've cut off the subclavian entirely."

"The collateral circulation in this region will carry on. And a good thing, too. Otherwise, this operation would still be an impossibility."

A heavily braided strand of silk came into his hand—as Julia once again anticipated the next step in the operation. Working with the tip of a small curved forceps, Andy opened a space under the subclavian, as far outwards as he could go, just behind the first large branch. Then, pulling the tough ligature taut, he tied off the vessel, setting the knots as hard as he dared without injuring the arterial walls. Then he cut entirely through the vessel, a short distance from this final ligature. No blood flowed from either end, as the distant one was closed by the ligature, the nearer one by the clamp he had already placed.

The whole room seemed to hold its breath as he eased the cut section of artery free from the vagus and recurrent laryngeal nerves and brought it over to the side of the pulmonary artery he had previously freed from the lung root. For a heart-stopping second he was afraid that he had erred in his estimates, for all the painstaking review of the region. And then the subclavian came free in earnest and touched the other vessel with no trace of tension. Andy let out his breath, one with the collective sigh of relief round the table.

"It's still one for the books," said Dale, in the barest of whispers.

The pathologist had summed up the thought in every mind. Above him, he could hear the stir in the gallery as tangible as actual applause would have been. Precision and knowledge had paid dividends so far. If the balance of the operation proceeded as smoothly, there could be no doubt about Jackie's cure.

"We'll rest for a moment," he said. "As soon as I strip the adventitia. It'll give the circulation a chance to adjust itself to what we've done so far."

The job of removing a cuff of the thin outer layer of the

artery took only a few minutes—and he was almost sorry when he tossed the scalpel on the used-instrument tray and stepped back. He had been dreading this break from the beginning—this emergence from his battle to save a life, from the absolute concentration that had held his own life at a safe arm's length. At least it's only a moment's pause, he told himself. I needn't risk meeting Julia's eyes a second time.

Dale Easton covered the great, box-like incision with a warm, damp pad, and joined Andy just outside the circle of light that still prisoned Jackie's inert body. At the head of the table Dr. Evans had already stepped up the pressure of his instruments, feeding the patient the greatest possible concentration of oxygen during this brief interlude.

"Have we bothered him much so far?"

Evans shook his head. "There's no real shock—and the oximeter reading has hardly varied."

Andy wrapped his hands in the sterile towel that Vicki Ryan offered with a long forceps, and murmured his thanks as the tall nurse pushed a stool against his legs. Only when he had settled on this temporary resting-place did he dare admit how tired he was. This unlocking of taut nerves was only a token of what lay ahead.

"It's well that we waited until tonight, when everyone was rested," he said generally. Actually this familiar circle of faces had never seemed more exhausted. Julia, he noted with quiet satisfaction, had withdrawn a little from the group, to replenish her stock of saline pads at the sterilizer. The next move is mine, he thought solemnly. If we've another word to say to one another, I must be the first to speak.

He turned to Dale, forcing lightness into his tone.

"Well, Doctor—would you care to switch to surgery, after tonight's sample?"

The pathologist's eyes gleamed above the mask. "As a student of the Bible, you'll remember the rich youth's remark. 'Almost thou persuadest me to be a Christian.' Almost, but not quite——"

The muted whine of a siren cut into Dale's murmur—a wailing that seemed to come from the street below the surgery windows, matched by a twin banshee approaching from the

north. Andy felt his spine tingle to that familiar sound, even
as he remembered that Tony Korff was on the sick list and
could plague him no more tonight. Above him he saw the
gallery of interns look up as one man—and watched two of
them slip out to check their wards.

"Emergency's getting some business, it seems——"

"That's a police siren, Andy."

"So it is, now you mention it. Who d'you suppose they're
trailing—our friend the bomber?"

The whining died, as though the police cars had turned a
corner or converged on a common rendezvous. Andy got to
his feet again, shedding the unanswered question. Even if
death had shown its face outside, he could afford to turn his
back for now. The world and all its contradictions slipped
into limbo as he squared off from the table again and held
out a gloved hand to Julia.

▼

The whine of the sirens reached the brewery office faintly.
Tony Korff stiffened for an instant, then shrugged off the
sound as he bent above the office safe. So far he had needed
no flashlight to guide his progress from street to loading
platform, from platform to office door.

He had left the last door open, if only to be doubly sure
that he was alone in the brewery. Enough dingy light spilled
from the street lamps outside to prove he was the only living
being within these walls tonight, save for the occasional
scurry of a rat. Trained as he was in this kind of nocturnal
adventure, he could sort each sound in advance, without
raising his eyes from the knob of Rilling's safe. He could bless
that training now—and the nerveless calm that always
invaded him, once a job was under way.

Six left, seven right, three left. The outer door of the safe
sighed open on noiseless hinges, revealing four inner knobs.
Rilling had said that the bottle was in the upper right-hand
compartment. He began to spell out the second combination

with hands that did not waste a motion, feeling the hot wine of triumph beginning to bubble in his throat. *Three right, three left, reverse spin.* His fingers seemed to have a brain all their own tonight. Even without the combination, he felt sure that he could open that second door in a matter of minutes—with time to spare for the signal from the quayside.

Another rat crossed the brewery floor outside the office: he could hear the creature's scratchy progress as it darted round the copper-shod circumference of one of the great vats. Those vats were his friends, he thought—towering in the faint wash of lamplight, closing him away from prying eyes outside. Beside him, on Rilling's carpet, his medical bag gaped ready to receive its precious burden. *Three right, seven left.* He could afford to laugh aloud as he remembered the salute of the bluecoat on the corner. Another half-hour, and he would take that same salute again, without breaking his stride. This time, fifty thousand dollars in cash would be packed among the tools of his trade. Fat wads of bank-notes, green and beautiful—and who cared if each packet bore the thumb-print of Mars? That fifty thousand was the key to his emancipation, the open sesame for every doorway he had stormed in vain.

When the inner safe opened at last he squatted on his haunches for a moment before he dared to explore its contents. This time he was forced to use his flashlight—and, for one moment of blind fury, he was sure that Rilling had out-witted him after all. The steel cylinder of the receptacle, jammed with papers of all kinds, seemed to mock his darting hand as he flung this useless ballast to right and left. Surely the safe contained nothing but trash—German-language news-papers wadded into the deepest cranny, a bale of old bills that seemed to disintegrate under his clawing nails. . . . And then his fears exploded into a sigh of relief. There, in the very depths, was the dark, squat bottle—ice-cold to his touch, and far too heavy to lift with a single hand.

He held the flashlight between knees that were suddenly fluid as jelly as he eased the bottle from safe to desk. The old fox had concealed it well—there was no denying that. He needed all of five minutes before he could collect the paper snow he had flung about the office, jam the safe again, and close both doors.

When he had finished he sat with his back pressed hard against the door of the safe, his eyes mesmerized by that rectangle of lead on the desk top. The flashlight, exploring its contours cautiously, assured him that the seal was tight, the bottle itself undamaged. Some of his confidence returned when he forced himself to his feet, though he needed all his will-power to close both fists round the bottle. Once he had moved towards the outer doorway—and discovered that his burden was really no heavier than a sashweight—he began to get back his swagger.

The dial of his wrist-watch hung on the stroke of nine as he inched his way down the pitch-dark stair. He would be punctual with his signal—but not so punctual as to seem anxious. Captain Falk of the *Baltic Prince* (who had received his written instructions hours ago) would have no cause for alarm when he picked up the wink of the flashlight across the river.

The heavy bottle had begun to tug cruelly at his wrists, and he dared to set it down on the bottom step while he paused for breath. A bar of light fell across this portion of the brewery floor, and he felt his lips part in a wolf grin as he located its origin, high up in the white bastion of the hospital just across the narrow alley. In the excitement of his search he had forgotten that the walls of surgery abutted on the brewery at this point. That rectangle of light spilled down from the operating theatre where Andy Gray was sweating at his trade.

Tony's grin widened. It was good to think of poor, plodding Andy at this moment. To admit, at last, that he hated Andy with all his heart. He cursed Andy fluently, in his best gutter German, as he felt his way down the flank of the first vat, the bottle cradled in one arm now, like a monstrous football. There would be ways to hurt Andy later, after he had stolen Andy's girl clean away and established himself in practice. A hundred ways to prove that he was Andy's superior, as a doctor and a man.

He was between two vats now, moving by instinct,

testing each step for hidden obstacles. Above and around him
he could hear the bubbling of the sour mash in the vast
copper receptacles. He breathed deep of the familiar, acid
stench of beer in the making. The miasma stirred his mind
with half-forgotten childhood nightmares. He had been born
in the shadow of a brewery much like this; his first youthful
battles had been fought, bare-knuckled and alone, under those
same dank walls; his first fumble at love's counterfeit had left
him spent and unsatisfied, in that same shadow, at the tender
age of fifteen. Somehow it was right and proper that he should
cut his last tie with the past in this sweating cave.

It was pitch-dark in the rear of the brewery, where the
floor sloped slightly towards the wide double doors that led
to the quay. He felt his way with extra caution here, for the
concrete floor was all but awash, thanks to the dank exhalation
from the river that purred under the pilings. The key
turned easily in the lock: he felt the door frame give under
his hand—and cursed in earnest when he sensed an obstacle
outside. A quick exploration identified the crossbar, placed
diagonally across the entire width of the door frame: he could
make out the silhouette of the bulky beam through the
cracks in the wood. Try as he might, he could not reach the
quay from inside the brewery. His only choice was to leave
by the warehouse platform and trust to the dark to hide his
movements as he cut back through the alley to signal from
the water's edge.

Who had placed that crossbar—and why? Even the
stupidest watchman should have realized it was useless as a
protection against prowlers, since it could be removed in an
instant from the outside. Besides, the stout Yale lock he had
just turned with Rilling's key was ample insurance that no
one could enter the brewery from the water side. He damned
his own stupidity anew as he backed among the vats and
began his slow, crabwise progress towards the loading
platform, on the far side of the building. If he had remembered to check his signal station before he entered the
brewery he could have removed that crossbar and saved
precious minutes.

And then, as he hesitated just inside the door to the

loading platform, a fresh hypothesis assailed him, causing the
sweat to burst from every pore. What if that crossbar had
been placed *after* he entered Rilling's office? What if a second
bar was in place across the warehouse platform, boxing him
in the brewery as effectively as a mouse awaiting the arrival
of the cat?

The scream of pure terror died in his throat as he turned
the hasp on the door that opened to the warehouse platform
—and, by extension, to freedom. The door swung wide,
revealing the damp cobbles of the street beyond, and the
humpbacked silhouettes of the tenements. He had already put
one foot on the loading platform before he saw that the
street was no longer empty. In that flash he knew why those
police sirens had sounded in the night—and identified the
contours of the two prowl cars that waited for their prey

"Come out, Korff! We've got you!"

He knew the voice instantly, though the speaker was deep
in shadows. Inspector Hurlbut, the Nemesis from Homicide.
He could picture Hurlbut perfectly, waiting at his ease behind
the bullet-proof windshield. The click of the gun hammer in
the dark was part of that unbearable nightmare. It was
climaxed instantly by the two floodlights that enfiladed the
platform from left and right, bathing him in cruel radiance,
pinning him to the wall as neatly as a pair of hatpins might
spear a cockroach.

"Come out, Korff—and hold up your hands!"

He screamed in earnest then as he slammed the door
behind him and reeled blindly into the dark maw of the
brewery. The spatter of gunfire followed him as he ran, but
he knew that he was safe—until Nemesis and company could
shoot away the lock. It was only when he recoiled violently
from the copper flank of a vat, and all but dropped the bottle
cradled in his arm, that his mind focused on a plan of action.

At all costs he must get rid of that bottle before he was
forced to confront Hurlbut and explain his presence here.
There were lies that might succeed in court, even now.
Thanks to his medical bag, he could pretend that he had
come here to answer an emergency call, that his patient had
mysteriously vanished, that he had backed away from those

floodlights in natural confusion. They'd know he was lying,
of course—but what could they prove, besides illegal entry?

Or so he reasoned while he ran, hearing the hammer blows
on the huge warehouse door, the whine of yet another siren
as a third prowl car rolled up outside. *Ditch this lead-wrapped
horror—and ditch it now.* His mind, jumping madly from end
to end of the gloomy brewery, fastened on the next vat, the
slow, pulsating murmur of the fluids within. He stood on
tiptoe, clawing at the copper tun with his free hand, making
sure that the vessel had an open top. Try as he might, he
could find no hand hold, no means of pulling his eyes level
with that mass of sour mash. But it seemed the only available
hiding-place, and there was certainly no time to lose.

He heard the warehouse door squeak ominously, as though
hinges and wood were parting company—and realized that
the police had begun working on the hasp with a crowbar.
I've still time to turn the lock and admit them, he told himself
wildly. Time enough to face up to Hurlbut and insist that I
lost my head just now.

By grasping the lead bottle in both fists and putting out
all his strength he found that he could toss it head-high.
More than enough leeway to clear the head of the vat. He
heaved both arms a second time—and gasped out his relief
when the heavy lead container slithered over the edge and
plunged without a sound into the bubbling cauldron. Then,
lest they find him here and guess that he had jettisoned his
burden on the spot, he groped his way towards the warehouse door.

When the explosion came, it bowled him head over heels.
Half shielded by the flank of the next vat, he knew that he
had escaped injury for the moment, even as the whole brewery
seemed to blossom with chromatic light. In that flash he saw
his error—and its fearful aftermath. Thanks to its great
weight, the lead-lined container had plunged through the
thick skin of mash that floated on the top of the vat. Once it
had pierced this soggy crust, there had been nothing to stop
its progress, since the liquid beneath had almost the con-
sistency of water. Striking the metal floor of the vat, it had
splintered its seal in earnest, dumping its lethal contents into

the active mash and splitting the copperplated vat as easily
as though the walls had been lined with cardboard.

He heard a babble of voices on the warehouse platform
and staggered to his feet again—eager for human contact
now, even with handcuffs attached. At that precise moment
the second vat, igniting from the first as naturally as a giant
Roman candle, split its sides with a mighty roar. For that
suspended moment in time, man and the elements he had not
yet tamed stood poised and waiting, immobile as some
tableau from the deepest circle of hell. In that moment Tony
Korff knew his first remorse, and a rage that transcended
fear. Obeying that burst of passion, he flung himself headlong
against the sundering copper wall of the vat, clawing with
both hands to stem the devil's cauldron he had opened here.
For one crazy instant he knew that he had triumphed over
time and chance. Then, as the flood of mash engulfed him,
he ceased to know.

VI

Andy Gray was tying a suture when the first explosion
rattled the surgery windows. Intent on the task at hand, he
did not even raise his head. Detonations from without (whether
they were man-made, or simply God's thunder) had always
rumbled into silence before. He felt the slight jar underfoot,
and sensed the alarm in his operating team. As the guiding
force of that team, he could not pause to give alarm a name.

"Steady, all," he said without inflection. "Clamp, please,
Miss Talbot."

The clamp had already come into his hand—the next link
in the delicate connection between blood vessels that would
save Jackie's life. For the past half hour the surgical team
had followed its textbook technique, with no important
deviation. The artery that would bring a fresh supply of blood
to Jackie's lungs was free and ready to do its part in the vital
union. The lung artery that would supply the only missing
link was prepared and delivered into the operative field. Now,

with the clamp ready in his palm, he moved down the exposed
barrel of the pulmonary artery and clamped down sharply,
precisely as he had controlled the flow in the subclavian. The
arterial wall was closed, as far back as he could manage. He
made sure that the jaws of the clamp were double-locked—
and held out his hand for the surgical scissors.

There had been no more explosions so far, and part of his
mind was obscurely grateful for the quiet that had settled on
the table at this climactic moment. The functioning part of
his brain, the dynamo that directed hand and eye in the
battle he was fighting against death, still held aloof from
outside threats as he poised the scissors for the next stroke.
The surgery windows rattled a second time.

Dale Easton spoke the uniformed thought aloud, as he
stood ready across the table. "Is the heat wave breaking, or
is it only Saturday night?"

"A bit of both, I'd say. Stand by to sponge, please——"

The scissors moved precisely, slitting the side of the
vessel between the clamps. Dale's fingers moved quickly
into the incision, sponging away the small amount of blood
that had gathered in the artery between the clamps. When
the pulmonary artery was ready, Andy delivered the end of
the subclavian into the operative field. For an instant he held
his breath, though every nerve in his finger ends told him
that both vessels were now prepared for anastomosis. Then,
with a conscious steeling of his mind, he delivered the subclavian into Dale's fingers, while he took up a fresh scalpel
and enlarged the cut he had already made in the lung artery.

"Sutures, Miss Talbot——"

The delicate needle was already in his palm, with the
slender strand of silk threaded precisely at the eye. This was
the most important, and the most difficult, part of the entire
operation. So far they had proceeded by the book. Their
technique had been a miraculous blending of tactile dexterity
with the facts of anatomy—those same tedious facts that most
interns had memorized and forgotten long ago. From this
point on the surgeon must do a solo performance, with
emphasis on the virtuoso skill at his finger ends. Somehow
these two super-active vessels must be joined and made one.

The slightest leakage near that man-made connection would be fatal.

Andy spoke to the microphone, without lifting his eyes. "We use a continuous suture on the posterior side. And another continuous joining on the anterior. Stay sutures will be placed at both ends as an added precaution——"

He felt his voice die—and, though he did not dare lift his eyes to the students' gallery at this point, he knew that he had lost most of his audience. It was a fact he could take on stride. It scarcely mattered if Martin Ash's interns had deserted the spectators' benches. Jackie's life was his only stake—and Jackie's chances were building with each tick of the clock.

He began to stitch the two blood vessels together, making them one with the same skill a housewife exhibits when she hems her daughter's first-term gown. The dark strand of silk served him admirably—a fragile barrier, but deceptively strong for all its gossamer texture. He counted the stitches with the slow-moving needle, checking them against his first notebook. The first stitch for the subclavian, matched by a stitch in the wall of the pulmonary. . . . He had remembered everything he saw. He had even placed the back row of stitches first—a manoeuvre that permitted him to work from the inside of the vessels themselves.

The third explosion sent the bottles in the medicine cabinet dancing and bathed the wide window in an orange glow. From a lower floor Andy heard the tinkle of breaking glass, a sudden clash of voices giving orders. He stepped back a pace from the table and folded his hands in a sterile towel, holding his team immobile without a word. Every eye in the room had moved to the anæsthetist's machine: even the probationer who was assisting Vicki knew that they were using an explosive gas.

"Will you take a look, Miss Ryan, and see what's wrong?"

No one stirred from the table as Vicki hurried to the surgery window. Andy's eyes dared to seek Julia's, but he read no sign of fear there. The discipline of the operating room, enforced ruthlessly over the years, was on his side tonight. Awaiting his orders, as always, she looked a picture of courage—though he was sure that Julia, like the others, was frozen in the common dread.

He had no need to look up to guess that the observers' gallery was deserted now. After that last blast, the lure of a fire-escape was more than these interns not on duty could resist. He was obscurely glad that the thick glass of the gallery had muted the panic rush to the corridor.

Vicki came under the cone of light again, her eyes wide above her mask. "The brewery's afire," she said. "From the inside. There are police cars in the alley now—and an engine working against the wall——"

Dale Easton did not stir, but his voice was taut. "No wonder the windows rattled. We're right across the street, aren't we?"

"Don't call it a street," said Andy grimly. "It's barely wide enough for a single car." Again he held the group steady with his eyes. "The tenement block is even closer, remember. God pity those poor devils in there, if they didn't wake in time——"

"Most of the hospital buildings are no safer. Including this one——"

"True enough. But we can't stop this operation now. Certainly not until we hear from Dr. Ash." Even as he spoke, Andy remembered the director's brief appearance in the gallery—and wondered if he had left for Long Island after all. He made his voice firm with an effort. "Shall we stop losing time? It may be precious later."

Dale Easton nodded, just as grimly. "Thanks for calling the score, Doctor."

"Ready, Dr. Evans?"

"Ready as I'll ever be," said the anæsthetist.

"Clamp, if you please, Miss Talbot!"

The sterile towel fell at Andy's feet unnoticed as he bent again above the operative field to continue the delicate stitching that would complete the anastomosis in time—if the surgery walls were still standing. Julia had already slapped the next instrument into his palm. He felt his heart swell with pride as the rest of the team moved in to take up their duties without a murmur. All of them knew that they must finish that delicate junction and close Jackie's chest before they dared remove him from the table. All of them admitted, just as calmly, that they must put their own lives on the balance until the job was done.

VII

Martin Ash was walking down the drive to his car when the first roaring detonation belched out of the alley like an inferno made visible. The shock of the displaced air rocked him on his heels, forcing him to embrace a lamp-post for support. Then, as the first blast subsided, he heard the crackling of flames at the bend of the alley, mingled with a scream that was not quite human. Sure that the tenement block had caught fire, he went down the narrow passage at the run—until two blue-coated figures barred his path.

"Better stay where you are, Doctor. It's the brewery."

"How did it happen?"

"Vat blew sky-high, I guess. The inspector's behind that prowl car. He can tell you more than I."

Ash hunched his shoulders and ran towards the sharp-etched silhouette of the automobile. Even from this distance the heat from the shattered brewery windows struck him like a blow: he needed all his control to avoid dropping to the pavement when a fresh blast, deep in the black and orange chiaroscuro of the building, shook the ground beneath his feet. Hurlbut, crouched in the shelter of a mudguard with a helmeted fire chief, waved an abstracted greeting.

"Hell on your doorstep tonight, Doctor. Sorry we couldn't stop him in time——" The inspector's voice was calm enough as he pulled Ash down beside him, just as a bit of flaming debris sailed overhead. "Of course it was only a crazy tip from our reporter friend. We had to let the fellow show his hand."

"Who do you mean, Inspector?"

"One of your doctors." Hurlbut's voice was still patient. "A fellow named Korff. Seems he had a hand in smuggling

out that chemical we were looking for—with Rilling holding
the bag, while he lived. I'm expecting more news later, from
across the river——" The inspector bit the sentence in the
middle, as though he had said too much too soon. "Unfortunately we weren't quite sure what he was doing inside the
brewery. Not until it was too late to stop him——"

"I still can't believe that Korff——" But Martin Ash felt
the protest die in his throat. For all his erratic brilliance, he
had always distrusted the refugee in his heart. He listened in
silence while Hurlbut described their patient stalking of the
quarry, Tony's panic flight, and the holocaust that had
followed. Try as he might, he could feel no anger or pity
now. Only a slow, numb realization of the threat that Tony's
greed had created.

"Where is he now, Inspector?"

"Spread-eagled on that wall inside," said Hurlbut grimly.
"What's left of him, at any rate—and it's no sight to write
home about. I'm afraid the fire'll do the rest, before we can
get the body out——"

A brace of hook-and-ladder cars had whined to a stop in
the alley mouth as they talked. Watching the firemen spring
to action, Ash tried hard to assure himself that they would
soon control the blaze before it could spread too far. But even
as he clung to that crazy hope another explosion seemed to
rock the whole brewery on its foundations, pouring fiery
debris into the street as a section of the wall buckled under
the impact.

"I must get back to the hospital——" His voice was
hoarse now, weighed with a fear he could not conceal. "We
should put our emergency plan to work right away."

The helmeted fire chief at Hurlbut's elbow spoke calmly,
without taking his eyes from the hook-and-ladder squad.
"The sooner the better, Doctor. How soon can you evacuate
the wing that comes out to the alley?"

Martin Ash hesitated. He had just remembered the heart
operation that Andy was performing in surgery. Unless they
sacrificed Jackie's life, it would be impossible to halt it now.
"There's an important job going on in the operating theatre,"
he said. "They can't finish for another hour, at least."

The chief looked up doubtfully at the great rectangle of lighted glass, a half-dozen storeys above them. "I hope the building's still there in another hour."

"Amen to that," said Ash—and backed away from the sirocco lash of the blaze.

Moving as in some waking nightmare, he saw that the firemen themselves were retreating before the fury of the holocaust. Still another explosion had blasted a fresh breach in the brewery wall while they talked. He paused for a second more to watch a tongue of flame lick out towards the ancient red brick wall of the old pathology building, to sear away its blanket of ivy as neatly as some giant blow-lamp. A jet of water from the nearest fire hose extinguished the blaze in a moment—but it was a warning of how the hospital itself would fare, if more than one vat exploded in unison.

His eyes moved down the curve of the hospital drive—faintly lit, at this angle, by the flaming horror behind the surgical wing. His car still waited, the keys were in his wallet. As he hesitated, the urge to fling himself at the steering-wheel and escape this mounting panic was almost more than he could bear. Then, with a muffled curse for his own weakness, he staggered through the wide-open door to the rotunda.

Strength and sanity returned with each step he took down the familiar corridor to his office. But his hands were still shaking as he poured himself a glass of water and drank it down. Then he settled at his desk and picked up the phone.

"Connect me with all the loud-speakers, will you, Operator? I must speak to the whole hospital at once."

He could feel the sudden fear in the girl's gasp of consent. Already the tension that radiated from his nerve-ends seemed to embrace the whole vast hospital, as though his staff and patients alike had expected his message.

"The microphone is ready, Dr. Ash. Will you try to speak more clearly?"

"*Your attention, please!*" His voice was still tight with excitement, and he fought hard to control it before he went on. No matter what the personal cost, he could not afford to show the terror he was feeling. Everything depended on his generalship now, on the smooth function of the disaster plan they had worked out months ago, as a safeguard against possible air raids.

"This is Dr. Ash. Emergency Plan A will go into effect at once." That was better, he told himself: the unhurried voice of experience, the man of science who had looked at death before and come back to tell the story. "All other work must be dropped. If you are in doubt as to details, study the blue-print which is in every chart book. All stretchers and litters will be sent, with all available orderlies and ambulatory patients, to the old wards—which are to be evacuated. Patients will be transferred to the fireproof wards, according to the details of the plan. All surgical residents will report to the emergency ward immediately—except for Dr. Gray and his team, who will await orders in their theatre——"

He found he had swallowed hard, after all, as he pictured the loud-speaker just off the surgery, and the probable effect of his words on Andy and Andy's assistants. But his voice had steadied before he continued. "Equipment from the regular operating rooms will be evacuated as rapidly as possible to the emergency ward. I repeat: Plan A is now in effect, and all concerned will report for their assigned duties."

When he replaced the telephone he found that his face was drenched with sweat. He summoned the operator a second time—and was pleased to find that the girl's voice, like his own, had steadied wonderfully in the execution of this routine broadcast.

"I must go to the O.R. for a moment," he told her. "Have someone take all calls for me until I can reach the emergency ward."

This time he dared to cross the rotunda itself, though it was hard not to break into a run. With no surprise, he noted that Father O'Leary was seated in his wheel-chair, smiling benignly at the sudden, ominous emptiness. There was something immensely soothing in the old chaplain's tranquillity— something that went beyond self and steadied both heart and mind. Ash had not intended to pause again, but he found that he had turned by instinct to the familiar chair.

"Things will be rather rough here for a while, Padre. We're evacuating the old buildings now——"

"I know, Martin. I heard your orders."

"You'd better let someone take you up to Schuyler Tower. You'll be safe there, I hope."

"I stopped worrying about my safety before you were born, Doctor."

Martin Ash frowned: it was quite like the chaplain to sit here, with the terrible patience of the old. "I'd much rather have you alive when this is over," he said quickly. "I'm on my way to the elevators now. Let me take you with me."

"You've more important things to do, Martin. The next orderly can wheel me over to emergency. That's where I'll be really needed, you know."

"But, Padre——"

"People will be afraid tonight," said Father O'Leary. "And where there is fear the presence of the Lord is needed." He had spoken the words simply, as a man might utter a fact that is beyond dispute. Now he raised his eyes to the great statue that towered above them both. "*He* can't go, so I'll be His deputy."

Martin Ash nodded. He had protested only from a sense of duty: Father O'Leary's job tonight was as clear-cut as his own.

"I'll see you in the ward, then, Padre. Mind you take care of yourself."

The priest put a hand on the surgeon's arm. "What about Andy Gray and Jackie? Will the operation be finished?"

"If Andy's still on his feet," said Ash. "I'm on my way to warn them now. The surgical wing is likely to be the first to go. It may have caught already."

"You know they'll stay, Martin. Just as you and I will stay——"

"I must warn them, just the same! There's my elevator now."

In the scrub room he stopped to don a mask and gown before he moved into the muted bustle of the theatre. In common with every trained surgeon, he could already sense the strain of the operation. If there was fear in that huddled group round the table it was not visible to the naked eye.

Andy Gray, tying off a suture deep in the operative field, looked up at last as his senior paused just inside the white surf of light that inundated the patient and the busy hands that hovered above him.

"Glad you're back, Dr. Ash. I was afraid you'd left for the island."

Martin found he was smiling under his mask. Andy's devotion to the task at hand, like Father O'Leary's, was vastly reassuring. "I had one foot in my car when the fire started," he said. "How are things going here?"

"We're about a third through the anastomosis."

"Will you need much more time?"

"Thirty minutes. Maybe forty-five. I can close with through-and-through sutures if necessary. But I must get this anastomosis right."

Martin Ash nodded and drew a deep breath. "I've just put Plan A into effect. I—thought you all should know."

The work round the table proceeded smoothly while he waited for Andy's reply. It was quite as though he had dropped in for a routine visit. As though the wall of glass in the observers' gallery still stood between them, shutting out all sound. Andy spoke without lifting his eyes.

"I thought you would, Doctor. That last explosion sounded like hell in the making."

"This building is almost certain to go," said Ash. "How soon we've no idea. We're already evacuating the old wards —and setting up an emergency in the new building."

Dale Easton spoke from his side of the table. "Does this business have anything to do with that stolen chemical?"

"The police are sure it does," said Ash—and he found that he was forcing his words now. "Korff was in on the smuggling, it seems. He paid with his life when the business backfired——"

Vicki Ryan gasped audibly. The others received his announcement with complete aplomb. Only the pathologist looked up from the small, sheeted body on the table.

"Is there no way of measuring the present state of this chemical?"

"We're praying it's spent its strength, of course. In that

case we'll be fighting a fire, and nothing more. But we can't be sure. That's why I came here to speak to you all——"

Andy reached for a fresh suture needle. "Are you suggesting we abandon this patient now, Doctor?"

"I'm suggesting nothing," said Martin Ash. "You're in charge here, Andy. But I do think you should all speak for yourselves, now you know the score."

"We won't know the score until we've closed," said Andy. "I, for one, intend to stay until the job's over. What about you, Miss Talbot?"

"We can't stop now," said Julia—and her voice was even steadier than Andy Gray's. "You know I'm leaving the hospital tomorrow, Dr. Ash. I couldn't go with my last job unfinished——"

"Nor could I," said Andy. "I'm sorry, Doctor. This has been a—a rather hectic day. I didn't have time to tell you I'll soon be setting up practice elsewhere."

Ash, watching the battle of glances across the table, read a message in Julia's eyes that he could not quite translate. So she'll go to Florida because she loves him, he thought quickly. Andy (because he loves nothing but success) will go straight uptown, to a career financed by Pat Reed. For an instant the impact of that discovery held his attention, blotting out the threat that waited just outside the operating-room door. I'd give anything to warn you, he thought. But you must learn your lesson first-hand—as I have done.

Aloud he said carefully, "You can excuse your circulating nurses at this point, I hope, except Miss Ryan, of course. We'll be needing them in emergency. Almost as much as I'll be needing Dr. Easton, the moment he's free——"

"Dr. Easton can join you now, if he likes," said Andy. "Miss Talbot and I can finish this between us, if Miss Ryan will assist——"

Ash glanced quickly at Vicki Ryan, but the tall nurse's gaze did not falter. "I go with the hospital, Doctor," she said. "We'll dissolve together."

"And you, Dr. Evans?"

The bulky anæsthetist shifted his weight on the high throne stool at the table's head. "Count me in too, Dr. Ash."

"What about it, Dale? Will you come with me now?"

The pathologist's voice was quite steady. "If you don't mind, sir, I'll stay with the team."

Ash drew back from the circle of light. Now, more than ever, he felt like an intruder. He heard his voice go on none the less. After all, he was still director of East Side General —even though he had just learned a valuable lesson in humility.

"I'd shut off that explosive gas, if I were you——"

"I already have, Dr. Ash," said the anæsthetist. "Not that it matters too much. We're sitting over a dozen tanks of cyclopropane in the storage room."

The windows throbbed as another orange flare shook the night outside, outlining the hunched figure of the surgeon and his assistant on the far wall of the room, dwarfing the overhead lights with its grotesque, surrealist day. Ash ducked his head by instinct—and left the room. Andy Gray, he noted, had gone on with his work, as calmly as though the hell brew outside had been kindled on another planet.

He's dedicated as I'll never be, thought Martin Ash. *Dedicated, and fearless—and utterly alone*. And then he remembered Andy's strange statement anent his future—a statement that had had no visible relation to the battle they were fighting round the table. Perhaps Andy Gray was not the man of iron he had just seemed. Perhaps he was frightened, too—and all too conscious of his loneliness.

The thought cheered him, for no reason he could name, as he stepped into the corridor of the emergency ward, ready to assume command. Plan A, he saw, had gone into gear without a hitch: an intern, with a casebook open on the desk before him, snapped to attention as precisely as though East Side General were under enemy fire.

"Cases moving on schedule, Doctor. And we already have casualties from outside. I've a fireman on the table now—will you have a look?"

Ash nodded and turned through the door of the first operating room—one of a series of emergency set-ups that extended down the whole side of the corridor. He had rehearsed this routine with his staff a score of times. It was hard to believe that this was not the overture to yet another drill.

"Serious?"

"Back injury, Doctor. He was thrown from the wall in that last cave-in——"

Ash stood at the man's side, noting with approval that the patient had already been prepared for the surgery that might still avert paralysis or death itself. Automatically, as though he were himself an intern, he reached down and pressed the man's foot upwards. Normally there would have been an instinctive reflex contraction of the muscles opposing such a motion. Here, those same muscles seemed dead, as if all control in that area had been lost. Dislocated vertebræ, he thought. Still, it doesn't look hopeless, if he's not too far gone with shock.

"Get fresh plasma started at once," he said. "And order whole blood from the bank. We'll want a quick X-ray, too, in case the cord is injured. Is Dr. van Pelt ready to operate?"

"Standing by now, sir. Will you take over the book?"

Seated beside his intern at the admissions desk, he found that he was in harness again, with no effort at all. He had come just in time. Patients began to pour in from the scene of the fire, almost before the spine injury could be transferred to the X-ray room across the corridor: other stretcher cases from the firemen's ranks, their pulses racing with shock, their faces pallid from smoke injury or the searing dart of the flames themselves. He could read the progress of the holocaust, even before the first tenement victims began to arrive in turn. Had he been less preoccupied, he might even have paused to wonder how long the ranks of fire-fighters could be filled, before the disaster swept all human opposition aside.

But there was no time for such imponderables now: the fire was the city's job, his the task of repairing the human debris in its path. He had put fear behind him long ago. Nothing mattered now but the next entry in his casebook, the next soot-blackened figure that paused for a fraction beside his desk and then moved on. Without so much as raising his head, he was sure that the whole hospital was in gear now, thanks to the spark he had generated.

Father O'Leary and a brace of receptionists had taken over the emergency switchboard, handling every call that did not require the director's own attention. These he answered briefly from his command post at the desk, without pausing in his check of the incoming casualties. The messages indicated that the evacuation of patients from the endangered wards was proceeding on schedule. Already the surgical building had been cleared, save for the group in the operating room. Ambulatory patients had been doubled up in the wards and other parts of the fireproof structures. Whenever possible, they had been allowed to go home—though most of these patients had been forced to remain, since their only habitations were the tenement blocks now engulfed by the blaze.

Martin Ash did not allow his mind to dwell on the threat to these human rookeries, though it was evident that many of the cases passing in review could have arrived from no other source. It's like a major train wreck, he thought—with beds within walking distance of the disaster. There was no mistaking the face of poverty that entered his door tonight—on foot, or moaning between the stretcher-bearers. The poor, he thought, must bear the brunt of every war—and this, after all, was war in its crudest guise.

He dared to glance at his watch. The injured were still moving past his desk in a steady line: he could hardly believe that he had sat here for half an hour now. His mind was still an efficient machine, classifying these battle casualties according to need. Surgical cases to the left, to the long file of operating rooms that had been running at full blast for a small eternity. Check the blood bank one more time—and praise Heaven that other hospitals had sent help long ago. Initial the first complete casebook of the less serious cases, from third-degree burns to simple shock.

He passed a hand across his eyes as the line jammed back upon itself, like an endless snake without destination or plan. In that pause he heard the steady hum of activity from the auxiliary store-room, where a dozen people worked with pulmotor and portable oxygen machines, administering artificial respiration to those overcome by smoke and heat.

The names in the casebook were legion now, doctor as well as patient. The visiting staffs, from every hospital in the city had inundated East Side General from the first alert. Thanks to the help of these outside doctors, there had been no delay in splint room or surgical cubicle. Despite some inevitable crowding—and the fractured nerves that went with haste everywhere—no life had been lost for lack of helping hands.

The dial of his wrist-watch hung on the stroke of ten when Martin Ash looked up impatiently into the grimy face of a fireman who hovered just outside the bustle that still overflowed the desk and backed into the corridors beyond. Surgeon and fireman stared at each other for a moment of silence. From where he's standing, thought Ash, I'm unreal as a ghost, and much too clean to be endured. The man's oilskins, shedding water like a seal's back, had already surrounded him with a private swamp. The fireman's blue-spiked jaw, moving at last, produced words that were not, at first, coherent.

"How are things going, Chief?" Ash inquired.

"I'm not the Chief, Doc. The Chief's got troubles of his own."

Martin Ash glanced down the long line of stretchers and walking wounded. "If I can be of help . . . ?"

"The surgical building's caught. Chief wants to know what about those lights in the big theatre."

"You mean the operating room? We've an emergency working there." Martin Ash glanced again at his watch. Andy is being as thorough as ever, he thought, even in the face of doom.

"Chief says you'll have another sort of emergency if you don't clear the wing pronto."

"Can't you give them any protection at all?"

"What else have we done this past hour?"

"We have orderlies standing by to bring the patient here, as soon as the operation is finished. We simply can't evacuate them now."

The fireman shook his head—and even here Ash noticed how utterly forlorn he seemed, standing in the midst of that man-made swamp. "Chief still thinks we better let that building go and try to save the others."

"Do what you can. That's all I ask."

"Hadn't you better pass the word along? It's their own lives they're risking up there."

"I tried that once," said Martin Ash grimly. "They're too busy to listen."

Another stretcher case moved up to the desk, and Ash forgot the fireman instantly. It's quite right, he thought as he made the next entry. Andy and his team were too busy to listen to the voice of reason. So, for that matter, am I.

He felt his heart expand in a wordless prayer while his busy fingers endorsed yet another entry. If Andy and company are alive this time tomorrow, he promised his Creator, I'll be Catherine's husband now and for evermore. If the hospital is spared—or even its shell—I'll move it uptown, if it's what she really wants.

The decision cheered him mightily. I've always been Catherine's husband, he thought—not too gloomily. It's both my cross and my reward. I was nothing when she found me— and I'll be nothing if she deserts me tomorrow. Pray God she won't abuse the privilege, when she makes that discovery on her own.

VIII

Thanks to the M.D. licence on her car, Catherine Ash had dared to push her speedometer past sixty on the Long Island span of the Triboro, ignoring the horns of other drivers as she zoomed between mudguards to gain the left-hand lane. Now, as she slowed to negotiate the long hairpin curve that led down to the East River Drive, she was conscious, for the first time, of a red glow to the south. Champagne still played its waltz in her brain, so the import of that ominous glow did not register at once. Sir Stanley Potter was a more positive threat at the moment. Not that she had minded Sir Stanley too much, on that drive to the city. Eluding his

rather fervid attempts to embrace her at every traffic stop
was part of tonight's madness—along with the resolve she
had made when he had first settled beside her in the roadster.

"I say, Catherine!"

"Yes, my dear?"

"Do Americans always drive as fast as this?"

"Sometimes they drive even faster."

"Then why are so many of you still alive?"

She shaved past a town car with inches to spare, and
laughed back at the chauffeur's icy visage. I'm my own girl
tonight, she told herself exultantly, and to hell with aftermaths. Tonight, at least, I know just what I'm doing. I'll
take him to the apartment and dismiss the servants: we'll be
there in ten minutes, if I can stay on four wheels. Once we're
alone, I'll call Martin and suggest he join us. If he consents
we'll have the nucleus of a party—and it won't matter in the
slightest if it's the sort of party he detests most heartily. If
he refuses. . . . Her mind made a pleasant hiatus as they
coasted to a stop at yet another traffic signal, and she felt
the boy's eager arm tighten round her shoulder.

"Tell me one thing, Catherine," he said as the light
winked green. "Where are we going, and why?"

"Where would you like to go most?"

"What about Twenty-one, for a refill? Or that place they
call the Stork?"

The mention of the two inevitable addresses disturbed
her a little. Somehow she had expected him to suggest her
apartment, or his own. Perhaps this was the celebrated British
reticence—their tendency to underplay every situation, even
when victory was in their grasp.

"Surely you know Twenty-one as well as you know the
Café Royal or the Ivy?"

"Sorry, dear lady. So sorry, really." She felt the tremor
in his voice and knew that he understood her perfectly,
without words. "Quite forgot it was your party, not mine.
After all, I'm only an invited guest."

She laughed at him, then, as they coasted up to the last
traffic lights before her turn into East End Avenue. "Have
you ever tried to park on Fifty-second Street at this hour?"

"There's nowhere one can park in Manhattan these days," he said dolefully. "Nowhere to pause for a quiet talk with a person one really likes——"

"There's a parking garage in our apartment building. And there's champagne on ice upstairs. Of course, if I can't tempt you——"

His hand closed on hers as it lay along the steering wheel, but she disengaged it gently as the traffic changed. "We can phone my husband at the hospital," she said. "Make it a real party——"

"Supposing he can't join us?"

"We'll have our party, anyway," she said steadily enough. It was Martin's fault, she told herself, for deserting her in favour of that other love, the hospital.

Sir Stanley let out his breath in a long sigh. She caught a glimpse of his profile—sharp-etched against that strange, pinkish glow to the south, as they swung round a bend in the river drive. He's really quite handsome, she thought, and quite appealing, too, even though he's still untouched by life. It might even be fun teaching him.

"We can only pray," he said.

"That Dr. Ash is available?"

"That our party is all you want it to be, Catherine."

Again she disengaged his gently insistent fingers from her wrist. "Play me some music, Stanley. We can start that party right now."

She just escaped smiling when he bent above the dials of the car radio, and she noticed that his hands were trembling. Poor lamb, she thought, you're having a wonderful time posing as an international black sheep. Will this be your first affair on our side of the Atlantic? Will you go back to your London club too shaken to boast of your conquest?

"Music, Stanley," she said gently. "Not news. There's too much news these days——"

"This is worth hearing," he said, and even in that wine-dimmed enchantment she noted the gravity of his tone. Then she, too, was listening to the news broadcast—so intently that she drove through the first traffic light on East End Avenue without seeing it at all. People have been saved by the bell ere now, she thought—even as she put down a crazy impulse to scream with laughter. Surely this is the first time an erring wife has been saved by her own car radio.

A fire of unknown origin in the brewery adjoining the East Side General Hospital. A fire that had spread instantly, to engulf the whole block of adjoining tenements and threatened, at this very moment, to sweep over the hospital itself. Even when the syrup-smooth voice moved on to speak of the weather and baseball scores she could not quite credit her ears. Martin is still there, she thought. He was right to stay at the hospital tonight. So right that I'll never question his judgments again.

"I must go to him at once," she said—and jumped the car through another light, with no knowledge that she had spoken aloud.

"I'll come, too, of course," said Sir Stanley Potter. She heard the voice from far off and turned to give him a startled look as he leaned forward in the seat to put a soothing arm round her.

"You needn't. This is my show, not yours."

"Surely I can be of help——"

Not any more, she thought. Aloud she said, gently enough, "I'll drop you at Twenty-one. It's right on the way."

"Suppose you can't get through?"

"With this licence I can cross any police line in New York."

He continued to argue, in his cultivated, earnest voice, a tone that seemed high-pitched to her now, almost strident. Actually she was hardly conscious that he existed, even when she braked reluctantly and leaned forward to open the door on his side. Sir Stanley Potter was only a name now—a temptation she had put behind her for ever. Nothing mattered but the next traffic light and that growing red stain, glimpsed now and again as the wall of skyscrapers opened to the south.

"But I say, Catherine——"

"Get out, please. I must hurry."

"I can't let you go on alone."

"Will you get out or must I call a policeman? There's one right there on the corner"

He got out with alacrity. Catherine Ash slammed the door and elbowed her way into the traffic stream, damning a too forward taxi in language that would have shocked her own ears at another time. She heard a faint cry behind her and realized that Sir Stanley had uttered a final, well-bred protest. Then she forgot him completely, in her race with time.

Once she had worked her way back to the drive she opened the motor in earnest and ceased to think at all until the great white bulk of East Side General blocked off the southern sky. Bathed in a hideous red glow, the hospital still managed to look aloof and self-contained, surrounded by chaos in the making. Catherine Ash felt the tears start into her eyes—and let them roll down her cheek unchecked. Somehow she had expected to see Martin's world in ruins: it was an unhoped-for relief to find its walls inviolate.

And then, as she drew closer, she saw that the flames had begun to lick away the ramparts of Martin's bastion, after all. Two of the old red brick wards had already crumbled under the onslaught of the fire: even as she strained her eyes into the orange flare, another building caved in upon itself, collapsing in a spout of crimson dust. The long, claw-like fireman's ladders vanished for a space in that cloud of debris, cut by the wild rainbows of a dozen fire hoses: at first glance the entire department seemed involved in the struggle to stem the blaze.

You must spare the hospital, she told them wordlessly as her car cut through the first police cordon. You must give me a chance to prove that I understand my husband—and my husband's dream. We can rebuild those walls tomorrow, no matter what the cost. Her brakes screamed, just in time to avoid a head-on collision with the road block on the edge of the esplanade. She vaulted the barrier as lightly as a schoolgirl and ran towards the crowd massed tightly behind the fire line just beyond.

Others were running, too, from all points of the compass, pulled towards the focus of disaster. She heard the hoarse shouts but dimly. Like the hiss of the water pumps and the crash of falling timbers, this human din seemed part of a diabolic stage setting without form or meaning. The exultant pulse of the fire itself was only a gigantic footlight trough, outlining the faces of the sweating firemen, striking highlights from the gold-stamped visor of a fire chief's cap as he sprang by instinct to bar her path.

"Stay where you are, lady!"

Catherine Ash strained hard against the rope that cut the narrow street from kerb to kerb. The crowd that hemmed her was quiet here, thanks to the fearful proximity of death. The faces turned towards the blazing tenement at the street's end were identical, straining discs, suffused by the same fearful glow.

Half the tenement was gone, she saw. People were still pouring from adjacent buildings, most of them half dressed, some with a few treasured belongings clutched in their arms. They seemed to move like sleepwalkers—and even as they stumbled out of the danger zone most of them paused to look back at a home they would never see again—an instinctive turning that twisted Catherine's heartstrings.

The burning building, she saw, was the rookery where the Aschoffs had lived so long. From where she stood, it seemed deserted. Catherine could only infer that Martin's parents had been evacuated long ago, along with the other inmates who now sat huddled in doorways farther up the street, adding their own human wailings to the roar of the flames. She had already turned back to the hospital when she heard a new note in that wailing, and recognized the voice at once. In another moment she had pushed her way into the smoke-stained throng, to take Mama Aschoff into the haven of her arms. Lamenting in her own tongue, seemingly blind to externals, the old woman did not recognize her at once. When Catherine had repeated her name she opened her tear-blurred eyes and clung to her daughter-in-law in earnest, as though her presence had brought new strength.

"I was away, Catherine. Only this moment do I return——" Her voice steadied: she was thinking in English now, without translating from her own tongue. "He is still in there. The neighbours are sure of it. No one thought to bring him out ——"

Catherine's eyes turned back to the tenement. The flames had already begun to consume the very walls of the building.

"Surely the firemen checked in every apartment before they——?"

The old woman's voice cut in patiently, with the same frightening, dead-level calm. "They have left Papa to die. Always they forget someone in times like these."

Catherine considered quickly. There was no time to send for Martin: she knew how busy he would be in the emergency ward. This was her responsibility—and hers alone. The realization steadied her instantly. Her voice was calm when she led her mother-in-law towards the fire line.

"We'll make them do something. Be sure of that——"

"I tried to go in twice, Catherine. The firemen only pushed me back."

"Stay right here. It's my turn now."

She was gone before Mama Aschoff could speak again—ducking under a fireman's arm and running towards a knot of helmeted figures all but hidden by the smoke that gushed from the axe-splintered façade of the tenement. She was shouting as she ran, in a raucous voice that had never belonged to Catherine Ash.

"There's an old man in there! On the second floor front. He's blind and can't get out——"

The assistant fire chief turned with a kind of weary patience, as though he half recognized her right to cross the fire line. "Everyone's out of that building, lady. We ordered them out as soon as the tenement caught."

"But he's blind. And nobody has seen him come out. It's Dr. Ash's father——"

A confused babble rose from the crowd against the rope a scant fifty feet away. "She's right, Chief!" a hoarse voice shouted. "Mr. Aschoff didn't come out with us. We all thought he was with his wife——"

The assistant fire chief turned towards the shout—and Catherine took advantage of that turning to duck beneath his arm and run towards the axe-harried tenement door. Without looking back, she knew that her boldness had given her a flying start, that these men in oilskins would only stand and gape as she dashed up the steps and into the building.

"Hold everything, lady!"

The shout had come too late. As she groped in the thick fog of smoke just inside she heard the assistant chief bellow on his own, and knew that the man had galvanized into action.

"Give me a wall of water! I'll have to go after her now."

She heard his feet clatter on the broken treads of the steps outside as she blundered deeper into the hall, groping with both hands for the stair rail. Already she was sure that she could outdistance him now: a sixth sense had warned her that the stairway rose to the left, with the first landing less than twenty steps above her. Even here the heat was a palpable thing: she remembered to bend almost double as she climbed, seeking the thin stratum of fresh air that still existed under the billows of smoke snaking down from above.

More than once she was forced to pause and gasp for that wisp of life-giving oxygen before she reached the first landing. From this height she could see how hideously the blaze had gained ground, reducing the whole basement area to a cauldron, latticing the stair well with a bright arabesque as the flames licked ever higher. In a few moments more that same stair well would be engulfed, collapsing the whole interior framework of the tenement into its glowing heart. Breathing deep (and feeling the smoke sear her lungs), she ran on, taking the stairs to the second floor in a dozen panting leaps. Even in this moment of sheer panic she could be glad for her frequent visits to the tenement. Thanks to her familiarity, there was no need to pause and count doors.

A window was torn from its hinges at the hall's end, creating a draught of a sort. As the smoke swirled away she saw that the hall itself was, as yet, untouched by the fire. The row of apartment doors looked immovable as time, and quite as solid. The door to the Aschoffs', like the others, was closed. She could only pray that it was unlocked: it was beyond her strength to smash the panel.

The fire below, working like a giant bellows, sucked a thick coil of smoke into the hall again, forcing her to drop on hands and knees before she dared approach the door.

Her hand found the knob, and she gasped out her relief when it turned smoothly. As the portal swung wide a blast of cool air struck her face. She did not understand its origin until she had moved into the room and felt a spray of water on her smoke-blackened hair.

Catherine Ash found that she could laugh, after all—though the laughter was coloured with hysteria. At both ends of the Aschoff living-room an overhead water pipe had burst under the fire, creating a small island of safety in this portion of the flat. Papa Aschoff was seated in his chair in the midst of this Heaven-sent lake: even in the flame-shot gloom she saw how quietly his hands were folded as he waited for death. Perhaps he's already dead, she thought. No one—not even the father of Martin Ash—could be quite so resigned to fate.

And then, as she took a step on the water-soaked carpet, the old man raised his head. His voice was part of his outer tranquillity—a serene whisper from the tomb.

"Why are you here, Catherine?"

"I've come to take you out," she said, and she could marvel at her steady tone. "They wouldn't believe you were still here——"

"You risked your life for that? The life of an old man isn't worth it."

"Martin is busy at the hospital," she said. "There was nobody else to come for you. Can you—get up from that chair?"

He rose with the question and tottered towards her, with one hand extended—the traditional gesture of the blind.

"I can walk. But you must go back without me."

"Don't talk, please," she said. "Save all the breath you can." Their hands met and joined; already she was leading his unwilling footsteps towards the door and the dense wall of smoke outside. "Will you do as I say, Father Aschoff? Nod, don't speak."

She saw the ancient head incline, and felt the hand she was holding tremble slightly. She seized her advantage quickly as she dropped to her knees just inside the doorway and pulled him down beside her.

"We must crawl down the stairs and hug the wall. There's too much smoke to risk walking."

He crawled obediently in her wake, from door to stair well. With that movement the heat smote them like a restraining hand. Catherine felt her heart plummet as she saw how rapidly the fire had invaded the lower stair well. Already the banister was ablaze down its entire length. Here and there the stair treads were twisted at crazy angles under that same blistering breath from the cellar. But there was no choice but to go on. Even if the stairway ripped loose and dropped them to the floor below, they must take their chance.

Parts of the outside wall had caved in while she worked her way upstairs. She could have looked down on the street outside, but a veritable wall of water blocked her view—a man-made cascade formed by a dozen interlocking hoses that seemed to dissolve in billows of steam almost before it could pour down the tenement's face. Through the hiss of steam and the crash of falling bricks she could hear the hoarse bellow of the assistant fire chief, as he shouted his instructions from the cavern below. Help, it seemed, was only a few yards away, but she must go through a furnace to reach it.

The treads were too hot to touch now—but she closed her fists round them as she inched her way downwards. Behind her, she could hear Papa Aschoff's laboured breathing, as he strove to match her snail-like progress. Another yard, and she felt a tread give under her weight—but it was too late to stop now. There was a rending sound at her left, a sound like death's own knell, repeated in a tearing crescendo down the whole length of the stairway. She went first, plunging head-foremost into blackness, twisting her body to one side as she saw the circle of the waiting fire net, forcing herself to clear the way for Papa Aschoff's heavily inert body.

The old man struck the net a fraction ahead of her own descent. Then they were both bouncing crazily in the canvas haven, just before the fire crew rushed them into the air again. She had a dim sense of moisture washing in a flood about her tired body, and knew that they had cut through the wall of water to gain the street beyond. Behind her she heard a sulphurous crash as the holocaust won its last victory in the stair well. At that precise moment blackness engulfed her.

When she opened her eyes she knew that she had only

fainted: her anxious hands assured her that she was unhurt, though her clothes and hair still smouldered. She was lying on a blanket between two stranded cars. On the cleared strip of pavement orderlies were waiting at either end of a stretcher. A man in white, whom she recognized as one of Martin's interns, bent over the stretcher with a stethoscope to his ears. Even before she could stagger to her feet she read nothing but reassurance in his intent eyes.

"Stay where you are, Mrs. Ash——"

"I can walk, I tell you!"

Something in her tone made the intern step back. She bent above the stretcher and looked down at Papa Aschoff's inert form, trying hard to match the old man's smile as his hand reached up and closed on hers.

"He isn't hurt badly, Doctor?"

"He isn't hurt at all, Mrs. Ash," said the intern cheerfully. "A bit shaken up after that jump: nothing a little injection of morphine won't cure. We're taking him to a hospital bed——"

"I want to see my husband," she said.

"Let me order you another stretcher, please."

"I can walk, I tell you."

Again the whiplash in her tone compelled obedience. She could even afford to smile as the intern jumped from her path.

"Just stay with the orderlies, Mrs. Ash. They're going to your husband now."

She never quite remembered crossing the esplanade or entering the wide brass doors that stood open to receive her one more time. Later she would recall how Mama Aschoff detached herself from the crowd to march proudly on the opposite side of the stretcher. Later still her senses would bring back the sharp, antiseptic smell of the corridor in the emergency ward, the bustle of white-coated men round the reception desk, and the line of patients (it was thinning fast, now that the tenements were cleared). A slow, patient line that paused, and moved, and paused again at the precise spot where her husband sat, dispensing his healing. Once her eyes had found Martin, she could see nothing else.

He's where he belongs, she thought, with all the shock of an original discovery. He's with his own people—helping them, as only he can help. What right have I to disturb him, even for a moment? Even if I've earned the right to walk at his father's side tonight?

The stretcher was beside the admissions desk now, the last item in the dwindling line. Martin looked up from his casebook with tired eyes, then rose to his feet. For a long, frozen instant, while he took in the tableau before him, he seemed to hesitate, as though he could not believe the evidence of his senses. Then he moved quickly forward and took her in his arms.

IX

In the surgical wing the operating theatre might have been a little world of its own—a private cosmos whose five inhabitants were clustered at one focal point, working in a realm where time hung suspended like a dream. None of them spoke as they worked. The anæsthetist and Vicki Ryan moved by instinct now, with no need for guidance; the three who were capped and gowned for surgery were part of that same steady rhythm, the iron compulsion that drove the team to its predestined end.

Andy Gray, feeling yet another suture slap into his extended palm, knew that he should thank God their luck had held so far, both on and off the table. But there was no time for prayer now—and still less for any thought that moved beyond the cone of light that had prisoned them all here for ever. The tension of this final anastomosis excluded hopes and fears alike. He scarcely felt the recurrent heaving of the floor beneath his feet, as the building shook in tempo with the disintegration of the brewery. If he heard the thud of the hoses just outside, as the firemen drenched the facing wall in a desperate effort to stave off ruin a moment more, the sound came through but dimly. The shouts of the firemen themselves and the confused, throaty rumble of the crowd behind the fire lines were a cacophony from another planet.

Now, as this endless operation was ending after all, he

was alone as he had never been alone. His brain had never been clearer, or emptier. There was no room there for distractions. Even the hand that had just offered him his final suture needle was part of the life he had excluded, by a sheer effort of the will. Loving the owner of that hand more than she could ever dream—and knowing just what he must say to her if they walked out of this room alive—he could forget her existence even now, as he poised the needle for its last thrust.

"Steady, all. It's nearly over."

His hands had already begun the final stitching, and he was quite unaware that he had broken the long, intent silence. His mind seemed to draw back a pace as his hands worked, watching the end product with a detachment that was soothing, all but god-like. The flash of the needle, as it drew the delicate silken strands from vessel wall to vessel wall, was the only reality in that æon of waiting.

Subclavian and pulmonary arteries were one now—so smoothly joined that he could hardly see where his task had begun and ended. If those sutures held, Jackie's blood would soon be pulsing here, ready to supply the oxygen lack that had doomed him from birth. He pulled the last strand taut and tied it off with steady fingers.

"Stay sutures, please."

They were already in his hand, the extra bulwarks that would protect the anastomosis itself. Placing them, and knotting the ends, was only a routine. He breathed deep, and knew that his respiration was echoed round the table. Their ultimate test was upon them—the release of the arterial clamps that would permit the circulation to reassert itself against the new, protective wall his surgery had created. If there was leakage, no matter how fragmentary the ooze, the operation must continue until that leak was stopped. Already the world was heavy on his shoulders—and the conviction that no man's luck could hold for ever.

He forced his fingers to release the first clamp—the one that held the pulmonary artery. When the passageway was free for the blood to surge through he clipped the ligature that held the ends of the subclavian clamp. The vessels distended dramatically, almost before he could lift the steel-jawed instruments from the wound—swelled and throbbed with the compulsion of Jackie's heartbeats. From where he stood, Andy could hardly believe his eyes. The snugly joined vessels, freed of their last restraint, might have been part of the anatomical chart beneath his hands.

"Standard equipment," said Dale Easton a little shakily. "How do you do it, Andy?"

It's holding firm, he thought. There isn't a trace of leakage anywhere. It's part of Jackie, now and for evermore. But he kept the exultation from his voice as he faced Julia across the table.

"Through-and-through sutures, please. There isn't time for more."

"They're ready now, Doctor." Her tone was as clinical as his own, yet he knew she was smiling beneath that mask.

Dale had removed the rib spreader when he returned to the wound. Thanks to the long, tough sutures Julia had begun to pass across the table it was a simple matter to close the incision in record time, drawing the threads through chest muscles and pleura, reinforcing them with a single strand which would bring the cut edges smoothly together to promote healing. With each thrust of the larger needle he could feel the world return in earnest. There was time to hear the roar of the fire now, more time than he needed to note the ominous pulsation in the wall that faced the alley, the fact that the floor beneath their feet had begun to tilt crazily, like the deck of a ship at sea.

"Skin clips, please——"

He closed the skin with these metal clips, since they could be inserted far more rapidly than the needle. As he placed the last one a jet of water sprang bodily into the operating theatre, shattering the glass wall of the observers' gallery and spreading a ready-made lake between that vantage point and the far window. With no real surprise, he saw the water translate into steam almost before it could strike the floor.

"Stretcher waiting, Doctor."

"Thank you, Miss Ryan. I think we can go now, if Dr. Evans is ready."

The anæsthetist removed the oximeter from the patient's ear lobe. "Oxygen tension has already risen," he said evenly. "The orderlies can have him now."

Moving as a team even now, they lifted Jackie among them and transferred him smoothly to the wheeled stretcher. A brace of sweating orderlies took over in the hall. The red undertone of terror died painlessly in Andy's brain as they dropped in the elevator to the main floor.

At the street level, where the door of the surgical wing opened into the quadrangle between the nurses' home and the pathology wing, a platoon of firemen waited to assume command, relieving Andy of responsibility so painlessly that he never felt the transition. He saw the fire line from the corner of one eye, and the massed humanity who had just raised a cheer. Cameras exploded in his face, but that, too, was part of the dream picture, now that he had emerged into the real world again.

Julia's fingers were twined in his when they walked into the shadow of the nurses' building—a blessed haven at this moment, shut off from the holocaust that still howled in the west. By common consent they paused in the deeper shadow of the entrance—where they had exchanged their first kiss, a scant twenty-four hours in the past.

"Were you frightened—really?"

Her eyes met his in the fire-laced gloom, and he read his answer in advance. "*You* weren't, Andy—why should I be?"

"Are you frightened now?"

"Not if you meant what you said to Dr. Ash."

"About leaving New York?"

"Tell me where you'll go next," she said, a trifle breathlessly. "I'd really like to hear the news, ahead of everyone."

"I'm joining Timmie in Florida," he said—and his voice was as quiet as her own. "Didn't you know that all along?"

She had known it, Julia realized now, with something like a shock, long before her final, desperate challenge. She had known it last night when he'd remembered the prayer of Maimonides:

May the love for my art actuate me at all times. May neither avarice, nor miserliness, nor the thirst for glory, nor for a great reputation engage my mind. . . .

Her eyes answered him without words as he bent towards her. Both of them laughed a little as they realized that she had not even paused to untie her surgical mask. The bit of gauze dropped to the walk unheeded as their lips met for the first kiss they had ever really shared.

x

Pete Collins emerged from the phone booth in the rotunda and mopped a soot-stained brow. Offhand, he could not remember when he had been happier—or wearier. In a way he was almost sorry the excitement was over, the fire beaten down at last, Korff's body (or what was left of it) on ice downstairs, the *Baltic Prince* in the hands of the harbour police. . . . He grinned broadly as he thought of that last item in tonight's events. Hurlbut had been unable to deliver his promised scoop on Korff—the refugee's own actions had prevented that, for a five-alarm fire had inevitably brought every reporter in New York on the run. The *Baltic Prince*— and the confession of its skipper, Captain Boris Falk—was something else again.

It would be months, of course, before that sinister trail was explored to the end, but the *Chronicle* had been promised an inside track when the story finally broke. Pete himself would write a series of articles exposing the smuggling ring— that was foreordained. It was the break he had prayed for ever since he received his first police card. A Pulitzer prize, his own column, and a columnist's salary were the very least he could expect.

Never, in all his experience, had a hunch paid off more handsomely. The more he pondered on that chance encounter with Korff, the more he was impressed by the refugee's

stupidity. It had been child's play for Hurlbut to stop the
messenger bearing Tony's note to the *Baltic Prince*; it had
been routine police procedure to set the trap in the brewery
and wait for Tony to walk in. . . . The refugee's death by
fire, too, had its symbolic overtone, the expiation of evil that
gave a neat ending to the front-page story he had just wrapped
up for the city desk.

He moved slowly towards the outer doorway, reluctant
to leave the scene of his triumph. At first glance the lobby
seemed deserted, save for the receptionist at the lighted
switchboard. When he saw the tall girl in evening dress
seated on the bench between the two marble pillars he
wondered how his roving eye had missed her. Surely there
was something familiar about the impatient tilt of her head,
the hot, angry eyes that had already nailed down his footsteps?

"Can I help you, Miss Reed?"

Pat Reed rose to her full height and favoured him with
an ominous stare. Pete returned the stare, unruffled. He had
been stared at in many languages during his long career, and
had survived each dagger.

"How did you know my name?"

"A newspaperman knows everything," he said. "Been
waiting long?"

"Only a moment, thank you."

"If you're looking for Andy Gray," said Pete judiciously,
"he just went down that corridor to emergency, with his arm
round his fiancée. I'm afraid they'll be operating till morning."

"Did you say his *fiancée*?"

He had expected to enjoy Pat's surprise. There was
something in that involuntary cry that touched his heart, case-
hardened though it was. Maybe you loved him after all, he
thought. Even if you do make over all your husbands in
your image. . . .

"They've been engaged for just an hour, so you couldn't
be expected to know. Didn't you realize that Andy is the
type who always marries his O.R. special?"

Her chin was up in earnest now: he knew that she would
never look handsomer or more dangerous. "Perhaps you can
tell me where to find Dr. Korff?"

"Dr. Korff is downstairs," he said. "On a slab in the morgue. Read the morning papers and you'll see why."

Pat Reed laughed aloud then—and the laughter sent a chill down his spine. There was no hysteria in her tone, and no pity whatever. The long, pale hands that reached for a cigarette were steady as a mannequin's. The eyes that met Pete Collins's as he snapped a dutiful lighter were inviting—and quite undisturbed.

"Apparently this isn't my night," said Pat Reed. "Would you concur in that, Mr. Collins?"

It was his turn to stare now. "How did you know *my* name?"

"I read the newspapers now and then," she said. "Even if I'm a bit behind tonight. Would you like me to drop you at your office—or farther uptown?"

The eyes that held his were all invitation. He felt his last good resolve melt in that incandescence, before he broke free.

"Sorry. I've a few loose ends to tie up here——"

He watched her go through the great brass doors with real regret. Not that he had really wanted that kind of diversion tonight—even a long-legged temptation like Pat. Tonight he would go home to his cluttered flat and enjoy his loneliness—along with four ounces of Irish whisky, a chapter of Voltaire, and his comfortable conviction that the world was mad. He turned as Father O'Leary's wheel chair came trundling down the hall from the emergency ward. Maybe the world's madness could be cured, if there were more men like the padre on deck—healers whose dedication matched that of Andy Gray and his brand-new betrothed.

"Isn't it past your bedtime, Father?"

The priest looked up and signalled to his orderly to stop the wheel chair. "I'm on my way, Pete. I stopped here to see someone."

"Who would you be meeting at this hour?"

"Someone who is always here." Father O'Leary lifted his eyes to the statue of Jesus that towered above them. "I wanted to give thanks for what happened tonight."

"Were you surprised when Mrs. Ash announced that she was rebuilding the hospital—and keeping it downtown?"

"I knew it all along, Pete," said the old priest softly. "So, I think, did Martin Ash. How else could it call itself East Side General?"

How else indeed? thought Pete. It would make a good story just the same. People always enjoyed reading about the generosity of the rich.

"Would you say that the evil were punished tonight—and the good rewarded?"

"It happens oftener than you think, Pete."

The reporter stood back to let the wheel-chair enter the elevator. He wished he could keep a little of the priest's assurance, his serene faith in the goodness of man—and man's ultimate salvation. Then, as the clock on Schuyler Tower struck midnight, he crossed the rotunda and took the steps that led downwards to the morgue.

There was still time for a beer with Otto and Dale Easton —and another of those arguments that proved how easily life could endure in the midst of death. Voltaire and the whisky would come later.